Joan Jonker was born an[...] [...] the charity-run organisation Victims of Violence and she lives in Southport with her son. She has two sons and two grandsons. Her previous Liverpool sagas have received warm praise:

'A hilarious but touching story of life in Liverpool' *Woman's Realm*

'You can rely on Joan to give her readers hilarity and pathos in equal measure and she's achieved it again in this tale' *Liverpool Echo*

'Packed with lively, sympathetic characters and a wealth of emotions' *Bolton Evening News*

'Mrs Jonker is blessed with the ability to write with a style which is at once readable while crafted with care and precision for her characters' *Skelmersdale Advertiser*

'As usual our Joan has come up with an easy-read story full of laughter and smiles – set in the colourful back streets of the 1930s' *Liverpool Echo*

'Joan Jonker has written a book worth reading; a book that will reduce you to tears – of sadness, but of happiness too' *Hull Daily Mail*

Also by Joan Jonker

When One Door Closes
Man Of The House
Home Is Where The Heart Is
Stay In Your Own Back Yard
Last Tram To Lime Street
Sweet Rosie O'Grady
The Pride Of Polly Perkins
Sadie Was A Lady
Walking My Baby Back Home
Try A Little Tenderness
Stay As Sweet As You Are
Down Our Street

Dream A Little Dream

Joan Jonker

HEADLINE

First published in 2000
by HEADLINE BOOK PUBLISHING

First published in paperback in 2000
by HEADLINE BOOK PUBLISHING

10 9 8 7 6 5 4 3 2 1

ISBN 0 7472 6384 1

Typeset by Avon Dataset Ltd, Bidford-on-Avon, Warks

Printed and bound in Great Britain by
Mackays of Chatham plc, Chatham, Kent

HEADLINE BOOK PUBLISHING
A division of the Hodder Headline Group
338 Euston Road
London NW1 3BH

www.headline.co.uk
www.hodderheadline.com

To Clare, who is not only my editor but also my sympathetic ear and my friend. And to all the staff at Headline for their help, friendliness and support. It has always been much appreciated.

And to my agent, Darley Anderson, who is one of life's gentlemen. Ever supportive and encouraging, and with a good sense of humour, it is a pleasure to be associated with him.

Dear Readers,
Dream A Little Dream is somewhat different from my other books, but I'm sure you will enjoy it. There are two baddies this time, who I know you will want to boo and hiss. I invented them, but there were times when I felt like boxing their ears! However, the other characters more than make up for them. You will need to keep a tissue handy.

My thanks to the many readers who have written to me. I get a lot of pleasure from reading your letters which are, without exception, always warm and friendly.

Take care.
Love,
Joan

Chapter One

'Mother, I don't want to go to a finishing school!' Abbie Dennison and her mother faced each other across the wide, highly polished mahogany table. 'I'd like to take a six-month course at a commercial college.'

Edwina Dennison's nostrils flared. She was a tall, thick-set woman with mousy-coloured hair which was swept back severely from her face and curled into a bun at the nape of her neck. She had a dull complexion, hard hazel eyes and thin lips that were seldom stretched into a smile. And her long thin nose added to her ever-present haughty expression. 'A commercial college? And what, pray, do you expect to learn there that would equip you for a life befitting our family's standing in the community?'

'I could learn shorthand and typing, book-keeping and—'

'We'll hear no more of this nonsense.' Edwina cut short her daughter's words. With her hands resting on top of one of the eight beautifully carved dining chairs which stood in uniformity around the table, she stared at her daughter. 'You'll continue to be educated as your father and I wish. You show little sign of ambition and left to your own devices would probably be quite happy serving behind a shop counter. A year at a finishing school will teach you deportment, etiquette and the art of conversation.'

'But Mother, that is not what I want!'

'Abigail, do not answer me back. You are a very ungrateful girl who does not appreciate the finer things in life that being a member of this family has given you. Now we'll hear no

1

more of this nonsense and you will go to your room and reflect on how lucky you are.'

Unnoticed by his wife and daughter, Robert Dennison was sitting in his favourite armchair which was set in the bay window and looked out on to the large garden at the back of the ten-roomed house. It was the place he found most peaceful to read his newspaper, away from his wife's incessant chattering. Had his youngest daughter not been the victim of her acid tongue, he would probably not have made his presence known. As it was, he swivelled the chair around to face them. 'Stay where you are, Abbie, please. I think there should be some discussion on what is, after all, your life. It is only right that your wishes are taken into account.'

'Robert, I thought we agreed the children's education should be left to me.' Edwina was not best pleased. 'I am their mother and know what's best for them.'

Her husband sighed. Usually he gave into his wife to keep the peace, but not this time. 'Abbie, will you go to your room while your mother and I discuss this? And don't look so downhearted, it's not the end of the world.'

'All right, Dad.' The girl smiled at him before leaving the room. If it wasn't for him, she would have a very miserable home life.

As soon as the door closed behind her, Edwina started. 'She's far too old to be calling you "Dad", and it's so working class. Why can't she call you "Father", as Victoria and Nigel do? And why is she so awkward and ungrateful? Any normal girl would be delighted at the chance of going to finishing school, but not Abigail, oh dear, no! Look what it did for Victoria. She moves with ease in all the right circles and her friends are from some of the richest families in Liverpool.'

'Oh, Victoria moves with ease in all the right circles, I'll grant you that. But that is all she can do. She doesn't have a job, she wouldn't know how to dust or wash dishes, and she can't even make a cup of tea. That is what finishing school did for Victoria. And what did Nigel's expensive education do for

2

him? Nobody will ever employ him because he refuses to work or get his hands dirty. I've tried to interest him in the firm's business because the idea was that he would take over when I retire. But when I make him come down to the office with me, he shows no interest whatsoever and just gets under everyone's feet. The youngest clerk has got more nous than he has.'

Edwina's nostrils were white and her head quivering with anger. 'How can you talk about your own children like that? Victoria is a daughter to be proud of. She's very pretty, always well-groomed and can converse with anyone. And Nigel is not a strong boy, never has been. He's only twenty years of age, and I'm sure that when the time comes for him to take charge of the business, he'll be well up to the task.'

Robert gazed at his wife and wondered how she could forget her roots. She'd been a lively, pretty girl when he started courting her. They lived in the same street of two-up, two-down houses, and she was called Edie then. Her family, like all the others in the street, had to struggle to make ends meet. But looking at her now no one would believe she'd worked in a factory until they'd married. And she made sure none of her snooty, middle-class friends ever found out.

Robert ran a hand across his forehead. He'd been working at the office all day and his head was filled with figures. That's why he'd come to sit in his favourite chair in the dining room, so he could read his paper undisturbed. Now he could feel a headache building up.

'I am not going to argue with you,' he told his wife. 'I shall not even raise my voice. That is something I should have done years ago. But because I was so busy building up the business to give you and the children a decent life, I allowed you free rein. That was the worst thing I could have done. It is too late to do much about Victoria and Nigel, you've spoiled them since I started earning decent money. But it's not too late for me to show some interest in my youngest daughter, and this I intend to do. By asking to go to commercial college, Abbie's shown she wants to do more with her life than swan around all day doing nothing, and I say she should be allowed to do as she wishes.'

Edwina was shocked. Her husband had never interfered before, nor spoken to her in such a challenging tone. 'And I say she should go to a finishing school,' she argued.

'The subject is closed, Edwina, so please let it drop.' How it stuck in his throat to call her by that name. 'And I do not want you discussing it with Abbie. I will tell her when we're having our meal, and I would advise you not to go against my wishes. You have a good life, one you could only have dreamt about in the old days. A house in Mossley Hill, plenty of money to entertain and buy the most expensive clothes, a live-in housekeeper, a daily cleaning woman and a gardener. Not bad for someone brought up in a two-up, two-down in Seaforth.'

'Aren't you forgetting you only lived a few doors away?'

'I have never denied my roots, and never would. I slogged my guts out, working to make something of myself. Missed going down to the pub with my mates for a pint, cut my smokes down to five Woodbines a day, anything to save a few coppers. Even when we got wed I used to deny myself things, but I always made sure you never went without. And I sometimes wonder if it was all worth it. You see, I was far happier when I was younger, even though my mother and father were as poor as church-mice. What we lacked in the way of food and clothes, they made up for with lots of laughter and love. I used to call them me mam and dad, as all the kids did, yourself included, and I still think the words have a ring of love about them, not as cold as Mother and Father.'

Robert sighed, asking himself why he bothered. Not once while he was talking was there a flicker to show his wife remembered those days. He shouldn't have expected any, knowing she'd spent the last seventeen years deliberately putting them out of her mind. She'd worked hard on losing her Liverpool accent, and the richer they became, the more of a

4

snob she became. And like a fool, he'd allowed her to change him, as well. At least on the surface she had. She'd be horrified if she knew he often frequented a small local pub near his office. And if she heard him in conversation with some of the workmen in the pub, sipping a pint of bitter and conversing so easily in the local dialect, she'd have one of the fainting fits she seemed able to bring about at will, and which confined her to bed for the day. But Robert had noticed these dizzy spells never occurred on a day she was entertaining some of her snooty friends. She was all sweetness and light then, playing the perfect hostess as if she had never known any other kind of life.

'I would very much like to go back to reading my paper now,' he said firmly, 'if you would kindly leave me alone to do so.'

As he swivelled his chair back towards the view of the garden, Robert didn't need to be told his wife was blazing with anger. He could hear it in the swish of her long black skirt, and the harsh closing of the door. Years ago, this would have upset him, and he'd have halted the argument with a kiss. But those days were long gone. There was no love or passion in their marriage now, it had been slowly killed by her aloofness. They shared the same bed because of the children, but they hadn't lived as man and wife since Abbie was born, seventeen years ago. Although Edwina never spoke the words, she made it clear that she had done her duty by giving him three children and found the act of lovemaking sordid.

Robert opened the newspaper and sought the article he'd been reading before the interruption, but he could no longer interest himself in it and let the paper fall to his lap. Resting his head on one of the wings of the maroon velvet chair, he closed his eyes and let his mind take him back in time. It was 1901, he was fourteen and had left school. Jobs weren't easy to come by, and he thought himself lucky to be taken on by a man who had a small furniture-removal business. The wages were low, only two bob a week, but his mother had said it was better than nothing and would tide him over while he looked for something that paid better. But Bob, as he was called then, loved the work because he was able to sit on the long seat at the front of the cart and watch the horse clip-clopping along. And after a few months, his boss, Will Lathom, let him take the reins and it was one of the most exciting days of his life. He became attached to Mr Lathom and Blackie, the horse, and he felt proud sitting on a cart that had high sides and bore the name of *William Lathom – Furniture Removals*. And he never did look for another job. He was a big lad for his age and capable of handling heavy furniture with ease, so they were able to take on more jobs and soon he was given a shilling a week rise in his pay. He'd been so proud that day, he remembered, when he handed his mother his wages. And the sixpence he got back as pocket-money made him feel like a millionaire.

He was so lost in thought, Robert didn't hear the discreet cough of the housekeeper and was startled when she appeared in front of him. 'I thought yer might like a cup of tea, Mr Robert.' She handed him a delicate china cup and saucer. 'A little milk and two sugars, just as yer like it.'

'Thank you, Agnes, that's very thoughtful of you.'

'Dinner will be in half an hour, sir.'

He smiled up at the woman who had been their live-in housekeeper for the last ten years. She was a good, hard worker, her cooking renowned, and the envy of all their friends. But her greatest gift, Robert thought, was that she smiled a lot and was very down to earth. She knew her place, but wasn't afraid to speak her mind if she thought she was right. She had been known to swear like a trooper on occasion, but housekeepers of her calibre were hard to come by, so even Edwina handled Agnes Weatherby with care.

'I'll drink my tea and then change for dinner.' Robert pursed his lips. 'On second thoughts, Agnes, I might not get changed for dinner tonight.'

'If yer don't feel like it, Mr Robert, then don't get changed.'

The housekeeper walked towards the door, muttering, 'Waste of bleedin' time anyway, if yer ask me.'

Robert swallowed a mouthful of tea before setting the cup back in the saucer. Then he chuckled and called after her, 'I agree, Agnes, it is a waste of bleedin' time.'

She turned with her hand on the door knob and a look of innocence on her chubby face. 'I never said no such thing, Mr Robert, yer must be hearing things.' Then she straightened the white cap on her head and smoothed her apron down over her ample bosom and tummy. 'It's either that, or I was talking to meself.' She gave him a broad wink then disappeared through the door to walk down the wide, expensively carpeted hall, to her domain. Nobody entered her kitchen without first knocking. Once there, she again addressed herself. 'Him and Miss Abbie are the only two sane people in the bleedin' house! The other three are away for slates and haven't a clue what life's all about. Lazy buggers, if yer ask me, more money than sense.'

Robert finished his tea and was placing the saucer on a mahogany side table when his eyes lit on the solid crystal ashtray. His wife disapproved of smoking and wrinkled her nose at the smell of tobacco, so for the sake of peace he used his study as a smoke room. But tonight he was going to change the rules. He would smoke his cigar here, and instead of changing for dinner, he would spend the time reflecting on the past. So when his cigar had caught, he puffed away contentedly and allowed his mind to go back in time, to when he was eighteen. There was one day which would always stand out in his mind, because, although he wasn't to know it then, it was the day that was to change his life.

Will Lathom had been complaining about feeling off-colour for some weeks, but had struggled to carry on working because he had plenty of orders and didn't want to let people down. But one morning when Robert called for him, Mrs Lathom invited him in and said her husband was ill in bed, and he'd asked her to say he wanted a word with Robert. It was plain to see the man was in a bad state, with a racking cough and high temperature. And worrying about the four removal jobs they had for that day certainly wasn't helping. The people would have all their belongings packed ready to move, and if he let them down, word would get around like wildfire that he wasn't reliable and his reputation would suffer.

Robert had stood at the bottom of the bed and tried to calm the man down. He said he knew the job inside out, and if he had help, he knew he could manage. There was a lad in his street who would be glad of a day's work, and if Will agreed, he'd pick the lad up and get started. That first day had been a nightmare. The young lad, Jeff, was willing enough, but wasn't used to handling furniture or breakables, and Robert needed eyes in the back of his head, making sure nothing was scratched or broken. But he was determined to show he could manage the round until Mr Lathom was better, so he and young Jeff ran themselves ragged in the process. And when he knocked at the Lathoms' house that night, an hour later than the usual time for finishing, he was almost dead on his feet. He passed over two pounds five shillings and sixpence that night, just for one day's work. It had been a busy day, granted, but even so Mr Lathom must be earning at least ten pounds a week. And that was after he'd paid Robert's wages and the bloke a few streets away where the horse and cart were stabled. So as he walked home that night, bone weary, Robert told himself that although the day had been hard, he'd learned something. That it was a mug's game to work for someone if you had the wherewithal to start your own business. It was a pipe dream, he'd never have the money to do that, but dreams didn't cost anything.

Will Lathom's health deteriorated and he was never able to return to work. So one day, a month after Robert had started to run the business on his own, the older man patted the side of his bed and told him to sit down. Then, with a catch in his voice, he said the doctor didn't give him much hope, so he wanted to sort his affairs out. He needed to make sure his wife and kids would be all right, so he had a proposition to put to

8

Robert. He had a bit of money put by, but he wanted to make sure his family had enough to keep the wolf from the door. So he asked if they could continue with the present arrangement for another six months, giving him time to build on his savings. Then at the end of that time he'd be prepared to sell the business to Robert for the sum of five pounds. That included the business and the horse and cart. And it would all be done legally, of course, drawn up by a Commissioner for Oaths.

The emotions that ran through the young man's mind that day would stay forever in his memory. Sadness that Mr Lathom was dying, because he'd grown really fond of the man. Then excitement that in six months he'd be his own boss. But after the initial sensation, came reality. He'd never be able to save five pounds in six months because he didn't have that much to himself once he paid his mam his keep. And he couldn't, or wouldn't leave her without because she was struggling as it was and would never manage on the pittance his dad earned.

He'd racked his brains on the walk home that night, but when he was putting the key in the door, he still hadn't found a solution. It would take a miracle, and who had ever heard of a miracle happening in Seaforth? Best to forget about it. He should have known it was too good to be true.

'Robert, what are you thinking of?' Edwina stood at the side of his chair, a frown on her face. 'Dinner is ready and you haven't even changed yet.'

'I decided not to bother changing.' He looked at her through narrowed eyes, remembering her as she was all those years ago, and now seeing what she had become. 'I've spent the time reminiscing about the old days, instead. I'd just got to the part where Will Lathom had offered to sell me his business for five pound, and I couldn't see a way clear to raising the money. D'you remember Will Lathom, Edie? I used to work for him before I started going out with you.'

Edwina flinched at his use of her old name. 'You would have been better employed making yourself respectable to sit down to a meal. What good does it do to hark back to the old days?'

'Oh, I often do it. And just lately I've been wondering if life wouldn't have been better if my mother hadn't struggled to help me raise that five pound. In gaining the wealth that we now have, we lost something that is far more important. We lost the ability to laugh and love. Sadly, there isn't much of either in this house. Our old neighbours in Seaforth would be green with envy if they saw us now, but I think they are the lucky ones. At forty-six I'm still quite a young man, with the needs of a young man. But I don't have the kind of loving wife who would find pleasure in satisfying those needs.'

Edwina heard the voices of her eldest daughter and son in the hall, and lifted a hand to silence her husband. What was the man thinking about, he was quite mad! 'The children are here, shall we take our seats at the table?' She glanced nervously at him as he took his seat at the top of the table. Surely he wouldn't bring up the bad old days and embarrass her? The children had no recollection of being poor because by the time Victoria was born, and Nigel two years later, they were living in a six-roomed house and were quite comfortably off. The horse and cart had long gone, and Robert had two motorised removal vans and employed four men.

'Good evening, Father.' Victoria smiled across the table. She was a very attractive girl who had inherited her mother's colouring, with mousy hair and hazel eyes. But she had a clear complexion and a fine set of white teeth. She had very good taste in clothes and chose those which showed off her slender figure and shapely legs to advantage. 'Have you been naughty? I do believe I smell cigar smoke.'

'Your father's had a busy day and needed to relax.' Edwina spoke before her husband could answer. It was to act as a warning to her daughter and also, hopefully, to soothe Robert. 'He spent an hour in his favourite chair and I'm sure he feels much better.'

'You work too hard, Father.' Nigel had the same mousy hair

as his sister, but there the resemblance ended. He was pale of face, with watery hazel eyes and a weak chin. Everything about him was effeminate. His mannerisms, mincing walk and high-pitched voice. 'You should leave the work to those you employ. That's what you pay them for.' He giggled like a girl, thinking what he was about to say was funny. 'After all, what's the point of keeping a dog and barking yourself, eh, what?'

Robert was saved from answering when Abbie entered the room. She came in smiling, like a breath of fresh air. 'I'm sorry I'm late, I didn't hear the bell.'

'That is no excuse,' Edwina said. 'You have a clock in your room and you know we dine at seven, not ten past.'

'Are you going to tell Agnes off, too?' Robert asked. 'As you remarked, it's ten past seven and no dinner on the table. Oh dear, oh dear!'

'Is somebody taking my name in vain?' Agnes pushed open the door with her hip, a huge soup tureen in her hands. While the housekeeper had told Robert not to change if he didn't feel like it, she had herself changed into a smart black dress with a white lace pinny tied around her ample waist. The white lace headpiece which Edwina insisted she wore when serving dinner had slipped sideways making her look slightly tipsy, and brought sly grins to the faces of Victoria and Nigel. Luckily Agnes didn't see them, or she wouldn't have thought twice about telling them off. 'I'm all to pot, tonight, so would one of yer serve the soup while I go and make sure the potatoes don't burn?'

'Really!' Edwina tutted. 'You do seem to be disorganised tonight, Agnes.'

The tureen now safely in the middle of the table, Agnes turned on her mistress. 'If yer didn't insist on me getting meself all dolled up like a dog's dinner, I wouldn't have had to leave the dinner to cook itself.' She looked pretty formidable with her hands on her hips and an 'I dare you' expression on her chubby face. 'I've only got one pair of bleedin' hands, so

11

it's up to you. Serve the soup yerself or take a chance on yer dinner being burned.'

'I'll serve the soup, Agnes.' Abbie scraped her chair back. She'd do anything for this woman who showed her more love than her mother did. Whose arms she'd run to when she was little and had fallen over and hurt herself. It was always the housekeeper who kissed her wounds better. And it was still those arms she ran to when anything went wrong or she thought she was being treated unfairly. 'I don't mind.'

'Thank yer, Miss.' With a withering look, the housekeeper left the room. 'Lazy buggers,' she chunnered on her way back to the kitchen. 'Won't even get off their backsides to feed themselves. If it wasn't for the master and Miss Abbie, I'd have told them where to put their bleedin' job and I'd be packing me bags right now.'

'Really, Mother, she goes too far,' Victoria said. 'You need to have words with her so she knows her place.'

'I would, darling, but she flies off the handle so quickly. And if she took it into her head to leave, we'd never get another housekeeper like her. There isn't one of my friends who wouldn't snap her up if she left here.'

'But Agnes isn't going to leave here,' Robert said, watching Abbie attending to the soup and feeling disgust that the rest of his family thought they should be waited on hand and foot. 'And anyone who upsets her will feel my displeasure. I hope I've made myself clear?'

Oh dear, Edwina thought, it seems as though everyone is deliberately being difficult tonight. But the fear of being humiliated by her husband made her change the subject quickly. 'Are you going out tonight, Victoria?'

'Yes, Charles is calling for me about half eight. He can't wait to try his new car out, so we're going for a run in it.' Victoria only ever mixed with those in the same social class as herself. She'd had several boyfriends, all sons of wealthy men, but in each case the courtship lasted no longer than a few months. Her reason was that they bored her rigid. But one

12

thing Victoria Dennison was not, and that was stupid. She pandered to her mother because she was the one who handed over her monthly allowance and it was easy to wheedle extra cash from her for a new dress or hat. But Victoria never lost sight of the fact that at the end of the day, it was her father who held the purse-strings. He could, if he chose to be awkward, make them all dance to his tune. So putting on her brightest smile, she said, 'You haven't seen Charles's new car, have you, Father? It really is very swish. We went for a run in it last night, just as far as the Pier Head because it was late, but everyone we passed turned their heads.'

Is that all you want out of life, for people to notice and envy you? Robert didn't speak the words but that is how he felt. For some unknown reason he was seeing his family in a different light today, and he didn't like what he was seeing. He must share the blame with his wife; he should have noticed sooner that spoiling the children wasn't the right recipe for making them kind and caring. Then he mentally corrected himself. Only two of his children had been pampered and spoilt. The youngest, Abbie, could easily have turned out the same way, but she hadn't; she was unspoilable. 'No, I haven't seen Charles's car, I'm usually in the study when he calls. Besides, you know I don't share his passion for cars. They are a means of transport to me, nothing more.'

Nigel, who spent the best part of every day in the company of his eldest sister, was sensitive to her mood swings. Why she wanted to be nice to Father he didn't know, but she must have a reason. 'Yes, it's a jolly spiffing car. You must tell me what speed Charles gets it up to tonight on the country roads.' He looked around to see if any face showed a spark of interest, and when he saw none, he tried something no one could argue with. 'I say, this soup is absolutely delicious.'

Robert laid down his spoon and using the heavy linen napkin, he wiped his mouth. 'I hope you pass that compliment on to Agnes, Nigel.'

13

'Oh, absolutely, Father! I'll tell her when she brings the dinner through.'

'Why not tell her when you help your sister carry the soup plates out? That would save Agnes making two journeys. And while you're there, would you ask her to serve me my meal in the study, please? I have a headache and need to be quiet.' Robert saw the look of disappointment on his youngest daughter's face and hastened to add, 'Before I go, I want you all to know that Abbie has expressed a wish to go to commercial college and I have agreed that she may.'

Victoria gasped. 'Commercial college! Whatever for?'

'If I remember correctly, Victoria, when you were her age it was your heartfelt wish to spend a year at finishing school. I never at that time asked "Whatever for?" Your wish was granted, and now I am granting your sister's wish. And I want it known that I am more than happy to do so.' Robert rose to his feet. He was still a very handsome man, tall and well-built. His raven-black hair was now grey at the temples and this gave him an air of distinction. His brows were black and bushy, his eyes a deep brown and he had a strong jawline. 'If you will excuse me, I will retire to the study. When the meal is over, Abbie, join me and we can discuss the way forward.'

There was complete silence until the door was closed behind him, then Edwina hissed, 'You little madam! You know that's going against my wishes.'

'It's what I want, Mother. I intend to go out to work, and to get a decent job I need qualifications. I won't get those at a finishing school.'

'Don't you dare talk to me in that tone. You have no thought for what I would like for you. You want this, and you intend doing that. Selfish, selfish, selfish! You are a very ungrateful girl, Abigail, and you may find you live to rue the day you went against me.'

'Oh, steady on, Mother!' Nigel said. 'If it's what Abbie wants to do, why not let her?'

'Keep out of it, Nigel,' Victoria said, sitting back in her

chair and crossing her legs. At twenty-two, she was four years older than her younger sister, who was not yet eighteen, and she had never felt any sisterly bonding between them. The difference in their ages meant they had different interests and little in common. It was only in the last year she'd noticed her sister blossoming into a very pretty girl. And envy had set in. For Abigail had inherited her father's looks and colouring. She had jet-black, thick luxuriant hair, black eyebrows perfectly arched, long black lashes, a slightly turned-up nose and a set of strong white teeth. All set in a heart-shaped face, above a body beginning to show signs of a firm bosom, slim waist and hips, and long shapely legs. Competition was something Victoria wasn't used to, and she'd be quite happy for her sister to be sent away to finishing school for a year.

'I'm not selfish, Mother, and I'm not ungrateful.' Abbie thought her mother was being very unfair. But then she'd noticed for years that she wasn't given the same treatment as her brother and sister. She hadn't worried about it because she knew her father loved her, but she couldn't bow down to pressure now, she had to stick up for herself. 'I don't know what you have against me going to commercial college. My best friend in school is going – her parents think it's a jolly good idea.'

'If, by your best friend, you mean Rowena, I'm not surprised her parents agree. They are no doubt looking to her to find a job because they are not particularly well off. You are not in the same position. You do not need to go to work.'

'But I want to! And what you said about Rowena wasn't fair. Her—' Abbie broke off when the housekeeper entered the room. 'Oh, I'm sorry, Agnes, I was supposed to take the plates out to save you a journey.'

The housekeeper could feel the tension in the air. She'd heard part of what the girl said, but not enough to know why she sounded so upset. The mistress had a face on her like thunder, but that wasn't anything new, she was a miserable cow at the best of times. Victoria was wearing that supercilious

15

expression that made Agnes want to clock her one, and Nigel was looking very uncomfortable. But it was the young girl's flushed face and tear-filled eyes that brought forth a reaction. 'What's wrong, Miss Abbie? Is someone having a go at yer?'

'No, I'm fine, Agnes, thank you.'

Victoria clicked her tongue. 'I really don't think it's any of your concern, Agnes. How dare you interfere in what is a private family matter! Now please remove these plates and bring in the dinner. I have a visitor coming soon.'

Chubby arms were folded under a voluptuous bosom as Agnes took her stand. 'Who was yer bleedin' slave before I came along, eh? I might work here, but I'll not be walked all over by an upstart like you. If yer want those plates removing, do it yer bleedin' self, 'cos I've finished fetching and carrying for you lot. I'm off to pack me bags.'

Edwina jumped to her feet. 'Please, Agnes, don't be hasty. Victoria didn't mean it to come out the way it did. We are all very fond of you and appreciate your work. We'd be devastated if you left us.'

'While yer were being devastated, yer'd be bleedin' hungry as well, 'cos there's not one of yer would know what to do with a pan. Except Miss Abbie, of course, at least she does try. But that's your hard luck, nowt to do with me 'cos I've had a bellyful and I'm off.'

Edwina caught up with her at the door. 'Please, Agnes, I beg of you. We'd be broken-hearted if you left. Come back and let Victoria apologise.'

'If she was sorry she'd have said so before now. And an apology is no good if it's got to be dragged out of someone. Perhaps she'll watch what she says in future, 'cos once words have been spoken, yer can't take them back.' The housekeeper pulled her arm free. 'She's looked down her snotty nose at me for the last time.'

There were tears streaming down Abbie's cheeks as she jumped to her feet. 'I'm going to fetch my dad because this is so unfair.'

'You stay right where you are,' Victoria warned. 'Or you'll be sorry.'

The girl ignored her and made for the door. 'I don't care what you say, I'm going for my dad.' She pulled the door open and walked straight into her father's arms. 'Oh Dad, Agnes said she's leaving us.'

'There, there, now, dear.' Robert gave her a brief hug before walking into the room. 'I don't need an explanation because I heard everything. I had left my cigars on the small table and I'd come to collect them. And I can honestly say I've never been so ashamed in my life. Victoria, you will come and apologise right this minute.'

'It's no good, Mr Robert, she wouldn't really mean it and what's the good of that?' Agnes was untying the bow in the back of her apron. 'Yer don't have to worry about me, I can walk into another job tomorrow.'

Robert ignored her words. 'Victoria, this instant!'

His daughter had been regretting her words since she realised Agnes was serious about leaving. She didn't want the woman to go, she was fond of her in her own way. The house was always immaculate, there were never any complaints about clothes being left on the bedroom floor instead of hung in the wardrobe, and there was no doubt she was a wizard in the kitchen. But having to say sorry to a person she looked on as her inferior, didn't come easily.

'I'm sorry, Agnes,' she said stiffly. 'I should not have been so rude. I would very much like you to stay.'

'Words are cheap, Miss Victoria, and not always sincere.'

Robert took the housekeeper's arm. 'Come to the study with me and we can talk in peace. My wife and daughters will see to the dinner, which I presume is ready to serve?'

'It is, Mr Robert, but I'm not serving it.'

'I don't expect you to. My wife is quite capable of seeing to her family for once. In fact, when she brings my dinner through to the study, she may as well bring a plate for you. For once in ten years, Agnes, you can be our guest.' The look he

17

gave Edwina before he led the housekeeper away held a warning that she would be advised to do as he said.

Robert handed the housekeeper a glass containing a generous measure of whisky. 'This is not a bribe, Agnes, I need a drink as much as you. I am so ashamed that a daughter of mine would talk to you in such a manner. But a lot of the blame lies at my door for not seeing that she and Nigel were growing up into snobs. If I'd been at home more, perhaps things might have been different, but when you have a business like mine, you have to keep a close eye on things. It was hard graft getting where I am; I'm not about to let others ruin it for me.' He held his glass high. 'Here's to me and you, Agnes, and no more talk of you leaving. If you went, Abbie and I would follow you. We couldn't do without you, and you must know that we are both very fond of you. What happened today was unforgivable and will never happen again, you have my promise.'

Agnes raised her glass. 'I'd have cried me bleedin' eyes out if I'd had to have walked out and left you and Miss Abbie. But I would have done it, Mr Robert, 'cos I've got me pride. I'll have no toffee-nosed little madam looking down her nose at me.'

'I rather think Victoria will have learned her lesson, Agnes. She does love to show off and act the lady, but beneath the surface she's not as cold as she appears. I don't think she would deliberately hurt anyone. But that is not to excuse her behaviour because there is no excuse for bad manners.' Robert sighed. 'It's been a rare old day today. I've spent much of it thinking about the past, when we were skint and happy. And I've been remembering my mam and dad. You'd have liked my mam, she'd have been right up your street. She was only the size of sixpenn'orth of copper, but she was wiry and all there on top. If she'd had a day like today, she'd have been waiting on the step for me to come in from work. And she'd have said, "It's been a right bleedin' day today, son, and that's the truth.

I'll tell yer all about it when ye're having yer dinner. That's if there's any arse left in the bleedin' pan" '

Agnes grinned and raised her glass. 'Ye're right, I would have liked yer mam. Me and her would have been the best of mates.'

Chapter Two

Abbie rapped lightly on the study door with a knuckle, and when her father answered she opened the door and popped her head in. 'Would you rather wait until tomorrow night, Dad, to have our talk? What with all the upset, and you having a headache, perhaps this is not the right time?'

'There's no time like the present, dear, so come on in.' He smiled at the daughter who held a special place in his heart, and waved her to a chair. 'As I said to Agnes, it's been a rare old day today.'

'She's not leaving us, is she, Dad? I couldn't bear it if she did. She's always been so kind to me, letting me sit in the kitchen when I come home from school, and listening to what I've been up to. And she's always interested and never loses patience with me, even when she's busy baking, or peeling potatoes. Never once has she said she didn't have time to listen, or chase me away. I feel as if she's one of the family, and I do love her.'

'She's not leaving, dear, but it was a close thing. If it had been one of the nights when I go straight from the office to the club, Agnes would have upped stakes and walked out of the door. And, frankly, I wouldn't have blamed her. She deserves to be treated with the respect she has more than earned in the ten years she's been with us. And I've given her my word it will never happen again.' Robert clipped the end of his cigar before eyeing his daughter. 'I know half of the story, but not the whole. I want you to tell me what caused Agnes to think you had been getting picked on?'

21

'It was nothing, Dad.' Abbie couldn't quite hide the catch in her voice. 'It's best forgotten, there have been enough bitter words spoken today. So let's put it behind us and start afresh.'

'If that's the way you want it, dear, but if ever you think you're been unfairly treated, come and talk to me. If you can confide in Agnes, then surely you can confide in your own father?'

She smiled. 'I can stick up for myself, you know! That is what started the trouble in the first place. If I'd known that would happen I would have kept my mouth closed. I'll be very careful in future.'

'No, my dear, it is best to speak your mind if you think you are in the right.'

Not when you've got two against you, it isn't, Abbie thought. She left Nigel out, because in his own way he had tried to defend her. But the scene in the kitchen when her mother had insisted that Victoria help serve the dinner, was still fresh in her mind. Tempers flared when her sister objected, saying she had no intention of ruining her nails, and she only changed her tune when her mother threatened to stop her allowance for a month if she failed to show some remorse. And while her sister had been complaining, Abbie listened and wondered why it didn't enter the older girl's head that what she was being coaxed to do, was something the housekeeper did automatically three times a day, six days a week – and all without so much as a thank you. But it would do no good to rekindle the argument now by speaking her mind. 'We've still got Agnes, Dad, and that's the main thing,' she said quietly.

'I'd have gone down on bended knee to her if necessary. She's a hard-working, decent woman, and while she's in my house I will not allow her to be treated like a skivvy.' Robert was thoughtful as he reached into his pocket for a handkerchief he didn't need, but the action gave him time to consider. 'She reminds me a bit of my own mother, does Agnes. They would have got on well together because my mother used to swear like a trooper, too!'

'Did she? I don't mind Agnes swearing because it doesn't sound bad coming from her. I think she's funny.' Abbie leaned her elbows on the table and her eyes were alight with interest. 'I don't remember my grandmother, or my grandfather. I wish I did. Tell me about them.'

'How far back can you remember, dear?'

'Erm, let's see now. I can remember playing in Balfour Road where we used to live. I had a friend and her name was Milly and we both had a doll's pram. We also had skipping ropes, but we weren't very good at skipping, not like the older girls in the street. And I can remember Mother taking me to school on the first day I started. I was petrified. But it wasn't so bad, 'cos Milly sat at the same desk as I did and the teacher was very kind.'

'Do you remember the removal vans I had at that time?'

'I think so. Were they a dark red with your name painted on in yellow?'

'That's right. They weren't as grand as the ones we have now, but they were a definite improvement on the horse and cart I started with.'

His daughter's face was now agog with excitement. 'You had a horse and cart, Dad? I didn't know that, you've never said.'

'I was only nineteen when the man I worked for sold me his horse and cart, and the business, all for five pound. It was something in those days, for a young lad to have his own business. And it was my mother who made it possible. For months she took in extra washing to help me raise the cash, and I scrimped and saved every penny I could lay my hands on. The day I passed the money over to the man who had been my boss, I had holes in the soles of my shoes, and not a farthing in my pocket, but I was as proud as a peacock because I owned my own business. And I've got my mother to thank for everything I have today. I'm just sorry she and my father didn't live long enough for me to repay them. Oh, I made life more comfortable for them when they were alive, and saw that they wanted for nothing, but I certainly didn't have the wealth I have today. I had visions of moving them to a nice house with a garden, but it wasn't to be. They died in the small two-up, two-down house I was born in. My mother was only fifty-six when she suffered a severe stroke and died within two days. My father, God bless him, couldn't get over losing her, and he died six weeks later of a broken heart.'

'Oh Dad, that's so sad! It must have been terrible for you.'

'It took me a long time to come to terms with it, Abbie, because they were the best parents anyone could ask for, and I loved them dearly. Everything I owned, I would have gladly given away to have them back again.'

'Did you live with them, Dad, or were you married then?'

'Your mother and I had been married about five years when they died. Victoria was three and Nigel one, so they will have no memory of their grandparents. You came along two years later.'

Part of Abbie's mind was asking why she was only hearing all this now. Surely at her age she should have been told about things like this. She knew that her mother's parents, Ada and Joe, had died because Nigel had once told her so. She'd ventured to ask about them a couple of times, but her questions had been brushed aside by her mother in such a manner as to suggest the subject wasn't one she ever wanted discussing. And tonight wasn't the time, either, because she could see sadness in her father's eyes and he was the one person in the whole world she wouldn't hurt. 'Tell me about the horse and cart, Dad.'

Robert shook his head to clear his mind. His plan had been to tell his daughter about his roots, and how he'd got where he was now. He thought it right that all three of his children should know, then perhaps his eldest daughter and son would realise the money they spent like water hadn't just dropped from the heavens above, it had been earned the hard way. And as they hadn't had to toil for the money themselves they should consider themselves lucky and not walk around as though they'd been born with a silver spoon in their mouths. But he hadn't imagined talking about his parents would be so painful. 'Blackie was the horse's name and he was quite a character. He had a mind of his own, did Blackie, and could practically talk. He could tell the time, too! If he wasn't back in the stable with his nosebag on by seven o'clock, he wouldn't half let us know. His head would be thrown back and he'd snort as if to tell us it was past his feeding time.'

'I wish I'd known him,' Abbie said wistfully. 'What happened to him, Dad?'

'He was getting old and a year after the war finished I gave him to a man who I knew would be good to him. I used to visit him when I was in the area and know he was well looked after until the day he died. I'd been saving hard because most of the removal firms were using motorised vehicles, and we were losing business to them. So I bought a good second-hand van and business increased so much, a year later I was able to buy a second van. And those are the two that you can remember. I worked on one with Jeff, who's been with me since the day I started on my own, and I had to employ two extra men for the other van.' Robert put a hand to his mouth and gave a dry cough. 'My dear, would you be an angel and make a pot of tea for us? Agnes usually brings one through about this time but she's been given the night off for obvious reasons.'

Abbie jumped to her feet. 'Remember where you're up to, Dad, because I want to know everything. I'm finding it very interesting, and I'm proud you've done so well. If I learn shorthand and typing, and book-keeping, I'd like to work for you, if you'll have me.'

'I'd be delighted, my dear.' And Robert really was thrilled that his daughter was showing such an interest. 'By the way, I still see Milly now and again.'

Her mouth gaped in surprise. 'But you never said, Dad! Oh, I'd love to see her, how is she?'

'Very well and very pretty. She left school at sixteen and works in an office in Dale Street. I call about once a month to

25

see the old neighbours, and I also take a trip down Memory Lane every month to see my mother's old neighbours who lived either side of her in Seaforth. They were good to her when she took ill; nobody could have been better looked after. Everyone turned out for her funeral because she was well-known and well-liked. She never turned anyone away from her door if it was in her power to help them. And they tried to look after my father when he was left alone, but he didn't want their help. Not that he didn't appreciate their concern, he did. But no matter what they did they couldn't give him back the one thing he wanted, and that was the wife he adored. He just wanted to be with her, so he pined away.'

'Oh, Dad, it's so sad. It must have been awful for you.'

'It's nineteen years ago now, but their faces are still fresh in my mind.' Robert gestured for her to move. 'Tea, my dear, please, my throat is parched.'

Edwina was in the kitchen when Abbie appeared, and the look she gave her daughter was not one of motherly love. 'What on earth have you and your father got to say to each other that is taking so long?'

'Nothing much, Mother. Just general conversation about this and that.'

'Would you kindly be more explicit about what this and that is?' Edwina's temper should have been directed at her eldest daughter for causing such an upset. But she knew it would be a waste of time because Victoria would just dismiss the matter with a wave of her hand and a look of disdain on her face. So she tried to take her anger and frustration out on her youngest daughter, who seldom answered back. 'If I thought you were telling tales, Abigail, I would be very displeased.'

'Tales, Mother? What tales would I have to tell? We've talked about Agnes, and you shouldn't be surprised at that, since Dad heard everything for himself.' Abbie usually tried not to upset her mother because of the lecture she was bound to get if she had done anything thought to be untoward. And that is why, she realised now, she was always the whipping-boy – because she made it easy by not answering back. But what she had heard in the last hour from her father about her paternal grandparents had given her a sense of belonging, and it had also given her confidence in herself. 'We've talked of nothing that would be of interest to you, Mother. Just general chit-chat, that's all.'

As she set about preparing a tray, Abbie could feel Edwina's eyes boring into her back. The silence was heavy, broken only by the hissing of the gas under the kettle. She began to hum, softly, feeling really uncomfortable. It shouldn't be like this, she told herself. Families should be loving towards each other, not always at loggerheads. So she held out an olive branch. 'Would you like a cup of tea, Mother?'

'I think not.' Edwina made her way towards the door. 'Wash the crockery when you've finished, we don't want Agnes to start complaining about dirty dishes.'

'No, of course not.' Abbie sighed. Why could she never find favour with her mother? Her sister and brother could do no wrong, while she couldn't please, no matter how hard she tried. Sometimes she felt like a stranger in her own home. She picked up the tray and when she reached the study door, she forced a smile to her face. At least she was sure of her father's love, and knew when she entered the room she would be greeted by eyes that would say they were happy to see her.

'Go on, Dad, carry on where you left off,' Abbie said, after pouring the tea and setting a cup down in front of her father. 'And don't leave anything out because I'm interested in everything you've done.'

Robert smiled. 'I hope this information you're so eager for doesn't mean you intend to start up your own business eventually, in opposition to me?'

'I'm not as clever as you, Dad, I couldn't do what you've done. And I can't see a woman driving a removal van, can you? No, I want to come and work for you. I'd like to learn the business inside out, so I can help you.'

27

'Your mother wouldn't be happy about that, my dear. You'll be eighteen in a couple of weeks and she'll expect you to mix in the same social circle as Victoria and Nigel where you would meet the type of young men she would find suitable for you to choose a husband from. She has high hopes of all her children making good marriages.' Robert had no such hopes himself, but he thought his youngest daughter should know all the options open to her. 'You need to think things through very carefully before committing yourself.'

'Is that what you want for me, Dad? That I marry a man from a good family with plenty of money?'

'All I want is for you to be happy, Abbie. I want that for all of my children.'

'As you said, Dad, I'll be eighteen soon, and I believe that's old enough for me to know what I want from life. I am not going to criticise any of my family, that would be unfair and futile, but suffice to say the life they enjoy would not be for me. I don't want to spend my time lounging around, and then marrying a man because he has money. When I do marry, Dad, it will be for love. But that's years off, and in the meantime I want to achieve something, to justify my being on this earth. If it means going against Mother, then I shall have to face that problem when it arises.'

'Are you absolutely certain, my dear? Have you given it plenty of thought?'

'I've known all along it's what I want, Dad! It's not something I've just thought of. You said Milly left school at sixteen – well, that is what I would have liked to do. But Mother insisted on the extra two years' private tuition, and I didn't have a choice. I know she had my welfare at heart, but I can't let her keep on running my life for me when I know I won't be happy. I'm sorry, Dad, because I know it will cause a lot of bad feeling, but I really am quite determined to make a stand on this.'

Robert gazed into his daughter's pretty face and his heart went out to her. She was very young and very tender-hearted.

No match for his wife's venomous tongue and her sister's scorn. 'I'll be standing right beside you, Abbie; you won't be alone. I'll tell your mother tonight that your future has been decided, and that you have my blessing. And tomorrow you can make enquiries on how to enrol at commercial college, and find out when their term starts.'

Abbie left her chair and flung her arms around him. 'Oh, thank you, Daddy! I won't let you down, I promise.'

Robert felt a lump form in his throat at the show of affection and her use of the word Daddy. She'd always called him that until Edwina decided it was too childish. Hugs and kisses, they were childish, too! And loud laughter was frowned on as being very common. In her quest for perfection, his wife had thrown out the very things that make a house into a home – love, warmth and laughter. 'I know you won't let me down, Abbie, and I admire your determination.'

Abbie returned to her chair with a smile on her face. 'Now I want to know how the business grew to what it is today, and how the auction houses came about.'

'Hard work and good fortune, I suppose. As you know, I have six furniture-removal depots across Lancashire, and they bring in enough money to allow us to live in comfort. Plus, I have a good manager in Jeff, who makes sure things run smoothly. He replaces vans when they are too old, and he can hire and fire. As for the auction houses, they are not something I intended, they just seemed to happen. It started in a very small way when I was asked if I would buy the contents of a house in Orrell Park. The elderly lady who lived there had died and her family didn't want her furniture. They weren't asking much for it, and I bought it more as a favour to them. I emptied the house and took the furniture to a second-hand shop, where I got four bob more than I had paid for it. Remember, this was 1924, and four bob was a lot of money in those days. A couple of weeks later the same thing happened, but this time I decided to sell the furniture myself. My thinking was that if the man in the second-hand shop could give me four bob over the odds for the other furniture, and make a profit himself, the money was better in my pocket, seeing as I had to remove the stuff. So I rented a small shop on Hawthorne Road in Bootle, and stored the furniture there until I had enough to open it up as a second-hand shop. It did very well because there were a lot of poor people in the area and I kept the prices as low as possible.'

As Abbie listened, she was filled with admiration for her father. He must have worked very hard, and yet his achievements were never mentioned! At least not in her presence. 'It's a wonderful story, Dad, you must be very clever. There's not many men could do what you have.'

'Ah, but I had the good fortune to have such a staunch friend as Jeff. From day one he's been there for me and he's never let me down. He's not afraid to speak his mind, either, which is what I like about him. If he thinks I'm wrong, he'll look me straight in the eye and tell me. And I listen to him because he has a good head for business. For instance, it was Jeff who told me that some of the furniture we were selling in the second-hand shop was worth a lot more than we were asking for it. I approached an antique specialist who is a member of my club, and after inspecting a few pieces he agreed with Jeff that they were indeed quite valuable. And so the idea was born for our first auction sales room in the city. I remember the first day as though it was yesterday. We had advertised the opening in the local newspapers and booked an auctioneer to handle the affair. Imagine our dismay when only ten people turned up, and they'd only come out of curiosity. Jeff and I often have a laugh about it, and he said it was a lesson to warn us not to get too big-headed.'

Abbie's eyes were wide and her mouth gaped. 'Only ten people, Dad! Oh, you must have been very disappointed.'

Robert chuckled. 'Agnes would have loved it there, the air was blue with my language. Not because we hadn't made any money, because that's hardly life-threatening, is it? No, it was because we felt foolish. Not so much Jeff, but I must have looked ridiculous, standing out like a sore thumb in my hard bowler hat, immaculate shirt and cravat, best overcoat with red carnation in the buttonhole, spats, kid gloves – *and* I was carrying a cane. The great businessman not doing any business.'

'Oh Dad, I know it probably wasn't funny at the time, but you describe yourself so well I can see you in my mind's eye and it must have been hilarious.'

'I can assure you I didn't find any humour in it at the time. I was all for closing the place down but Jeff persuaded me to give it a couple of months. The auction was only going to be held every two weeks, and he said there was no need for me to go along, he would attend to it. Once again he was right, Abbie, because in three months the business was up and running and has never looked back. And as you know, we started a similar scheme over in Chester five years ago, and that is also very successful.' Robert took out his fobwatch and pulled a face. 'That's all for tonight, young lady, it's very late. Besides, I think you know all you need to know about the business for the time being.'

'Can I ask a favour of you, Dad?'

'Of course you can. And if it is in my power I will grant it.'

'Will you take me to see Milly's house one day? I'd love to see her.'

Robert lowered his head. This youngest daughter of his was really stirring up a hornet's nest. Her young friend Milly was part of the past that Edwina had gone to great pains never to mention. It was as if seven years in Balfour Road had never been; she had erased them from her mind. And whether by word or deed, she seemed to have been successful in erasing them from the minds of her two eldest children. Victoria and Nigel also had friends in the street where Milly lived, but they appeared to have forgotten them. Yet was it right that Abbie should be encouraged to also forget the friends of her childhood? No, there was no justification for that. She had a right to choose her own destiny. 'Yes, I'll take you down to see her one night. I'm sure she'll be delighted because she never fails to ask after you. But I'll have to let her know when you're coming and that may take a week or two, so you'll have to be patient.'

He was smothered in kisses. 'You are the best father in the world, and I do love you.' Abbie picked up the tray and made for the door. 'I'll wash these before I go to bed. Goodnight and God bless.'

'Goodnight and God bless, my dear.' Robert sat deep in thought when his daughter had left. Then he spoke to the empty room. 'I've tried to be a good father, and on the whole I believe I have. But I've also been a coward, and turned a blind eye when I should have put my foot down. Because of that, my two eldest children are snobs who spend their days playing tennis, swimming, shopping for clothes they don't need, or going to afternoon tea dances. They don't know any other kind of life, and I must take the blame for that. Now my youngest child wants to be free to lead a different life, one I would dearly love her to have. But she'll have to fight every foot of the way to get it. Unless I do what I should have done in the first place, and that's to be master in my own home.'

Edwina was sitting up in bed pretending to read when Robert entered the bedroom. She was wearing a plain white cotton nightdress, longsleeved and buttoned to the neck. She would never show an inch of flesh if it was possible to cover it. And her face revealed she was not in the best of tempers. 'You have been shut in that study for over two hours, Robert,' she said shrilly. 'What could a seventeen-year-old girl possibly have to say that would hold your attention for so long?'

'It was a very enjoyable two hours, Edwina.' Robert pulled off his cravat and placed it on top of a tallboy. 'I discovered that Abbie and I have a lot in common.'

When he didn't offer any further information, her nostrils flared. 'More in common than with myself and your other two children?'

'Good gracious, Edwina, aren't you being a little dramatic? What is so wrong with a father spending some time with his daughter?' Robert studied his wife's pinched face before picking up his cravat and walking through to his dressing-room. What on earth had happened to them? They'd been madly in love with each other once, now they were like strangers. The girl he'd fallen in love with was a happy person, full of joy and laughter. A working-class lass from a working-class family, who spoke, like himself, with a Liverpool accent. Now that girl had grown into a woman and changed beyond all recognition. Gone was the loving nature, the laughter and the Liverpool accent. He had changed too, but his change had been brought about by necessity. Mixing with wealthy business people, it had been important to learn to speak, dress and live as they did. But underneath he hadn't changed so much he'd forgotten where he came from or those who had once been his friends.

Robert was very thoughtful as he undressed and hung his clothes in the built-in wardrobe. The love he and Edwina had shared was long gone, but since they both lived under the same roof, surely they could at least be pleasant with each other? But there was no point in asking himself this question when the only one who could answer it was his wife. God knows he had tried many times over the years to get close to her, but to no avail. For the sake of harmony in the house, though, he was prepared to try again.

Edwina lowered her book when she sensed Robert standing at the foot of the bed. 'Did you want to say something?'

'I would like to know where the hell we went wrong, Edie?'

She closed her eyes at the use of her old nickname. 'I don't know what you are talking about. What has gone wrong?'

'You, me, the children – everything. When I leave work each day, I don't come home, I come to a house where my belongings and my family just happen to be. Because it isn't like any home I have ever known, where there is love and laughter, and where the family sit together and discuss things.

33

I never understood why you suddenly took a dislike to my making love to you, but I went along with it because I would never force myself on you. That I could have tolerated, if we had remained friends. But we are not even that, Edie, and I'd like to know why? There are times when I think you actually hate me, and if it weren't for the fact that I'm the one who supplies the money to enable you to have the lifestyle you revel in, you wouldn't care if you never saw me again.'

Edwina closed the book and put it on the bedside table. 'Now who is the one being dramatic. Of course I don't hate you, Robert, you are being childish.'

'What are your feelings for me, then?'

Edwina looked down at her clasped hands. 'You are my husband.'

'In name only, Edie.' He could see anger flare in his wife's eyes. 'That was your name when I met you, so why are you ashamed of it now?'

'Because it's all in the past and I don't want to live in the past.'

'Is that why you never visit your old friends and neighbours, because they wouldn't fit in with your new life?' Robert knew what he was going to say would hurt her, but it was something he should have said years ago. 'Even your own mother and father? Are you really so ashamed of them?'

Edwina's face drained of colour. 'Why are you doing this to me? It will serve no purpose to go over all this again. We have a good life – why can't you leave things be? Anyway, my mother and father are probably dead by now.'

Robert shook his head sadly. 'I daresay you would like them to be, to ease your conscience, but I can assure you they are very much alive. I visit them once a month, as I do all my old friends. I take them a food hamper from Coopers and make sure they don't go short of coal in the cold weather.' His sadness now turned to anger. How could this woman erase everything from her mind, even her elderly parents, and live with herself? Never once, in the last seventeen years, had she been to see them or mentioned their names. 'I blame myself for allowing you to forget your duties. I should have insisted you keep in contact with your parents, even carrying you there if that was the only way to get you to visit them.' He took a deep breath and blew the air out slowly. 'You've told the children that they're dead, haven't you?'

His wife couldn't meet his eyes. 'I thought they would be.'

'Thought or hoped? Didn't you once acknowledge to yourself that every child has a right to know and love their grandparents, and the grandparents have the right to know their grandchildren? Especially as you were their only child, and when you deserted them they had no one. And the sickening thing is, they ask about you and the children every time I visit them. I used to make excuses for you at first, believing you would come to your senses eventually. But you can only make excuses for so long and expect them to be believed. I don't like telling lies, and apparently I'm not very good at it. Because one day your mother took my hand and said, "It's all right, Bob, you don't have to lie to me and Joe. We're just glad you come to see us, and very grateful". Two lonely old people, Edie, who at best only have a few more years left to them. If you can live with yourself, knowing that, then the heart that beats inside of you is a heart of stone. My feelings for you, right now, are of sadness, pity and disgust.'

'I don't know what you had hoped to gain by raking all this up, but if you have finished castigating me, I would like to go to sleep. It's been a very trying day.'

'I'm afraid you're going to have to force yourself to stay awake a little longer, because I still have much to say.' Robert couldn't remember being as angry as he was now. 'I am the provider and master of this house and I intend taking more of an interest in what happens. There will be some changes, I can assure you. I have two children who are so idle they don't make any contribution to either this house, or to society as a whole. They take everything for granted and expect to be waited on hand and foot. They look down on people who have to work for a living, as though it's something to be ashamed of. And what gives them the right to think like this when they come from the working class themselves? Because they've never been told the truth. I have no intention of laying the law down unless it becomes necessary. So I'm going to leave it to you to suggest to Victoria and Nigel that they get involved in charity work. Perhaps helping children in the Cottage Homes, by taking them gifts of toys or clothing. Or they could visit the poor in almshouses and hospitals. There are thousands of poor people in Liverpool who need help, even if it's only a visit to show somebody cares about them. And seeing the poverty in which some people are forced to live, might just change our children's outlook on life, and make them appreciate how fortunate they are. It might even make them more sympathetic to the plight of others.'

Edwina was livid. 'I notice you don't include your precious Abigail in this noble charity work you have in mind for Victoria and Nigel. I wonder why?'

'I don't need to! Abbie will be starting at commercial college at the beginning of their term, and eventually she will find herself a job. She intends to do something useful with her life and I admire her for it. And I'll make sure she is allowed to follow the course she's set out for herself without interference from anyone in this house. I hope I make myself clear?'

'Quite clear! And now, if I am allowed to speak, I want you to know that your plans for Victoria and Nigel will be met with stiff opposition. There is no way they will do this charity work you have in mind. It's quite out of the question.'

'That's a pity, because I refuse to keep on giving them generous monthly allowances if they do nothing to deserve them. You are responsible for protecting them from the realities of life, so I suggest that it would be in the interest of both parties to seriously consider what contribution they can make to society. You are going to have to go along with me on this, Edwina, and any other proposals I may make in the future.'

'This is not like you, Robert, to be so hard.'

'I hope you understand that I mean every word. As I said earlier, I intend taking more of an interest in my family and my home. I want to hear laughter in the house instead of sarcasm, a smile in the place of a sneer, and most of all I want more care and consideration shown by every member of the family. Are you going to help me achieve this, Edwina?'

'I have run this house to the best of my ability, and with you being away so much I'm the one who has had to make the decisions. Now, it seems, you don't think I've made a very good job of it! That I don't care!'

'Do you care enough for us to be at least friends? To be pleasant with each other and show respect? To support any decision I make, even though it might not be popular with the children? I would not be unreasonable and of course would always discuss things with you first. If you were against any suggestion I made, we could argue the toss until we reached a suitable compromise. But once an agreement had been reached between us, I would expect you, as my wife, to stand firmly behind me. Can I have your word on this?'

Edwina wasn't convinced her husband meant what he said. In a day or two he'd be so tied up in his business the whole episode would be forgotten. Then she remembered her parents. She had felt a stab of guilt when he said they were still alive, but how could she be expected to look after this big house and go visiting. And she salved her conscience by telling herself she wouldn't be doing them a favour by inviting them here, they'd feel out of place and uncomfortable. But the mood Robert was in tonight, if she continued to thwart him, he wouldn't think twice about telling the children their grandparents were still alive. And she couldn't bear the thought of them condemning her. So she kept her true feelings to herself, and said, 'Shall we wait until something crops up that doesn't meet with your approval? Then we can discuss the situation and take it from there?'

Robert was less than satisfied. 'If you deliberately go against my wishes, I will have no hesitation in taking over completely. That means I will attend to paying the household bills and the staff wages, and you and the children will have to ask me for every penny. It may sound harsh, but it's the only way I can get you to understand I mean every word I've said tonight. You have a choice. Work with me in harmony, or suffer the consequences.'

Robert slipped off his dressing gown and laid it over the back of a pale pink velvet, elaborately carved chair. Then he climbed into bed and turned on his side, away from his wife. 'Sleep on it, Edwina. Goodnight.'

Chapter Three

Agnes Weatherby was bending over the large, scrubbed kitchen table, a voluminous apron covering her ample figure and her sleeves rolled up to the elbows. Her hands were covered in flour as she moved the rolling pin back and forth over a piece of pastry which would be made into a mouth-watering apple pie and served with cream for the family's dessert. She heard the back door opening and a smile covered her face. 'Good morning, Kitty. How are you this fine morning, sunshine?'

'Morning, Aggie.' Kitty Higgins put her scruffy bag down at the side of the sink. She was a small woman, as thin as a rake. The second-hand coat she'd bought at Paddy's Market about five years ago, which was now of an indistinguishable colour, hung on her like a scarecrow. But although she looked as though a puff of wind would blow her over, she was wiry, and a damn good worker. She needed to be, because at forty-five she was the sole breadwinner of the family and if she didn't work, she and her invalid husband would be thrown out on the streets. They barely made ends meet on the money she earned, because once the rent was paid there was only enough left for pennies for the gas and a bag of coal, but at least they had a roof over their head. 'That walk tires me out, queen. I'm all in before I bleedin' get here!'

Agnes kept the smile on her face while she sighed inwardly. For the sake of one penny, this woman had to walk three miles, and although she might moan now and again, as everybody did, she had never once blamed her circumstances on the husband she idolised. 'It is a long walk, Kitty. I wouldn't fancy it meself every morning.'

'Beggars can't be choosers, queen, so it's Hobson's choice. There's many a one in the cemetery would swap places with me.' The little woman eyed the pastry and licked her lips. 'Meat or apple pie?'

'Apple, sunshine, and I'll make sure there's a bit over for you to take home. And before I forget, there's some pork and vegetables in the larder, left over from yesterday. They'll do for a meal for you and your feller.'

'I don't know what me and Alf would do without you, queen, we'd bleedin' starve to death. "Our guardian angel" is what he calls yer, and he's right.' Kitty stood on tip-toe to reach an overall hanging from a hook behind the door and chuckled as she slipped it on. It was miles too big for her, and she looked comical. 'I could get the bleedin' army in here with me, and have a knees-up into the bargain.'

'Did you have anything to eat before yer left the house?' Aggie asked. She worried about Kitty because anyone with half an eye could see she was under-nourished. 'And don't bother telling lies because I can always tell.'

'I didn't have time, queen, I got up late. I just had time to see to Alf and swallow half a cup of tea.'

'Then sit yerself down and I'll make a fresh brew and some toast.'

'But what if Miss Edwina comes in? She wouldn't be at all happy.' Kitty couldn't afford to lose this job. She'd never get another one with a housekeeper like Aggie, who made sure she didn't go home any day empty-handed. 'She can be a right snotty bugger at times.'

'I don't think she will be today, somehow.' The housekeeper nodded her head knowingly. 'Yer see, sunshine, yer didn't half miss a treat last night. Yer wouldn't believe the shenanigans what went on. If it hadn't been for Mr Robert persuading me to stay I'd have been out of that bleedin' door with me coat on.'

'Go 'way!' Kitty's eyes widened. 'What happened, queen?'

40

'Wait till I make a couple of rounds of toast and a pot of tea, then I can rest me feet while we're having a natter.' Agnes was nothing if not efficient. Within minutes they were sitting down with a large plate of golden-brown toast on the table and two cups of piping hot tea. But she could see Kitty's eyes going to the door that led into the hall, and knew she was afraid of being caught out. 'Don't worry, sunshine. Mrs Dennison hasn't stirred yet, nor have Miss Victoria or Mr Nigel. We're all right for ten minutes. Mr Robert was out early because he's got something on in Chester today, and Miss Abbie left just before you came.'

Kitty reached for a round of toast, and when she took a bite the butter oozed out and ran down her chin. Oh, what luxury, she thought. Some people don't know they're born, being able to have butter spread so liberally. 'Tell us what happened, queen.'

'Well, yer might know it was Miss Victoria what started it.' The housekeeper related the incident from the very beginning. 'I only asked Miss Abbie if someone had been having a go at her, and that's when the sparks began to fly.' Before adopting the posh voice and haughty pose of Victoria, she said, 'Get a load of this. "I really don't think it's any of your concern. How dare you interfere in what is a private family matter. Now please remove these plates and bring in the dinner. I have a visitor coming soon." Well, I wasn't going to be spoken to like that by no one, so I told her to remove the bleedin' plates herself!'

Kitty gasped. 'Yer didn't, did yer?'

'I said a lot more, sunshine, like telling them to get their own bleedin' dinner 'cos I was off to pack me bags as I'd had a bellyful of them.'

'Ooh, wouldn't I love to have been there to hear that! She's a snooty cow, that Miss Victoria, and it's been on the tip of me tongue many times to tell her to sod off. But I can't afford to lose me job, so I have to keep me gob shut and take everything she wants to throw at me.' Kitty helped herself to another piece of toast. 'What happened then, queen?'

'Miss Edwina begged me to stay, saying her daughter didn't really mean what she said. But the bold one sat there without saying a word, posing like a flipping mannequin. So I said no, I was leaving. Miss Abbie was crying and said she was going to fetch her father, and when she opened the door, there he was standing there. He'd heard every word and he made Miss Victoria apologise, then took me through to his study and gave me a glass of whisky. He said he was ashamed of his daughter, and if I left, him and Miss Abbie would follow me.' Agnes leaned her elbows on the table and grinned. 'And how about this, sunshine? He ordered his wife to see to the family's dinner, and while she was at it she could bring two plates through to the study. One for him and the other for yours truly.'

'Well, I declare! Put the bleedin' flags out and declare it a national holiday.'

'That's not all. He gave me the night off and the family had to wash their own dishes. So I went next door and spent a couple of hours with Tilly. And to round the day off, she had six bottles of milk stout stashed away in the scullery and we ended up in a very happy frame of mind.'

'You jammy bugger!' The smile suddenly dropped from Kitty's face. 'Yer'd better watch out for that Miss Victoria, though, queen, 'cos she'll have it in for yer now. It must have killed her to have to apologise to yer, and she'll be looking for ways to get her own back. So yer'll need to have eyes in yer backside from now on, mark my words.'

Agnes's body shook with laughter. 'So every time I see Miss Victoria, are yer suggesting I turn me back on her, bend down and drop me bloomers? You haven't seen my backside, sunshine. If yer had, yer wouldn't wish it on anyone – even Miss Hoity-Toity.'

'If it was me, she wouldn't even notice 'cos she never looks at me. Never by a word or a nod does she acknowledge my existence. If I didn't move out of her way, she'd walk through me. Now I know I'm thin, and if I stand sideways yer can't see me, but she makes me feel like an invisible woman.'

Agnes glanced at the large round clock on the wall and pushed her chair back. 'I think yer'd better make yerself visible now, sunshine, and start on the fire in the drawing room. If anyone notices ye're running a bit late, tell them I needed yer to help me out in the kitchen. If I'm asked I'll say I didn't sleep very well last night 'cos I was too upset.' She watched the cleaner pick up the heavy bucket which contained all the articles needed for raking the ashes out, and washing and polishing the large fireplace in the drawing room. And as she often did, Agnes wondered how someone who didn't have a pick on her, could cope with the heavy work she was required to do in this big house. 'I'm going to start on their breakfast now 'cos they'll be down any minute. So you get a move on in the drawing room so it's ready for them to retire to. And when they ring for their eleven o'clock tea and biscuits, I'll give yer the aye-aye and we'll join them. Not in the same room, mind, but I don't see why they should have all the fun.'

The little woman turned at the door. 'Fun did yer say, queen? They don't know what fun is. I've been working here for five years now, and I've never once heard a good belly laugh.'

'Kitty, don't you know that only people as common as muck enjoy a belly laugh?' The housekeeper adopted a haughty stance and looked down her nose. 'Really, Mrs Higgins, you must have been brought up in the gutter.'

'And that's where me and my Alf will end up if I get the sack from this job, Agnes Weatherby. It's all right for them what are on friendly terms with the boss. But what I'd like to know is, what have you got that I haven't?'

'A big bosom, tummy and backside. That's without taking into account me legs which are as big as tree trunks, arms that would put a navvy to shame, and hands like ham shanks. Does that answer yer question, sunshine?'

Kitty lowered the bucket. She'd have to work like the

clappers to make up the time she was wasting, but the devil in her couldn't resist. Lounging against the back of the door she crossed her feet at the ankles like she'd seen Miss Victoria do. Then she lifted a thin hand to within six inches of her face and opened two fingers as though holding a cigarette holder. 'I say, old girl, you don't have a very high opinion of yourself, what ho!'

Her lazy drawl in a posh voice, so in contrast to the raggedy clothes she had on, had Agnes doubled up with laughter. 'Get going, yer silly cow, or we'll both end up being given the bleedin' sack.'

'Has Father gone *completely* mad?' Victoria's eyes were giving out sparks as she crossed a shapely leg. 'I have no intention of doing as he asks, and I'm quite sure I speak for Nigel, when I say that.'

'Steady on, Victoria, I think we should discuss the matter at some length before dismissing it out of hand.' It was so rare for Nigel to disagree with anyone, both mother and sister looked taken aback. 'After all, Father has always been more than generous with us, and I think we should try to please him.'

'I have no intention of going into poor houses to visit sick people! Heaven only knows what sorts of diseases we could pick up. No, it is out of the question.'

For the first time in years, a sense of unease entered Edwina's head. Had Robert been right all along, in saying the children should have been made aware of their background from the time they could understand? Then she mentally shook her head, not allowing the idea to take root. She'd done a good job with the children, they were a credit to her. And she couldn't understand why Robert wasn't equally proud of them. Then she conjured up a picture of his face last night, full of determination. She had no doubt he meant every word he said, and if certain things didn't change he would carry out his threat.

'I have to tell you, Victoria, that your father made it quite clear that unless you and Nigel found a worthy cause where you could be usefully employed for one or two days a week, he would take over the running of the house himself. That would mean I'd no longer have control over the money; he would pay all the outgoing expenses. Any money we needed, we would have to ask him for.'

'He's bluffing, he wouldn't do it.' Victoria waved a hand as though dismissing the idea. 'I will call his bluff.'

'He was not bluffing, Victoria,' Edwina said. 'So if you refuse to do as he asks, then on your own head be it.'

Victoria was livid. She was so used to having all her requests for money granted without question, she had no intention of allowing the system to be changed without strong resistance. And when she spoke, her voice raised, her anger was evident. 'And you, Mother? Did you just stand like a servant and let Father dictate to you? Really, you do surprise and disappoint me.'

A knock on the door had Edwina lifting both hands for silence. 'Not one word,' she hissed, 'we don't want the servants knowing our business.' Then she called, 'Come in, Agnes.'

The housekeeper carried the tray to a table at the side of Edwina. Her eyes appeared to be concentrating on the tray and its being deposited on the table without mishap. But she could feel the tension in the air and sly glances took in the stony expressions on the faces of the two women. 'Shall I pour, Miss Edwina?'

'No, thank you, Agnes, I'll attend to it. You go about your business, I'm sure you have lots to do.'

With a nod, the housekeeper left the room. She closed the door behind her but didn't move. She'd heard the raised voices before she'd knocked and knew Mr Robert was the target of their anger. This wasn't fair, because he was the one who put the finest food on the table, silk sheets on the beds, and had provided furniture fit for a palace. And if it wasn't for him they wouldn't be sitting there now being waited on hand and foot.

Agnes sighed, and was about to walk away when she heard Miss Victoria speak. It was the venom and sarcasm in her voice that had the housekeeper rooted to the spot.

'I don't know why you kowtow to her, Mother – she's only a servant, after all. She gets paid for the work she does, has a room to herself and eats the same food we do. Where else would she be so well off? She's a good cook, I'll grant you that, but she could easily be replaced. And don't forget what happened yesterday. A silly little incident, brought about by herself, and she threatens to leave! I'd have let her go, and good riddance. But no, everyone is at great pains to coax her to stay. And as a result, Nigel and I are to be penalised. Well, I for one would be glad to see the back of her.'

Agnes moved away from the door, muttering, 'Oh, yer would, would yer? Well, I won't give yer the bleedin' satisfaction, yer jumped-up little madam. I'll go when Mr Robert asks me to go, and not one minute before. Now I know the way yer talk about yer father behind his back, and me, I'll bloody well haunt yer.' She climbed a flight of stairs to see Kitty on her knees polishing the spindles of the ornate staircase. And with the scene came the comparison. This little woman, half-starved, was forced to work just to keep a roof over her head. Apart from the husband she adored, all she had in her life was toil and worry. And yet those three downstairs didn't even pass her the time of day because she was only a skivvy. Not worthy of a smile or a kind word. But if Agnes had to choose between Kitty and Victoria for a friend, she knew who'd she'd choose any day. Kitty was more caring and sympathetic than the daughter of the house would ever be. 'Come on, sunshine, it's time for a cuppa and one of me scones what I've just taken out of the oven. They're still hot and they'll be just the job with some butter.'

'I'll clear me polish and dusters away first, Aggie.'

'Leave the bleedin' things where they are. With a bit of

luck a certain person might trip over them and break the nose she's so fond of looking down.' When the housekeeper took hold of Kitty's arm, and could feel only bone, her anger increased. Why was life so bloody unfair? Not that she had any worries herself, she'd never married and only had herself to think about. But surely fate could have been kinder to Kitty Higgins? 'I'll take the blame if anything is said. After all, I had a very big upset last night and I haven't got over it yet.'

When they were seated facing each other across the kitchen table, Kitty said, 'Yer should be careful what yer say, queen, 'cos yer never know who's listening.'

'That cuts two ways, sunshine. They should be careful what they say in case *I'm* standing outside the door listening.'

'Nah, yer wouldn't do that!' Kitty closed her eyes as she bit into the hot scone on which a generous portion of butter had melted. What luxury, what bliss. If only her Alf could have one of these while they were hot and oozing real best butter. 'As I said, you wouldn't do nothing like that.'

'Would and have, sunshine! I've just heard Miss High and Mighty Victoria say she'd like to see the back of me. They say eavesdroppers never hear good of themselves, and that is probably right, but at least I heard the truth. I know where I stand now.'

'Pay no attention to her, queen, she's not worth it. Hasn't got a good word for anyone and a slapped backside wouldn't go amiss.' A picture flashed into Kitty's head, of Mr Robert with Miss Victoria across his knee, smacking her with a slipper. The image was nearly as pleasing as the scone. 'That's something I'd like to see,' she mumbled through a mouthful of crumbs. 'The queer one being taken down a peg or two.'

'It'll happen one day, you mark my words. All it needs is for her to insult the wrong person and she'll end up getting her face slapped.'

Kitty lifted her cup. 'I'll drink to that, queen. But you steer clear of her 'cos if she can cause trouble for yer, she will. And I wouldn't want to work here if you left. Yer see, ye're me best

47

mate, I don't bother with no one else.'

There was affection in the housekeeper's smile. 'Don't yer start worrying about me leaving, Kitty, 'cos I ain't going nowhere. Miss Victoria can do her damnedest, she won't get rid of me. Not while Mr Robert and Miss Abbie are here. They're like family to me and I love the bones of them.'

'D'yer love the bones of me, queen?'

'There's nothing else of yer to love, is there? Ye're a bag of bleedin' bones! I'm going to have to start trying to fatten yer up, 'cos yer worry the life out of me. D'yer know what, sunshine, yer shadow's got more meat on it than you have.'

Kitty thought this was funny. 'Oh, you are a one, Aggie! Just wait until I tell my Alf what yer said, he won't half laugh.'

'While ye're at it, yer can tell him I want yer to bring a basin in with yer tomorrow so I can fill it with thick, nourishing soup. It'll put a lining on yer tummies.'

'Is that what the family are having tomorrow for starters?'

Agnes nodded, a sly smile on her face. 'They don't know it yet, but yes, that's what they're having for starters.'

'But I thought Miss Edwina gave yer a menu every day?'

'She does, she brings it in every night for the next day. And tonight the menu will probably start with a consommé, which they usually have on a Thursday. But with a little wangle here, and a little lie there, I bet she'll leave this kitchen thinking what a clever woman she is to have thought of having barley broth for a change.'

'Ye're a bleedin' caution, you are, Aggie!' Kitty grinned. 'There's no flies on you, they're all ruddy bluebottles.'

'Then I'll have to make sure none of them fly into the soup, won't I, sunshine?'

Robert took out his fobwatch and turned to the man standing beside him. 'I'm off for lunch now, and I think I'll go straight home afterwards. You don't need me here, do you?'

'I'm not even needed meself for a couple of hours, the auctioneer's two assistants do all the work. There's only the books to see to when the auction's over, and that's no problem. The bidding has been quite brisk so I think you'll find we've had a good day.' A few years ago Jeff would have been too embarrassed to look his boss in the eye when similar conversations like this took place, and many times he'd wished Robert had never confided in him. But not any more. His employer had been open and honest, and after a few visits to the large, richly furnished house in Mossley Hill, Jeff not only understood, but sympathised. 'You go and enjoy your lunch, Bob, I can manage things from now. I'll have the books ready for your inspection tomorrow.'

Robert nodded to the auctioneer, then walked through the double doors donning his beige bowler hat. He stood outside the building breathing in the fresh air as he pulled on a pair of soft leather gloves, then made his way to the black Bentley saloon car parked nearby. Tall and well-built, he cut a handsome figure in his well-fitting expensive clothes, and many an eye was turned in his direction. And he was in a happy frame of mind as he turned on the ignition and the car purred into life. He only came to Chester one day in a month, and it was a day he always looked forward to.

Five minutes later, Robert pulled up outside a very ordinary house in the middle of a terrace of other ordinary houses. There was a handkerchief-sized garden and a short path leading to the front door. The windows were neat, with pure white net curtains hanging behind gleaming panes of glass, and the brass knocker shone so brightly he could see his reflection in it. Before he had time to knock, the door was opened by an attractive woman in her forties whose smile told him he was welcome. 'Come in, Robert.' She closed the door then turned and lifted her face for a kiss. 'It's good to see you.'

'And it's good to see you, Maureen, my dear.'

'Hang your coat and hat up, while I nip through to the kitchen and take our dinner out of the oven.' Over her shoulder, she called, 'I've got some nice gammon, to have with egg and tomato.'

'And chips I hope!' Robert followed her through the small living room to the kitchen. He felt more at home in this house than he did in his own. 'If there's no chips I'll take my custom to the café down the road.'

'Oh, you and your chips! Honestly, you're like a little boy sometimes.'

'When I'm with you I feel young, you have that effect on me. I come to your door an old man, with all the worries of the world on my shoulders. But when I step over the threshold I am rejuvenated and feel as free as a bird.' Robert chuckled. 'A very young bird.'

'An old man indeed!' Maureen Schofield wagged a finger in his face. 'It so happens that I am only a year younger than you, and I refuse to think of myself as an old woman. So don't you be putting years on me. I prefer to think we are both in the prime of life.' She shooed him through the kitchen door and back into the living room. 'Sit down and read the paper while I peel a few potatoes to make some chips for you. I couldn't bear to see a grown man cry 'cos he doesn't get what he wants.'

'Why can't I stand and watch you? We get little enough time together as it is, I would hate to waste any by sitting twiddling my thumbs.'

'Sit down, Robert, and do as you're told. I'll have the meal on the table much quicker if I'm left on my own. Ten minutes at the outside.'

Robert spent the time reminiscing. It was three years now since Maureen came into his life, and it was by pure luck that he was the one who called on her, and not Jeff. An elderly neighbour of hers had died, and the family had asked her if she would see to the selling of the furniture as they lived some distance away. She had contacted their office in Chester and as he'd been there at the time, he agreed to come along and give a valuation. That was how easily the friendship came about. Robert took to Maureen right away, she was so warm and friendly and had a good sense of humour. They'd got

50

talking and he learned she was a spinster, by choice and not necessity. She was born when her mother was turned forty, and by the time she was old enough to have a social life, both her parents were frail and needed looking after. Because she loved them so much, she put her own life on the back burner and cared for them until they died. She was thirty by that time, and all the friends she'd had in her teens were married with families. When she was telling Robert this, there'd been no self-pity in her voice, no regret that the best years of her life had passed her by, and he found himself being drawn to her. She worked in a shop, and as Wednesday was half-day closing, he'd said casually that as he was in Chester every fourth Wednesday, he might pop in one day for a cup of tea. For months he made excuses, that he was just passing the bottom of the road, or he was calling on someone in the next street. Lame excuses, as they both knew. Then he took to calling every fourth week without making excuses, and Maureen took to looking forward to seeing him.

'Elbows off the table, please.' She smiled down as she placed a plate in front of him and one on the opposite side of the table. 'You were miles away then.'

'Yes, my dear, I was reliving the last three years. It doesn't seem that long since I first knocked on your door. The time has flown over.'

'It hasn't gone without incident, though, Robert. I've got many more grey hairs in my head now than I did then.'

There was affection in his smile. If he had to describe Maureen in one word, it would be bonny. She was by no means fat, but she had a full rounded figure, and such a happy, bonny face. 'I think I've grown more grey hairs than you, my dear.'

'I've no intention of counting hairs! Now get that meal down you, and if you leave as much as one chip, I'll have yer guts for garters.'

'Message received and understood.' Robert speared a chip and bit half of it off. 'They used to be a luxury when I was a

51

kid. My mother would send me for a pennyworth of chips with plenty of salt and vinegar on. On a hard-up day, when she was skint, she'd make that penn'orth of chips into sandwiches for me and me dad, and herself. And I can still remember how I relished the taste of those chips. They were hard times for us, and all our neighbours, but they were good times as well.'

'Stop talking and eat your dinner, Robert, before it goes cold.'

'This gammon is very tasty, my dear.'

'That's one of the advantages of working in a grocer's shop. I can pick out the rashers I fancy, knowing they have been freshly cut.'

They carried on eating in silence until their plates were clean. Then Robert licked his lips and patted his tummy. 'Very enjoyable, as always.'

'I've kept the kettle on the boil on the hob, so there'll be a nice cuppa ready for you in just two minutes.'

Robert watched as she picked up a knitted square to cover her hand before lifting the heavy kettle. 'I wish you would allow me to pay to have that grate removed, Maureen, and a smaller one put in its place. Not only would it save you blackleading that huge thing all the time, it would also give you more space in the room. I could have the work done by a skilled fitter who would be quick and efficient. The room would be a mess for about three days, but think of the advantages. And it would make me very happy if you would accept my offer.'

Maureen put the kettle back on the hob and returned to her chair. 'I am very fond of you, Robert, and I treasure the few hours we have together each month. My life would be empty if I didn't have them to look forward to. You know I am happy to be your confidante when you feel the need to talk, and that my shoulder is here for you to cry on. And when you need comforting, my arms will always hold you. I have no one else in my life, and I value what we have together. But I will never take, or allow you to spend money on me. I would feel like a kept woman, a mistress, and I couldn't live with that. My parents bought this house at a time when it was unthinkable for working-class people to own their own home. They scrimped and scraped, went without to raise the money so that when they died, I would have some security. So I don't have to worry about paying rent, and my wages buy me what little I need. I don't possess many worldly goods, but I have no need of them. What I do have need of, is my independence and my pride. I would lose both if I accepted money from you. I know you mean well, and I do appreciate your thoughtfulness, but it would spoil what we have, and I don't want that.'

Robert reached across and covered her hand. 'If I have hurt or insulted you, it was unintentional, I assure you. You are one of the most open, honest and kind people it has been my fortune to know and I have the greatest admiration for you. A short while ago you said I was like a little boy, and there's nothing a little boy likes better than to give and receive presents. But I will never again make a suggestion that displeases you if you will, just once, humour me.'

Maureen's blue eyes twinkled as she raised her brows. 'Humour you? I thought that was something I often did! What about the plate of chips you've just eaten? They weren't on the menu today, I only made them to humour you.'

'What I have in mind is far more serious than a plate of chips, my dear. It's something that has been nagging in my head for quite some time. I have great affection for you, and I believe you return my feelings?' Robert waited for her nod, then continued, 'Yet if anything happened to stop me coming here, neither of us have a single thing to remember each other by. No photograph or memento to remind us of the happiness we've shared for the last three years. That saddens me, because you have given me so much joy. You filled a void in my life and helped me keep my sanity.'

'And don't you think you did the same for me? We have helped each other, Robert, and please God, we will continue to do so for a long time. So no more talk of anything happening to prevent you coming – you are making me sad.'

'Are you not prepared to humour me, then?'

'I'm not saying yes until I know what it is. Otherwise I might find a man at my door tomorrow morning with a toolbox, come to take my grate out.'

Robert grinned. 'I think you've taught me the error of my ways on that one, my dear. No, what I had in mind, and what I would dearly love, is for us to buy each other a gift. Something we can use every day so our thoughts are always with each other.'

Maureen looked doubtful. Everything he had was expensive – his clothes, fobwatch, cuff links, tie-pin and the huge black saloon car standing outside her house which the neighbours must wonder about but never mentioned. She couldn't buy him anything that would compare with what he already had. 'Don't think I'm feeling sorry for myself, Robert, but any gift I gave you would have to come from Woolworth's.'

'I've told you many tales about our housekeeper, Agnes, so as you seem to think I'm a snob, I'll answer you as she would. "I don't care if it's a bleedin' penny whistle, sunshine, it's still a gift. And if it's not good enough for yer – well, that's too bleedin' bad. Yer can sod off and yer'll get bugger all in future".'

Maureen's head fell back and she roared with laughter. 'How I would love to meet Agnes, she sounds a treasure.'

'She is that! Dead funny and as straight as they come. Her and Abbie are the two people who make life worth living. Anyway, back to the subject in hand. I know what I would like from you, my dear. It wouldn't be too expensive and it's something I would use every day.'

'And that is?'

'A cigar clipper.'

'But you've already got one. You don't need two, surely?'

'I want one that has been given to me by your fair hand. It will go with me everywhere and you will be constantly in my thoughts.'

'If that is what you want, but I warn you it will not be as good as the one you have. And for that reason I don't want you buying me anything expensive, otherwise you will embarrass me.'

'That is one thing I will not go along with, Maureen. And before you argue, please listen to my side. Every time I come here you have a meal ready for me. I have offered to bring groceries with me to help out, but you stubbornly refuse. So while it is all right for you to give to me, I am not allowed to give to you. Is that fair?'

'Good heavens, Robert, I'd be a poor one if I couldn't give you a meal. I'd be cooking for myself anyway, so a little extra makes hardly any difference.'

'I wonder why I don't believe you? Can you honestly say you would buy gammon for yourself, rather than streaky bacon?'

Maureen tried to keep her face straight but it didn't come off. 'Oh, all right, you win. But don't you dare buy me anything too expensive.'

'We'll see, my dear, we'll see. Now how about you making our cup of tea, then we can sit holding hands while we have a cosy chat. You can tell me everything you've been up to since I last saw you.'

'That should take all of two minutes, Robert, because as you well know, I lead a very uneventful life. Of course I could invent something to keep you amused, but I'd need time to do that and there isn't enough now. However, if I put my mind to it in the next four weeks, I'm sure my imagination can come up with a few incidents to keep you happy.' She smiled and pinched his cheek then went to pick up the kettle. 'I'll leave the washing-up until you've gone; it'll give me something to do.'

When Maureen came through carrying two steaming cups of tea, Robert was sitting on the couch looking very much at home. He patted the space beside him and said, 'Leave the cups on the table and come and sit next to me. We only have a little time left, let's not waste it.' When she was seated, he put an arm across her shoulders and pulled her close. 'Now I am happy. You chase away my cares, my darling Maureen, and if I had one wish, it would be for you to play a bigger part in my life.'

Her head resting on his shoulder, Maureen looked up at him. 'It isn't possible, so let's be grateful for what we have.'

'If it were possible, would you come to me?'

'Yes, I would. But wishes and dreams are not going to make it happen, Robert. You have a wife, even if it is in name only. And I am not a marriage-breaker, although there are many who would see me as a scarlet woman. But I honestly believe we are doing no wrong. Everyone needs some love and affection in their lives and that is what we are giving each other. No one is being hurt by it.'

'I know what you're saying is true, but it doesn't stop me wishing. I would give you the earth if I could, buy you anything your heart desires.'

'Robert, I am a forty-five-year-old virgin, and I work in a grocer's shop. That was my life when you came into it, and it is still my life. We agreed then that our relationship would be purely as friends, and no one would be hurt by it.'

'It was easy to say that then, dear, because I didn't know I was going to fall in love with you – that you were going to become so important to me. I'm sorry, but it would have been easier to stop rain from falling than stop myself being drawn ever closer to you.'

'And don't you think the same thing has happened to me? I love you, Robert, and have done for some time. If you only knew how much I look forward to your visits, and how I count the days and hours. But we can't change things, so why don't we just settle for what we have? I couldn't bear you not to be part of my life, I would be lost without you.'

'You'll never be lost, my darling, because I'll always be here. Whatever your terms, I will abide by them, and love you all the more for your honesty.' He kissed her hair. 'That's the first time you have ever said you love me, and you've made me very happy.'

Maureen reached for his hand. 'We've become very serious, so why don't you make me laugh by telling me more of what Agnes gets up to? And I want to know how Abbie is and how today's auction went. There's so much I want to hear, so come on, Robert, let me share the happenings in your life.'

'I left the auction before it was over, as you know, but I would hazard a guess that we've had a particularly good day. Abbie is to go to commercial college to learn shorthand and typing, book-keeping and general office work. She met stiff opposition from her mother, but I put my foot down. You'd like Abbie, she's a lovely, bubbly girl, full of fun.' Robert ruffled Maureen's hair. 'And now to our indomitable housekeeper. My eldest daughter can be a pain in the neck, a real snob. Well, she looked down her nose once too often for Agnes, and was told, "Take yer own bleedin' plates out, 'cos I'm packing me bags. And yer can see to yer own bleedin' dinner, 'cos I ain't." And she would have gone, too, if I hadn't smoothed things over with a glass of whisky. I wouldn't have blamed her either, she deserves more respect than that. As she said to me, "I'd have cried me bleedin' eyes out if I'd had to leave you and Miss Abbie. But I would have done, Mr Robert, 'cos I've got me pride. I'll have no toffee-nosed little madam looking down their nose at me!" '

'Good for Agnes! I've never met the woman but I know I'd like her.'

They chatted about different things, keeping the conversation light, until it was time for Robert to leave. Then they stood in the hall, their arms around each other, and kissed. Neither of them said a word, but both were aware that the kiss was warmer and more loving than usual. Robert sighed. 'Four weeks today, my dear. Take good care of yourself.'

'And you, Robert, you take care.' Maureen watched him walk down the path then closed the door and leaned her back against it as the tears rolled down her cheeks.

Chapter Four

'I couldn't believe my ears when Mother told me. Can you imagine me going into a poor house, or workhouse, whatever they call them? I'd come home crawling with lice and heaven knows what else.' Victoria was wearing a petulant expression as the wind played with the strands of hair that had worked loose from the pretty floral voile scarf she had covering her head. 'I'm of the opinion that Father has gone completely mad, because if he was in his right mind he'd know I would never entertain such an idea.'

Charles Chisholm didn't answer as he changed down a gear to navigate the bend in the country lane. There was no traffic on the road, but he wasn't taking any chances with his beloved MG drophead coupé. His father had bought it for his twenty-third birthday last week and he was the envy of all his friends. He'd spent a couple of hours polishing it that afternoon and there wasn't a fingermark on the bright blue bodywork, the chrome fittings sparkled and you couldn't see the windscreen it was so clear. He'd even had the black soft top up, so a maid, standing on a chair, could dust it. He was so proud of it, and had expected Victoria to be very impressed. Instead, she was sulking and hadn't even passed comment.

'Charles, are you listening to me?'

He glanced sideways. She looked stunning as always. Elegant, poised, make-up perfect and dressed from head to toe in expensive clothes. She was just the right person to go with his car. But he wished she would take that frown off her face.

'What did you say, darling? I'm new to this car and I'm afraid I need to concentrate.'

'I was talking about Father, and his stupid idea that I should do charity work! I mean, do you really think that's me?'

'No, I must admit I can't see you in that role, my sweet. But my mother, and a couple of her friends, they do a little charity work and they find it very rewarding. But not everyone is cut out for it.'

Victoria showed an interest. 'I didn't know that, Charles, you've never mentioned it. What exactly is it that your mother and her friends do?'

'I'm not quite sure, my love, you would have to ask her. As far as I know they visit poor people in hospital, and they take them flowers, or fruit. There's probably more to it than that, but I honestly don't know. Mother seems to enjoy the work, but whether it would suit you is a different matter.'

Victoria was now definitely interested. Perhaps things weren't as black as they seemed. The Chisholms were a very rich and influential family, and she couldn't see Annabel Chisholm going near anyone who was dirty or disease-ridden. 'I'd rather you didn't mention it was Father's idea, Charles, but would you make a few enquiries for me, darling?'

He put a hand on her knee and squeezed. 'Of course, my sweet. I'll ask Mother over breakfast tomorrow. Now, can we please have a smile on that pretty face? You've looked miserable since I picked you up, and you haven't even said how spiffing the car looks.'

'It looks lovely, and you look very handsome behind the wheel.' Victoria was feeling decidedly more happy. She'd been going out with Charles for several months now and had been trying to coax him into revealing his intentions. So far she hadn't met with success, but she wasn't going to let him slip through her fingers if she could help it. He would be an excellent catch, rich and terribly good-looking. If she could land him, she would live a splendid life of luxury. Never again would she have to ask for an allowance, she'd have money to burn. She would be mistress in her own house, with servants to do her bidding. But she wasn't the only one with designs on him, he was fawned over by several of her friends. No dinner party was complete without Charles Chisholm, particularly if there was a daughter in the house seeking an eligible husband. So she had to persuade him that by choosing her, he would be getting an excellent wife who would be an asset to his business and social life. And he had just handed her an ideal way of getting closer to him – through his family. It would do her cause no harm to ingratiate herself with his parents. To let them think her desire to do charity work was out of the goodness of her heart. And who knows, one day she might even thank her father for starting a chain of events which led to her catching the most eligible bachelor in their circle of friends.

'Darling, you look so handsome I could kiss you.' Victoria made up her mind she was going to woo the man who could give her the life she craved. So she fluttered her lashes and asked in a coy voice, 'Would you think me a wanton hussy if I ask you to find a secluded spot to park? Somewhere romantic, under the shade of a tree perhaps, where we could kiss without being seen.'

'Oh, I say, that's a jolly good idea,' Charles said, bucking up no end and thinking Victoria wasn't such a bad old stick after all. She'd been out with several of his friends and they said she was cold enough to be an iceberg. Hopefully he would be able to tell them how wrong they were. 'I'll pull in here, my sweet.'

Victoria wasn't a romantic or sentimental person. Aloof and cool, she didn't like being kissed or fondled. She'd earned the name 'iceberg' by keeping her suitors at arm's length. A peck on the cheek was as far as she would allow most of them to go. The odd few who had managed to reach her lips had left her totally unmoved, and unresponsive. But she hadn't set her sights on any of them with regard to marriage. With Charles, however, she was prepared to suffer the sloppy kisses and boring caresses. At least until she had his ring on her finger.

When Charles put his arm across her shoulders she looked into his eyes and smiled. 'It is very peaceful here, don't you think?'

'The only thing on my mind at the moment is your promise of a kiss. So come here, my pretty, and send shivers down my spine.'

Victoria offered her lips and moaned softly as though enjoying the experience. The sound seemed to please Charles, so she repeated it each time his lips covered hers. She was unmoved, there was no thrill of excitement for her, but her pleasure came from hearing his heavy breathing and low groans. She risked opening her eyes slightly, and seeing his flushed face, coupled with the sounds he was making, filled her with a sense of power. A few words now wouldn't go amiss. 'Charles, my darling, I really am very fond of you.'

'Oh, yes, my sweet, the same goes for me. You are absolutely adorable.'

Victoria smiled. If this is what it took to snare him, then she'd go along with it. After all, the reward at the end would be well worth a few kisses and caresses. But while she was thinking this, Charles was becoming more and more amorous. No longer content with her kisses, his hand began to stray down to her breast and he groaned as he fondled it. 'God, Victoria, you have a beautiful body. It's enough to send a chap wild.'

'Thank you, my darling, I'm happy you think so. But you are being naughty, I did only promise you a kiss.'

'No red-blooded man would be content with that, Victoria.' Charles was now letting his hand stray down her leg, and with one quick movement it was under her dress and moving over her thighs.

'Charles, you go too far!' Victoria swept his hand away and feigned indignation. But under the surface she was delighted. It wouldn't be long now before she had him in the palm of her hand. 'I don't know what on earth my parents would think, or yours.'

'Oh, come on, Victoria, how would they ever know?'

'I'm not worried about our parents, Charles, I am in control of my own life. And I will not give myself to any man but the one I marry.'

'We've been courting for months now, so who is to say I will not be that man?'

'To be courting and to be betrothed are two very different things, Charles, as you should well know.' Victoria was satisfied that tonight she had taken one step towards her goal. And she didn't want to spoil it by acting too quickly. 'And now, darling, can we carry on with our journey, please?' She leaned sideways and kissed his cheek. 'I find you very attractive, Charles, and it would be so easy to fall in love with you.'

He opened his mouth at the same time as a voice in his head advised caution. And without wondering why, he heeded the warning and switched on the ignition.

Agnes climbed the stairs to call Kitty for her afternoon cup of tea, and found the cleaner sitting on the top stair with her head in her hands. 'What's wrong, sunshine?'

'I don't know, Aggie, I just came over all funny, like. I had to sit down because I was frightened of falling arse over elbow down the bleedin' stairs.'

'Come on, I'll help yer down. Leave all yer cleaning tackle, it'll come to no harm. All the family are out, so there's only thee and me.' Agnes put her arm around the thin waist and half carried Kitty down the wide staircase. 'I called Pete in earlier for his cuppa, and he's in the back garden now, trimming the hedges.'

'He's a good gardener, isn't he, queen?'

'He can turn his hand to anything, love, and he's a nice bloke into the bargain.' When they reached the kitchen, Agnes pulled a chair out from the table. 'You sit there, sunshine, and I'll pour yer tea out. And I'll give yer a little treat, seeing as ye're not feeling too good. I bought meself a small bottle of whisky, and a drop in yer tea will buck yer up in no time.'

A smile came to the face that was far too gaunt to be healthy. 'Don't blame me if I end up doing an Irish jig on me bleedin' head, will yer?'

'Kitty, yer don't look as though yer've got the energy to wink, never mind standing on yer head. I am worried about yer because yer don't look a bit well. I don't like the colour of yer at all.'

'I'll be all right, queen. I just went a bit light-headed, that's all. I can't afford to be sick and that's the bleedin' top and bottom of it.'

'Kitty, yer'll be working yerself to a standstill if ye're not careful. I know they say hard work never killed anyone, but it would if yer not getting enough to eat and ye're walking six miles a day.'

'It's that bleedin' walk what gets me down, queen, and I admit it. But I haven't got the shilling it would cost me to get the tram here and back every day. And if I got a job nearer home I'd miss all the tit-bits I get from you, so I can't ruddywell win, can I? Besides, it's not that easy getting a job, there's too many people out of work. Where I live, there's kids running round with no shoes to their feet, rags on their backs and their heads are walking with fleas, the poor buggers.'

Agnes set a cup in front of the cleaner. 'There's a good measure of whisky in there, so get it down yer. While ye're drinking it I'll do yer an egg on toast. And ye're not walking home tonight, I'll give yer the penny fare.'

'Ooh, don't do that, queen, yer'll get into trouble with Miss Edwina if she knows ye're feeding me. And I can't take no money off yer, either, 'cos with yer living in and getting all yer food and everything, I know yer don't get much wages.'

'A penny isn't going to skint me, sunshine, so don't let that worry yer. And with regards to making yer a bite to eat, I'll clear that with Mr Robert when he comes in. He won't mind, he's got a heart of gold.'

'I'm just a worry to everyone, aren't I, queen? But I'd

rather yer didn't say anything to Mr Robert in case he thinks I'm not up to the job.'

'You don't know him like I do, Kitty, he's a real gentleman and very kind. Not like his ruddy wife, she wouldn't give yer a spot if she had the measles. It's easy to see where Miss Victoria gets her airs and graces from, they're both stuck-up cows. Mr Nigel's not so bad, though. He's a bit of a cissy, and as thick as two short planks, but at least he's got a heart, not a swinging brick.' Agnes was at the stove poaching an egg while she was talking, and she had her back to Kitty. So she didn't hear the low moan that came from the little woman before her head dropped on to the table.

'Here yer are, this will give yer a bit of strength.' When the housekeeper turned and saw her friend sprawled out, she nearly dropped the plate with fright. 'Oh, my God!' She wasn't very good with people who were ill, she never knew what to do. So she put the plate down and hurried to the kitchen door. Her eyes travelled over the large garden but there was no sign of the gardener. So she shouted at the top of her voice, 'Pete, will yer come quick, I need yer help!'

Pete came from between the trees in the orchard at the bottom of the garden, rubbing his hands down the side of his working trousers. 'What is it, Aggie?'

'It's Kitty, she's just flaked out. I haven't touched her 'cos I was too frightened.' Agnes wrung her hands. 'Oh God, I hope she hasn't died on me.'

Pete brushed past her and headed for the figure huddled over the table. He felt Kitty's forehead with one hand and her pulse with the other. 'She's fainted, that's all. Have yer got any smelling salts?'

'In the drawer here.' Agnes opened one of the drawers in the huge Welsh dresser which covered the whole of one wall. She took out a small bottle and passed it over. 'Don't put it too near her nose 'cos it's awful strong.'

Pete smiled. 'Go and teach yer grandma how to milk ducks, Aggie.' He removed the stopper and waved the bottle about six inches away from Kitty's nose. When there was no response he moved it nearer and was heartened to see her eyelids flicker. 'There yer are, love, yer'll be all right in a minute. Just take it easy.'

It was a few minutes before Kitty came around enough to lift her head. Her voice feeble, she asked, 'What happened?'

Agnes sighed with relief. 'Yer passed out on me, that's what happened. Frightened the bleedin' life out of me, yer did. I thought yer were dead, and if yer do that to me again, so help me, I'll kill yer.'

Kitty, her face as white as a sheet, tried to raise a smile. 'So if I don't die of me own accord, yer'll kill me, eh, Aggie? I'll be dead whichever way it goes.'

Agnes turned to the gardener. 'Thanks, Pete, I don't know what I'd have done if you hadn't been here. Will yer help her over to me rocking chair while I find a stool for her feet? She's not doing no more ruddy work today, and that's for sure.'

'I've got to, Aggie, I haven't touched the dining room yet.' Kitty was getting agitated. She daren't lose this job, otherwise she and Alf would be turfed out on the streets. 'I'll be all right when I've had a bit of a sit-down.'

Agnes stood before her, hands on hips and head tilted. 'Listen to me, Kitty Higgins, yer'll do as ye're told. There's no more work for you today, and that's final. I'll give the dining room a quick flick over while the dinner's on the go, and no one will be any the wiser.'

'Are all the family out, then?' Pete asked. 'I haven't seen sight nor sound of them.'

'They're all out for the day, but they'll be home soon to get dressed for dinner. It's a great life for some, eh, Pete? Talk about the idle rich!'

'I dunno, Aggie, I wouldn't change places with them. I mightn't have much money, but I'd rather have my little house than live in this mausoleum. I wouldn't swap wives with Mr Robert, either. At least my missus knows how to laugh and enjoy herself. I think Mrs Dennison's face would crack if she smiled.'

'Ye're better off than we are,' Kitty chipped in. 'At least you don't see much of them, working in the garden all day.'

Agnes spun around. 'Listen, Tilly Mint, will yer put yer feet on that footstool and sit back in the chair? I'm going to chase Pete now 'cos I'll have to put a move on with the dinner. And while I'm doing that, you can try and eat that poached egg on toast, save it going to waste. Then yer can close yer eyes and have a nice little snooze. I'll give yer a shake when it's time for yer to go home. There's no hurry tonight 'cos yer'll be going on the tram.'

'Ye're spoiling me, queen, so don't blame me if I expect yer to let me have a snooze every afternoon. I could easy get used to the good life, yer know. Before yer know it, I'll be expecting to have tea in the drawing room.'

'Sod off, sunshine, there's enough lazy buggers in this house. I'm only spoiling yer now 'cos ye're not well. But don't come the wounded soldier every day 'cos it won't wash.' Agnes felt her heart turn over when she looked down at the little woman who was so scrawny and badly dressed, she could be taken for a tramp. 'Have yer bite to eat, then close yer eyes, sunshine, a little sleep will do yer the world of good.'

'Yer won't forget to wake me, will yer, Aggie?'

'How can I forget to wake yer when I'm in the same room as yer, listening to yer snoring yer bleedin' head off?'

Kitty grinned. 'I love you, Aggie Weatherby.'

'And I love you too, sunshine.'

Agnes was taking the roasting tin out of the oven when she heard Mr Robert's car drive down the side of the house to the garage. She glanced across to where Kitty was still sleeping peacefully and put down the piece of cloth she used to prevent her hands getting burnt. Some nights Mr Robert came into the kitchen to say hello before making his way to his room to change for dinner. If the cleaner woke up to find her boss bending over her, she'd have a fit. Perhaps I should have woken her up sooner, Agnes thought, but I didn't have the heart because she needed that rest. Anyway, Mr Robert won't mind, but I'd better warn him. So the housekeeper opened the back door and stepped out, closing it quietly behind her.

'Good evening, Agnes, it isn't often you come out to welcome me.' Robert was feeling happy and contented, as he always did after an afternoon with Maureen. 'I appreciate your thoughtfulness.'

'Can I have a word with yer, Mr Robert?'

'Need you ask, Agnes? Come on, let's go indoors.'

'Before we go indoors, if yer don't mind.'

'Not trouble with the family again, I hope?'

'Nothing to do with me or the family, Mr Robert, it's about the cleaner.' Her hands clasping and unclasping, Agnes poured her heart out about the woman she thought deserved everything but had nothing. Mindful of the time, and the dinner being ruined, the words poured from her mouth. And she left nothing out. The invalid husband, the three-mile walk to and from work every day and the pinching and scraping to keep body and soul together. 'I help her when I can, Mr Robert, but it's not enough. To tell yer the truth, I always give her the leftovers from the day before's dinner and I think that's all the food she and her husband have. Perhaps yer think I'm doing wrong in giving her something that isn't mine, but it would only go in the bin anyway, so it isn't really stealing.'

Robert took a deep breath. 'Agnes, are you telling me this little woman walks here every day to save a penny?'

'No, she doesn't save a penny, 'cos she doesn't have a bleedin' penny to begin with! Oh, I'm sorry for swearing, but I get so mad. She works her socks off every day keeping this big house like a palace, and she's killing herself into the bargain. She's asleep on the chair in the kitchen and I was supposed to wake her up when it was time for her to leave. But I've let her sleep because the poor bugger is worn out. When she fainted today, it was through overwork and lack of nourishment. I'd bet a pound to a pinch of snuff that she and her husband sit in the dark 'cos they can't afford a penny for the gas meter. And I'll also bet their grate doesn't know what a fire is.'

'Why didn't you tell me this before, Agnes? You know I would have helped.'

'Because she thought she might get the sack.'

'But who on earth would sack the poor woman?'

'If you don't know that, Mr Robert, then there's no point in me telling yer.' Agnes sniffed up. 'Anyway, I've probably ruined the dinner, standing here talking, so I'd better get in. Would yer give me a couple of minutes to wake Kitty up, please, so she doesn't get upset?'

Robert nodded, too angry to trust himself to speak. He paced the ground, kicking at loose pebbles to relieve his feelings. To think that someone working in his house was so poor they couldn't afford a penny tram fare, nor to feed or clothe themselves properly. He often had a few words with the cleaner, but he was seldom home when she was there. He had noticed she was skinny, but thought nothing of it. It was his wife who gave Kitty her orders, she was around every day and must have some sort of conversation with the cleaner. And being a woman, surely she should have seen all was not well. But then, knowing Edwina, as long as the work was being carried out, she wouldn't give a damn if the person slaving away was dying, if it didn't interfere with her life.

The kitchen door opened and Agnes beckoned him in. He stood for a second to compose himself, then walked into the kitchen with a smile on his face. 'Hello, Kitty, what's this I'm hearing about you? I believe you gave Agnes quite a scare, fainting on her like that.'

'I don't know what came over me, Mr Robert. I didn't do it on purpose, 'cos I wouldn't upset Aggie for the world. She's me best mate, yer see.' Every part of the thin body was shaking with a mixture of fear and embarrassment. In all the jobs she'd had, she'd been treated with contempt and this had led her to believe she was in a lower class than others. Particularly the people you worked for. 'I'll be all right tomorrow, though, Mr Robert, and I'll be here as usual. So if Miss Edwina worries about the house not getting cleaned, tell her she won't need to get another cleaner in 'cos I'll definitely be here.'

How Robert kept the smile on his face he would never know. Why had he been so blind not to have seen this woman wasn't fit to be working? The face and hands had hardly any flesh on them, and although the long black raggedy skirt covered most of her legs, the little he could see looked far too frail to carry the heavy, down-at-heel boots. 'Kitty, my dear, there is no question of our getting another cleaner. Now, if you'll just sit for a little while longer, I would like to have a word with Agnes.' He walked towards the door leading into the hall and indicated he wanted the housekeeper to follow. Once outside he put a finger to his mouth as he heard movement coming from upstairs. 'Agnes, I want you to fill a basket with sufficient food to last Kitty and her husband a few days.' He kept his voice low. 'Just throw in anything that is nourishing and tasty. That includes tea, sugar, bread, butter and milk. Then I want you to take it out to my car and place it on the back seat. While you're doing that, I'll go upstairs and tell my wife I'm running the cleaner home because she's not well.'

The housekeeper's eyes widened. 'Ye're running her home, Mr Robert?'

'She's obviously not fit to go on a tram, and it's the least I can do. I will tell my wife she is not well, nothing more. I know you're worried about the dinner, but it won't take long to get some things together for Kitty to take home. I'll have my meal in the study, later.'

Agnes put a hand on his arm. 'Mr Robert, ye're gentleman. And I thank yer, 'cos I've been worried sick about her. She never complains, but I've watched her fading before me eyes and I didn't know what to do.'

'You don't worry in future, Agnes, you come to me. Now,

let's both go about our business.' Robert took the stairs quickly, and when he opened the door of the main bedroom it was to find his wife standing in front of the dressing-table mirror, running a comb through her hair. 'Start the dinner without me, Edwina, I'm running Kitty home as she is out of sorts.'

She looked puzzled. 'Kitty?'

'Yes, Mrs Higgins, our cleaner.'

'Surely she is capable of making her own way home?' Edwina was clearly annoyed. 'You can't be expected to act as a chauffeur to one of the servants. The very idea is ridiculous!'

'Nobody is expecting anything, Edwina, I'm doing it because the woman is obviously ill and distressed.'

'If she is ill, then she is of no use to us and must be sacked. I'll look for another cleaner first thing in the morning.'

'Is that all the sympathy you have for a woman who has worked for us for five years, with never a day off? Who has obeyed your orders without question and done everything asked of her?'

'Good heavens, Robert, she's a servant! And servants are paid to take orders.'

'How much is she paid?'

'Twelve shillings a week.'

Robert closed his eyes and tried to control his rising temper. 'Twelve shillings a week. That's two shillings a day to clean this house from top to bottom, clean your shoes, and Victoria's and Nigel's, and be at your beck and call each day.'

'Nobody is forcing her to do it. I'll have no problem finding another cleaner.'

Robert walked slowly towards her, his eyes blazing. 'Oh, you'll have problems, Edwina, I promise you. And I am the one who will make them for you, if you attempt to sack Kitty and replace her with someone else.'

His wife stood her ground. 'If she's as sick as you say, and doesn't come in tomorrow, I'll have no alternative but to find someone else.'

'No alternative? Have you forgotten how to pick up a duster,

71

Edie? I remember well how you used to scrub your mother's front step every Saturday afternoon. And you'd think nothing of shaking the mat out in the street. In those days you would have had sympathy for someone like Kitty, because you weren't much different then to what she is now.' Robert shook his head, asking himself why he was wasting his breath. 'If you had any decency left, you would be down in the kitchen now, seeing if you could do anything to help a woman who has pulled her guts out working for you. But as you seem devoid of decency and sympathy, I will leave you with something to think about. In future, *I* will hire and fire staff – *you* will have nothing to say in the matter.' He walked towards the door. 'I'll have my meal later, in the study.'

'I can walk from here, Mr Robert, yer don't have to take me all the way home.' Kitty didn't want him to see the poor conditions she lived in, she'd be too ashamed. He was a nice kind man who wouldn't look down his nose at anyone. But their lifestyles were worlds apart. 'I'll be all right, honest, so let me out here and you go home and have yer dinner.'

'Kitty, are you afraid of being seen with me?' Robert guessed what the problem was but he'd made up his mind to help her, and he had to do it in a way that wouldn't look as though he was doing it out of pity. So he took his eyes off the road for a second to smile at her. 'I know what it is. You're frightened your neighbours might think I'm your fancy man.'

Kitty's mouth gaped and she looked stunned. Fancy her employer saying that! Then she began to chuckle. 'I should be that bleedin' lucky, Mr Robert. Fancy man indeed!' Oh, wait until she told Alf, that would bring a smile to his face. And when he saw the basket of food, he'd think it was his birthday and Christmas all rolled into one.

'This is my street, Mr Robert, yer can stop here.'

'I said I'd run you home, Kitty, and that's what I propose to do.' Robert drove the car around the corner and glanced at the number on the first house. 'I think Agnes said you live in number thirty-five, is that correct?'

The little woman was stumped. This man was her boss, she couldn't demand he stopped the car. 'My husband won't be expecting me to come home in style, Mr Robert, and he'll get a shock.'

Robert braked to a halt. 'I was born in a street like this, Kitty, and grew up in a house exactly the same as these. My parents didn't have two ha'pennies to rub together, either. So if your furniture's falling to pieces and the paper is hanging off the walls, I'll feel quite at home. I'm not a snob, so don't treat me like one. And now, before I drive down and park outside your front door, there's a little matter I'd like to clear up first. I didn't realise you haven't had a rise in wages since the day you started working for us. You should, of course, have had at least two increases, and I take full responsibility for the error. So I want you to take this pound note as part payment of the money due to you. We'll sort the rest out when you feel able to return to work.' He pressed the note into her hand. 'Take it, my dear, you have earned it.'

Kitty stared down at the note but it was blurred by the tears filling her eyes. She hadn't had a pound note in her hand for seven years, since her Alf had to pack in work because of ill-health. It was a fortune to her, but she wasn't sure she was really entitled to it and her pride took over. 'Mr Robert, all this talk about owing me back money, yer've just made that up, haven't yer? Yer see, I'm not very bright, but I'm not behind the door, either. You've never had anything to do with paying me wages, and I'll bet yer've never known what I was getting in all the time I've worked for yer. Miss Edwina is the one who sees to the staff getting paid, and I don't believe a word yer say about these rises I'm supposed to have had. So, while I'm beholden to yer for the food, I'd rather not take money I'm not entitled to.' She held out her hand towards him. 'Please take it back, Mr Robert.'

'That and cut my throat are the last things I'm likely to do,

73

Kitty.' Robert dropped right back into the Liverpool accent. 'Ye're a stubborn bugger, just like Agnes. Yer flippin' pride will be the death of both of yer. Well, let me tell yer something, and every word is the truth. There was a man once, his name was Will Lathom, and he held out a helping hand to me. My pride didn't stand in the way, I can tell yer. I grabbed it with both hands and it's Will, God rest his soul, I've got to thank for being where I am today. So take the pound, Kitty, because pride is not going to feed you and yer husband, or keep yer warm. And don't look on it as charity because it's far from it. We owe yer a lot more than that.'

Kitty didn't know whether to laugh or cry. Cry because he was so good, and she could tell he meant what he said. Or laugh, because if she closed her eyes and shut out the car and his expensive clothes, he sounded just like anyone who lived in the narrow street. She pushed the pound note into her pocket and grinned at him. 'If yer don't watch out, Mr Robert, we'll have yer swearing next.'

'My mother invented half the swear words, Kitty, so yer can't teach me anything. And now let's find number thirty-five.'

Alf Higgins was sitting in the chair when he heard the key in the door. He'd been watching the clock for half an hour now and was getting worried because his wife was usually home by now. He wished she didn't have to do that long walk every day; it was taking it out of her, he could see that.

'I'm home, love, and we've got a visitor.' When Kitty came in she was a bag of nerves, seeing the room as others would see it. There was little furniture because everything they'd had of any value had been pawned years ago. But at least it was clean. 'This is Mr Dennison, Alf, he brought me home in his car. The whole bleedin' street came out to see us, and I felt like waving me hand like what the Queen does.'

Robert grinned as he put the basket on the table and turned to shake hands. 'Pleased to meet you, Mr Higgins. Your wife can be as stubborn as a flaming mule when she feels like it.

74

She wanted me to drop her off around the corner and I had to be firm with her. She's been under the weather today, so I suggest she has a few days off work.'

Alf's face showed his concern. 'What's wrong, pet?'

'Just off-colour, love, that's all. If it was serious I wouldn't be here now, would I?' Kitty waved to the couch. 'Sit down, Mr Robert, and take the weight off yer feet.'

Just before he sat down, Robert noticed one of the springs sticking up out of the cushion, and he moved a little to avoid it. His mam used to have a couch like this and it could be lethal to sit down without taking care. Many's the sore bottom he had from that old horse-hair couch. 'I believe you don't enjoy good health, Mr Higgins?'

Alf shook his head. He was as thin as a lath, but you could see he'd been a handsome bloke when he was younger. He had vivid blue eyes and a thick mop of prematurely white hair. 'I haven't worked for nearly seven years now. I used to be a stevedore at Seaforth docks, but I caught some sort of infection off a cargo we were unloading and the doctor signed me off. I thought it would only be for a few days, but I never did pick up.'

'And didn't the doctor send you to hospital, or tell you what was wrong?'

'Oh yeah, I was in hospital for a while, and they said my lungs had been affected and there was little they could do.' Alf's laugh was hollow. 'They recommended plenty of fresh air. Now I ask yer, plenty of fresh air! With the factory chimneys smoking non-stop around here, there's fat chance of that.'

Kitty was hovering by the side of his chair. 'We don't do so bad, though, love, do we? We've got each other, and that's what counts.'

'But I should be the one going out to work, not you! How d'yer think I feel sitting here all day while you're out slaving to keep us? And just look at yer, pet, ye're wearing yerself into the ground.'

'Well, she's going to have a few days' complete rest, with plenty to eat to put some flesh on her bones,' Robert said. 'A lie-in every morning with no worry about dashing out and walking those three miles. Honest to God, I had no idea you were doing that, Kitty, or I would never have allowed it.'

'It's not your fault, Mr Robert, it's just the way things are. But I can't afford to take no time off work, and that's the top and bottom of it. The rent man has to have his money every week or he'll have us out on the street. Besides, Miss Edwina can't do without a cleaner and I don't want her taking no one else on in me place.'

'It might not always appear so, Kitty, but I am the master of the house. No one will take your place, I promise. But I insist you take a few days off. It's Wednesday today, so I suggest you take it easy until Monday. I'll call at eight o'clock on Monday morning, and if I consider you fit for work, I'll take you in.'

'Do as Mr Dennison says, pet.' There was tenderness in Alf's eyes as he reached for her hand. 'I don't want to see yer getting ill, ye're all I've got.'

'Don't be going all soppy on me in front of me boss,' Kitty said. 'Wait until he's gone and then yer can get as soppy as yer like.'

Robert was moved by the scene. These two had nothing in material possessions. The furniture was only fit for the scrapyard, and a rag and bone man wouldn't even give them a balloon for their clothes. But what they did have, was their love for each other. This made them far richer than he was.

'I've had an idea, Mr Higgins, which might interest you. Why don't you come with Kitty on Monday morning? We have a very large garden, and there are no smoking chimneys for miles. You could get as much fresh air as you wanted, and I'm sure Agnes would be delighted to keep you supplied with food and drink. Does the idea appeal to you?'

Kitty clapped her hands. 'Oh, that would be bleedin' marvellous! It would do you so much good, Alf, 'cos yer seldom go over the door. And yer'd have Pete, the gardener to talk to – I bet yer'd enjoy that.'

'I'd like it very much, Mr Dennison, thank you.'

'Good! Now that's settled I'll leave you in peace. Make the most of your few days of freedom, Kitty, and I hope to see you looking better on Monday. And you are not to worry about a thing – I forbid it.'

Alf got to his feet. 'Thank you for looking after my wife today, I appreciate it very much.'

'It was nothing less than she deserves.' Robert could see a group of children around his car and thought a hasty retreat was in order. He had no objection to them looking, they were only kids after all, and a car down their street would be a rarity. But the last time he had felt benevolent towards a group of boys, it ended up with one of them snapping his windscreen wiper. 'Don't bother coming to the door, Kitty, I'll see myself out.' He donned his hard bowler hat and smiled at the couple who were now holding hands. 'Until Monday, then.'

Chapter Five

Robert was thoughtful as he parked his car in the garage. He didn't relish telling his wife she would be without a cleaner until Monday, and he expected sharp words would be exchanged. But he didn't regret his actions and would do the same thing again if the occasion ever arose. On the drive home, he'd been picturing the size of his house and the work involved for one little woman to do. There were ten large rooms and the wide staircase was almost the size of two of the rooms. Plus there was his study, the bathrooms and cloakrooms. Far too much for one person, and his own common sense should have told him this. What was needed was a junior maid to help Kitty with the work and he'd like one in place before Monday.

Agnes was washing the dinner dishes when he entered the kitchen, and as she dried her hands her eyes were anxious. 'How was she, Mr Robert? I've been on pins, waiting for yer.'

'I've told her to stay off until Monday, and get plenty of rest. I'm picking her up, but if I don't think she's well enough, she must stay off longer.'

Agnes dropped her eyes. There'd be skin and hair flying when Miss Edwina heard; she'd already been in the kitchen ranting and raving. She blamed the housekeeper for not sending the cleaner home instead of crying to Mr Robert and getting him involved. 'Your wife won't be happy about that. Who's going to do the cleaning until Monday? I'll help as much as I can, but I can't do Kitty's job as well as me own.' In her mind she was thinking it could easily be done if everyone pulled their weight. But there was fat chance of that. They were too bleeding lazy to lift a cup. 'Anyway, as long as Kitty's all right, that's all I'm worried about. I'll take the rest as it comes and to hell with everyone. Of course it goes without saying that the last remark doesn't include you, Mr Robert.'

'I've decided to take on a junior maid to help with the cleaning. I was going to say a scullery maid, but she'd have to be a maid of all work. I'm feeling rather tired now, it seems to have been such a long day, but I'll put my mind to it tomorrow and set the wheels in motion.'

'I've heard of a fourteen-year-old girl who's looking to go into service, Mr Robert, but I don't know if she'd suit.'

'D'you know the girl personally?'

Agnes shook her head. 'Never set eyes on her, wouldn't know her from Adam. But yer know I'm friendly with next-door's housekeeper, Tilly, don't yer? Well, it's her sister's girl and she was telling me about her the other day. I didn't ask no questions 'cos I wasn't really interested, but I can slip next door and find out, if yer like. It can't do no harm to ask a few questions, and at least we'd know what sort of a family she's from.'

'I would like you to do that, Agnes, and if she's suitable it would speed things along.'

'I'll serve yer dinner first, yer must be starving. You go and get yerself changed and I'll bring it through to the study in, say, fifteen minutes?'

'I'm not getting changed tonight, it's hardly worth it. So I'll just swill my hands and face, which should take five minutes.'

Robert heard his wife's voice as he passed the drawing room, and although he couldn't hear the words, her tone implied she wasn't in the best of tempers. As he took the stairs two at a time, he visualised her face. There would be no smile, there seldom was, her eyes would be blazing and her nostrils flared. And if Victoria was in the room with her, she would be agreeing with every word her mother said. He'd have to keep a close eye on Kitty when she came back, because both mother and daughter could be very spiteful.

Tilly Woods' eyes widened when she opened the back door. 'Yer haven't been given another night off, have yer, yer jammy bugger?'

Agnes grinned as she pulled out a chair from the table that was identical to the one she had in the kitchen next door. 'No, this is strictly business.'

'I was going to say I'll have to take a leaf out of your book and throw a tantrum with the Mistress, see if she's as obliging as yours.' Tilly sat down opposite and folded her arms. She was in her early forties, the same age as Agnes, and she had a pleasantly plump figure topped by a face that was rarely without a smile. 'Strictly business, eh? Does that mean yer've come to cadge the recipe off me for me mouth-watering pastry?'

'Sod off, Tilly Woods, my pastry knocks yours into a cocked hat any day.'

'Yer crusty pastry might, but my flaky pastry beats yours by a mile.'

'We'll call a truce shall we, and agree that we both make bloody good pastry? And I wouldn't say no to a piece of apple pie to eat with the cup of tea I know ye're just dying to make me.'

'Ye're not backwards in coming forward, are yer? Cheeky mare, yer face would get yer the ruddy parish!'

'I don't want the parish, Tilly, I'm not greedy. I'll settle for a nice slice of apple pie.'

'No can do, sweetheart, 'cos the family had rhubarb pie tonight. And everyone commented on how delicious it was.'

'Well, I think it was most inconsiderate of them, 'cos I don't like rhubarb. They're like my lot next door, only ever think about themselves and to hell with what I want. Still, I suppose I could force meself to eat a piece seeing as it's all yer've got.'

Tilly was at the sink filling the kettle when she asked over her shoulder, 'What is the business yer were talking about? Or was it only an excuse to scrounge a piece of me pie what yer know is better than anything you can make?'

'No, I came to ask about that niece of yours. Yer know, the one you said was looking for a job in service. Well, Mr Robert is looking for a junior maid and when I mentioned what you'd told me, he asked me to make some enquiries. It wouldn't be live-in, though, so it might not be what she's looking for.'

Tilly raised the gas under the kettle and returned to her seat. 'She doesn't particularly want to live-in, it's just that there's no jobs around for her to pick and choose from. There's an awful lot of people out of work, yer know, Aggie, and her mother could do with her bringing a few bob in each week. She's got three other children to clothe and feed, and her husband only brings home buttons. He works at the docks and some weeks he only gets taken on for two or three days. They're having a struggle and she needs Jessie working.'

'Is that the girl's name, Jessie?'

'Well, Jessica really. And she's a little love. Very pretty, pleasant, well-mannered and thoroughly nice. I'd be made-up if Mr Robert would give her a chance, and me sister, Edna, would be over the moon.'

'Tilly, don't clock me one for asking yer these questions, but I need to know all about the girl before I ask Mr Robert to see her. Yer said she was fourteen, is that right?' Agnes was sitting with her hands in her lap and her fingers crossed for luck. She waited for her friend's nod, then asked, 'Is she willing to work hard and take orders?'

'I don't see much of them, 'cos as yer know I only get the one day off. But I know she looks after the three children when our Edna goes out to do a few cleaning jobs, and she does the housework, washing and ironing. I'd say she wasn't frightened of hard work, but then she's never worked in a house the size of next door, nor encountered anyone like Mrs Dennison.'

'I'd show her the ropes, sunshine, and I'd keep her away from Miss Edwina as much as I could until she was used to us and the house.' Agnes was beginning to get her hopes up. 'If she's willing to work, and she's pleasant, I think it's worth a try, don't you?'

'I'd recommend her, Aggie, and I wouldn't do that unless I had faith in her. And yer can tell Mr Robert she's as honest as the day's long, and trustworthy.'

'How soon could you get in touch with her to arrange an interview? We could do with someone right away 'cos Kitty's gone off sick for a few days. The girl wouldn't be thrown in the deep end, I'd be there to help her.'

Tilly looked at the clock and saw it was ten past eight. 'Nip next door and have a word with Mr Robert. If he's interested, I'd go tonight. They live in the Dingle and I could get a tram right to the end of their street.'

Agnes pushed her chair back. 'Right, I'll get cracking before the grass grows under me feet. I'll be back as soon as I can, and I'll come on the tram with yer.' She got to the door then turned, a mischievous grin on her face. 'Yer can wrap that piece of rhubarb pie up for me, I'll have it for me supper.'

'It sounds promising, Agnes.' Robert swivelled his chair from side to side as he tapped his fingers on the top of his desk. 'It's an advantage to have someone who's recommended.'

'Highly recommended, Mr Robert. If Tilly says she's a good girl, then yer can take that as gospel. I've been friends with Tilly Woods for nigh on ten years, and I'd stake me life on her.'

'And you're prepared to go with her to see this girl and make arrangements for her to call here as soon as possible for an interview?'

'Yeah. If we're lucky with trams we could be there and back in just over an hour.' Agnes had something on her mind and it was her firm belief that instead of bottling things up, you should get it off your chest. 'Mr Robert, would you

83

interview her? I know I shouldn't say it, but Miss Edwina can be a bit off-putting. The girl is only fourteen and this will be her first job. I'd hate her to be frightened off and I think it would be better all round if you were to see her.'

'I intend to, Agnes, so have no fear.' He grinned. 'I'll treat her with kid gloves.'

'If she can come tomorrow, what time should I say?'

'Shall we say ten o'clock, when breakfast is over? I don't have anything important on tomorrow so I'm all right for time. And if the interview goes well, as I'm sure it will, would you ask if she'd be prepared to start right away?'

'I'll have an idea when I see the girl, Mr Robert, and if I feel she's right for the job and would fit in, I'll suggest she comes ready to start, just in case. And I'll have to dash off now, before it gets too late. I'll let yer know how we get on when I get back. Will yer still be in here?'

'Yes, I'll do some work on the books to pass the time. But before you go, Agnes, what sort of wages would a girl her age be expecting?'

'Fourteen and untrained, I'd say she'd start on three bob a week in a factory.'

'In case her parents ask, shall we say four shillings a week? With a sixpence rise when she's experienced in the job.'

'It's going to be bleedin' midnight before we get out, Mr Robert, if yer keep on talking,' Agnes huffed as she bustled to the door. Then, remembering something, she turned with a huge grin on her face. 'My old ma used to say the only ones on the street at that time of night are cats and loose women.' She closed the door with Robert's laughter ringing in her ears.

It was a quarter to ten when the housekeeper knocked on the study door again. She was thanking the Lord above that she hadn't bumped into any of the family. Miss Edwina would lay a duck egg if she knew what was going on behind her back. Mind you, it served her right. If she didn't look as though there was a bad smell under her nose when she was talking to you, and was more pleasant and friendly, then it would be easy to be friendly back. So if she wasn't liked, she only had herself to blame.

Robert opened the study door. 'Come in, Agnes, my dear. Have you been associating with the cats or the loose women?'

Safe now, knowing that Miss Edwina never came to the study, Agnes could feel herself relaxing. 'Oh, yer can laugh, Mr Robert, but me and Tilly are not past it, yer know! In fact, we were accosted by two fellers so yer can put that in yer pipe and smoke it. They were a bit of all right, too. The only thing was, they expected us to pay them instead of the other way round.'

'You and Tilly are two very attractive women, Agnes, and it wouldn't surprise me in the least if you were approached by two men. What does surprise me is that you haven't been snapped up long ago. You'd have made good wives and mothers.'

'I didn't want to be snapped up, Mr Robert. When my Ben got killed in the war, I didn't look at anyone else. I loved him, yer see, he was the only one for me. And Tilly was the same, she lost her boyfriend in the war. We're good mates, and we often sit and talk about the boys we loved and lost. We don't get miserable, we just like talking about them.'

'Sit yourself down, my dear, and tell me how you got on.'

'Oh, yer should see her, Mr Robert, she's a little beauty. Her name's Jessie, and she's polite, well-mannered, and everything yer could wish for. She was so excited about coming for an interview for a job, she said she won't sleep tonight. Her parents were over the moon, too! But I couldn't tell them about the hours she'll be working if yer do take her on, 'cos yer hadn't told me.'

'*If* I take her on, Agnes? Will I have a choice? I've got a feeling I'd be a very unpopular man if Jessie wasn't a member of our staff tomorrow morning.'

'Nah, yer wouldn't be unpopular, Mr Robert. It's your house and your money, I've got no say in the matter. Though I might think, privately like, that yer were tuppence short of a shilling, and I might call yer for everything under me breath. But none of those things are going to happen 'cos when yer set eyes on her, yer'll want to adopt her, never mind setting her on as a scullery maid.'

'My goodness, you must have been very impressed, Agnes.'

'I was very impressed, and still am. I'm also ruddy tired, and me feet are talking to me. So I'm going to see if there's any dishes want washing, then I'm off to me bed. And I'll bet I'm asleep before me flaming head hits the pillow.'

'Goodnight, Agnes, and thank you. I'll see you in the morning.'

'Goodnight and God bless, Mr Robert, sweet dreams.'

There's little chance of that, Robert thought as the door closed on the housekeeper. I've got a feeling that as soon as I set foot in the bedroom the fireworks will start. He didn't mind a discussion, even if it got a bit heated, but the trouble was, his wife wouldn't let up. She would harp and harp, until he sometimes felt like taking her by the shoulders and giving her a good shaking. Perhaps that's what she needed to shake her out of the life of fantasy she'd created for herself, and back to reality. She lived in a dream world which at times frightened him, but while he'd been sorely tempted at times, he knew he would never lay a finger on her.

Edwina didn't even wait until the bedroom door was closed before venting her anger. 'Am I not allowed to know what's going on in my own house? First, against my wishes, you take it upon yourself to run the cleaner home because she's not feeling well. Then you shut yourself in the study without informing me of the situation regarding the length of time she could be away from work, and who is to do the cleaning in the meantime. Then, without a by-your-leave, Agnes mysteriously disappears and we are left to see to our own supper. I will not tolerate such behaviour and demand an explanation.'

'I do not intend to raise my voice, Edwina, so listen

carefully as I answer each one of your complaints. Firstly, you ask if you are not allowed to know what's going on in your own house. Surely you should have said "our" house, as it is also the home of the children and myself. Then you rant on about my running Kitty home against your wishes. Against *your wishes*, Edwina? Pretty soon you'll be expecting me to ask permission to light up a cigar! And if I have to weigh your wishes against helping a sick woman, you will lose every time. I have given Kitty leave to stay off until Monday. I will be calling for her, and if I think she's not fit for work she'll have her paid leave extended further.' Robert kept his voice even, determined he wasn't going to demean himself by shouting. 'Agnes didn't mysteriously disappear, she had gone on an errand for me. You see, I have decided to take on a young girl as a maid of all work, to help Kitty or Agnes where necessary. I should have seen the need for this a long time ago, but unfortunately it took the present situation to shake me into action. Anyway, a young fourteen year old is coming tomorrow to be interviewed for the post. She comes highly recommended, is from a good family, and I am hopeful she will be suitable.'

There was open dislike in his wife's eyes. 'You did all this without consulting me? How dare you!'

'And who, exactly, do you think you are, Edwina?'

'I am the mistress of this house.' The words were spat out. 'When I interview this girl tomorrow, if I find her common, uncouth or ill-mannered, she'll be sent packing. I'll have no one who doesn't know their place, or appreciates how lucky they would be to work here.'

'What you are suffering from, Edwina, is illusions of grandeur. And the sooner you dispel those illusions, the better it will be for yourself. The young girl who is coming tomorrow, whose name, incidentally, is Jessie, will be very much the same as you were at her age. Did you ever consider yourself common, uncouth or ill-mannered? I don't think so. Anyway, *I* shall be interviewing Jessie, so your feelings don't enter into it.' Robert slipped off his jacket and draped it over his arm. 'End of discussion, Edwina, I don't want to hear another word.' He walked through to his dressing room, and as he opened the double doors to his wardrobe his eyes lit on the small bed in the corner. He never thought it would come to this, but it had been a long day, so much had happened, and he was very tired. The woman in their bed treated him like an unwelcome stranger, and the thought of sleeping next to her filled him with despair. So after hanging up his jacket and waistcoat, he returned to the bedroom. 'I shall be sleeping in the dressing room tonight, and I'm sure that's one thing I'll be doing right in your eyes. Goodnight.'

'Mother, I left my black court shoes out to be cleaned, and they're just as I left them. They haven't been touched.' Victoria sat down with a disapproving look on her face. 'And Nigel tells me his haven't been cleaned, either. It's just isn't good enough!'

Before his wife could answer, Robert said, 'Good morning, Victoria, Nigel and Abbie. Or have we dispensed with civilised behaviour?'

'Of course not, Dad.' Abbie left her chair to give him a kiss. 'Good morning.'

'I'm sorry, Father,' Nigel said. 'How very rude of me. Good morning to you.'

Victoria gave a curt nod. 'Good morning.'

'To save any further words on the subject, there is no one to clean your shoes as Kitty is unwell. But I'm sure Agnes will show you where the shoe polish and brushes are kept.'

'Ah, what's wrong with Kitty?' Abbie asked. 'She's not very ill, I hope?'

'No, my dear, she's suffering from fatigue. Been overworked for too long.'

'Overworked!' Victoria didn't see the warning sign in her mother's eyes. 'If the wretched creature isn't up to the job she shouldn't be here.'

'Don't be horrible, Victoria,' Abbie said with feeling. 'Kitty is not a wretched creature and she can't help being sick. She's very nice and I like her.'

'You never were fussy about the people you liked,' Victoria sneered. 'Some of the friends you've had have been most undesirable.'

Robert banged the handle of his knife on the table. 'I will not have remarks like that at the breakfast table. While you sit here on antique chairs, with solid silver cutlery in front of you and expensive clothes on your back, waiting to have your breakfast served to you, there are thousands of people in this country who are worrying about where their next meal is coming from. You are so selfish you disgust me. If you are not satisfied, or think you are badly treated, then may I suggest you find somewhere else to live?'

Abbie had her head down, her lips were moving but no one heard her saying, 'Dad's right, you are selfish. You don't care about poor Kitty.'

Meanwhile, Agnes was just about to push the door open when she heard Mr Robert's voice. She felt a wave of pity for him, because more than most, she knew exactly how spoilt they were. The silver tray she was carrying was heavy with matching silver dishes, filled with bacon, eggs, liver, sausages, kidneys and tomatoes. And once these were on the table, she'd have to make a few trips back and forth to the kitchen for their toast and marmalade and pots of tea. There were three in that room who didn't know they were bloody well born. And it would give her great pleasure to tip the tray and its contents on their laps and wave them goodbye. It was Mr Robert and Miss Abbie that kept her here, and she'd stay as long as they needed her.

Taking a deep breath, the housekeeper pushed open the door with her hip. 'Good morning, breakfast up,' she called in a bright and breezy voice, as she set the dishes out on the long mahogany serving table. 'I'll fetch yer toast now.'

'Agnes.' Victoria's voice was silky and persuasive. 'Would

you be an angel and clean my shoes for me?'

'Oh, I say, old girl,' Nigel said, red in the face with embarrassment at his sister's nerve. 'You can't expect Agnes to clean your shoes.'

'She can expect what she likes, Mr Nigel, but she won't bleedin' well get it.' Agnes was equally red in the face, but it was with anger, not embarrassment. 'I've got me hands full without cleaning ruddy shoes.' With that, the housekeeper stormed out, muttering under her breath that someone needed a bloody good hiding.

'How dare you.' Robert could scarcely contain his anger. 'What arrogance!'

'She gets paid to work here, doesn't she?' Victoria didn't see anything wrong with her request and wasn't in the least repentant. 'So why shouldn't I ask her to clean my shoes?'

'Yes, Agnes gets paid to work here, and she works hard for her money. What do you do, Victoria, to earn the very generous allowance you get?'

Edwina spoke for the first time, in an effort to defend her daughter. 'Robert, you'll be pleased to know that Victoria has already set the wheels in motion for the charity work you were keen for her to get involved with. Apparently Mrs Chisholm and some of her friends visit the poor in hospital, and Charles is getting some information today on how Victoria can join their group.'

'Charles and I are getting quite close, really.' Victoria was thinking the day wasn't far off when she could tell her father what to do with his money. 'In fact, I think the day is fast approaching when he'll pop the question. So don't be surprised, Father, if Charles asks for my hand in marriage.'

The expression on Robert's face when he looked at his daughter was one of pity mixed with disbelief. Charles Chisholm, by his own father's admission, was a lady's man who loved them and left them. There'd been a rumour several years ago when Charles was only about seventeen, that he'd got a young parlour maid into trouble and it had cost his father dearly to pay the girl's family off to avoid publicity. This tale had been the talk of the Athenium Club for months and had never been denied by George Chisholm, who was an extremely wealthy shipping merchant. His son seemed to settle down after that and there was no further scandal. That is until he reached the age of twenty-one, and then gossip flared about his liking for older women. Particularly married women who had little to fill in their days and enjoyed the excitement of a clandestine affair. There was no sign that Charles Chisholm was ready to give up his lifestyle and settle down to marriage. But it wasn't up to Robert to repeat rumours to his daughter, so he said, 'I'll be prepared if he does approach me.'

'I've got some news, too, Dad.' Abbie looked and sounded happy. 'Miss Gillespie has given me the morning off to enrol at the commercial college. She said it was best to do it as soon as possible, in case there are a lot of applications for the subjects I'm interested in. They only take on so many for each class, you see, and I'd be very disappointed if my application was turned down. I've set my heart on it.'

'I'm sure there'll be no problem, my dear. If you come home later with a smile on your face, I'll be very happy for you.'

'Yes, Abbie, I hope you get what you want,' Nigel said, ignoring the set faces of his mother and elder sister. 'Good luck!'

'Thank you, Nigel.' Abbie gulped down a few mouthfuls of tea, then patted her lips with the heavy linen napkin. 'I'm off. I don't want to be last in line.' She planted a kiss on the top of her father's head as she passed his chair, then waved to the other members of the family. 'See you later!'

'When will she start to act like a young lady,' Edwina tutted, 'instead of a child?'

'I think Abbie has a good head on her shoulders,' Nigel said. 'She knows what she wants and is going after it. Good luck to her, I say.'

Robert found himself being pleasantly surprised by his

son. For years he'd agreed with everything his mother and older sister said, and wouldn't have dared to offer an opinion. Yet several times in the last few days he'd risked their wrath by opposing them. And each time it had been in defence of Abbie or Agnes. Could it be he was at last becoming his own man and breaking free from the unhealthy, stifling relationship that bound him to his mother and sister? Robert hoped with all his heart that this were so. Nigel was twenty-one soon and he had never had a proper girlfriend. If he went out to a social gathering it was always in the company of Victoria who, in talking down to him, had others doubting his ability and intelligence. The consequence was that no one expected him to have anything of interest to say. He was well-liked, but not taken seriously.

'If you'll excuse me, I'm going along to the study.' Robert was looking at his son as he pushed the chair under the table. Had he been too impatient with him, expecting too much too soon? He hoped not, but it was possible. 'Nigel, when you've finished breakfast, perhaps you'd like to come along to the study for a chat? We don't seem to spend much time with each other lately.'

'Yes, Father, I'd like that.' The young man's face showed his pleasure. 'I'll finish my tea and be along in five minutes.'

Robert made a detour to the kitchen to find Agnes. Her sleeves were rolled up to the elbows, and she was taking her temper out on the huge heavy frying pan she was scrubbing. Plunging it in and out of the hot, soapy water, she was muttering under her breath what she'd like to do to 'the stuck-up cow'. Robert chuckled and told himself he wouldn't need two guesses to know who she was talking about. He knew he shouldn't see any humour in his housekeeper calling his daughter names, and it wouldn't be tolerated in their neighbours' houses, where servants were treated as such. But then, being a fair man, he had to allow that most households didn't have a daughter as disrespectful as Victoria.

'Agnes, I'll be in the study when the young lady comes.

Would you be kind enough to bring her along to me?'

The housekeeper glanced at the large, round kitchen clock. 'She should be here any minute, Mr Robert. But I'll keep her here for five minutes talking, to settle her down, like, so she's not so nervous. Then I'll bring her to yer.'

'Sit down, Nigel.' Robert waved to a round-backed, maroon leather chair. 'I won't offer you a cigar because I believe you don't smoke.'

'I have never tried a cigar, Father, but I do smoke the odd cigarette. Would you object to me having one now?'

'Not at all.' Robert placed the heavy crystal ashtray between them, then held his lighter to the cigarette in his son's mouth. 'I don't recall ever seeing you smoke.'

'You know Mother doesn't like the smell of tobacco, so I don't smoke in her presence. I usually confine myself to the odd whiff in my bedroom.'

Robert puffed on his cigar, wondering how to word his questions so his son didn't think he was being criticised. He wanted to get to know his offspring, not frighten him off. 'How is life these days, Nigel? I know you are involved in plenty of social activities, but do you find them satisfying and fulfilling?'

'I used to, Father, but not any more. I'm finding them dreadfully boring.'

'Then why continue?'

Nigel concentrated on the smoke coming from his Turkish cigarette to avoid meeting his father's eyes. 'What else is there? I'm not qualified for anything else.'

'Oh, come now, son, you should have more faith in your abilities than that! If there is something you would like to do, then tell me and I'll help you all I can.'

'I wish I had as much faith in myself as Abbie has in herself. I think she's jolly brave and I really do admire her, Father, for wanting to do something with her life.'

'If you feel like that, why don't you do as she has? There's not a thing standing in your way, Nigel. If you set your mind to something, and are really determined, then there's nothing you can't do.' Robert hoped Agnes wouldn't knock on the door for a while yet. Now he and his son were talking, he wanted something constructive to come from it. 'Don't be afraid to talk to me, son, I really am interested in your welfare.'

'I wish I had the nerve to do what Abbie's done, but I haven't. You see, I'm not as clever as she is, and I'm afraid of being a failure. I know I'm a disappointment to you and that saddens me. I want you to be proud of me, Father, but I don't know how I can do that.'

'Am I to understand that lurking within you, is the desire to accomplish something you believe would make me proud of you? I assure you, Nigel, that you should have no concern for sadness. You are my son and I am proud of you. But if I am to be totally honest, I would have to say I believe you are wasting your life. For your own sake, I would like to see you involved in some work that gave you a sense of fulfilment. You are lacking in confidence now, but that would soon change if you found your niche in life.'

'I haven't got the guts, Father, I'm a coward. I'd be afraid of the humiliation if I started something and didn't succeed in making it a success. Remember my stint at your offices in the city? I was a disaster, an absolute disaster.'

Robert got to his feet to open a window and let out some of the smoke. 'Nonsense! Why do you use words like coward, disaster and humiliation? I was disappointed you didn't take to the work, and I readily admit that. But it wasn't the end of the world. However, now we are on the subject, perhaps you can tell me why you didn't fit in? You are not stupid, your school and college reports confirm this. Never below third in class, which is quite an achievement. I left school before I was fourteen and my school report was never as glowing as yours. I think tenth was the highest I ever got, and I thought that was good. So why are you so unsure of yourself?'

For the first time, a smile lit up Nigel's boyish face. 'It

could be that you are a hard act to follow, Father. You are so self-assured, always in control. And for the short time I lasted in the city office, I thought I was being compared to you and didn't measure up.'

While his son was speaking, Robert was seeing things through his eyes. Why hadn't he realised how difficult it would be for Nigel? The son of a successful businessman, having to be shown the ropes by junior clerks? No wonder he had an inferiority complex. 'This conversation should have taken place a long time ago, son, and I take responsibility for the fact it didn't. Now I have a greater understanding of your feelings and needs, we must forget about the past and look to the future. Unfortunately, though, we're going to have to leave it now because I'm interviewing a young girl for the position of scullery maid. Agnes and Kitty have far too much to do and I want their load lightening. Hopefully this young girl will fit the bill. She comes highly recommended. Agnes has seen her and is very impressed, so all the signs are good.'

'How is Kitty, Father? Is she really ill?'

'Worn out with hard work, son. She has an invalid husband whom she has to support. They are literally living from hand to mouth and I felt quite ashamed seeing how little they have compared to what we take for granted. I'll give them whatever help I can, and I'll make sure that when she comes back to work her life will be made easier with a junior to help.'

'I was going to say I realise how lucky we are, but it hasn't anything to do with luck, has it? It's all down to your hard work.'

Robert pushed his chair back and stood up. 'I heard Agnes outside a few minutes ago, but she must have known we were in conversation and didn't want to interrupt. Will you tell her I'm free now? But before you go, how would you like to come to the club with me later? I have a few ideas in my head that might interest you and we wouldn't be disturbed there.'

'I would like that very much, Father. Give me a call when you're ready.'

'One thing more, Nigel.' Robert smiled when his son turned. 'Remember when you used to call me "Dad"? I really much prefer it, if you don't mind.'

'I prefer it myself, Dad.' Nigel left the study feeling more of a man than he ever had. With his back straight, he whistled as he made his way to the kitchen.

Chapter Six

'Come in!' Robert swivelled his chair around as the door opened. 'I'm sorry you were kept waiting, Agnes, but Nigel and I had things to discuss.'

'That's all right, Mr Robert, we had a cup of tea while we were waiting.' The housekeeper had an arm across the shoulders of a young girl, and she now pressed her forward. 'This is Jessie. And this, sunshine, is Mr Robert.'

The girl had her head lowered, and she was visibly shaking. 'Good morning, sir.' There was a catch in her voice that told of the fear inside of her. 'I'm very pleased to meet you.'

Robert took in the coat which was far too old-fashioned for a young girl and was frayed at the cuffs and pockets. The shoes too were well worn and scuffed, but it was plain to see they had been cleaned and polished in an effort to make the best of them. 'Don't be frightened of me, Jessie, I'm not going to eat you. And if you'll look at me, you'll see I don't have two heads.'

When the girl lifted her head, Robert found himself looking into eyes that were as blue as the sky on a summer's day. And they were set in a face of such beauty, he was taken aback. Agnes had said the girl was pretty, but there was more to this child than mere prettiness. 'See? Only one head.'

A shaky smile briefly lit up her face. 'I'm sorry, me mam said I hadn't got to be nervous, but I can't help it. This is me first job, yer see.' When Jessie realised what she'd said her hand flew to her mouth. 'Oh, I didn't mean to say that, honest! I meant if I get the job it will be me first one, sir.'

Robert smiled. The girl had the job as soon as she'd walked through the door, but it wouldn't do to say so. Nor would it do to get too familiar, which might give her the impression that working in this house was going to be easy. 'Then I think you should sit down and we can find out if we suit each other.' He glanced at Agnes, who still had her arm across Jessie's shoulders. 'Would you leave us for ten minutes, Agnes, please. I will ring for you when the interview is over.'

'Yes, Mr Robert.' The housekeeper gave Jessie a quick squeeze. 'Yer'll be all right, sunshine, just act natural and I'll see yer in a bit.' As she left the room, she cast her eyes Robert's way. And if he'd been asked to interpret the message he read there, he'd say Agnes was telling him in a nice way that if he didn't treat the girl right he'd have her to answer to.

'Sit down Jessie, and tell me something about yourself. There's no need to be nervous, I'll just ask you a few questions and all you've got to do is answer. Can you do that?'

'Yes, sir.'

'I know you have never worked for an employer before, but if you were able to choose a job, where would you choose to work? I know most children have an idea what they would like to be when they leave school, so what was your dream, Jessie?'

'Well, sir, one day I wanted to be a nurse and help sick people, then the next day I wanted to be a film star and have lots of money.' There was a hint of laughter in the girl's voice when she said, 'And I've dreamed of being a shop assistant in one of the posh shops in Liverpool. Like Bunney's or Hendersons' in Church Street. I've never even set foot in the shops, but I can tell from the outside that they'd be really posh inside.' She met Robert's eyes. 'They were only dreams, sir, and dreams don't often come true, do they?'

'You are very young, my dear, with plenty of time for more dreams. And you must never give up on them, always keep the flame of hope alive. But being a scullery maid is vastly different to anything you've mentioned. It's hard work, you would be at everyone's beck and call and you would have to learn to take orders. Do you think you could do that?'

'Oh, yes, sir! Me mam said no matter where I go to work I've got to do as I'm told. Always be polite, pleasant and respectful, that's what she said. Oh, and I'm to tell yer that I'm honest, hard-working, punctual and would never let yer down.'

Robert had difficulty keeping his face straight. 'I'm sure you are all of those things, Jessie. But are you prepared to take orders?'

Her head nodding vigorously, the girl said, 'Of course I am. If people are nice to me, I would always be nice back.'

'Say the person giving you an order wasn't nice to you? Say they were bad-tempered and barked an order at you, what would you do?'

'The truth, sir?'

'Yes, Jessie, the truth. You see, we are badly in need of a junior maid, and I don't want to take on someone who is only going to last a week.'

'Right! Well, what I'd have to do, sir, is bite me tongue and get on with it.'

This time Robert didn't try to hide his smile or the laughter that accompanied it. He had a strong feeling that beneath the shy exterior, there lurked a happy girl with a mischievous fun-loving personality. She was just what the house needed, but did she need the house and the problems that went with it? 'Very well answered, my dear. But as you may be biting your tongue more often than you would like, may I suggest you don't bite too deeply? Perhaps it would be better to just clamp your lips together and wait until you can pour out your troubles to Agnes or Kitty. Agnes is your best bet, because she is not afraid of anyone. If she thinks she's in the right, even the Lord above wouldn't change her mind. So if you have any problems, or are not sure of anything, always go to the kitchen.' He grinned. 'That's what I do! If I've had a busy day and feel full of cares and woes, I sit on the corner of the kitchen table and unburden myself to Agnes. And I always leave the kitchen a brighter, happier man.'

I like him, Jessie thought, he's nice. 'So can I have the job, then, Mr Robert?'

'I think we'll take a chance on each other, shall we? Has Agnes told you anything about the members of the family you will have to serve?'

Jessie nodded. 'There's you, Mr Robert, and yer wife is Miss Edwina. Then there's Miss Victoria, Mr Nigel and Miss Abbie. The cleaner is called Kitty, and the gardener is Pete. And Miss Aggie said if I got the job she'd show me around the house before finding me an overall to start work. She's very kind and said she'll help me find me feet.'

'The wages are four shillings a week, Jessie, and the hours are eight until six, Monday to Saturday. You will have your meals here, of course, and we will provide you with working clothes. Does that satisfy you?'

The girl was more than satisfied. Her mam would be over the moon with the extra money each week. She would be able to cut down on the cleaning jobs she had and wouldn't be tired all the time. 'Yes, thank you.'

'I'll take you along to the drawing room now and introduce you to my family. All except Abbie, who is still at college. Then I'll have to leave you in the capable hands of Agnes, as I have to go out.'

Jessie looked down at her coat when she stood up. Wanting to look as smart as she could, she ran a hand down the front to smooth out the creases. 'I've already met Mr Nigel, and he was ever so friendly.'

'Yes, my son is very easy to get along with. But I have to warn you that my wife and Miss Victoria are not so easy. They have very high standards and are rather strict. But if you do as you're told there shouldn't be any problems.'

As soon as Robert opened the drawing-room door, the conversation inside stopped. He hesitated briefly, knowing Nigel had, without thinking, mentioned that he'd met the new maid. His wife would be furious that he'd taken on a new member of staff without her approval, and he wondered whether he should put the shy, nervous young girl through the ordeal of meeting her and Victoria. He quickly decided it would be worse for Jessie if she met them when he wasn't present. So he opened the door with a flourish and motioned for the girl to enter. 'I want you to meet Jessie who is to be our new junior maid. Jessie, this is my wife, Miss Edwina and my daughter, Miss Victoria. Nigel you have already met.'

Jessie could feel the coldness of the two women in the room. They were looking at her as though she was something the cat had dragged in. But she remembered her mother's words about being polite, so she bent her knees in a little curtsy and managed a weak smile.

'What is your name, girl?' Edwina asked, coldly.

'Jessie, Miss Edwina.'

'I've already been informed of that. But I presume you have a second name?'

Robert stepped in before Jessie could answer. He knew what his wife had in mind and it saddened and disgusted him. Because she couldn't hit back at him, she would take her spite out on the young girl by calling her by her surname. 'It makes little difference, Edwina, as she is to be known as Jessie. And as she will be taking her orders from Agnes, you have no need to bother your head. The whole idea of the exercise is to lighten the burden for Agnes and Kitty, so it is they she will be accountable to. And myself, of course.' He looked down into a face that was no longer smiling, and eyes that held a look of bewilderment. The poor child had only been in the room a few minutes and in that short space of time she had been robbed of the joy and happiness she'd been filled with at getting her first job. Why, oh why, did his wife get satisfaction out of humiliating a fourteen-year-old girl who was unable to answer her back? She could see by the child's clothing that she came from a poor family, but instead of showing understanding she showed nothing but scorn. 'Jessie, run along to the kitchen and Agnes will tell you what to do.'

Robert waited until the door was closed, then, eyes blazing

with anger, he looked from his wife to his daughter. 'How dare you treat a young girl so abominably? You looked at her as though she'd just crawled from under a stone. And for the life of me I can't think what either of you have ever done in life which gives you the right to act as though you're a cut above the rest.'

'Good grief, Father,' Victoria said. 'She's only a servant girl, after all.'

'Steady on, Victoria!' Nigel uncrossed his legs and leaned forward. 'I think Jessie's a very nice young girl. She was very pleasant when I spoke to her earlier, and she's certainly very pretty.'

'Keep out of it, Nigel.' There was a warning in Edwina's voice. 'You have no idea how servants should be treated. Show them the slightest weakness and they'll play on it. Give them an inch and they'll take a yard.'

'Stop this senseless bickering,' Robert said. 'I have told you that no one in the family, apart from myself, is to give Jessie an order. Agnes will tell her what her duties are and make sure the work is done properly. And while all the staff slave to keep this establishment running smoothly, you can carry on with your useless, idle lives. It shall be as I said, and I brook no argument.' He turned to his son. 'Nigel, I have a phone call to make which will take about ten minutes. Would you get the car out of the garage in readiness, please, so we can be quickly on our way?'

Nigel followed Robert from the room. He knew his mother and sister would be very critical of his father and he had no desire to hear, or be part of it. They seldom had anything good to say about anyone, and for a long time now he'd wearied of their wickedness. But he'd put up with it because he had nothing else to fill in his time. He was hoping that would change in the near future. His determination had grown in the last hour, since he'd first met Jessie. A fourteen year old working to earn money, and here was he, nearly twenty-one and never worked or earned a penny in his life.

'We'll go in the smoking room, Nigel, we can talk better there.' Robert led the way, feeling so good to have his son with him. 'The reading room is very quiet and you have to talk in whispers or suffer raised brows from the members who wish to peruse the daily papers.'

'I say, you can tell it's a men only club with the various smells of tobacco.' Nigel looked around the richly appointed room as he sank into a deeply upholstered, brown leather wing-back chair. 'But the best smell, Dad, is the smell of old wood. I prefer that to a woman's perfume any day.'

'I think that would depend upon the woman wearing the perfume, son.' Robert nodded his head in greeting to another club member. 'When the right one comes along you certainly won't have the smell of old wood on your mind.'

'I want to get my life sorted out before then. When you said earlier to Mother and Victoria that they led useless, idle lives, you could have included me in that. I'm not proud of it, but it's the truth.'

'Perhaps I shouldn't have overreacted as I did, because heaven knows I should be used to it. But I object to anyone being humiliated, and that's what they were doing to Jessie. Poverty doesn't make anyone an inferior being.'

'I went through the kitchen to the garage, and you'll be pleased to know that Agnes and Jessie were sitting at the table enjoying a cup of tea and a good laugh. I quite envied them, actually, and if I hadn't been coming with you, I would have joined them.'

Robert was surprised and pleased by the change in his son. What a pity he himself hadn't tried harder and sooner. They'd lost a lot of time but he hoped to make up for it now. 'The telephone call I made was to Jeff. I'll tell you what we discussed and you can say if it interests you or not. And I want you to be honest, and not say something because you think it's what I want to hear. It's your future, your life, I'm only here to help if I can.'

'I know that, Dad, and I appreciate it. Now, I'm all ears.'

'I've known Jeff for over twenty years, when neither of us had two ha'pennies to rub together, and I trust him implicitly. He knows the business inside out, from the removal side, the auctions, how efficiently the offices are run, and he sees to all the bookwork himself. I couldn't manage without him. And he was a lad who left school at thirteen, like myself, with no proper schooling or qualifications. He has grown with the business, which was easier than it would be for anyone now who joined the firm and had so much to learn. And I've asked him if he would take you on board. Not to sit in an office and look at books or filing cabinets, but to be by his side every day, watching what he does and how he does it. Not to interfere or get involved, but to learn gradually, by experience, every aspect of the business. And you couldn't have a better teacher or work with a nicer man.'

Nigel was sitting forward, his eyes alight with interest. 'Oh, I could work with Jeff, Dad, I think he's a topping bloke! But are you sure that's what he wants – me under his feet all the time? Whenever he turns his head I'll be there, breathing down his neck.'

Robert was being drawn to his son more with each passing minute. The lad was conscious he hadn't lived up to his father's hopes last time and was trying to make sure it didn't happen again. 'I think you're quick enough to keep from under his feet, and are too polite to breathe down his neck. Besides, Jeff doesn't mince words, he'd soon tell you to shove off. And before you give me your answer I'd like you to know he isn't offering to help just as a favour to me. He said he'd be pleased to have you working with him.' Robert stroked his chin as he pondered whether to tell his son what Jeff's last remark had been. Would he be putting Nigel under a lot of pressure, or would he be giving him a goal to aim for? He quickly decided on the latter. 'As a matter of fact, before he put the phone down, Jeff said he'd waited long enough to see *Robert Dennison and Son* above our offices and on our vans.'

Nigel's mouth gaped in surprise. 'He said that? It was jolly decent of him, Dad! But I've got to prove myself worthy first, and I've a long way to go. But I'll try not to let you or Jeff down. I'll do my utmost to justify your faith in me.'

'I'm sure you will, Nigel. And now shall we celebrate by having lunch in town? I'll ring home and tell them not to expect us. That is, if you haven't made other arrangements?'

'No, Dad, I had nothing planned. Every day is very much like the day before, with nothing to look forward to the day after. I need something to stimulate my mind and body, and spending each morning in the drawing room talking about the lives of our friends, followed perhaps by a game of tennis, is hardly stimulating. I've felt for a long time that the life I was leading was useless and there was nothing to look forward to. But today all that has changed and I feel on top of the world. My heart is thumping and I'm having a hard job stopping myself from grinning like a Cheshire cat.' Nigel took a deep breath before saying, 'And the one thing above all that has made me so happy, is that you and I are sitting here, talking like father and son. That means a lot to me, Dad.'

'And that's how it will be from now on, I promise you,' Robert said. 'Abbie always comes to me with her problems, and I want you to do the same. I want us to be a close family, that's all I've ever wished for.' He took out his fobwatch. 'I'll have to ring home before Agnes prepares the lunch. I'll only be two minutes.'

'Before you go, Dad, can I ask you something?' Nigel's smile was shy and boyish. 'When can I start work?'

There were a few raised brows from members of the exclusive club who were seated nearby, when Robert's laughter rang out. It would be hard to say who was the happiest, he or his son. 'Will Monday be soon enough?' He sat down again and leaned forward. 'I'm picking Kitty and her husband up at eight o'clock, so I could run you down to Jeff's first. Or is that too early for you?'

'No, that's fine, I'll ask Agnes to give me an early call.' Nigel's forehead was creased. 'Did you say you were picking Kitty's husband up as well?'

Robert nodded. 'He's a sick man and I thought a couple of hours in the garden would do him good. Heaven knows the garden is big enough, and fresh air is free.'

'That's very generous of you, Dad. No one mentioned it to me.'

'Ah well, you see, that's because no one knows. I haven't told anyone because I'm aware that your mother will raise the roof. She says I'm too soft with the servants and far too familiar. I wouldn't be swayed by her views, because if I can help someone I won't ask permission to do so. But every time she lectures me I get a headache, so I take the easy way out. However, I will have to tell Agnes and Pete, so they can keep their eye on Mr Higgins.'

Nigel watched as his father crossed the room, his back ramrod straight and his gait that of a man who had confidence in himself. He was a handsome man, and a good and kind one. I want to be like him when I'm older, Nigel thought. And I'm going to work hard to make him proud of me. Then came another thought that had crossed his mind many times over the last few years. Why were his mother and Victoria so different in nature to the man who provided them with the best that money could buy? They didn't appreciate him, in fact they appeared at times to actively dislike him. But then there were very few people they did like, even those they fawned over and called friends. They never laughed, seldom even smiled, and they never saw good in anyone. If it wasn't for his father they wouldn't have any staff at all because they were so badly treated.

Robert came walking towards him rubbing his hands. 'Everything's taken care of. Oh, and Agnes said, "No matter where yer go for lunch the bleedin' food won't be as good as what I'd be giving yer, so there!" '

Nigel chuckled. 'Agnes is very funny, isn't she?'

'My dear boy, Agnes is a treasure and should be treated as such. Now, where shall we find food as good as hers?'

Abbie knocked on the study door when she came home from school, and her face was aglow with excitement. 'I had to come and tell you, Dad. I couldn't keep it bottled up until dinner-time.'

'I don't need to ask, it's written all over your face. But I'll ask anyway. You were successful, then, my dear?'

'Signed up for every class I wanted, Dad! Shorthand, typing, book-keeping and general office work. I'm so thrilled I don't know whether I'm coming or going.'

Robert held out his arms. 'Come and let me give you a kiss of congratulations. I'm so pleased for you, and very proud. I think you should be rewarded, so what would you like me to buy for you?'

Abbie moved back from him and gazed into his eyes. 'I don't want you to buy me anything, Dad, I have everything I need. But there is one thing you could do that would make me very happy.'

'You only have to name it, my dear.'

'Take me to see Milly, please? I know you said you would, and you always keep your promises, but I've set my heart on seeing her soon.'

'I haven't had time to visit or call on her and her parents yet, I've been rather busy the last day or so. I'll definitely make an effort on Monday or Tuesday, though, and you have my word on that.'

'I can't wait to see her. We were very good friends you know, Dad, and never once did we have an argument or fall out.' Abbie grinned. 'Well, maybe a little one over a skipping rope, or who was better at hopscotch. But it only ever lasted five minutes and then we'd see the funny side and double up laughing.'

Robert smiled, remembering how close the two young girls had been. 'A right pair of gigglers you were, my dear. And I think it right you meet up again. A good friend is a friend for life.'

'My friend Rowena isn't of the same opinion. When I told her about Milly, she said we'd be like strangers after not seeing each other for ten years and wouldn't have a thing in common.'

But because Robert had been seeing Milly on a regular basis during those ten years, he was in a better position to judge. 'I think Rowena will be proved wrong, Abbie, but just let's wait and see, eh?'

'Yes, OK, Dad.' She flung her arms around his neck and planted a noisy kiss on his cheek. 'I'll have to hurry and get washed and changed for dinner, otherwise I'll be blotting my copy book. And I don't want any dark clouds spoiling this day for me.'

'Oh, before you run off, my dear, did you happen to come through the kitchen when you got home?'

Abbie shook her head. 'I came to the front door and used my key to let myself in. Why?'

'I wondered if you'd met Jessie, our new junior maid. She joined the staff this morning and I've left her in the capable hands of Agnes to be shown the ropes. She'll be helping Kitty with the housework mostly, but she can also give Agnes a hand when needed. She's only fourteen, as pretty as a picture and a likeable lass. This is her first job, so naturally she's shy and more than a little frightened. Unfortunately she got a very cool reception from your mother and Victoria, which I could see upset her. So I'm hoping you and Nigel will make up for their rudeness by showing Jessie we are not a family of ogres. I know I don't have to tell either of you to be nice to her, because it isn't in your nature to be otherwise. She needs this job, and Agnes and Kitty need the help she can give them.'

'Ah, the poor thing!' Abbie felt a wave of sympathy. It must have been a terrible ordeal for a young girl, facing two women who no doubt looked down their noses at her. 'I'll slip along to the kitchen now and welcome her.'

Robert tapped a finger on his temple before standing up.

'I'll come with you. I need to tell Agnes about some arrangements I've made for Monday, so I'll do it now while I think on.'

Edwina and Victoria were seated at the dining-room table when Nigel made his appearance. Taking his usual chair next to his sister, he said, 'Good evening. I thought I was late, but I see Father isn't here yet.'

Victoria turned her head and raised her brows. There was sarcasm in her eyes and in her voice. 'Where on earth have you been all day? Mother and I were beginning to think you'd left home.'

Abbie, watching from the opposite side of the table, saw her brother's face flush as he gave a nervous smile. They're going to make fun of him, she thought, like they always do. Why does he allow them to tease him, and make him the butt of their cruel jokes? He never stands up to them, but he might with a little help. 'I've been out all day, too,' she announced suddenly, 'but I don't suppose you gave a thought as to whether I'd left home or not. Probably because you couldn't care less whether I did or didn't!'

Three pairs of eyes fastened on her. 'I wasn't talking to you, I was talking to Nigel,' Victoria said. 'So kindly keep your thoughts and remarks to yourself.'

'Oh, am I not entitled to join in a conversation then? Perhaps you'd like me to sit quietly and suck my thumb, or, better still, make myself invisible?'

'Don't be impertinent, Abigail,' Edwina frowned. 'You speak when you are spoken to, and not before. Do I make myself clear?'

Nigel hastened to defend his younger sister, and surprised himself by the depth of his feeling of injustice. 'Oh, I say, Mother, that was uncalled for. Abbie has as much right to speak her mind as any other member of the family.'

'We have a mutiny on our hands, Mother,' Victoria drawled. 'What shall we do to punish them?'

'Punish who?' Robert entered the room and turned to close the door behind him. 'It all sounds very serious.'

'It was in fun, Father.' Victoria turned on the charm. 'We were having a light-hearted conversation, that's all.'

'Well, I'm glad everyone's in a happy mood,' Robert said, taking his seat, 'because this is a day for celebration. I presume you've heard Nigel and Abbie's good news, Edwina?'

His wife looked flustered. 'We've only just sat down, so there hasn't been time for the passing on of news.'

'Only time to talk of punishing someone?' There was a smile on Robert's face, but the eyes that stared down the table at his wife were hard. Why did she think he was stupid enough to fall for her lies? 'Still, be that as it may, this is a day for celebrating. I'm sure you'll be happy to know Abbie has succeeded in signing on at the commercial college, Edwina, and I know you'll be delighted for her and wish her well. But before you do, there's another piece of absolutely brilliant news for you. On Monday, Nigel is joining the family firm. It has been agreed by all concerned that he will begin his training working alongside Jeff.'

While Robert was watching the stunned disbelief on the faces of his wife and eldest daughter, Abbie rounded the table and put her arms around Nigel. 'Oh, I'm so happy for you! Just think, both of us in the one day!'

Nigel pushed his chair back so he could stand up and give his sister a big hug. His face was alight with pride as he gazed down at her. 'It's something I've wanted to do for a long time, but you spurred me into action. I couldn't have my kid sister working while I sat on my bottom all day doing nothing. And Dad has been very good. I really am indebted to him for giving me another chance.' His arm still around Abbie, he glanced at his mother. 'It's marvellous news, isn't it, Mother?'

Her face showing no animation, but fearing a reprimand by her husband if she didn't answer, Edwina ground out the words through clenched teeth. 'Yes, marvellous.'

'I wouldn't get too carried away,' Victoria said, her top lip curled in a sneer. 'You'll probably last a couple of weeks, like you did last time. You are not cut out to work, Nigel, and the sooner you realise that, the better.'

Robert thought it time to intervene. 'You have made it very obvious that *you* are not cut out to work, Victoria, but please don't try and make Nigel's decisions for him. I can assure you he is capable of knowing what he wants and more than capable of carrying it out. And I've another little surprise for my son, so will you sit down Nigel, please?'

While her brother sat down, Abbie hurried back to her chair. Her pretty face agog, she asked, 'What is it, Dad?'

Robert was savouring every word he was about to say. 'We all know Nigel is twenty-one in a couple of weeks, which is a big milestone in a man's life. Well, I've decided to bring his birthday forward because his present will make life easier for him when he starts work.' He met his son's eager eyes. 'I'm going to buy you a car. Only a small Austin to be going on with, but it will take you everywhere you want to go. You can come with me to the garage in the morning, and if they have one in, we'll take delivery right away.'

Nigel was stunned. His mouth was working but his emotions were running so high he could only stutter, 'I don't know what to say, Dad.'

'I do!' Victoria's eyes were blazing. 'I wasn't given a car for *my* twenty-first, so if anyone deserves one it should be me. I'm nearly two years older than Nigel, Father, or had you forgotten?'

There was a knock on the door and Robert lifted his hand for silence. 'We'll discuss this later.'

Jessie opened the door and stood aside to let Agnes pass with the heavy soup tureen. The girl's eyes were everywhere, taking everything in so she could tell the family when she got home. She should have finished work by now, but because she was late starting she offered to make the time up by helping in the kitchen. That meant she would get a full day's pay and her mam would be over the moon.

111

'Shouldn't Jessie have left by now, Agnes?' Robert asked. 'I don't want her parents to think we're overworking her.'

'She wanted to stay, Mr Robert, to make up for the time she lost this morning.' The housekeeper was well aware of the tense atmosphere. What a bloody happy family this lot were! Then she mentally corrected herself. Three of the family were smashing people, it was the two stuck-up bitches who spoilt it. The faces they had on them now, anyone would think they had a sour lemon in their mouths. 'The girl's doing very well, Mr Robert, she's quick and picks things up in no time.'

'As long as she doesn't pick things up that don't belong to her,' Victoria said. 'You should keep your eye on her because you'll be held responsible if anything goes missing.'

As Agnes was later to tell Tilly Woods next door, if she hadn't already put the soup tureen on the table, she would have emptied it on someone's head and taken great delight in doing so. 'I'll pretend yer never said that, Miss Victoria. Wicked words thought of in a wicked head and spoken with a wicked tongue. And to think you went to a finishing school which was supposed to make a lady out of yer! I'm glad I went to a corporation school – they taught us manners there and it didn't cost nowt.'

The housekeeper went to stand beside Jessie who, thankfully, was so busy eyeing the ornaments and curtains, she didn't hear all that was said. 'Jessie will be watching me serve the dinner, Mr Robert, is that all right? It's the only way she'll ever learn.'

'Of course, Agnes.' Robert had managed to keep his temper under control simply because he could tell from the young girl's face that she hadn't heard what was said. 'She is in your care and is to take orders from no one else.'

With a satisfied nod of her head, the housekeeper put her arm across Jessie's shoulders and led her from the room. But had she lingered for a few seconds outside the door, as she often did, she would have been more than satisfied when all hell broke loose.

'I am ashamed of you!' Robert was on his feet, his curled fists resting on the table. He was so angry the veins in his neck were standing out and his face blazing. 'I am ashamed to say that you are my daughter. The sooner you marry and leave this house, the better.'

'Agnes was right, you *are* wicked,' Abbie shouted. 'How could you say such a horrid thing about Jessie when she's never done you any harm? I don't like you, Victoria, you aren't a nice person.'

'I agree with what my Dad and Abbie have said.' Nigel touched his sister's arm so she had to turn and face him. 'You've said many hurtful things, Victoria, and I've let them go over my head. But you are getting worse and I can no longer stand by and say nothing. What you said about Jessie was bad. To accuse a young girl of being a thief on the first day she starts working here, shows you have an evil streak which will one day get you into very serious trouble.'

'For heaven's sake, what's all the fuss about?' Victoria didn't turn a hair. 'I didn't say the wretched girl was a thief, I merely hinted that she could be. And if anything does go missing, don't say I didn't warn you.'

'Could we please put a stop to this shouting,' Edwina said faintly. Not for all the tea in China would she speak against her eldest daughter. 'We don't want to fill the servants' mouths.'

'If, by servants, you mean Agnes and Jessie, then I think your dear daughter has already filled their mouths for them. And if they come back and find the soup hasn't been touched, then that is something more for them to talk about. So do your wifely duty, Edwina, and serve the soup while I dispense some home truths to our eldest offspring.'

When her mother rose to do as her father had asked, Victoria knew she didn't have any immediate support. So she kept her voice level. 'Father, I don't need any lectures, thank you.'

'Oh, but you do! I'll get this over quickly so we can all eat our meal, perhaps not in peace because that word seems out of place in this room, but in quietness. So I'd like to go back to your remark about wanting a car. You said if anyone deserves one, it's you. Now I'd like you to tell me why you think you deserve a car.'

'Because I'm the eldest, that's why!' Victoria was losing patience. Why couldn't the man see why it should be her getting a car, and not Nigel? 'I would have thought that would be obvious to you, Father. You pride yourself on being a fair-minded man, but in this instance you seem to be bloody-minded.'

'I wouldn't like you to think I'm not a fair-minded person,' Robert said, in a deceptively mild tone. 'So, I'll do the same for you as I have for Nigel. And as I will do for Abbie when the time comes. The day you find a job, and start work, I will be more than happy to buy you a car. You see, my dear Victoria, that will be the day you have earned one.'

Victoria's nostrils were white with temper. How dare her father talk down to her! 'Clarissa Chisholm has a car and she doesn't have to work for it. It gives people the impression we can't afford one!'

'Select your words carefully before you speak them, Victoria, because many of them do not apply. For instance, forgetting the family as a whole, can you, as a fully grown adult, afford to buy yourself a car?'

'Not on the allowance you give me, no! But Clarissa didn't have to pay for her own car, her father bought it for her. So why can't you do the same for me? Surely it's not too much to ask?'

'I have three things to say to you, Victoria, and I do not want a reply to any of them. What I do want, though, is your silence and the whole subject closed. Firstly, because your mother wants you to mingle with the right sort of people, hoping you will marry into a wealthy family, you receive twice the allowance your brother and sister get. This money is frittered away on clothes, hairdressing and manicures. To ask for more would be a waste on my part and greed on yours.

114

And we come now to the Chisholms. They are one of the wealthiest families in Liverpool, money and business passed on for the last three generations. They were born into wealth, they know no other kind of life. But we Dennisons are a different breed. You see, we were born into poverty and only through sheer hard work, and the loan of five pound, have we reached the position we are in now. We will never be on the same social scale as the Chisholms and, quite frankly, I wouldn't want to be. That isn't to say I don't have a high regard for Mr Chisholm senior, because I find him an honest, down-to-earth man who is popular with all the club members.'

Robert took a deep breath and let his eyes travel around the table. Victoria wasn't even giving him the courtesy of showing interest, preferring to examine each of her nails in turn as though bored rigid by the sound of her father's voice. This irritated him into saying, 'I hope I have made my position clear, Victoria, and my words haven't fallen on deaf ears. And lastly, if by words or looks, you ever again humiliate Jessie in my presence, you can expect me to retaliate and belittle you in front of her. You have been warned.'

Chapter Seven

When Alf Higgins climbed out of the car and looked around him he was taken aback by the size of the house and the garden. He'd never been to his wife's place of work before, and while she was always talking about it, and the wonders within, he hadn't visualised it being so huge. It was a flipping mansion, and the garden was as vast as a park. 'It's a big place yer've got here, Mr Robert.'

'Yes, it is, Alf, and I'm glad I don't have to do the gardening because it's a full-time job. But it's very enjoyable to sit in on a summer's afternoon.'

Kitty came scurrying around the car. She'd been in the back passenger seat while her husband was given pride of place sitting in the front with her boss. And she could tell by his face that he had enjoyed every minute of it. 'I'll go straight in, Mr Robert, otherwise Aggie will have me guts for garters being late on me first day back.' She looked nervous as she glanced at her husband. 'Will my Alf be all right if I leave him with yer?'

'Of course he will, Kitty, I'll take good care of him. I can see Pete down at the bottom of the garden, so I'll introduce Alf to him, then bring him back for a cup of tea.'

Kitty wasn't so sure about this. She was grateful to Mr Robert for his kindness, and it was really good for Alf to get out of their tiny house for a while and enjoy a change of scenery. But her fear was that Miss Edwina would take exception to him being here and cause trouble. And the little woman wasn't going to let no one make a fool of her Alf, even

117

if it meant losing her job. 'If you say so, Mr Robert.'

'I do say so, Kitty.' Robert could almost read her mind. 'And you are not to worry about a thing, because Agnes has everything under control. Now go and meet Jessie, whom I'm sure you'll like and who will be a great help to you.'

Still the little woman was reluctant to move. She squeezed her husband's hand and smiled up at him. 'I'll see yer soon, love.'

'Yes, pet. And don't worry, I'll be all right. I'm a big boy now, remember!'

Kitty's thin legs covered the ground to the kitchen door. Then, after one last look back, she took a deep breath and pushed the door open. 'Good morning, queen! I bet yer thought yer'd seen the last of me?'

Agnes's grin stretched from ear to ear. 'I've missed yer, sunshine. The place has been as quiet as a bleedin' graveyard without you nattering away all day.'

Kitty looked at the young girl standing by the table. 'And you're Jessie, are yer, queen? Well, I'm glad to make yer acquaintance. How are yer settling in here?'

Jessie grinned. She only had to look at Kitty to know she was going to like her. 'I still can't find me way round yet 'cos there's so many rooms. But me mam said it's only natural, and I can't expect to learn everything in a couple of days.'

'I've been here five years, queen, and I still haven't learned everything.' Kitty's chuckle turned into a full-blown laugh. 'I got used to the house in a couple of weeks, but I'm blowed if I can get the hang of some of the people who live in it.'

'I've got a few tales to tell yer later, over a cup of tea.' Agnes pursed her lips and nodded her head to infer that what she had to say was ripe for the telling. 'Yer see, it doesn't pay to play silly buggers and take days off, 'cos yer miss all the excitement.'

'I didn't get sick on purpose, queen, I couldn't bleedin' help it! And I wouldn't have stayed off if Mr Robert hadn't been so idimant.'

The housekeeper's head fell back and she roared with laughter. 'I didn't know Mr Robert was sick as well!'

'He wasn't sick.' The cleaner's eyes narrowed in puzzlement. 'He wasn't, was he?'

'You said he was!'

'I never said no such thing!' Kitty looked at Jessie for support. 'I never said he was sick, did I, queen?'

Jessie was really enjoying the exchange. She didn't know what it was about, but she did know that since Kitty arrived the kitchen was a much warmer place. But she thought it wise not to take sides. 'I don't know, I wasn't really listening.'

'I think yer've gone soft in the head, Agnes Weatherby. Yer've missed me that much yer've gone doolally.' The cleaner adopted a dramatic expression. 'Yer should be down on yer hands and knees thanking me for coming back in time to save yer from the men in white coats. Them what cart people off to the looney bin.'

'Don't be getting carried away, Tilly Mint, yer'd never make a Greta Garbo. And it was you what started all this by saying Mr Robert had been so idimant!'

'That's not the same as saying he was sick, is it? Bloody hell, girl, yer can be as thick as two short planks sometimes. It's a good job yer can cook, 'cos yer'd never get a job doing anything that needed brains.'

'So although idimant sounds like a sickness, it isn't?'

'Of course it's not, yer daft ha'porth! Ooh, do I have to spell it out for yer? Idimant means, er, means, er, means determined, like, yer know.'

'No, it doesn't! *Adamant* means determined, sunshine, and that's the word yer were after.'

Kitty looked puzzled, then the penny dropped. 'Well, I'll be buggered. Yer've been pulling me bleedin' leg all this time, and I fell for it. Yer daft nit, we could have had the landing and stairs done by now!'

Agnes kept her face straight with great difficulty. Oh, how good it was to have the little woman back. 'Yes, and you won't

119

half cop it off Miss Edwina if the landing and stairs are not done before she comes down to breakfast. Yer'd better get yer overall on, and yer skates, and go like the clappers. Jessie's got all yer cleaning utensils ready and she's waiting for the off. Just tell her where to start and make sure there's nothing lying on the floor when the family come down. Mind you, there's only two up there. Mr Nigel went out early with his father, and Miss Abbie left just before you came. And eh, guess what? Miss Abbie had her breakfast in here. She said it was more homely than sitting on her own in the dining room.'

Kitty screwed up her thin face. 'Aggie, will yer shut yer cake-hole, please? Or are yer keeping me talking deliberate, like, so I get into trouble with the queer one?'

'Now would I do that to you, who's me best mate! If I hear one raised voice out there, sunshine, I'll be out like a shot with me broom in me hand and clout anyone who dares to upset yer.'

'Come on, queen, let's go.' Kitty winked at Jessie. 'Once Aggie starts gabbing there's no holding her. She'll talk till the bleedin' cows come home, only stopping for a breath every now and again. She can't help it, though, poor bugger. I reckon when she was born, instead of crying, she came into the world reciting her two times table.' She pulled Jessie to a halt at the bottom of the stairs, to add, 'And d'yer know what, queen? She never did get past her two times table. Ask her what three times three are and she's got to count them on her fingers.'

Agnes crept out of the kitchen behind them and watched as they walked up the stairs. Kitty was holding her long black skirt up so she wouldn't trip up on it, and the sight brought a smile of affection to the housekeeper's face. 'The elastic's gone in the leg of yer knickers, Kitty,' she called softly. 'I can see yer've got yer best blue ones on today, is it someone's birthday?'

Kitty's head went down as she lifted each leg in turn for inspection. Then she spun around and stuck her tongue out. 'Thought yer had me there, didn't yer, soft girl? Well, as yer can see, I've got me pink ones on and the elastic has got more bounce in it than you have, so there, clever clogs.'

Agnes looked at the far too thin legs, and filled up with emotion. How anyone with so little flesh on them could come out to work every day, and work hard, was beyond her. She deserved a bloody medal, and that's a fact. But the housekeeper knew the last thing Kitty wanted was pity. 'Just look at the state of yer legs! They remind me of knots in cotton.'

Just then they heard a door closing on the landing and three pairs of eyes looked up to see Edwina walking towards the stairs. 'Oh, I see you've decided to show your face today, Kitty.' There was no smile, no greeting and no enquiry about the cleaner's health. 'Am I to be told why you are so late starting, and setting a bad example to the girl?'

While Kitty and Jessie stood rooted to the spot, afraid to even blink, Agnes stepped on to the first stair. 'Oh, they're not just starting, Miss Edwina. They've been hard at it for nearly an hour now. I'm sure yer'll find the dining room meets with your approval, and the two cloakrooms. It's a wonder yer didn't hear them moving the furniture about – I could hear them from the kitchen! Still, I expect yer had a busy day yesterday and being overtired yer dropped into a deep sleep.'

Edwina didn't quite know how to react. She'd look a complete fool if she made an issue out of it and was proved to be wrong, but she was sure there'd been a hint of sarcasm in the housekeeper's voice. 'You can rest assured that I will check it has been done to my satisfaction.' She made her way down the stairs, a hand trailing lightly over the wide mahogany bannister. 'If I am not satisfied there will be some explaining to be done.'

'I'm sure yer'll find everything gleaming.' Agnes, following closely on Edwina's heels, turned to give a thumbs-up sign to the woman and girl standing halfway up the stairs with their mouths agape. 'I'll bring yer breakfast through now, and Miss Victoria's, 'cos she should be down any minute. And I'll eat me hat if yer tell me yer can find a speck of dust anywhere.'

'Holy sufferin' ducks! I've bleedin' well had it now!' Kitty wiped the back of a hand across her brow. 'There'll be a layer of dust on everything in there, and the Missus will go over every inch with a fine-tooth comb. She'll be on her hands and knees looking for something to complain about and I'm the one that'll get it in the neck.'

'Why?' Jessie asked. 'She won't find any fault with the dining room 'cos me and Aggie gave it a good do. We used that much elbow grease, we were sweating cobs when we'd finished. It looks a treat and everywhere's shining so much yer can see yer face in it.'

Kitty studied the fresh, pretty young face before cupping it between her hands. Standing on tip-toe, she kissed one of the rosy cheeks. 'Oh, thank you, queen, yer've saved me life. And me mate, Aggie, of course. I love the bones of both of yer.'

Jessie grinned. 'Aggie said yer'd be made up. She wanted it to be a surprise for yer.'

'It was a surprise all right. Trouble was, she should have told me before I nearly had a bleedin' heart attack! I really thought I was for the high jump.' Kitty's thin face broke into a smile. 'Still, all's well that ends well, eh? And I'll tell yer what, queen, I'll pay you and Aggie back with interest.' Looking a lot happier, the little woman jerked her head upwards. 'Let's get up there before Miss High and Mighty comes out of her room. I've faced one dragon this morning, I don't fancy facing another. Especially one what breathes bleedin' fire.'

'Yer do a good job in the garden, Pete, it looks a real treat.' Alf Higgins breathed in the fresh air, feeling better than he had done for years. Standing beneath fruit trees in beautiful surroundings, with two men to talk to – well, he felt uplifted. 'Yer've got it well set out with the orchard, vegetable plots, lawns and flower beds. It must have taken years to get it in shape like yer have.'

'I worked for the people who lived here before Mr Dennison

bought the house. So it's nigh on twenty years now. And I've been lucky with me bosses, they've let me have the run of the garden, to do what I like.'

'Every man to his trade, Pete, that's my belief,' Robert said. 'I'd never had a garden before I came here and didn't know one plant or bush from another. And as I know my limitations, I was happy to leave everything in your capable hands. As Alf said, the garden is a treat, and I spend many hours either sitting in it, weather permitting, or gazing through the window and admiring your handiwork.'

'It's not like work to me, Mr Robert, more a labour of love. I'm at peace with meself out here, and I can think of no other job I would get as much satisfaction from.' He began to chuckle. 'My wife says I think more of this garden than I do of her. And when I told her the flowers don't nag me like she does, she threw a cushion at me.'

'It could have been worse,' Robert said. 'The cushion could have been attached to the couch!' He raised his brows at Alf. 'Do you want to come and have a cup of tea, or would you prefer to spend more time out here?'

'I'm enjoying the fresh air, as long as I'm not in Pete's way.'

'Not at all. I'll bring him in when Aggie calls me for me morning cuppa. He's better filling his lungs with fresh air than his ears with women's chatter. Twenty minutes' break morning and afternoon, that's enough for me. Yer won't get nicer people, or better workers, than Agnes and Kitty. Their only fault is that they are of the female sex and inclined to be talkative.'

'I happen to be glad my wife is of the female sex,' Alf laughed. 'I'd look well being married to a feller, don't yer think?'

'It would raise a few eyebrows,' Pete admitted. 'But I'll say one thing for yer wife, and Agnes, they're a right pair of comediennes. Sometimes the things they come out with have me doubled up with laughter, and they're sitting there poker-faced. That makes it even more comical because their expressions are funnier than the jokes!'

There was a look of pride on Alf's face. 'Kitty has always been full of fun; even when times have been hard she'll think up some lark to put a smile on me face. She was very pretty when she was young, as dainty as a doll. And she could dance the legs off anyone.'

'You've got a good wife and a good marriage, Alf, so you have a lot to be thankful for.' Robert gave him a friendly pat on the back. 'And now I'll have to leave you because I have a few calls to make today. But I'll be back in time to run you and Kitty home, save you waiting around for trams.' He looked knowingly at the gardener. 'Perhaps you could bring a chair out in case Alf gets tired standing.'

'I'll be all right, Mr Robert, don't you worry about me. As long as Pete doesn't mind, I'd prefer to watch him. It was always a dream of mine, when I was young, to have a garden. And this is the nearest I've ever got to it.'

'I'll have yer pulling carrots up if ye're not careful,' Pete joked. 'I've had orders off Aggie that she'd like some for the dinner tonight, as long as they're big enough.'

'I can see you two are getting on well, so I'll be away.' Robert waved a farewell and hurried to the car. His first call was to be to a jeweller's in the city to choose a present for Maureen. He had in mind a gold, heart-shaped locket that he could have engraved with their names on the back. Either that or a gold wrist-watch. As he switched the ignition on, Robert told himself he would have a better idea when he was in the shop and could look at several pieces of jewellery before deciding. If it was up to him, he would buy both a locket *and* watch, but he knew Maureen would refuse to accept two expensive gifts. She was a proud woman who guarded her independence, and for this he admired her. The fact that he had money meant nothing to her; she liked him for what he was, not what he had.

As he drove down Smithdown Road, Robert told himself he

must put a couple of hours in at the office to keep on top of things. And, of course, to see how Nigel was faring. He wasn't going to interfere, but he wanted his son to know he was interested in what he was doing. Then, after lunch he'd keep his promise to Abbie and make a call to the Jamiesons'. Milly would be at work, but her mother, Beryl, should be home in the afternoon preparing a meal for the family. He knew he would get a warm welcome, he always did. There'd be a cup of tea in his hand before he'd had time to sit down. And it was a house he could relax in, and go back to being Bob Dennison, who had once been the proud owner of a horse and cart.

'Go down the garden for us, sunshine, and tell the two men that the tea is up.' Agnes lifted the heavy iron kettle and poured boiling water into the dark brown teapot. 'And tell Pete if he doesn't get a move on, and the tea is stiff, it'll be his own fault.'

Jessie pulled a face. 'I'll tell him the tea is ready, Aggie, but I won't tell him to get a move on 'cos that would be cheeky and he wouldn't like me for it.'

'No, ye're right, sunshine, and I'm out of order encouraging yer to be cheeky. If yer mam knew, she'd have me life.' Agnes opened a drawer and took out a tea strainer. A pet hate of hers was finding tea leaves floating on the top of her cup. The only time she didn't use the strainer was when Tilly from next door told her fortune from the tea leaves left at the bottom of her cup. Not that anything Tilly ever forecast came true, but it passed an hour away and was a good laugh. 'Just give them a big smile, sunshine, and ask them if they'd honour us with their presence.'

When Jessie had left, Agnes turned to where Kitty was sitting at the table. 'She's been well brought up, that girl, and a credit to her parents.'

'She's not half pretty, as well.' Kitty was sitting on the edge of her chair so her feet wouldn't dangle, and she was resting her elbows on the table. 'That blonde hair and bright blue eyes

125

will have the fellers chasing after her in a year or so. And another thing, Aggie, she's a damn good worker. I've only got to ask her to do something and it's done before yer can say Jack Robinson. She leaves me bleedin' standing, I can tell yer.'

'I should think so! She's twenty-five years younger than yer, sunshine.'

'Did yer have to say that, queen? Now yer make me feel as old as the ruddy hills! I know I am as old as some hills, but yer don't have to remind me of it.' Kitty curled her fists and rested her chin on them. 'Ay, queen, just out of curiosity, like, who was this Jack Robinson feller? And who was it said he could work that fast yer eyes couldn't keep up with him?'

'How the hell do I know! That saying is as old as the ruddy hills yer were on about.'

'That's another thing, queen. How does anyone know how old hills are? I mean, like, the only way yer'd really know is if yer had a shovel and yer built the bleedin' thing yerself!'

Jessie came running in then, her childish giggle bringing smiles to the faces of the two women. 'They're coming when they've scraped the dirt off their shoes, Aggie. And Pete said to remind yer that he likes his tea strong enough to stand the spoon up in.'

'Yer can tell Pete to sod off, sunshine, 'cos he'll get the tea as it comes out of the pot.'

'I heard that, Aggie.' Pete took off his peaked cap and hung it on the hook behind the kitchen door. 'If yer loved me like ye're always telling me, yer'd make sure I get me tea exactly as I like it.'

'Fussy bugger!' Kitty clicked her tongue on the roof of her mouth. 'Yer don't have to worry about my Alf, Aggie, 'cos as long as it's wet and warm, he'll drink it.'

When her husband smiled down at her, he was seeing the eighteen-year-old girl he'd fallen in love with. 'We don't have much option, do we, pet? On hard-up days we're counting the flipping tea leaves!'

'Well, sit yerself down, Alf,' Aggie told him. 'Seeing as ye're a visitor, yer can have yer tea weak or strong, whichever yer prefer. And as a special treat I've made a batch of scones which I'm now going to take out of the oven. Butter them while they're still hot and I guarantee they'll melt in yer mouth.'

'Ay, you, don't be spoiling him!' Kitty waited until her husband was sitting beside her then linked her arm through his. 'And yer can keep those greedy eyes off him, Aggie Weatherby, 'cos he's mine.' She laid her thin face against his shoulder. 'Aren't yer, love?'

Alf pretended to give this very serious consideration. 'Now yer know, pet, I've always said I wouldn't swap yer for all the tea in China, or all the money in the world. But I've never said nothing about Aggie's hot scones, now have I? I mean, like, yer can't say yer prefer one thing when yer haven't tried the other! According to you, these scones are out of this world, so I think I should consider me options before making a statement.'

'Don't start getting big-headed because ye're sitting in a posh house, Alf Higgins, comparing me to hot scones. The bleedin' scones will be wolfed down in five minutes, while I'll be here for ever. So think on in case I turn the tables on yer and find meself another feller what will appreciate me.'

While Jessie filled the teacups, Aggie set two big plates in the middle of the table and plonked herself down. She pushed a lock of her white hair behind her ear, hoisted her ample bosom, then leaned her elbows on the table. She glanced across to see the look of love being exchanged between Alf and his wife, and she couldn't help feeling sad. They were both as thin as rakes, and it just didn't seem fair. If you put the two of them together they wouldn't come up to her weight. 'Muck in, Alf, and pretend ye're at yer granny's. There's ten scones so it works out at two each.'

'That's right, love, you muck in as Aggie said. We only get twenty minutes' break, and there's five of those minutes gone already.' Kitty could feel her mouth watering as she spread the best butter on to a scone. It was melting as she put it on, and she gave her husband a dig. 'This is the gear, isn't it, eh? Aren't yer glad Mr Robert invited yer for the day?'

Alf didn't answer straight away. There was a look of pure bliss on his face as he tasted best butter for the first time in years. Then he nodded. 'I've got a lot to thank your boss for. It's a treat enough just getting out of our house for the day and being driven in a posh car like a proper toff. But to be able to walk in a lovely garden, and be fed like a king, well, it really is something.'

'I've told Alf that Mr Robert wouldn't mind him coming down now and again if he enjoys it so much.' There was butter trickling down Pete's chin and he wiped it away with the back of his hand. 'What do you think, Aggie?'

'Mr Robert wouldn't mind in the least, he'd be only too pleased that someone was getting enjoyment out of the garden. But it's not him yer'd have to worry about, is it? If Miss Edwina got wind of it, she'd probably have something to say. Yer know what a miserable cow she is, she wouldn't give yer a drink if yer were dying of thirst.'

Kitty's head was nodding vigorously. 'Or the lend of last night's *Echo*! She'd even stop yer breathing in the fresh air if she could.' A smile of mischief crossed her face. 'Hands up all those who wouldn't shed a tear if she stopped breathing? And no bleedin' lies, either!'

Alf pointed a stiffened finger at her. 'Now that wasn't a very nice thing to say, love. There's many a true word spoken in jest.'

'Oh, I think God will forgive her this time, Alf,' Agnes said. 'Perhaps she shouldn't have said anything so drastic, but if the truth's known, there's not one person in this kitchen who even likes the woman of the house. We all love and admire her husband, but we can't stand her because she thinks she's better than anyone else.'

Pete, who had never been known to gossip or criticise

anyone, nodded his head. 'I don't wish her dead, I just wish she lived somewhere else.' His eyes lighted on Agnes. 'By the way, Aggie, the carrots yer wanted are outside. They're not a bad size, either. And yer've got Alf to thank, 'cos he picked them.'

Kitty gaped. 'Yer didn't, did yer, love? Oh, I hope yer haven't been overdoing it 'cos I don't want you laid up sick.'

'He hasn't been overdoing it, Kitty, I made sure of that,' Pete said. 'It's not hard work picking carrots, it doesn't require any strength.'

'Anyway, take a look at yer husband, sunshine,' Aggie said. 'He's got colour in his cheeks which he didn't have before.'

'Do I get a say in this?' Alf laughed. 'If anyone is interested in how I feel in meself, I can honestly say I've never felt so well for a long time. I love being in the garden, Pete is a smashing feller to work with, and to top it off, Aggie's scones really are something to write home about.'

'That just leaves me and Jessie,' Kitty said. 'Can't yer think of anything nice to say about us two?'

'That's easy, I don't have to think. You are the love of my life and I wouldn't part with yer, not even for Jean Harlow. And as for Jessie, she's pretty enough to be on the lid of a box of Cadbury's chocolates. Does that satisfy yer, pet?'

Kitty gave it some thought before looking at the young girl. 'I think I'm happy with that, queen, but what about you?'

'Ooh, yeah, I'll say!' Jessie rolled her big blue eyes. 'I mean, Cadbury's are the best chocolates yer can buy, aren't they?'

'It's that bleedin' long since I tasted any chocolate, queen, I wouldn't know. But I'll give yer a little compliment meself. As soon as I clapped eyes on yer I knew we were going to get on. It's a pleasure working with yer.'

Jessie's face lit up. 'It's a pleasure working with you, Kitty, and Aggie. I've only been here a few days and already we're mates.'

Agnes glanced at the clock. Time was marching on, and if

Miss Edwina came in now there'd be hell to pay. But there was one thing she felt she had to say. And it was to the young girl who had fitted in so well in so short a time. 'It would be a hard one to please what didn't like yer. Yer haven't said a word out of place, or put a foot wrong, since the hour yer started. And there's not many young ones yer can say that about. So welcome to the family, sunshine, and long may you reign.' Her palms flat on the table, she pushed herself up. 'It's back to the grind now, so get moving. Except you, Alf, yer can sit here as long as yer like.'

He shook his head. 'I'll go with Pete and get some fresh air while I can. I'm beholden to yer for feeding me, Aggie, I appreciate it.'

'I'll be feeding yer again at lunchtime, and then on our afternoon break. In fact, by the end of the day yer'll be sick of the sight of me.'

'Never in a million years, Aggie! How could I ever be sick of someone who has been so kind to my wife for the last five years. I think ye're a hero.' He bent to kiss Kitty. 'I'll see yer later, love.'

'Ay, hang on a minute.' Agnes banged a fist on the table causing the cups to rattle in the saucers. 'How come, if I'm the hero, she's the one what gets the kiss? I'd say that was not flamin' well fair! Or as Mr Nigel would say, that's not cricket, old boy!'

With a grin on his thin, but still handsome face, Alf walked around the table. 'I did think of it, Aggie, but I thought if I attempted to kiss yer, yer'd clock me one.'

'Kisses off men are short in my life, Alf, so help yerself.' Agnes tilted her head and offered a cheek. And when she felt his lips, her round chubby face broke into a smile. 'Made my day that has! I'll have to think of something tasty for yer lunch.'

Pete poked his head back into the kitchen. 'We'll have no favouritism here, Aggie. What he gets, we all get.'

'Sod off, Pete, and go and see to yer potato patch. Yer'll get what ye're given and like it.' Agnes hugged herself and smiled at Kitty. 'It's nice to have friends, isn't it, sunshine?'

'It certainly is, queen, yer can't beat it.'

Jessie rocked on her chair, looking relaxed and happy. 'I've really enjoyed meself today. I'm going to like working here.'

Robert turned in Balfour Road and slowed down to glance at the house the family had lived in before moving to Mossley Hill. He'd been happy there, with a wife who still loved him. She'd started to put on a few airs and graces, but he hadn't thought anything of it. After all, moving from a tiny house to a six-roomed one was a step up in the world and most women would have felt proud.

As he pulled up outside the Jamiesons' house, Robert shook his head. It was ridiculous to blame the house for the change in his wife. If a person had their feet on the ground, money didn't change their personality. Anyway, what had brought these thoughts into his head? He'd had seventeen years to get used to his wife's coldness, and she couldn't humiliate or hurt him any more because he'd gone past caring. So it was useless to dwell on what might have been.

Beryl Jamieson opened the door with a towel in her hand. 'Bob, it's lovely to see you! Come on in, yer don't need to stand there like a lemon waiting to be asked.' When he was in the hall, she closed the door behind him. 'Go through to the living room and I can talk to yer while I finish taking some clothes out of the dolly tub.'

'Have I come at a bad time?'

'Don't be daft, I'm always happy to see yer.' Beryl was the same age as Robert, but she'd kept her slender figure and pretty face. Her fair hair was peppered with strands of grey, but they were the only signs of middle age. 'It'll take me five minutes to finish off in the kitchen, then I'll make a cuppa and yer can fill me in with yer news.'

Robert laid his bowler hat on the sideboard and took a seat on the couch. 'I don't need a reason to call on you, I do it because we're old friends. But I have a special reason today.'

Beryl came through from the kitchen. 'Blow the washing, I'll do it later. Yer've got me interested now. What's so special about today's visit?'

'Abbie is pestering me to bring her down to see Milly. She's got a bee in her bonnet about it and I'll get no peace until she has her way.'

Beryl leaned forward and rested her elbows on her knees. 'Why now, Bob, after all this time? It's been ten years.'

'That's my fault entirely. You see, she didn't know I'd been visiting you over the years and see Milly quite often. When I told her last week she was surprised, and her surprise quickly turned to wanting to see her old pal again.'

Beryl sat back in the chair. 'Doesn't Edie know yer come, either? Has she got so big for her boots she's forgotten all the old friends she knew?'

Robert nodded. 'Ever since we moved to Mossley Hill, if I mention Arthur Street or Balfour Road she clams up tight and refuses to discuss it. I have told you over the years that our marriage isn't perfect, but the truth is, we haven't any marriage at all. She's my wife and I really don't like talking about her, but right now I think you deserve an explanation. And I think I'd better begin at the beginning.' He gave a deep sigh. 'Before the war started, I'd worked like hell to build the business up. And we were doing well. When Victoria was born, and two years later, Nigel, I was able to give Edie enough money for everything she wanted. And I could afford to give my mam and dad a few bob each week. Life was good, even though I was working all the hours God sent. Then the war started and me and Jeff were expecting to be called up any time. But in nineteen fifteen, they didn't call us up, they requisitioned the horse and cart, with Jeff and myself, for war work. Which meant transporting war materials from factories to the docks. There was more to it than that, but I won't go into details or I'll be here all day. We were paid handsomely for it, so I'm not complaining. And it meant we weren't in the firing line like thousands of other poor buggers.'

Robert reached into his top pocket and took out a cigar. 'Do you mind, Beryl?'

'Not at all, you make yerself at home.'

'You may remember it was in nineteen fifteen, when Edie was pregnant with Abbie, that we moved into this road. She was delighted, and I was glad to have been in a position to afford it. But there was a war on and everyone had to pull their weight, so I was working all hours and saw little of my wife and children. I remember thinking Edie seemed to be changing, becoming more aloof and a bit hoity-toity, but I thought it was just a phase and she'd grow out of it. However, as time went by, our relationship went from bad to worse. If I went near her she would move away, as if she couldn't bear to be close to me.' Robert was quiet for a while, watching the smoke from his cigar spiral towards the ceilling. Then in a voice that told of his despair, he continued. 'The final break came after Abbie was born. I wasn't allowed to touch her and in bed she turned from me as though I was a leper. I stupidly put it down to her being depressed after the birth, and assumed that as time went by we would get back to normal. It wasn't to be, though, and we haven't lived as man and wife for seventeen years.'

Beryl gasped. 'The bitch! I always thought she was a cold-hearted snob, but I didn't think she was that bad.'

'There's worse to come, Beryl, I'm afraid. You see, I was so busy during the war I didn't have much time for visiting, but I always popped into my mam's whenever I could. And at the same time I'd call to see Edie's parents, Ada and Joe. I was only ever there a few minutes because I wanted to spend as much time as I could with my children. I was never at home during the day, but I took it for granted that my wife would be visiting her parents regularly and taking the children. It never dawned on me that she never went near them. Anyway, when the war was over, I didn't have a business any more and had to start again from scratch. I still had Jeff with me, thank God, and the pair of us worked our socks off for the next five years until we had a thriving business. I was so busy I didn't have time to fret over the state of my marriage, hoping it would sort itself out eventually. And with this in mind, I bought the house in Mossley Hill. As you know, by this time my mam and dad had died, leaving a big gap in my life. The horse and cart had gone, too, to make way for motorised vans. And as I was able to employ men to do the hard graft, and Jeff was there to supervise the whole operation, I decided it was time to take an interest in my home and family. Unfortunately I had left it too late, because my house was not a home, my wife was not a wife and my children didn't know what it was like to have a mother's love.'

Beryl leaned forward and touched his knee. 'Bob, take a break and I'll put the kettle on.'

He shook his head. 'I'd rather get it off my chest now I've started. You see I've been blaming myself for all of this, and it's been hell living with the guilt. But I will no longer take the blame because the only thing I've done wrong is to work like a slave to give my family the best. And I mean the best. Sadly, in the process I have lost my wife and my eldest daughter. You wouldn't know them now, Beryl, they've changed completely. My wife thought the name Edie wasn't grand enough, so she's now Edwina. She and Victoria are the biggest snobs you are ever likely to meet. If you aren't rich, they would look down their noses at you. Both are cold, conniving and humourless. When I tell you Edie hasn't been to visit her parents for nearly seventeen years, it will give you an idea of what she's like. And Victoria is exactly the same. Neither of them would be seen dead in Arthur Street, or Balfour Road.'

Beryl gasped. 'I don't believe it! Never been to see her parents? How could she be so cruel, Bob?'

'I didn't know for years, Beryl, because Ada and Joe never mentioned it. They used to ask after her and the children, but I thought nothing of it. When we moved to Mossley Hill I used to ask Edie if she'd been to Seaforth, but she always had the excuse there was too much work to do in the big house. And she got away with it because I was too busy making money to see what was happening in my own family. But I finally blew my top last week and told her I still visited the old neighbours and her mother and father. I tried to get through to her that Ada and Joe are old now and the least she can do is visit them while there's still a chance. And it was her reaction to this that finally killed any respect I had for her. She looked at me as though I was a stranger and said she thought her parents would be dead by now.'

'Oh, my God, what's wrong with the woman? She's not normal! No daughter with any feelings at all would want to forget their parents!'

'There's worse to come, my dear. She has led our three children to think their grandparents are dead. Abbie and Nigel would be devastated if they knew the truth. Victoria, unfortunately, is like her mother, a complete snob. Any mention of coming from a two-up, two-down would have her reaching for the smelling salts.' Robert smiled, but there was no warmth in it. 'I'm sorry to burden you with my problems, Beryl, but I need to get it off my chest to someone, and you were always a good listener.'

'Look, I'm going to put the kettle on, Bob, so you sit back and light another cigar. I've loads of questions to ask yer.'

Robert reached for the cigar case in the inside pocket of his coat. It was when he put a hand in his suit pocket for the clipper that he thought of Maureen. He'd taken a very short time to choose her present. They had a wide selection at Boodle & Dunthorne's but one of the first lockets the assistant brought for his inspection was the one he knew instinctively would be her choice. Not too plain and not too fancy. He had left it to have both their names engraved on the back and would pick it up in a week's time. If only things were different, how happy he would be to spend the rest of his life with her. She would give him the warmth and love everyone needs in their life. Instead, he had to be content with a few hours every fourth Wednesday.

Beryl came bustling in. 'I'm sorry I've got no cakes to offer yer, Bob, but I haven't been to the shops today.'

'A cup of tea is fine.' Robert extended his hand and relieved her of the cup and saucer. 'I can't stay much longer because I want to make my usual two calls to Arthur Street. And before I do, I need to stop at the tobacconist's shop by the Gainsborough to get tobacco and cigarettes for the men, and a mixture of sweets for the ladies.'

'You're a good bloke, Bob, and yer deserve a lot more happiness from life than ye're getting. Don't yer think it's time to put things straight?'

'I intend doing that, my dear. The children have every right to know about their grandma and grandad, and, God knows, Ada and Joe have a right to see the only family they have left. How I will do it I don't know because it is going to come as a shock to the children. Victoria I have no fear about, because she and her mother are as thick as thieves and wild horses wouldn't drag either of them to Seaforth. But my worry is that Nigel and Abbie will turn against Edie for keeping the truth from them. I wouldn't like that to happen, but for my own sanity I have to do what I think is right.'

'Yer'll have to put yer house in order before Abbie comes down here, Bob, because Milly might let it slip. She knows yer see Edie's folk, 'cos she's asked me a few times why yer couldn't bring Abbie to see her when yer were down this way. I told her, which I thought was right, that she probably had new friends now. I wasn't to know any different, and Milly wouldn't see any harm in asking Abbie the same question.' Beryl leaned across to put her empty cup on the table. 'And that's no way for the girl to find out she still has grandparents. It would be a big shock for her and that wouldn't be fair.'

'I have every intention of telling Nigel and Abbie tonight. I don't relish the thought, because I feel I am as guilty as my wife. My weakness in allowing the situation to carry on for

136

so long has deprived Ada and Joe of the love of their grandchildren and the pleasure of watching them grow into adults. I can't bring back those lost years, but I can make sure that no further time is lost.'

'Do it, Bob, and then yer'll be able to live in peace with yerself. To hell with what yer wife thinks, she's not worth worrying about. And you are not as guilty as she is, for Ada and Joe are her parents, not yours.' Beryl saw the worry in his eyes and tried to shake him out of his sadness. 'Milly will be over the moon when I tell her Abbie's coming. How about Wednesday night, about eight, and I'll make sure she's in. And Bill will be made up to see you, he's always asking after yer.'

'How is Bill? And young Kenny?'

'My husband is fine, and at sixteen my son is taller than him. I can't keep the lad in clothes or shoes, he grows out of them in no time.'

Robert handed his cup over before standing up. 'I'll look forward to seeing them all on Wednesday.' After fastening his overcoat he reached for his bowler. 'Thanks for listening to me, Beryl, I really didn't mean to unburden myself to you. I think it was seeing the old house and remembering how much happier those days were.' He gave her a peck on the cheek. 'I'll see myself out, you go back to your washing.'

Beryl didn't move for several minutes after he left. He was a lovely bloke, and it was sad the way his life had turned out. It just went to prove, she thought, that money really can't buy you happiness.

Chapter Eight

They stood on the pavement outside the Higgins' house and Alf thrust out his hand. 'I can't thank yer enough, Mr Robert, I feel as though I've been on me holidays.'

It had been a mixture of a day for Robert. He'd been happy when he walked into Jeff's office and saw Nigel looking calm and settled, as though this was just another day at work. Then there'd been sadness when telling Beryl of his troubles. He probably wouldn't have opened his heart to her if it wasn't for Abbie wanting so badly to see Milly. There'd also been a bout of anger against his wife for putting him in this position. But all that was his worry and had nothing to do with the man standing before him who got enjoyment just by being in a garden.

'You must feel free to visit whenever you're at a loose end, Alf,' he said to the other man. 'I won't be able to chauffeur you, but the trams are handy. Pete would be glad of your company and the helping hand you gave.'

Trams cost money, though, Alf thought, and that is something we don't have. But to say that would sound as though he was hinting. 'Thanks, Mr Robert, I'll remember that. I will call up some time, but I won't make a nuisance of meself.'

'Are yer coming in, Mr Robert?' Kitty was standing on the step with the key in her hand. 'I could make yer a cuppa.'

'No, thank you, Kitty. I've told Agnes to keep the dinner back fifteen minutes and if I'm later than that there'll be some rumbling tummies and long faces.' He doffed his bowler and

139

opened the car door. 'I'll see you tomorrow. And I hope to see you in the near future, Alf.'

The couple waved as his car pulled away from the kerb. 'That is one hell of a nice bloke,' Alf said. 'It's a pity there aren't more like him.'

Robert saw them in his rearview mirror, their arms around each other's waists, and he felt a pang of envy. They probably thought that with his wealth he could have anything in the world he wanted. How wrong they would be.

Knowing he was cutting it fine for time, he drove as quickly as he could. But when he entered the kitchen and saw the housekeeper's face, he knew he was responsible for holding things up. 'Very late, am I, Agnes?'

She tilted her head and rolled her eyes. 'They've been sat in the dining room like stuffed dummies for the last quarter of an hour.'

'Then I won't bother changing. I'll just rinse my hands in the cloakroom and be in my chair in five minutes.'

'Miss Edwina's face is like thunder, so perhaps yer better had change, Mr Robert.'

He turned at the door, shrugged his shoulders and spread out his hands. 'Then her face will go with my head and my heart, because both are ready to burst. So don't be surprised if you hear fireworks, Agnes, just be ready to duck.'

The housekeeper grinned as the door closed behind him. There was nothing like a bloody good row to stir the old brain box, and if she'd read Mr Robert right, he was ready if one should start. She raised her eyes to the ceiling and prayed that if there was to be a row they'd wait until she was serving dinner. She'd go mad if she missed anything.

Edwina was sitting up perfectly straight, a very disapproving expression on her face. 'It really isn't good enough, Robert. You've kept the whole family waiting twenty minutes and you haven't even changed.'

'You are right on both counts.' Robert took his seat and glanced at each of his children. 'Good evening.'

The only replies came from Nigel and Abbie, and they were accompanied by smiles. 'Not to worry, Dad,' Abbie said. 'We won't starve.'

'We might not starve, but some of us will be late for appointments,' Victoria said, a haughty expression on her face. 'It really is inconsiderate of you, Father. Charles is calling for me in half an hour.'

'Then I suggest you telephone him and ask him to make it a little later. The whole family cannot revolve around you and your social life. You may use the telephone in the study if you wish.' Robert unfolded his napkin when the door opened and Agnes came through. 'Ah, here is the dinner. Perhaps you'd like to make your call while the soup is being served.'

'No, it is hardly worth the effort.' Victoria knew if she persisted she would look a fool that evening when Charles turned up late. He was never on time; sometimes he'd turn up an hour late, giving a cock and bull excuse she didn't believe for a second. Although this annoyed her, she never let it show. Never made an issue of it because she knew Charles would just turn on his heel and walk away. So until she had his ring on her finger, she would continue to be sweet and understanding, to convince him she'd make the ideal wife. That he was a philanderer was well-known to her, but once married to him and his money she wouldn't care. She'd be delighted if he found his pleasures elsewhere. 'He can wait in the drawing room if need be.'

Robert moved aside to let Agnes ladle the soup on to his plate and sniffed up, his face showing appreciation. 'Smells delicious, Agnes.'

'Made from home-grown vegetables.' She looked suitably pleased at the compliment. 'Except for the onions – I had to buy them. Pete doesn't seem to have much luck with them.'

'There was a strange man in the garden today, Robert,' Edwina said. 'Victoria and I thought he looked shifty and up to no good. Pete will have to be told he's not to invite this person again. Or any of his other cronies.'

Oh dear, here it comes, Agnes told herself. I thought it was too good to be true, 'cos this one doesn't miss a thing. Fancy her saying Alf looked shifty and up to no good, though – that just showed what a bad mind she had. The housekeeper carried on serving, but held her breath waiting to hear what Mr Robert had to say.

'The man in question is no stranger; he happens to be a friend of mine who was here at my invitation. And if you thought he looked shifty, then you were letting your imagination run away with you because he's a decent chap.' Robert tasted the soup and made a sound of pleasure. 'Excellent, as always, Agnes.' He wiped his lips on his napkin before looking down the table at his wife. 'I gave Alfred an open invitation to come any time he pleases, so you will no doubt be seeing him in the garden again. And I would be most displeased if anyone were to question his presence.'

That's telling them, Agnes thought as she made her way out of the room with the soup tureen. Mr Robert had been throwing his weight around over the last week, and not before time. Still, better late than never, eh?

For a few minutes the only sound in the room was that of the silver spoons coming into contact with china. Then Robert pushed his plate away and leaned his elbows on the table. This was a habit that irritated his wife as she thought it was bad manners. But common sense told her she would be unwise to mention the fact right now.

'So how was your first day at work, Nigel?' Robert asked. 'You appeared to be getting on so well with Jeff I didn't like to interfere.'

'It was a pleasure working with him, Dad, he's so patient. There was an extra chair at his desk for me and everything he did he explained to me. He probably only got through half the work he usually does, because every entry he made in the books he gave me all the details of what it was for, and why it went in that particular ledger. I really think I learned a lot today, although I know I've got a long way to go. I may be as green as grass right now, but I'm convinced it will all come together with Jeff's help. He's very efficient, anyone with half an eye could see that, but he's also very humorous and I'm going to enjoy working with him.'

'Good! That's what I was hoping to hear. If you are not going out tonight, I'd like you to come along to the study and go through a few things with you myself. Call it homework if you like. Then tomorrow you can surprise Jeff with your knowledge.'

'I haven't any plans for tonight, Dad, so I'd like that.'

'And you, young lady.' Robert turned to Abbie. 'I'd like you to come along and make a list of books you'll need for starting at college next week. I believe you mentioned you had to have one on shorthand?'

'Yes, there's a few books I need. I've got a list upstairs so I'll bring it along to the study after we've eaten.' She gave her father a broad wink. 'I noticed you never asked me if *I* had any plans for tonight. I'll surprise you one day and say I've got a date.'

'I'd be delighted, my dear, because I worry that you don't have much social life. A young girl your age should have plenty of friends, male and female.'

Had he been able to read her thoughts, Robert would have found out that she didn't try to make friends because she would be afraid to bring anyone home to suffer the indignity of being eyed from head to toe by her mother. The one friend she had, Rowena, had never said it in so many words, but she wasn't comfortable in the Dennison house. 'As I said, Dad, I'll surprise you one of these days.'

'It won't be a surprise, my dear, it will be a pleasure.'

'Oh, it will be a surprise, Dad, 'cos I'm hanging back for Prince Charming. And when he calls for me he'll be riding a white charger and will lift me off my feet to sit behind him, and he'll carry me off to a beautiful castle in the country.'

Ignoring the snorts of derision coming from his wife and eldest daughter, Robert covered Abbie's hand and grinned.

'That would make me a very happy man, as long as he didn't take you too far away from me.'

'Dad, wild horses wouldn't take me far away from you.' Abbie heard the tuts and snorts and decided not to ignore them this time. If they wanted to sneer, she'd give them something to sneer about. So, letting her eyes move from her mother to Victoria, she said, in a very clear voice something she'd never said in front of anyone before – not because she hadn't wanted to, but because the air of hostility in the house didn't encourage words or acts of affection: 'You see, I love you too much.'

The words lifted Robert's heart and brought a lump to his throat. 'And I love you, too, sweetheart.'

Robert and Nigel left the dining room together and went along to the study, while Abbie, growing more excited as the time drew nearer, dashed up the stairs to get her list of the books she would need when she started at commercial college. It was only fourteen days off, and the time would fly over.

'If you wish to smoke a cigarette, son, then do so because I will be lighting my after-dinner cigar.' Robert wasn't looking forward to the next half-hour, but it was something he couldn't put off any longer. Not only couldn't put it off, but didn't want to. He glanced at his son through the smoke rising from his cigar and wondered how he would take the news.

The study door burst open and Abbie came in waving what appeared to be a form. 'Here it is, Dad, names of books and shops that stock them.'

'Leave the form on the desk, my dear, we'll go through it later. I want you to sit down now as I have something of great importance to tell you and Nigel. It is something you should have no need to be told, you should have been aware of it all your life. When you hear what I've got to say, I hope you won't think too badly of me for leaving you in the dark for so long, thus depriving you of something very precious.'

'You would never do anything to hurt us, Dad,' Abbie said.

'So whatever it is, Nigel and I won't think badly of you.'

Nigel could see the concern in his father's eyes. 'What is it, Dad?'

'You are both aware that my parents died many years ago, although neither of you will have any recollection of them. Victoria was a little lass of three when they died, Nigel was only one and you weren't even born, Abbie.' Robert paused, praying he could find the right words. 'Have neither of you ever wondered about your mother's parents?'

'Well, I know they died a long time ago, Dad,' Nigel said. 'But that's about all.'

'And you, Abbie, have you never wondered?'

'Yes, I did, but when I mentioned it to Nigel a few years ago, he told me they had died.'

Robert sighed. 'They are not dead. Your Grandma and Granda are still alive and living in the same house your mother was brought up in.'

While Abbie gasped, Nigel's face drained of colour. 'I don't understand. Does Mother know they are still alive?'

'Yes, she knows.' Robert's cigar had gone out and he placed it in the ashtray. 'Before I say any more, I want your promise that you will not confront your mother until I've had a chance to tell her about this conversation. Do I have your promise?'

Nigel looked stunned. 'You mean Mother lied to me?'

'I wasn't aware your mother had deliberately lied until now. I believe she thought that by not ever mentioning them, you would automatically think they had passed away.' Robert ran a hand across his brow. 'I must take some of the blame because I should have insisted she visited her parents and taken you with her.'

'Are you saying that, knowing they were still alive, she hasn't visited her own parents since we went to live in Balfour Road?' Nigel was shaking his head in disbelief. 'But why, Dad?'

'That is something only she can answer. I visit them on a regular basis and have done since we moved out of the little

145

house in Arthur Street. She wasn't aware of this until I told her last week. And as you will have noticed, the air between us since then has been decidedly cool. Over the years my relationship with your mother has been going downhill, but since being told I keep in touch with all my old friends and neighbours, including her parents, things have reached a point where I can no longer keep quiet. Her parents, Joe and Ada, are old now and haven't many years left to them. She refuses point blank to visit them, but I'll no longer allow her to deprive them of the pleasure of knowing their own grandchildren.'

Tears rolled slowly down Abbie's cheeks. 'That's wicked, Dad. Our Grandma and Granda are still alive and she never told us? How *could* she?'

There was colour in Nigel's face now, brought about by his rising anger. 'I'll tell you why she's disowned them. They're not good enough for her – she's ashamed of them!'

'I asked you for a promise before, which you never gave,' Robert said. 'Can I have it now before any more is said?'

'You have my promise, Dad,' Nigel said. 'But I'll never forgive Mother, never!'

'Me neither.' Abbie wiped the tears away with the back of her hand. 'I won't say anything, Dad, not until you tell me I can. But I'll never feel the same towards her, and I hope God pays her back for being so cruel.' A thought struck her. 'Does Victoria know?'

'That is a question I can't answer. But I will try and make you see why I think your mother has behaved the way she has. When we were poor, we were as happy as any married couple could be. She was a good wife and was always kind and helpful to our neighbours. It was when I started to make money that she gradually began to change. They say money doesn't always bring happiness, and in our case this has proved to be true. The more money I earned, the bigger the house we lived in, the greater the change in your mother. In my opinion she has reached the stage now where she believes she has never known any other life than the one she enjoys now. And this is what she wants our newfound friends to believe. Our life before we moved into Balfour Road has been erased from her mind, and that includes family and friends. In my heart I can feel some pity for her because she has lost more than she's gained.'

'I can't feel pity for her, Dad, because she deliberately lied to me,' Nigel said, 'and about something that affected my life and the lives of her own parents! I would never have neglected them if I'd known they were still alive, and I am determined now to make it up to them. I mean, what must they think of grandchildren who never come to see them?'

'Ada and Joe know the whole story, Nigel, I've never kept anything from them. Even though your mother has treated them so badly, they never fail to ask after her, and yourselves.' The worst over, Robert picked up his cigar and held his lighter to it. He puffed on it several times until the tobacco had caught, then faced his children again. 'What I have just done is about the worst thing I've ever had to do in my life. It hurts me to criticise the woman who is my wife, and your mother. And I ask you not to repeat to her anything we have talked about. I am not being deceitful or underhanded, but I need to find the right time to bring everything out into the open with as little unpleasantness, and hurt, as possible. In the meantime, though, I must ask you if you would like to see your grandparents?'

'Need you ask, Dad?' Nigel said. 'As soon as you said they were still alive I made up my mind to see them as soon as possible.'

'Me too!' There was determination on Abbie's face. 'I can't wait!'

'I called on Mrs Jamieson today, and we arranged for me to take you to see Milly on Wednesday night about eight. I could ask Agnes to have dinner ready an hour earlier and we'd have time then to call at Arthur Street first, to meet your grandparents.'

As Abbie hugged him and rained kisses on his face,

Nigel said, 'I'm coming with you, Dad.'

'Of course you are, son, I never thought otherwise. And you have a treat to come before then. Have you forgotten you can pick up your new car tomorrow?'

'I certainly haven't. I think Jeff must have been sick of hearing about it. I'll go for a spin in it tomorrow night, then I'll drive behind you on Wednesday night because I'm not quite sure if I'd find the way on my own.'

'That's a good idea because I'll probably spend an hour or two at the Jamiesons' and it would save you hanging around.'

'Oh, I'm coming to see Milly as well. I'd love to see her and her parents again.' Nigel suddenly smiled. 'Do you remember the mate I had in Balfour Road – Bobby Neary? I might give him a knock and see how he's getting on.'

'You could take him for a spin in your car.'

'Good grief, no! I'll park the car well out of sight. I wouldn't even mention it because he'd think I was bragging. Don't you remember how outspoken Bobby was, Dad? He was forever in trouble at school for saying exactly what he thought. I don't think a day went by that he didn't get told off for it. Unless he's changed a lot, he wouldn't hesitate to look me straight in the eye and tell me I was a big-headed swank.'

'Ooh, I remember Bobby Neary!' Abbie giggled at the memory. 'He used to pull my hair and I used to kick his legs to make him let go.'

Robert sat back in his chair feeling contented. He didn't have to worry about these two children, they both had their feet on the ground. And, hopefully, after Wednesday a new life would open for them. A life in the real world. There would be storms ahead when Edwina found out what he'd done, but it would be too late for her to stop it. And usually after a storm came the sunshine.

'Why must we have dinner so early, and why wasn't I consulted?' Edwina, who lived in a fantasy world of her own, hadn't even noticed the difference in Nigel's attitude towards her. It wasn't open hostility, but he seldom spoke to her whilst looking into her face. Abbie she wouldn't notice anyway, never did. She thought of her as the black sheep of the family; the one who took after her father. 'I shall be forced to have strong words with Agnes.'

'I gave Agnes instructions this morning whilst you were still asleep, so it would be pointless you having words with her,' Robert said. 'It so happened that in the course of conversation over breakfast, I discovered that Nigel, Abbie and myself had all made arrangements to go out early this evening. So as we are in the majority, the obvious thing was to have an early meal. Heaven knows why it should interefere with your plans, seeing as you have little of importance to do. However, if it doesn't suit you and Victoria, you can retire to the drawing room and Agnes will serve you at whatever time you say.'

'It's very unusual for the three of you to be going out on the same night, at the same time.' Edwina eyed her husband with suspicion. Since the night he'd told her he still visited their old friends, and her parents, there'd been no conversation between them. He had slept in his dressing-room that night, and continued to do so. Those arrangements suited her, for she felt nothing but revulsion when he was near her. In her warped mind, she saw him as an enemy. One who wanted to spoil what they now had by bringing back into their lives people whom she wanted to forget. People who didn't measure up to the standard of living she was now used to. People who wouldn't know how to dress or behave at a dinner party or soirée. And if her husband thought he could put her to shame by reminding her of the past, then he was sadly mistaken. But a part of her mind warned her that he could make life unpleasant, even alienate her son if he decided to spread tales. And she wouldn't want that because she needed Nigel and Victoria on her side. 'Nigel, where are you off to without saying a word?'

Nigel had spent the last two nights tossing and turning, and when sleep finally came, it was fitful. He could not come to terms with his mother having told him a deliberate lie. And not just a white lie, as most people do sometime in their lives, but one that had robbed him of the love of his grandparents. For they did love him. He could remember being bounced on his Granda's knee, and his Grandma singing him a lullaby. Many happy memories of his boyhood had come back to him in the last two nights and he found it hard sitting at the table with his mother and trying to act as though nothing had changed. 'Really, Mother, I'm twenty-one years of age next week, a little too old to have to account for my movements,' he said stiffly.

'There's no need to bite Mother's head off,' Victoria said, wondering what on earth had got into her brother. He was usually so placid and falling over himself to please. 'It was a perfectly harmless question.'

'Then I'll give a perfectly harmless reply. I am going for a spin in my new car, as Charles did when he first got his. Except mine is an Austin, not an MG.'

'Yours is a car to get you around in your work, Nigel,' Robert said. 'The luxury of an MG will come later.'

Agnes came in then to serve dinner. She hadn't a clue what was going on and was filled with curiosity. But it would all come out in the wash, eventually. All she did know was that when she had told Miss Edwina that the dinner was to be earlier than usual, the mistress of the house had looked as though she was going to burst a blood vessel. She demanded that the housekeeper ignore her husband's order and serve the meal at the usual time. But Agnes had refused, saying it was more than she dare do. There was definitely something in the wind, but what?

Robert had suggested that Nigel park his car on the main road and join him and Abbie in the Bentley. Two cars driving down Arthur Street and stopping outside his in-laws' house would bring every neighbour to their doors. One car was rare, but two would definitely cause a sensation. They were used to seeing his so wouldn't give it a second thought.

As he switched off the engine, Robert had a moment of doubt. He hadn't called to warn Ada and Joe that they would be seeing their grandchildren, he had thought it would be a nice surprise. Now he questioned his decision, wondering if it would be too big a surprise. But he didn't pass his thoughts on to his children, they were apprehensive enough. 'Stand away from the window so they can't see you,' Robert said, smiling at them as he lifted the knocker.

It was Joe who opened the door. 'Hello, Bob, we weren't expecting you tonight.' He was small and thin, was Joe, and a little stooped. But his thatch of pure white hair sat on top of a face which was kind and welcoming. He saw Robert wasn't alone and smiled at the two people with him. 'Good evening to yer.'

Robert had taken his bowler hat off and was holding it in his hand. 'Can we come in, Joe?'

'Of course yer can, son! Yer know ye're always welcome in this house. And yer two friends are welcome, too. But yer'll have to take me and Ada as yer find us, we weren't expecting visitors.'

A woman's voice called out, 'Who is it, Joe?'

'It's only me, Ada,' Robert called back. 'I've got two people with me, but don't go rushing around and putting your false teeth in, they'll take you as they find you.'

'Oh, fancy catching us on the hop!' The old lady was standing on tip-toe in front of the mirror, patting her wispy white hair into place. Like her husband she was small and frail-looking, with deep wrinkles on her cheeks and forehead. But her eyes were alert. She turned when Robert pushed Nigel and Abbie into the tiny living room.

'Someone to see you, Ada.'

There was a smile on her face and words on her lips to tell him off for bringing visitors without warning them. But the words stayed silent and the smile left her face. She stared at

151

the two youngsters, her hand covering her mouth. Then she called, 'Joe, Joe, come here!'

Thinking there was something wrong, Joe pushed Robert aside to get to his wife's side. 'What is it, sweetheart?'

Her voice a mere whisper, she asked, 'Don't yer know who they are?'

Joe looked puzzled. Then, his watery eyes narrowed, he studied them. It was Nigel he recognised first, by his colouring and his facial likeness to someone he had thought the world of but hadn't seen in seventeen years. And when he looked hard at Abbie who, with her dark colouring was so like Robert, he cried, 'Oh, my God, sweetheart, it's our grandchildren.'

When Nigel saw tears begin to roll down the two lined faces, he moved quickly. Taking Ada in his arms, he held her tight. 'Hello, Grandma.'

Abbie was trying to swallow the lump in her throat and willing herself not to cry, when Joe came towards her with his arms outstretched. 'Yer were a babe in arms last time we saw yer, sweetheart, but ye're so alike yer dad I couldn't mistake yer.'

She flung her arms around his neck, wanting to hug him to death, but he was so frail she was afraid of hurting him. 'I'm sorry, Granda, but we didn't know.' She sobbed into his shoulder. 'We'll make it up to you, I promise.'

'Don't fret, sweetheart, we know the ins-and-outs. Bob has always told us the truth. And he's kept us up to date on all yer doings and Victoria's, 'cos he never stops talking about yer.'

Robert was standing by the door, his hat still in his hand. He had never felt so emotional in his entire life. He was watching four people whom he had robbed of seventeen years of knowing and loving each other. And what a feeble excuse he had for his actions. A grown man who didn't want to upset his wife! What a pathetic creature he was. Through eyes blurred with tears, he watched the scene before him.

'Grandma, let me introduce you to Abbie, your granddaughter.' Nigel smiled as he watched his sister walk into arms that couldn't wait to hold her. Then he turned to hug Joe. 'It's been a long time, Granda, since you used to bounce me on your knee. As soon as you opened the door it all came flooding back. You used to take me to the swings in the North Park, and you'd buy me an ice cream from the dairy on the way.'

Joe was so happy he thought his heart would burst. He and his dear wife had given up hope of seeing their grandchildren again before they died. Yet here were the younger two, and as loving as could be. For Ada's sake he wished their mother, Edie, and her first grandchild Victoria, were with them. But when somebody gives you the stars, you don't ask for the moon as well.

'Sit down, Bob,' Ada said. 'Yer've given us such a surprise we're forgetting our manners. Take yer coat off and make yerself at home.' She gave an impish grin. 'Yer can put yer feet on the mantelpiece if yer like.'

Abbie looked at the high black range and giggled. 'I don't think he'd be very comfortable, Grandma.' The word came easily and it felt good. 'There, I've said it. Grandma, Grandma, Grandma! And, Granda, Granda, Granda! Oh, I'm so happy, and I'm going to love you and spoil you both.'

'Yer father has always spoiled us, sweetheart. We'd have been in Queer Street often only for him. Food, coal, baccy and sweets, he's kept the wolf from the door often.' There was affection in Ada's eyes as she looked at the man who had married her daughter but was more like a son to them. 'But tonight, Bob, yer've given me and my Joe the best present in the whole world.'

'It won't be a one-off present, either, Ada,' Robert told her. 'I'm sure you'll see a lot more of the youngsters from now on.'

'There's nothing we'd like better, Bob, but we'll understand if they can't make it 'cos it's a long way for them to come.'

'It's not, you know.' Nigel's chest swelled with pride. 'Dad bought me a car yesterday for my birthday, so it won't be a problem getting here. I was going to suggest that if you would like to, I could take you out for a run on Sunday. Perhaps you'd like to go to Southport?'

'We've never been to Southport,' Ada said wistfully. 'The furthest my Joe and me have been is into Liverpool on the tram. But I'm not complaining, mind, 'cos we're lucky compared to some. At least we still have each other.'

Nigel was sitting on the edge of his chair, his face eager. 'So you would enjoy a trip to Southport, Grandma?'

'Southport is a place the toffs go to, son, and me and Joe don't have the right clothes to mingle with the hoity-toity.'

Joe wasn't going to sit by and see his beloved wife pull herself down. 'Sweetheart, we are as good as anyone else. Even better than some.'

'We're as good as anyone who hasn't got a bleedin' suit to their name, Joe!' Ada's hand flew to her mouth. 'Oh, I'm sorry, I'll have to watch me language.'

'Oh, that's all right,' Nigel said with a chuckle. 'We've got someone in our house who swears like a trooper. We love her and think she's hilarious.'

Robert knew what the problem was. 'Ada, you don't even need to get out of the car if you don't want to. It's just a run to Southport and back, to make a change from being in the house. In fact, we could all go. I wouldn't mind a run out. We can use my car because it holds five people comfortably. You'd like that, wouldn't you, Joe?'

'It would make a change from these four walls, lad, but it's up to the wife.'

'That's settled then, Ada, no argument. We'll pick you up about three and have you home again for six. And now we'll love you and leave you, until Sunday.'

'I would offer to make yer a cup of tea,' Ada said, 'but I haven't got enough milk. We weren't expecting company, yer see.'

'That's all right, my dear, you see Abbie's got another pleasant meeting in front of her. I've promised to have her at

Balfour Road about now, where she's meeting her old school-friend for the first time in ten years.'

'Oh, that's nice for yer, sweetheart.' Ada held her arms wide and Abbie walked into them as though it was the most natural thing in the world. 'Give yer Granda a kiss 'cos he'll be counting how many I get. He'll get jealous and sulk all night if I get one more than him. Men can be proper babies, yer know, sweetheart, especially when they're getting older. So give him two to be on the safe side. And then get off to meet yer friend. I bet she's on pins waiting to see yer, like I'll be on pins from now until Sunday.'

After emotional farewells, the trio made their way to the front door. There, Robert handed the car keys to Nigel. 'You and Abbie get in the car, I've just remembered something.' He stepped back into the hall, turned a surprised Ada and Joe around and steered them gently back into the living room. There he took a white five-pound note from his wallet. 'Before you start, Ada, just listen to me. You and Joe are like a mam and dad to me, and it gives me great pleasure in treating you as such. And now you are going to enrich the lives of my children. So take this and buy whatever bits and pieces you need for the house, remembering you'll be having visitors regularly from now on and won't want to be caught on the hop, as you call it. And I know you and Joe like nothing better than rummaging around the stalls at Paddy's Market, looking for bargains, so with a few bob in your pocket you might just pick up something there to wear on Sunday. I wouldn't care if you and Joe looked like tramps, and neither would the children. But I know you would.' He placed the note on the sideboard. 'Do it to please me, because I love you very much.'

Chapter Nine

'There's a knock.' Beryl gave the room a once-over to make sure everything was where it should be. 'You open the door, Milly, it'll be Bob and Abbie.'

'Ah, aye, Mam!' Milly was shaking inside in case her old schoolfriend had changed and gone all posh. 'I wouldn't know what to say, I'd feel daft! You go, please?'

'Oh dear,' Beryl said, rising from her chair. 'Yer've talked about nothing else since you knew Abbie was coming, and now she's here you won't even let her in!'

'Go on, love,' Bill, her husband said. 'Yer can't leave them standing on the step.'

Beryl ran her hands over the front of her dress as she walked down the hall. It was a double-fronted house, with the two front rooms as sitting rooms. But they were seldom used as the family preferred to sit round the table in the kitchen. She'd given one of the rooms a good going over today, though, just in case they decided to take their visitors in there.

Robert laughed when he saw the surprise on her face. 'You've got more than you bargained for, Beryl. Nigel insisted he wasn't going to be left out.'

'I'm glad, 'cos it's lovely to see him. He's grown into a big lad, hasn't he? The last time I saw you, Nigel, you were still in short trousers.'

'I'm twenty-one soon.' Pleasant memories were flooding Nigel's mind. 'Can I still call you Auntie Beryl?'

'Of course yer can, love.' Beryl stepped down on to the pavement and gave him a peck on the cheek before turning

157

with a wide smile on her face to Abbie. With her hands on the girl's shoulder, she said, 'It does my heart good to see you, Abbie. And what a bonnie lass yer've grown into. Mind you, the odds were on your side 'cos yer've got yer dad's looks and he's a handsome blighter.' She heard her husband calling and hustled them inside. 'They're all dying to see yer.'

Abbie stood inside the kitchen door and looked across the room to where Milly was standing with her hands clasped in front of her. They eyed one another up shyly, then as though by silent consent, they ran to meet up in the middle of the room. With their arms around each other and giggling like they used to do, it was a happy sight for the onlookers. 'Hey, look at you, kid,' Milly laughed. 'Yer went and grew up! I'd have known yer anywhere, though, because yer haven't changed that much.'

Abbie searched her friend's face. The fair hair wasn't in plaits like it used to be, it was cut in a fashionable short bob and suited her. Her complexion was rosy and her blue eyes as full of devilment as they'd always been. Even when she was getting told off by a teacher for talking in class she never looked scared like the other girls did. 'You've changed though, Amelia Jamieson,' Abbie said cheekily. 'Where's your blinking plaits?'

'If you tell me where yer Shirley Temple curls have gone, I'll tell yer where my plaits went. And that's on the kitchen floor when me mam decided to take the scissors to them when I was going for an interview for me first job. She made such a mess of me hair I had to go to the hairdresser's to get it cut properly.'

They made an attractive couple standing together holding hands. Both girls were the same height, both with slim figures maturing into womanhood. Abbie began to giggle, and in a childish voice, said, 'If I lend you my skipping rope, Milly, will you let me play with your top and whip?'

Milly pouted her lips. 'Only if yer let me have a go on yer scooter. I'll only go to the bottom of the street on it, honest injun.' She stamped her foot in pretend anger. 'Ye're a meanie, you are, Abbie Dennison, and I'm not going to be your friend any more. So there!' Once again she stamped her foot, bringing forth laughter from those watching.

Then Beryl said, 'Did yer not notice we've got another stranger in the camp, Milly? If you say hello to him, and yer Uncle Bob, then perhaps we can all sit down.'

'Hello, Nigel.' The girl became shy and couldn't think of what to say. The last time she'd seen this man he was a ten-year-old boy in short grey trousers and he used to chase after her to pull her hair. The best she could come up with was, 'You haven't half grown tall.'

'And you've grown very pretty, Milly,' Nigel told her. 'Pretty as a picture.'

'Ay, what about me?' Bill Jamieson asked with a smile. 'All these compliments flying around and not one's come my way!'

Abbie went to give him a kiss. 'Next to my dad, you're the most handsome man in the whole wide world, Uncle Bill.'

'That's more like it, I hate being missed out.' He winked at his wife. 'My one used to pay me compliments, didn't yer, love? But what was it yer said to me the other night? That we were getting too old now to be soppy?'

'D'yer know what, Bob? The older he gets, the dafter he gets! Because the mirror doesn't tell him he's handsome, he expects *me* to tell him. I'm supposed to lie through me flaming teeth, just to keep him happy!'

'Well, I'm going to take him for a pint now, Beryl, so I won't forget to throw the odd bit of flattery in now and again.' Robert was thinking how easygoing the talk was in this house compared to the one he lived in. No stiff, unnatural conversation here, just a happy family being themselves. 'Is that all right with you, Bill?'

'I thought yer'd never ask, Bob! We'll leave the young ones to catch up on old times. Is Nigel coming with us?'

'Can I follow you on?' Nigel asked. 'There's something I'd like to do first. But where will you be if I need to find you?'

159

'Turn left at the bottom of the road and yer'll find us in the first pub yer come to. Yer can't miss it, it's on the corner of the street.'

When the two men had left, Beryl cast an enquiring glance at Nigel. 'Have you got a heavy date that yer dad doesn't know about?'

He blushed, hoping she didn't dig deeper and find he had never had a date with a girl. At his age, it was normal to have a girlfriend. 'No, Auntie Beryl, I haven't got a date. I was hoping to meet up with Bobby Neary, if that's possible. I'd really like to see him again for old times' sake and to find out how life is treating him.'

It was hard to say whose laugh was the loudest, Beryl's or her daughter's. 'Yer won't find Bobby in, son, he's out every night, jazzing. With his blond hair sleeked back, his dance shoes under his arm, he's a real lady-killer. Takes a different girl home every night and yer never see him with the same one twice.'

'So he won't be in, then?'

'Not a chance, love.' Beryl chuckled. 'His mam said she's given up on him and doesn't think he'll ever settle down. She told me in a joke that she'd thought of tying him to a chair with the clothes line, just to keep him in one night, then decided he'd probably bite through the rope. "If he had to miss one night's dancing, I think he'd have a bleedin' heart attack." That's what Rose said. It's all he lives for.'

'He can't half dance, though, Mam,' Milly said. 'He's the best I've ever seen, and all the girls swoon over him.'

'You go to the same dance halls, do you, Milly?' Nigel asked, more eager than ever to see his old friend. 'Local, or in town?'

'Right now, Bobby Neary will be thrilling some girl with his dashing waltz or passionate tango. And it's only a matter of yards from where you're sitting. He'll be in Balfour Hall on the corner of the street.'

160

'Why don't you go down there?' Beryl asked. 'Give him the surprise of his life.'

Her daughter pulled a face. 'Mam, nothing in this world would surprise Bobby Neary. Anyway, it's dark in the hall, Nigel would never recognise him.'

'Well, you and Abbie go with him! Yer've no need to stay once yer've got the two boys together. Do you dance, Abbie?'

'Never been to a dance in my life, Auntie Beryl, and neither has Nigel.' Abbie decided Bobby Neary sounded just what her brother needed. Someone of his own age who enjoyed life, who would get him out of the stifling relationship with his mother and older sister. 'But I don't mind going with them so he can see his friend.'

Milly was looking at her with mouth agape. 'Yer mean to tell me yer've never been to a dance! What the heck do yer do with yerself then?'

'Not much,' Abbie told her truthfully. 'I'll tell you about it some time. Right now, though, let's go with our Nigel.' She reached for her friend's hand. 'I've found you again – let's help him find his old mate.'

'They'll charge yer at the door, yer know,' Beryl said. 'Yer'll not get in for nothing just because yer want to see someone in there.'

'That's all right, Auntie Beryl,' Nigel told her. 'I've got money on me. We'll be back before you know it, because if Bobby's as keen on dancing as you say, he won't want to be bothered by me. But at least I can try and make arrangements to see him another night.'

'OK, come on, then.' Milly jerked her head. 'We won't be long, Mam.'

'Don't worry about that, sweetheart, yer might just get a click. If yer do, though, make sure there's something other than fresh air between his ears. Not like the last boy yer brought home, he was as thick as two short planks.'

Her daughter grinned. 'He was nice-looking though, and yer can't have everything, Mam.'

161

'It helps to have a brain, sweetheart,' Beryl said, wanting, like every other mother, only the best for her beloved daughter. 'Now go on, poppy off.'

'You go in, I'll wait out here,' Abbie said. 'Nothing usually puts the wind up me, but I just can't bring myself to go in there.'

'Don't be such a daft nit.' Milly took her arm in a tight grip and dragged her forward. 'It's usually crowded so yer won't even be noticed.' She gave Nigel a knowing look. 'It's tuppence each to get in and there's a man on the door to take yer money. You pay while I drag yer suddenly shy sister in – by the hair if necessary.'

Nigel wasn't feeling very brave himself, but he knew there was a first time for everything and if he wanted any sort of life at all, he had to make the effort. He took a silver sixpence from his pocket and handed it to the man standing just inside the door. 'Three, please.'

The man put the money in a box before spotting the two girls. 'Hello, Milly, ye're late tonight.'

'These are two friends of mine, George, who I haven't seen for ten years. So we've been gabbing. Tell me, is Bobby Neary here?'

'That's a daft question,' the man chuckled. 'Have yer ever known him miss a Wednesday yet? Dance mad, he is.'

'Well, we won't hold him up for long. My friends just want a word with him.'

Abbie held on tight to her friend's arm when they entered the darkness of the hall. 'Don't you dare leave me.'

Milly's eyes were travelling over the dancers. Some couples on the floor were learners and just walking around, while the good dancers twisted and swayed as though dancing on air. Then she saw who she was looking for. 'There he is, dancing with the dark-haired girl in the blue dress.'

While Nigel stared as though he didn't believe his eyes, Abbie gasped, 'That's not Bobby Neary, surely?'

'The one and only,' Milly laughed. 'The world couldn't cope with two like him.'

'He's a very good dancer,' Nigel said, remembering the boy who didn't care whether his trousers had a hole in them, or whether he had a tide-mark around his neck. 'Who would have thought it?'

'He's not a bad-looking lad,' Abbie said. 'He used to be smaller than you, Nigel, but I'd say you're about the same height now.'

'The record's coming to an end,' Milly said. 'I'll nab him as he leaves the floor.' She waited until the dancers were returning to their seats, then walked on to the floor and put a hand on the arm of the unsuspecting young man. 'Hi, Bobby.'

'Milly! I've been looking out for yer. Will yer have the next foxtrot with me?'

'I haven't come to dance, Bobby, I've got a surprise for yer. Someone yer haven't seen for a long time is waiting to meet yer.' Without further ado, or explanation, she pulled the lad to where Nigel and Abbie were standing. 'Well, is this a surprise or not?'

Bobby, shoulders and eyes on a level with Nigel's, stared hard. It only took a couple of seconds for recognition to dawn. 'Well, I'll be darned. Nigel Dennison!' He looked as pleased as Punch as he thrust out one hand and gripped Nigel's arm with the other. 'Me old mate! Me old slide-down-the-embankment-and-tear-our-kecks mate! Well, I never expected to see you again – I thought yer'd forgotten I existed. I know yer've gone up in the world 'cos I see yer dad's posh car now and again.' His face split into a wide grin. 'I thought yer'd gone all stuck-up and toffee-nosed.'

Nigel's cup of happiness was overflowing. In the space of an hour or so, he had been reunited with his beloved grand parents, and now the only real friend he'd ever had was smiling and looking genuinely pleased to see him. 'I'm sorry to disappoint you, Bobby, but stuck-up and toffee-nosed I am not! And anyway, when have you ever worried what a person had or didn't have? You weren't that fussy at school if I remember rightly. When you were getting the cane off the history teacher, I never heard you say that if you had to be caned, you would prefer the headmaster did it.'

Bobby was so pleased to see his old friend he was rubbing his hands and grinning like the cat that got the cream. 'It's great to see yer, mate.' He glanced down at Abbie. 'Is this yer girlfriend?'

Abbie found her voice. 'It's not that flipping dark in here, Bobby Neary! Would yer like me to show you the bald patch on my head where you pulled my hair out?'

'Well, I'll go to the bottom of our stairs.' Bobby was really taken aback. 'If it isn't little Abbie! Only ye're not little any more, yer went and growed up. Well, well, well! I'll tell yer what, kid, yer couldn't half run. By the time I caught up with yer, I didn't have enough strength to pull yer flipping hair.'

Abbie pointed an accusing finger. 'You could have fooled me! I wouldn't let you see it, but I sometimes went home crying.'

'If I promise not to pull yer hair, will yer have this dance with me? I did ask Milly, but that would mean you dancing with yer brother and I know yer wouldn't want that.'

'I'm sorry, but I can't dance. And neither can Nigel.'

'Can't dance!' Bobby's voice rose in disbelief. He looked at Nigel. 'What the heck have yer been doing with yer life, mate? Everybody can dance!'

'Everybody but me and Abbie,' Nigel told him with a grin. 'But we can both ice-skate.'

'Ice-skate! Yer can't ruddy ice-skate on this floor, mate!'

Abbie was chuckling inside. 'I can do hand-stands, Bobby.'

'Well, you could certainly do that here, and I'm sure all the blokes would love yer to. But I think George would take exception and throw yer out.'

'Look, we don't want to spoil the night for you,' Nigel said, 'so why don't you have a dance with Milly while we watch.

164

Then we'll go and leave you to trip as many light fantastics as you like.'

'No, yer don't have to do that. I don't mind missing a few dances, honestly.'

'I never thought the day would come when I'd hear you say that, Bobby Neary,' Milly said. 'I've seen yer here when yer were dying of a cold, with a bright red runny nose, when yer should have been at home in bed. Then another time, at Star of the Sea, two of yer fingers were in splints 'cos yer'd broken them at work. But even that didn't stop yer dancing.'

'I don't dance on me nose, or me fingers, clever clogs. Anyway, come and finish this dance off with me, and don't gab all the time 'cos it puts me off me stroke.'

Brother and sister watched Bobby lead Milly on to the dance-floor. 'He hasn't changed a bit,' Nigel said fondly. 'Always laughing and full of fun.'

'Don't lose him now you've found him again,' Abbie told him. 'You need a good mate, someone who can take you to places and show you how to have a good time. You've been stuck with Mother and Victoria too much and have been missing out on life, so grab the chance while you've got it. I know I'm going to.'

'I don't think I'll be seeing much of Bobby, not if he goes dancing every night. Just look at him, he's really very good. And Milly doesn't have any problem keeping up with him, either.'

'If you and I intend to get any enjoyment out of life, then we're going to have to learn to dance, Nigel, like everybody else our age. Rowena goes dancing but I've never been with her because I knew if I asked Mother I'd be scoffed at for going to such common places. But I don't care what she says now, I'm going to start enjoying myself. So, brother dear, you and I are going to learn to dance as well as Milly and Bobby can.' She saw her brother look at the dancers with dismay, and giggled. 'No, I don't mean making a fool of ourselves here. There are dancing schools where you can have private tuition, and that's what we need. We'll have a word with Dad, and if he approves we can find where the nearest dancing school is. Does that appeal to you?'

Never as outgoing as his sister, Nigel looked apprehensive. 'Would we be able to go together?'

'I don't know any more than you do, I've never even thought about it before. But I imagine we could be taught as a couple, and that would be great. We could practise at home, then, and learn much quicker.'

This cheered her brother up. 'That sounds great, Abbie, as long as we go together.'

The dance finished and Milly and Bobby joined them. 'Yer don't know what ye're missing, Abbie. Dancing is a wonderful feeling.' Milly linked her friend's arm. 'If yer've got a good partner who's light on his feet, it's like floating on clouds.'

'I hope that's not a dig at me, Milly Jamieson.' Bobby put on a bulldog expression. 'I'm noted for me light feet, and all me partners tell me they feel as though they're floating on clouds.'

'That's because the stuff yer put on yer hair smells so strong it probably makes them feel light-headed,' Milly said in an effort to take him down a peg or two. She began to sway from side to side. 'Like this, yer see.'

'Keep still, yer daft nit, ye're making me feel seasick.' Bobby spread out his hands to Abbie. 'I suppose yer know this mate of yours is two sheets to the wind? She works in an office, too, but I'll never know how she keeps her job. Mind you, for all we know she wheels the tea trolley around.'

'Where do you work, Bobby?' Nigel asked. 'I remember you used to say you wanted to be a train driver.'

'I'm at Owen Peck's, the wood merchants. Been there since I left school. Do you work?'

Nigel thanked heaven he was able to say, 'Yes, I work for my dad.'

'Have you got a Bentley, too?'

Once again Nigel was thankful he didn't have to tell an

outright lie. 'No, I am not the proud owner of a Bentley. Not yet, anyway.'

'Don't be so ruddy nosy, Bobby Neary,' Milly said. 'Yer'll be asking him how much he earns next.'

'No, I'll leave that until the next time we meet. He's caught me unawares tonight, but it won't happen again. I'll have a list of questions for him next time. Like when is he going to pay me back the bull's-eye I gave him? He needn't think he can give me the old one back 'cos he'll have licked all the colour off by now. So I want a new bull's-eye, or I'll settle for two liquorice sticks instead.'

'I bet you'd be childish enough to eat them, too!' Abbie was completely relaxed now and enjoying the exchange. 'I remember you always had something stuck in your mouth.'

'I still have.' Bobby pushed out his tongue. 'See, it's been stuck in me mouth all me life and I'm quite attached to it, if yer see what I mean.'

'Ye're wasting yer time trying to get one over on him,' Milly said, knowing from experience how sharp the lad was. 'He'll have the last word if it kills him.'

'I wouldn't, yer know, not if it was going to kill me. I'm too young and too good-looking to die. Think what some poor girl would be missing if I did?' He squinted an eye at Nigel. 'Have you got a girlfriend?'

'Not as yet.'

'Yer've got yer head screwed on, then, mate. Girls are nothing but a blinking nuisance. Most of them talk fifteen to the dozen, and it's always a load of rubbish. Like how high their heels are, or this dress they've seen in a shop window which they're going to save up for 'cos they just know it'll suit them. Yer can be putting yer whole heart and soul into a dance, really carried away with it, and out comes this silly voice nattering about nothing at all. They're a waste of space, girls are. I don't know what God was thinking about when He made them.'

'I know why He made them,' Abbie was stung into saying.

167

She knew he was only acting daft and didn't really mean what he said, but she wasn't going to let him get away with that. 'He made them just for you to dance with. I mean, you'd look silly dancing around the floor on your own, wouldn't you? So girls do have their uses.'

Milly too went to the defence of all females. 'And what about yer mam? She was a girl once, yer know. Isn't she the one who puts that sharp crease in yer trousers what yer could cut yer throat on? And doesn't she iron yer shirts, makes sure yer have a clean hankie in yer pocket, feeds yer and gets yer up for work every morning? And believe me, everyone in the street knows what a holy terror yer are to get out of bed 'cos yer mam's got a voice that would wake the dead.'

Bobby was shaking with laughter when he looked at Nigel. 'That's another thing about girls, they can't take a joke. Me mam's the same. Every morning I tell her I'm up but she won't believe me and keeps bawling her head off. She reckons if she can't hear the springs on the bed going, then I'm not up.'

'So all the time she's bawling her head off, you are up?' Nigel asked.

'Well, it's like this, yer see, Nige, from one man to another. I'm not actually *out* of bed, but I am giving it careful consideration.'

The shortening of his name brought a vivid memory back to Nigel. It was in the early days of his friendship with Bobby and they were fighting over an ollie. 'You've just had a certain expression on your face, and d'you know what it reminded me of?' he asked.

'Ronald Colman or James Cagney?'

Nigel shook his head. 'We were only about seven, I think, and we were having a game of ollies near St James's School. You accused me of cheating and an argument broke out. You got yourself in a right paddy, and I can remember the words as though it was yesterday. Your face the colour of beetroot, you shouted, "What sort of a name is Nigel, anyway! It's a cissie's name and ye're getting Nige off me, whether yer like it or not." And to my mother's annoyance, whenever you called for me, you always asked, "Is Nige coming out to play?" '

There was a burst of laughter from the four of them. Then Bobby said, 'I hope ye're not going to hold that against me for the rest of me life? Or is that the reason yer looked me up, just to tell me off?'

Nigel shook his head. 'No, I really wanted to see you. And anyway, I've never really liked my name, so Nige suits me fine.'

'Well, at last yer got something right. That makes a change.' Milly's tongue darted in and out so fast Bobby didn't know whether he was seeing things.

'If you keep picking on me, Milly Jamieson, I'm going to tell me mam on yer and she'll sort yer out. And yer know yerself she's got a voice like a foghorn. When she tells yer off, yer know yer've been told off good and proper.'

'Look, we'll be going,' Nigel said. 'Otherwise you'll miss every dance. But is there a night you don't go out, so we can get together and have a good chinwag about the old days?'

'There's nothing doing on a Sunday, so how would that suit yer? Yer could come to ours, 'cos I know me mam would like to see yer.'

Abbie remembered they were going out on Sunday and quickly reminded her brother. 'Don't forget we're seeing Grandma and Granda on Sunday.'

'I hadn't forgotten, but that's in the afternoon. We should be home about six, or seven at the latest. So I'll give you a knock about eight, Bobby, is that all right?'

'That's fine.' He followed them to the door. 'It's been really great seeing yer, Nige, and you, Abbie. I've often thought about yer over the years, but I didn't know where yer'd gone to live or how to get in touch with yer. And it proves how glad I was to see yer, when I've missed four dances through yer.' A cheeky grin on his face, he slapped his friend on the back. 'But you know me, mate, I'm not one to bear grudges.' He

169

waved them off and returned to the dance-floor in time for a two-step. Many of the girls' heads were turned hopefully towards him, as he was very popular. Not only because he was such a good dancer, but his blond-haired, blue-eyed good looks were a great attraction. However, Bobby Neary didn't choose a partner for her looks. He didn't care if a girl had a face like the back of a tram, as long as she could dance. Oh, and didn't talk the ear off him, either.

Robert looked through his rearview mirror to make sure Nigel was still keeping up with him, then turned his attention back to his daughter. 'So, you've both had an enjoyable evening, my dear?'

'Enjoyable is only one of the words I can think of, Dad. There's marvellous, exciting, very emotional and extremely funny. I really fell in love with Grandma and Granda, they're kind, gentle and very loving.' Abbie thought for a second before saying, 'You would think they'd be bitter, the way they've been treated, but they're not. I don't believe they've got an unkind thought in their heads. And Nigel and I are going to make it up to them for the time we've all lost.' Once again she considered the words in her head before she allowed them through her lips. 'Are you going to tell Mother?'

'Yes, of course, I'll have to tell her. If she isn't asleep when we get home, and I think the timing is right, I'll tell her this evening. But I must ask that you and Nigel do not say anything that she feels is condemning her. She is what she is, my dear, and recriminations will not serve any purpose. We all have to live in the same house, and it would be better for all concerned if we can at least be pleasant and civil to each other.'

Abbie didn't want to spoil a perfect day so she brought a little lightness into the conversation. 'It was really good seeing Milly and her family again, Dad, and we've pledged to be best friends for life. You know I'm seeing her on Sunday, don't you? That's after we've been to Southport with Grandma and

Granda. I'm really looking forward to that, it's going to be a lovely day.'

'Nigel seemed very happy about meeting up with Bobby again. I bet he got a shock, you turning up at the dance hall.'

'He didn't know me at first, he asked if I was Nigel's girlfriend. Oh, and by the way, he said he's always called your son Nige, and he's not going to change now 'cos we're posh. He is so funny, and he'll be good for Nigel.' Abbie repeated the whole conversation they'd had in the darkness of the dance hall, and when Robert was driving through the gates and down the side of the house to the garage, he was laughing loudly.

'So, you and Nigel are going to learn to dance to keep up with your friends? I think that's an excellent idea. You find a good teacher, my dear, and I'll willingly pay for your lessons. And the day won't be far off when you can take to the dance-floor and give Bobby and Milly the surprise of their lives.'

'Oh, Milly might get a surprise, but not Bobby Neary 'cos I don't think anything would surprise him. He's so easygoing, got an answer for everything. He seems to get on well with Milly, and if I'm not mistaken he's got a soft spot for her. Even though he said girls are nothing but a blinking nuisance and he doesn't know what God was thinking about when He made them, I've got a feeling he isn't completely immune to Milly's charms.'

They were out of the car when Nigel drove up behind them. He slid from behind the wheel and faced them with a grin on his face. 'What a day, eh? One of the best in my life.'

'I'm glad about that, son, and I think you're in for many more. Now, shall we creep through the kitchen and up the stairs in case the rest of the family are asleep? You two go first and I'll follow.' He waited until they were on the far side of the kitchen, then chuckling inside, he said softly, 'Goodnight, Abbie. Goodnight, Nige.'

There was a look of astonishment on his son's face until he heard his sister giggling. 'Oh, she told you?'

Robert nodded. 'I must say I rather like it. And I think Jeff would, too!'

Nigel grinned. 'I'm rather partial to it myself, Dad, it sounds more friendly. Goodnight, and thank you for today.'

Chapter Ten

Robert could see a glimmer of light under the bedroom door when he reached the landing, and he felt his heart-rate quicken. He wasn't looking forward to telling his wife what he was responsible for today, even though he knew he shouldn't feel guilty about doing something he thought was right for his children and their grandparents. Keeping them apart for seventeen years was unforgivable, and it was she who should feel guilty. Not only for letting it go on, but to lie in the process. Nevertheless Edwina was his wife and he didn't get any pleasure out of hurting her. Even though she hadn't been a real wife to him for seventeen years.

He had just turned the knob on the door when the light went out, and he knew the action was deliberate. It was her way of saying she didn't want to talk to him. But, unfortunately for her, he was determined not to be put off. He wanted everything out in the open, and he wanted to do it tonight instead of it lying heavily on his mind for another day. He reached for the wall switch and flooded the room with light. 'Edwina, I know you are not asleep, so would you kindly sit up as I need to talk to you.'

His wife pulled the bedclothes up to partly cover her face. 'Whatever it is can wait until tomorrow. I am very tired.'

Robert took a deep breath. 'I asked you once and you refused; I will not ask a second time. I am *telling* you that unless you want the whole house to hear what I have to say, you will sit up and listen.' He waited a few seconds, then when there was no movement he strode to the door and threw it open. 'Right! If that's the way you want it, that's the way you shall have it.'

When a muffled voice said, 'Give me time.' Robert closed the door and stood at the end of the bed to watch his wife huff and puff as she pushed herself upright. She was forty-five years of age but looked like an old woman with a lace bed-cap pinned over her hair and an old-fashioned nightdress covering her from neck to fingers and toes. It was when she pulled a sheet up to her chin that Robert lost patience. 'I know two women your age and compared to you they look like young girls. Even your own mother has more go in her than you do. Well turned seventy, she still does all her own housework and keeps the house like a new pin, while you sit on your backside all day, do sweet Fanny Adams, then have the nerve to complain of being tired.' He ran his fingers through his thick black hair and sighed. He didn't want to lose his temper but she really would try the patience of a saint.

Edwina peered at him through narrowed eyes. 'Then I don't know why you don't go and talk to one of your women friends. They would no doubt be more interested in what you have to say than I am.'

'I have no intention of being put off track by a remark like that. You may think what you wish, it really doesn't affect me in the slightest. I'll say what I have to say, then retire and leave you to the sleep you so badly crave.' Once again he ran his fingers through his hair and asked himself why he was bothering. What he had to say, and what he had done, would have no effect on her and wouldn't change her one iota. But she had a right to know, and he could live in peace with himself. 'Today I took Abbie and Nigel to see their grandparents.' He saw the sheet being gripped by her fingers and he heard her gasp. But he carried on. 'It was a wonderful experience for all of them and a joyous sight to behold. The only thing that marred the occasion for me was the knowledge that it was something I should have done many years ago. Anyway, the children are delighted that their grandparents are

174

still alive and will be visiting them on a regular basis. Sadly, Victoria has not been included in this rejoicing. I think you know why.'

'All this just to spite me,' Edwina hissed. 'Well, if you think I'm going to let you change my way of life, then you are very much mistaken. So if you have said what you wanted to say, I would like you to leave now and let me sleep.'

'Oh, I haven't finished yet, there's more to come. You see, Edwina, I have had a busy day with my son and daughter. Abbie has been reunited with her schoolfriend, Milly, and Nigel met up with his old mate, Bobby Neary.'

The growl started in Edwina's chest, came up her throat and out of her mouth. She was seething with anger. 'How dare you! How *dare* you bring these people back into our children's lives! I will certainly discourage them from associating with the likes of the Jamiesons or those Nearys. And none of them will *ever* cross the threshold of this house. Do you understand?'

'I haven't been able to understand you for a long time, Edwina. I think most reasonable people would have trouble understanding why a woman would disown her own parents and friends. But then you are not a reasonable, or rational person, are you? As far as I am concerned you can go your own sweet way, as long as you don't try and interfere in my life, or my son and youngest daughter's. They've found their true friends again, and are delighted. You put a blight on their happiness and I'll come down hard on you. And you would be wise to heed my warning.' Robert spun on his heels and walked towards his dressing-room where he would sleep on the single bed. But as he reached the door, he turned. 'Oh, by the way, here's another little item for you to think about. As they never fail to do, your mam and dad asked me how "our Edie and Victoria" are. Sleep on that if you can. Goodnight.'

'Ay, I've got a nice surprise for yer, sunshine.' Agnes smiled at Jessie as the girl hung her coat on the hook behind the door. 'Mr Robert ordered them by phone yesterday morning, and they were delivered half an hour ago.'

Kitty, who had arrived a few minutes earlier, was sitting at the table having a cup of tea. 'Ye're going to look proper posh, queen. But if I catch yer looking down yer nose at me I'll clock yer one.'

'Are you two pulling me leg?' Jessie asked, a huge grin on her face. 'If yer are, I'll think of something to pay yer back.'

Agnes nodded to the dresser. 'Have a look at what's in the parcel over there. If they don't fit yer, me or Kitty will have them.'

Jessie giggled. She was twice the size of Kitty, and Aggie was three times the size of her, so what could possibly be passed on to either of them if it didn't fit her? Still thinking she was having her leg pulled, she picked up the parcel and carried it to the table. Gingerly, she parted the brown paper covering to reveal a square cardboard box. 'I know it's a joke, so tell me what it is before I open it and have a heart attack.'

'Pass it over, queen, and I'll show yer what's inside.' Kitty took off the lid and lifted out a white lace pinny which she held out by the waist straps. 'How about that, then, eh? And look, this is to go with it.' A matching white headpiece was produced and passed over to Jessie, who looked stunned. 'She's lost her bleedin' voice, Aggie! She'll probably lay a duck egg when she sees what else is in the box.'

'Are these for me?' The girl's voice was choked. 'They're lovely.'

'Show her the rest, Kitty,' Agnes said. 'Don't be making a meal out of it.'

'Patience never was one of your virtues, Aggie Weatherby. Making a bleedin' meal out of it, indeed! Here yer are, queen, a nice black dress and a pair of black stockings.'

It was all too much for Jessie. 'But why? I mean, why would Mr Robert want to buy these for me?'

'For the same reason he bought me a new dress, overall and apron. And why he bought Kitty a new dress and overall. Because he's a good boss, that's why.' Agnes nodded to stress

176

how good she thought their boss was. 'But ye're not to wear them in the morning when ye're helping Kitty with the heavy housework. You'll put them on in the afternoon when ye're helping me in the kitchen, and when they're expecting guests and you answer the door to them.'

'They'll think they've come to the wrong bleedin' house,' Kitty said, draining her cup before pushing her chair back. 'Hurry up and finish yer tea, queen, so we can get cracking. I don't fancy being ticked off by her ladyship. She doesn't half get up my nose the way she goes around all the woodwork with a finger to make sure we haven't missed an inch. And the look on her clock, anyone would think she had a rotten egg under her nose.'

'She's got nothing better to do with her days, sunshine, so I wouldn't worry about her.' Agnes was laying rashers of bacon in the frying pan ready to start the breakfast when she heard movement from upstairs. Sometimes Miss Edwina would let her know she was preparing to come down by pulling a cord in her room. This would set off one of the row of eight bells on the kitchen wall. Most days though, she came down unannounced, hoping to catch the staff doing something they shouldn't. 'I wouldn't swap my life with hers for all the tea in China. What I would like that she's got, though, is a husband like Mr Robert, and children like Mr Nigel and Miss Abbie. The woman doesn't know how lucky she is and she doesn't deserve them.'

'Ye're right there, queen.' Kitty's nod was emphatic. 'It's a pity she can't be poor for a few weeks. Yer know, without two ha'pennies to rub together. No food in the pantry, no coal for the fire and no penny for the gas meter. Then she might appreciate what she's got here.'

'She should have to work as hard as my mam,' Jessie said, with feeling. 'See how she'd like scrubbing floors for people, just to buy food so the family don't go hungry.'

'Oh, I think she's probably known what it is to be poor,' Agnes said. 'I've worked for them long enough to know they haven't always had money.' The housekeeper was remembering what Mr Robert had told her about his mam and dad. But that had been told in confidence and she wasn't going to repeat it. 'I find that people who are born into money don't act so high and mighty as those who acquire it later in life. I may be wrong, but I don't think so.'

Kitty carried the bucket as far as the door before turning. 'If anyone should know, it's you, queen. Ye're very knowlickable when it comes to the well-off.'

Agnes tutted. 'Did you not learn anything at school, sunshine? It's not knowlickable, it's knowledgeable.'

A slow smile crossed Kitty's thin face. 'What have I just said, queen? A proper bleedin' know-it-all, that's what yer are.'

Agnes raised a clenched fist and winked at Jessie, who was standing behind the cleaner. 'Hit her for me, sunshine, ye're nearer than I am.'

'No fear!' The girl shrank back in feigned horror. She was getting used to the two women now, and their humour. 'Little as she is, she'd have me guts for garters.'

'I don't wear no garters, queen,' Kitty said, her shoulders shaking with laughter. 'I keep me stockings up with a piece of string.'

Agnes was determined to get the last word in, so she followed the cleaners into the hall. 'My mam always made me wear a clean pair of knickers every day, in case I had an accident and ended up in hospital. It would be the price of yer, Kitty Higgins, if you had an accident and ended up in a hospital bed. Think how bad yer'd feel if yer woke up to find a doctor trying to undo the piece of string.'

'Nah, I wouldn't feel bad, queen. I mean, when I woke up I'd be unconscious, wouldn't I, so it wouldn't make no matter.' With that Kitty trundled up the stairs, followed by a giggling Jessie -- and leaving the housekeeper gazing after them with her hands on her hips and telling herself she might have known the little woman would have the last word. However, the day was young, and there was plenty of time to get her own back. But whatever she did would have to be good; she didn't want to be left with egg on her face.

Sitting at the breakfast-table, Victoria waited until the door closed on Agnes before asking, 'What on earth is wrong with Father? Why would he want to involve anyone in this family with all those dreadfully common people?'

'They are not dreadfully common people, Victoria, certainly my parents are not.' Edwina seldom disagreed with her eldest daughter, but the things Robert had said to her last night had been playing on her mind. She didn't feel guilty, nor did she intend changing the way things were. But to admit to her parents being common would be admitting that she herself had at one time also been common. 'But I do agree that he is being stupid in the extreme to encourage any sort of friendship between Nigel, Abbie, and people who, at one time, just happened to be our neighbours. But your father is in a difficult mood, Victoria, and we must tread very carefully because he holds the trump card, and that is money.'

'He has been very inconsiderate in his timing, Mother, because I was going to suggest having the Chisholms to dinner one night. Charles and I are getting on very well, and it would help the courtship along if the two families became closer. We could also invite the Thompson-Brownes to make the numbers up.'

'I see no reason why Robert would object to you having a dinner party. He has spent money on a car for Nigel, so it would be churlish of him to refuse you. I know he finds dinner parties boring, but he'll just have to grin and bear it.' Edwina turned a piece of toast over before buttering it. The bread was a lovely golden brown, absolutely perfect. But she had to find fault with it. 'The bread is very lightly toasted today, not quite to my liking. I'll have to have a word with Agnes and ask that she be consistent.'

'Not harsh words, Mother, you know how easily Agnes can

179

be upset. And she is so good at preparing for dinner parties. I remember the last time we had one, the guests were raving about her pastry. They said it was so light it melted in the mouth. And Bernice Thompson-Browne said she'd snap Agnes up if ever she was looking for a new post.'

'I wouldn't put it past Bernice to try and poach her from us. Each time she comes she visits the kitchen to compliment Agnes in glowing terms on the dinner. But I think we're pretty safe with our housekeeper. Not because she cares for you and me, but because she is very fond of Robert.'

'I wonder if I should broach the subject over dinner tonight? Or do you think the timing is bad? It's just that it would take two weeks to arrange a night for the dinner party, by the time a date is decided which suits everyone.'

'Why would it be bad timing? Your father won't know I have told you what he's been up to behind my back. So be pleasant, ask him nicely and he can't refuse. Especially as you and Charles are practically engaged.'

'Hardly that, Mother, but getting closer, I think. I'm twenty-two years of age, and it's time I found myself a husband. Oh, I've had several suitors after my hand, but I wouldn't be bettering myself if I'd married them. I'm ambitious, Mother dear, and marrying into the Chisholm family would be a real achievement. A definite upward move.'

'And you really love Charles, don't you, dear?'

Victoria bit back a sigh of impatience as she turned her head to roll her eyes at the ceiling. Really, her mother could be so naive sometimes. Love had nothing to do with her wanting to marry Charles. In fact, his conversations bored her stiff, and although she encouraged his passionate advances, they left her cold. 'I am fond of him, Mother, but I'm even more fond of his money. I could live in luxury for the rest of my life, waited on hand and foot.'

'His father has control of the money, Victoria, and it will be many years before he retires and Charles takes his place. And he's quite a hard man, is George Chisholm.'

180

'I get on very well with him, Mother!' Victoria bridled, but she wished it was true. Charles very seldom took her to his home, and even then it was at her insistence. His parents were pleasant enough but there was no warmth there. And not for a minute did she believe the excuse his mother made for turning down her offer to help with the charity work. They had plenty of volunteers at the present time, Annabel Chisholm had told her, smiling sweetly. But she'd be the first they called on if the need arose. Although Victoria had been seething at being turned down, she didn't let it show and gushingly told Annabel she quite understood. Anyway, it was Charles she was trying to entice, not his parents. 'He is certainly not mean with money where Charles and Clarissa are concerned. They only have to mention they like something and it's there. I have no doubt whatsoever that when Charles marries, he will be set up in a suitable residence, complete with staff and a very generous allowance.'

'Then speak with your father tonight,' Edwina told her. 'Get it settled, then you can start planning.'

'I'd like a new dress for the occasion, Mother, I want to make a good impression. Shall I mention this to Father as well, or would that be going too far?'

Victoria's craftiness paid off, as she knew it would. 'I have some money put aside – I'll buy the dress for you,' Edwina said. 'You get your father's permission for the dinner party and we'll take it from there. By the way, how many people are you thinking of?'

'I thought eight would be a nice round number. The Chisholms, Thompson-Brownes, you and Father and Charles and I.'

'What about Nigel and Abbie? Would you be asking them?'

'Not if I can help it!' Victoria gave a snort. 'I don't think they'd come anyway. Nigel has been decidedly cool with me for the last week or so, and Abbie has always kept her distance.'

'If I might offer a little advice, dear, I believe if there is no invitation for your brother and sister, there will be no dinner party. Your father would be furious if you left them out.'

'Then I'll extend an invitation and keep my fingers crossed that they'll refuse.' Victoria was sure her father would agree and was already planning ahead. Charles was calling for her tonight so she could ask him to get a date off his parents when they'd be free. Once she had that she could telephone the Thompson-Brownes. 'I want it to be a perfect night, Mother, so Charles's parents can see I would make a suitable wife for their son. And I'll ask Agnes to put on a feast such as they've never seen before. Oh, I can't wait to see Father so I can start preparing. It will be an important night for me in regards to my relationship with Charles, so everything must be carefully planned, right down to the last detail.'

The housekeeper came in then to take away the breakfast dishes. 'Oh Agnes, I want you to spare me an hour tomorrow to help prepare a menu for a dinner party. I'll let you know in the morning what time will suit me.'

'I'm sorry, Miss Victoria, but it'll have to be a time to suit me!' Agnes stacked the dirty plates on to a tray, keeping her eyes averted so her anger wouldn't show. Cheeky madam! She'll tell me what time will suit her! Well, she can go and jump in a lake for all I care. 'This is a big house to run, and I have a routine. If I didn't stick religiously to that routine, then yer'd be getting yer meals all hours. And tomorrow is the day I give my living quarters a good clean through.' There were two very large attic rooms at the top of the house, and Agnes used one as a bedroom-cum-sitting room. She didn't expect the cleaner to do her room, she did it herself, and the staircase leading up to the attic. 'The best time will probably be around two o'clock, but I'll let you know when I serve lunch.'

The housekeeper picked up the tray and turned towards the door. 'Unless yer'd rather write the menu out and just hand it to me?'

'No!' Victoria was telling herself not to lose her temper. She needed the experience of this woman, and giving in was a small price to pay. 'It's for a special occasion, Agnes, and I couldn't do it without you. So whatever time suits you, that'll be fine.'

Later, the staff were having their morning break, and Agnes told them what had been said. 'The bleedin' stuck-up bitch!' Kitty was wishing she had the housekeeper's nerve. 'I'm glad yer told her where to get off, queen.'

'That was cheeky of her,' Jessie said. 'Yer work hard enough as it is, Aggie.'

Pete gave his opinion in a slow drawl. 'Someone should have taken her across their knees when she was younger and given her a good hiding. Never does a tap all day and expects to be waited on hand and foot.'

Agnes, her nerves calm now, said, 'There were two women in that dining room who think of no one except themselves. They love no one, and no one loves them. Two unhappy, lonely women. I pity them.'

Victoria's face was stretched in a smile, but close inspection would show it didn't reach her eyes. 'Father, can I ask a favour of you?'

Robert found he couldn't warm to his eldest daughter, but he was determined not to make fish of one and flesh of the other. 'Of course you can. What is it?'

'I'd like to ask Charles's parents to dinner one night. And perhaps the Thompson-Brownes. Just a small gathering, with Nigel and Abbie of course.'

'Count me out,' Nigel said. 'Dinner parties bore me stiff.'

'And me!' Abbie said. 'I've only ever been to one, as you well know, Victoria, and I swore I'd never go to another.'

Robert was probably the only one who saw the gleam of satisfaction on his eldest daughter's face. She doesn't want them there, he thought. In fact, if they'd said yes she would have found a way, over the next few days, of putting them off. 'What is this dinner party in aid of – something special?'

'No, nothing special. It's just that Charles and I have been seeing a lot of each other and I thought it was time for the families to become better acquainted.'

'I am very well acquainted with George Chisholm, I see him several times a week at the club. But that is by-the-by. If you and Charles are serious about each other, then I agree the families should get to know each other. So go ahead and plan your party, but definitely not on a Wednesday which coincides with my visit to Chester.'

'Thank you, Father, that's very sweet and generous of you.' Victoria stretched a leg to touch her mother's foot under the table. It was her way of saying they'd won.

'I can't speak for my parents, Victoria, but I will certainly ask them.' Charles had parked his car down a country lane, with not a house in sight, just fields. He was running a finger up and down Victoria's cheek, but with each downward stroke he strayed further towards the neckline of her dress. 'But I warn you, they have a very wide circle of friends and a full diary.'

'Charles, would you say I was your girlfriend?'

He grinned. 'Well, we certainly see each other nearly every night, so I suppose you are a girlfriend.'

'I don't mean just a girlfriend, I mean *your* girlfriend.' She could feel his finger now inside the neck of her dress and working towards her bosom. She noted too, the gleam in his eyes, the shallow breathing and his air of excitement. The time was fairly near when he would promise her anything she asked for. 'Kiss me, Charles.'

'Oh, yes.' He put an arm around her to draw her near, while his free hand slid down into her brassière and cupped a breast. 'Mm, that feels good, Victoria. You have a beautiful body, enough to send a bloke crazy.'

'Beautiful enough for you to want me to be your girlfriend?'

'Oh, yes!' In his eagerness to see what he could now only feel, Charles pulled so hard on the neck of her dress he ripped the button off the back, giving his hand the freedom to roam. His breath coming in short gasps, he caressed the full breast, watched by a pair of eyes that were cold and calculating. She had never let him go this far, and she wanted something in return.

'Charles, my darling, I shouldn't let you do this unless you truly are my boyfriend. I am not some cheap common tart.'

'I really am your boyfriend.' Charles at that particular time would have promised her the earth. He tugged again at her dress until both breasts were exposed. 'Beautiful, my darling, beautiful.' He tried to slip his hand under the skirt of her dress, but she pushed it away. 'You can't stop me now, I'll be in agony. I want you, Victoria, please!'

But his pleas fell on deaf ears. Victoria had a plan, and giving herself to him was not part of it. 'I have no intention of losing my virginity to anyone unless their intentions are honourable. And certainly not in the confines of a small car.'

'You're a tease, Victoria. You flirted and led me on, and nice girls don't do that.'

'Nice boys don't expect to make love to a woman who isn't their wife.' She cupped his face and kissed him. 'Did you mean it when you said I truly was your girlfriend?'

'You think I tell lies?'

'No, darling, of course not. It's just that if you are serious about me, then a car isn't the place to try and seduce me. It would have to be a bedroom in a first-class hotel, and I'd expect a bottle of champagne at the side of the bed.'

Charles wasn't the soft touch he made himself out to be. He was well-experienced in the wiles of women. He could have a girl, or woman, whenever he wanted. Married women sought his attention for thrills, to pass away a dull afternoon. Or he could buy the favours of high-class prostitutes. He could afford to pay them whatever they asked to carry out his sexual fantasies. So why should he settle down when he was enjoying life so much. Perhaps in ten years' time, when his father would be expecting an heir to carry on the family name and tradition, but not yet. He'd only paid court to Victoria for so long because she was a challenge. Never slept with a man

185

before, a virgin. And heaven knows, she was ripe for the picking. 'So you want to do it in style do you, my love? A top-class hotel, a bottle of champagne, and a man crying out for you. And that is what you deserve, the very best. Just say the word, my sweet, and I'll arrange it as soon as possible.'

'Not before the dinner party, Charles, I'll be too busy up till then. But as soon as it's over and my mind is free, you can book us into the finest hotel under the name of Smith.' She stroked his cheek. 'I'm sure you can persuade your parents to make an evening free the week after next. Now, that's not too long to wait, is it, my darling?'

The crafty minx must think I'm stupid, Charles thought. But she was still a challenge to him, and he would coax his parents into attending an event they wouldn't enjoy at all. It would be worth it to brag to his friends that he was the one who deflowered Victoria Dennison.

Chapter Eleven

Ada was back and forth to the window like a cat on hot bricks while Joe shook his head at her impatience. 'Bob said three o'clock, sweetheart, and it's only half two. Sit down and relax for half an hour.'

'I can't relax, I'm all wound up. I can't wait to see the children again.' Ada looked at her husband with pride. He was wearing new trousers, shirt and cardigan, and the tie around his neck was neatly knotted under his Adam's apple. None of the clothes were brand new, they'd come from Paddy's Market, but they were of good quality and condition. 'Yer look very handsome, Joe Brady, a proper toff.'

'And you look beautiful, sweetheart, I could fall for yer all over again.' He eyed with appreciation the pale blue jumper and navy blue skirt, and the black flat-heeled court shoes she'd spent hours polishing to try and get the scuffmarks off. 'That five pound off Bob was a godsend. I feel good enough to go out with them now, but I wouldn't have done in my old clothes, I'd have felt ashamed.'

'Yer should never feel ashamed of what yer are, Joe. I mean, what have yer got to be ashamed of? Yer worked hard until yer were sixty-five, with never a day off, and no one could do more than that. And if Bob heard yer he'd go mad.'

'Our Edie must be ashamed of us, otherwise why would she have stayed away for seventeen years?' The old man shook his head sadly. 'I keep asking meself why. Have we failed her in some way?'

'No, we ruddy well haven't! It's not us, it's her. The best we can do is forget her, she's not worth our tears. And God knows we've shed enough of those over the years. But I'll tell yer something I've never mentioned to yer before. Our Edie is not a good daughter, but I'll bet a pound to a pinch of snuff she's an even worse wife. Oh, Bob's always cheerful and ready with a joke, but there's times I've seen pain in his eyes. He strikes me as a man unfulfilled, like someone who isn't getting the right sort of love and affection. He does from the two youngsters, yer can see they adore him. But that's not quite the same thing. And today has proved to me that what I've been thinking for a long time, is true. Because if things were right between them, like they should be between man and wife, she'd be coming with them this afternoon.'

'Yer've never talked like this before, sweetheart. I'd be very upset if I thought Bob wasn't happy in his marriage. He's been so good to us over the years, better than any son. In fact, in my eyes he is our son.'

'Yes, we've got to count our blessings there. And it's through him we've got to see our grandchildren again at last. Two of them, anyway.'

Joe, whose chair was facing the window, sprung to his feet. 'They're here, sweetheart.'

His wife flew into the hall, pulling her jumper down and smoothing her skirt. The smile on her face when she opened the door told of her happiness. 'It's good to see yer. I thought today would never come.'

Abbie wrapped her arms around the frail figure and kissed her on both cheeks. 'Grandma, you look so pretty!' Then she caught sight of Joe standing by the living-room door. 'And who is that handsome man I see?'

Nigel was getting impatient standing on the step. 'Come on, Abbie, give someone else a chance.'

When kisses and greetings had been exchanged, Robert was at last able to enter the house to pass on his compliments. 'You both look splendid. I bet you'll be the best-looking couple in Southport.'

Ada pushed him playfully in the chest. 'D'yer think if me and Joe pretend we're not together we might get a click?'

'If a woman so much as glanced at Joe, you'd scratch her eyes out, Ada Brady. You're a one-man woman.' Robert looked from the elderly couple to his two children. There were three generations in the small room, and his heart was full that he'd been able to bring them together. 'Get your coats on and let's be on our way.'

When Ada reached for the coat hanging ready over the back of a chair, Nigel took it from her and held it out for her to slip her arms in. And Abbie helped Joe on with his. There were tears glistening in his faded eyes, but he wasn't going to spoil the day by allowing them to fall. 'It's been a long time since me and the wife were waited on, isn't it, sweetheart?'

'It is that, love, but I could get used to it if I was coaxed enough.' Ada fastened the buttons on the navy blue coat which had cost five shillings at the market. It was in quite good condition, but then it should be, five shillings was a lot of money. And Joe's black overcoat cost seven and six, which was a fortune!

When Robert was opening the car doors, several neighbours came out to stand on their front step. 'Hello, Bob, how's things?' one woman called.

'I'm fine thanks, Betty, how's the family?'

'Everyone's fine, even that lazy sod of a husband of mine.'

'Take no notice of her, Bob.' Another woman, her arms folded across her tummy, was shaking with laughter. 'That's not a husband she's got, he's a gift from God. She doesn't know she's born. I've told her I'll swap hers for mine, then she'd really know what a lazy sod is.'

Florrie, another neighbour, said, 'If it's lazy sods we're talking about, I'll bet my husband would beat theirs hands down. He's that bleedin' lazy, he doesn't even turn over in bed. I'm waiting for the day when he asks me to breathe for him.'

Nigel, who was helping his grandparents into the car, had his ears cocked. His dad was obviously very well liked in the street he was born in. That was because he hadn't changed, was still the same person he'd always been. He didn't put on any airs and graces. 'Granda, would you rather sit in the front seat, and I'll sit in the back with Grandma and Abbie?'

'No, son, I'd rather sit with the wife. You sit in the front.'

When they were all settled, Robert waved to the women. 'Betty, Nellie, Florrie, look after yourselves and remember me to your husbands.' He slid into the driver's seat and turned to make sure those in the back were comfortable. Abbie was sitting in the middle so her grandparents could look out of the windows, and the happiness on the three faces brought a lump to his throat. 'Right, off we go.'

Robert decided to drive down the Dock Road so Joe could see the big ships being loaded and unloaded. And it turned out to be a good decision because the old man was excited as he pointed out the various ships to his wife, telling her their country of origin. 'That's very interesting, Joe, how do you know all this?'

'I've always been interested in ships, Bob; they fascinate me, even though I've never set foot on one. So the week I retired from work, I bought meself a book which tells everything about them, in words and pictures. The number of funnels they've got, the colours of the flag they sail under, the knots they do and even the tonnage. And I'll tell yer, lad, I've had me money's worth out of that book, it's helped pass many hours away.'

'I'd like to see that book sometime, Granda,' Nigel said, turning his head to smile at the old man, who, with his wife, was giving a lot more meaning to life. He felt a sense of belonging now that he hadn't felt since he was a young boy. 'You'll have to show it to me and explain the difference in the ships and what part of the world they come from. It's all part of my education, and you can be my teacher.'

Joe looked as proud as a peacock. 'I'll do that, son, and get a real kick out of it. My wife is so fed up with me trying to get her interested in the book, she's threatened a few times to throw it on the fire.'

Ada leaned across Abbie to cover her husband's hand. 'Now yer know I wouldn't really do that, love, I've only ever said it in jest. I wouldn't dream of throwing something on the fire that means so much to yer.'

'It doesn't mean as much to me as you do, sweetheart.'

'Away with yer, yer'll have the children thinking ye're a soppy old man.'

'Ah, no we won't, Granda!' Abbie felt like hugging them both to her, to make up for some of the love she'd lost in the time she didn't even know they still existed. But she knew they were sentimental, like herself, and that they'd end up weeping buckets. 'I think it's lovely when people express their feelings for someone. If that means being soppy – well, I hope the man I marry is very soppy.'

'Better make sure of that before you marry him, my dear, otherwise you might get a big disappointment.' Robert's tone was light, but there wasn't a person in the car who didn't know that he was speaking from experience. 'Once you get the ring on your finger there is little you can do if you find things not to your liking.'

'There's always divorce, Dad!' Nigel was laughing so his words wouldn't be taken seriously, but he'd been asking himself recently how much longer his father could tolerate the life he was leading. That the marriage was loveless was plain to anyone who was in the company of his parents for five minutes. They never exchanged a look that said they even liked each other, never mind loved each other. Never kissed, hugged or held hands. And Nigel didn't need anyone to tell him it was all down to his mother. He couldn't remember the last time she kissed him, or his sisters, or showed any affection. In fact, she didn't seem capable of any emotion. His father was always civil to his wife, even though she was disrespectful, constantly complaining and humiliating him at every opportunity. 'I know a divorce is not easy to come by, but at least it's worth a try and better than two people living together in misery.'

'Oh, I don't think it'll come to divorce with yer grandma and me,' Joe said. 'I mean, the ruddy book doesn't mean that much to me.'

Robert had turned the car around and they were driving back the way they had come. Through Seaforth, then Waterloo to Crosby. Now it was Ada's turn to point excitedly through the windows at the big posh houses. 'I'd buy yer one of them, sweetheart, but they'd be a bit big for the two of us.'

Joe laughed. 'We could always get a cat and dog to help fill the place up.'

Nigel sat back in his seat only half listening to the conversation. He was carrying a dark secret around and it was weighing heavily on his mind. Yesterday, after dinner, he had retired to the drawing room with his mother and Victoria. He didn't feel at ease with them now, and would have preferred not to be in their company. But he was in the drawing room before he realised his father had gone to his study to enjoy a cigar, and Abbie had gone straight up to her room. While he was thinking up an excuse to leave, his mother had asked him to go to her bedroom and bring down the book from the side of the bed. He'd picked up the book and was on his way out of the bedroom when he noticed the light was on in the dressing-room. The switch was inside the dressing-room, and it was when he was reaching in to flick it off that he noticed the single bed was made up and a pair of pyjamas were folded neatly on top. This had saddened him so much, he'd run down the stairs, practically threw the book at his mother and left the room without bothering to make an excuse. And it had preyed on his mind ever since. He knew things were not good between his parents, but for his father to be reduced to sleeping on a tiny bed in his dressing-room was just too much to take in. How long had things been this bad? And Agnes must know his parents were no longer sleeping together because she'd be the one to make the bed up. His mother certainly wouldn't, she'd consider such a menial task beneath her.

'That was a deep sigh for such a young man,' Robert said. 'It sounded as though you have the troubles of the whole world on your shoulders.'

'No, not at all.' Nigel didn't realise he had sighed. There was no way he would want to add to his father's worries. 'It was a sigh of contentment, Dad. Being chauffeured in a very comfortable car, in the company of my father, sister and grandparents. What more could a man ask for?'

'Well said, son.' Ada leaned forward to pat him on the back. 'I couldn't have put it better myself. It's a day me and Joe will spend the whole week talking about. And the neighbours will be knocking first thing in the morning, wanting to know all about it.'

'Then we'd better make sure you have plenty to tell them,' Robert said. 'In fact, you'd better write it all down so you don't leave anything out. You see, although we arranged this as an outing for you and Joe, it's also a treat for my two children. Nigel was twenty-one a few days ago, and Abbie is eighteen in two days' time. I bought Nigel a car for his birthday, but so far Abbie hasn't made up her mind what she'd like. However, both were quite definite they didn't want a party. So to celebrate a number of occasions, I thought we'd have tea at Matti and Tissot's on Lord Street. Does that meet with your approval?'

'Ooh, er,' Ada said. 'Is that as posh as it sounds, son?'

'Nothing is too posh for us, my dear. I promise you'll love it.'

Ada wasn't so sure. 'Do all the ladies wear hats?'

Abbie giggled and squeezed the old woman's hand. 'Grandma, I haven't got a hat on. So if they throw you out, they'll have to throw me, as well.'

They were now driving through the country and the big houses with their massive gardens had Ada gasping. 'Just look at that one, Joe, isn't it beautiful!'

'It is that, sweetheart. Our whole street would fit into the garden. Whoever lives there must be rolling in money.'

Just in time, Nigel bit back the words that would tell them the Dennisons' back garden was just as big. He didn't want to hurt them by letting them know the daughter who had disowned them lived in the lap of luxury.

The delight shown by Ada and Joe at everything they saw, made the day especially happy for Robert and his children. He parked the car and they strolled along the promenade, stopping at the marine lake to watch the swans gliding gracefully by. Then they walked to Lord Street with its expensive shopping arcades. Everything was new and exciting for the old couple. The shops weren't open as it was Sunday, but Ada was fascinated by them. 'My God,' she said, giving Joe a dig in the ribs. 'Look at the price of that dress! It's more than we get to live on for a year, and there's no more than three yards of material in it. If anyone paid that for one dress they must have more bleedin' money than sense.'

Robert was standing behind them, highly amused. He stuck his head between theirs and said, 'They'd want their bleedin' bumps feeling, wouldn't they, Ada?'

She pulled a face at him. 'Ay, ye're not supposed to be listening, so if yer hear me swear it's yer own look-out.'

Nigel and Abbie were looking in a jeweller's window near by. 'How can Mother not want to see the two wonderful people who are her father and mother?' Abbie asked. 'I'll never be able to understand her. I love the bones of them.'

'What I can't understand is why she is so different from them,' Nigel said. 'They are warm, affectionate and funny, and she's so cold and aloof. It's hard to believe she's their flesh and blood.'

'I'm glad Dad never let them down, or they'd have been on their own all these years without a soul to call on if they were cold and hungry. I'm proud of Dad, he's a smashing man and I love him very much.'

'I'm proud of him, too. He's a truly remarkable man.' Nigel would have loved to confide in his sister, but it wouldn't be fair to worry her. Nor would it be fair on his father. 'He's put up with more than you or I will ever know.'

Robert called to them, 'Come along, time for Matti and Tissot's and their delicious, mouthwatering cakes.'

Ada hardly opened her mouth during the next hour. Her eyes were agog at the fashionable coats and hats on the people sat at tables around them. And they spoke so far back she kept nudging Joe's knee to make sure he wasn't missing anything. When Betty and Florrie called in the morning she was relying on him to remember what she'd forgotten. Not that she was likely to forget anything, the afternoon had been a real eye-opener for her. I mean, how could she forget the bone china cups they were drinking from, the real silver cutlery, the serviettes and the two glass stands on the table covered with cakes the likes of which she'd never seen before? And although the cakes really were delicious, it has to be said the three Dennisons got more pleasure out of watching her changing expressions.

Ada's quietness lasted until they were back in the car, then right through the drive home she had them in stitches. Adopting a haughty expression, and posing with a pretend cigarette-holder between her fingers, she took off one of the women who'd been sat at the table next to theirs. 'Oh, my dear, I know! It was ab-so-lute-ly dreadful!' Then she lowered her hand and leaned forward to impersonate the woman's companion. 'I could not believe it, darling, I was truly horrified! One doesn't expect that sort of behavior from a friend, does one?'

After waiting for the laughter to die down, Ada moved to the table situated on the other side of them. Her fingers laced together under her chin, her voice sugary sweet, she drawled, 'My dear Dorothea, Guy is quite the most charming man. A real poppet.' To which darling Dorothea's companion answered, 'Yes, I agree, Penelope, the man is charm itself. And very popular, I might add. Always invited to the best parties – and the gels simply *adore* him!'

Ada bent her head and hugged her tummy as she rocked with laughter at her thoughts. 'I can't see that lot having a jars out, knees-up do, what us common folk have. I can imagine the look on their faces if they were offered a bottle of milk stout and a brawn sandwich. They'd reach for the smelling salts and take to their bleedin' beds.'

Robert took a hand from the steering wheel to wipe his eyes. 'You don't envy them, then, Ada? Wouldn't swap places with them?'

'Swap places with them! Not on your nellie I wouldn't! They don't know what life is, that lot. They're too polished for my liking. And I'll tell yer what, this Guy feller might be charming but he's not a patch on my Joe.'

The love for his wife shining for all to see, Joe said, 'And for all their fancy clothes and their posh talk, you'd knock spots off them any day.'

Ada had quite enjoyed talking posh, and decided to have another go. To practise it, like, ready for the neighbours tomorrow. 'Oh, my darling Joseph, that is so sweet of you! But next time we have a party we really must invite Guy, he is so charming and such a poppet.'

The car turned into Arthur Street with loud laughter coming through the open windows from five happy people. 'It's been a grand day, Bob,' Joe said as he was being helped out of the car. 'Me and Ada will be talking about it for a long time to come.'

'There'll be many more days, Joe, so while you're talking about this one, you can be looking forward to the next. Now you go inside while I fetch something from the boot.'

When Robert entered the living room with two large brown bags, Ada was being helped out of her coat. 'Ye're going to stay and have a cup of tea and a bite to eat, aren't yer.' She'd bought a quarter of boiled ham, which was a rarity in the small house, and some cakes and biscuits. And she still had plenty left out of Bob's five pound note to entertain visitors for the next month or so. That the visitors would be her grandchildren filled her heart with joy. 'I can't promise yer china cups or posh cakes, but the cups will be clean and the cakes from Allerton's.'

'Of course we will.' Robert placed the bags on the table and began to undo his coat. Not for the world would he disappoint her. He'd got to know her very well over the years and was aware that she would have bought food she wouldn't normally buy, just for their benefit. 'Nigel and Abbie will be going straight to Balfour Road from here, so a sandwich will make up for them missing their dinner.'

Ada rolled up the sleeves of her jumper and said briskly, 'Well, move those bags off the table so I can make a start.'

'I'll give you a hand, Grandma,' Abbie said. 'I can make quite a good pot of tea, and I'm capable of buttering bread.'

'Just hold your horses, Mrs Woman! Aren't you curious as to what is in the bags?' asked Robert.

'Of course I am, but I wasn't going to say owt in case yer reminded me it was curiosity what killed the ruddy cat. But seeing as it was you what brought the subject up, what is in the flaming bags, anyway?'

Robert put his two hands in one of the bags and pulled out a bottle of whisky and a bottle of port wine. Then he ripped the other bag to reveal six bottles of milk stout. 'I want us all to have a celebration drink. Then what's left I'll leave for you and Joe to finish off.'

'My God, son, there's enough there to keep us drunk for a month!' Joe was staring at the whisky. 'I've only ever seen a bottle of whisky that size in a shop window or behind the bar in a pub.'

'Only the best for my favourite people,' Robert said. 'And who else would I celebrate with but those I love so much? While we are all together, I thought it would be nice to have a drink to celebrate the children's birthdays.'

Ada rolled her eyes. 'We haven't got no glasses, Bob.'

Robert bent his head to smile into her face. 'We are not Dorothea, Penelope or the very charming Guy, my dear.

Whisky is whisky whether it's in a glass or a cup. Believe me, it tastes just the same.'

'I'll get the cups.' Ada jerked her head at her granddaughter. 'Give us a hand, will yer, sweetheart?'

While Robert and Joe opted for the hard stuff, Ada, Abbie and Nigel chose the port wine. And they lifted their cups in a toast. 'Many of them,' Joe said, before spluttering when the strong liquor hit the back of his throat. He patted his chest and croaked, 'By, it's strong stuff, that is.'

'Then sip it, yer silly bugger!' Ada tutted before turning on her sweetest smile. 'Me and Joe wish yer good health, happiness and a long life.'

Nigel and Abbie weren't to know it, but they were thinking exactly the same thing. If their mother could see them drinking port out of a cup she'd look down her nose in disgust. Their dinner wine was drunk from long-stemmed pure crystal glasses that sparkled and changed colour in the light. But the atmosphere around the dining table at home was never as sparkling as the glasses. Nor was it as warm as that in the living room of the small terraced house.

'Now a drink to wish them well in their careers. Abbie was determined to do something useful with her life, and I'm happy to say she starts at commercial college this coming week. And Nigel, my son and heir, is now on the staff at Dennison's, which is what I have always wanted. Very soon the name will be changed to Dennison and Son.'

'Uh, uh!' Abbie shook her head and sent her dark hair swirling. 'You're not leaving me out of it. I intend to learn all about your business, Dad, and then it'll have to be Dennison, Son and Daughter.'

Robert chuckled. 'If you say so, my dear. I'm beginning to realise that what you want in life you will go after and get. And for that I take my hat off to you.'

Ada was so excited she was hopping from one foot to the other. 'Oh, I'm so happy for all of you. And for me and Joe, too!' Then a serious note crept into her voice. 'Yer dad has

198

worked very hard all of his life, and he's been very good to a number of people who were down on their luck. Nobody knows that better than me and my Joe. But there are some who don't appreciate what he's done, or how kind he is.'

'Hear, hear!' Joe said. 'He's one in a million, is your dad. And it does my old heart good to know he's got you two behind him.'

'Me and Abbie are not behind him, Granda, we're standing by his side.' Nigel drained his cup in the hope the port wine would swill away the lump in his throat. 'If I turn out to be half the man my dad is, I'll consider myself lucky.'

'Hey, come on.' Robert held out his empty cup. 'Do the honours, Nigel, and pour another drink before we start getting maudlin.'

'I don't want no more to drink.' Ada fastened her eyes on Joe, as though daring him to object to what she was about to say. 'And neither does my husband. We'll have a quiet one tonight when we're on our own. I'll get cracking and make some sandwiches, otherwise it'll be time for the young ones to leave before they've had a bite to eat. And we don't want their friends to hear their tummies rumbling, do we?' She began to chuckle at a thought. 'Yer've heard them say someone's all fur coat and no knickers, well they'd be saying about you that yer had a big flash car and empty bellies.'

She bustled out to the kitchen with Abbie, laughing her head off, following her. 'Tell me what you want me to do, Grandma, and we'll be finished in no time.'

The three men in the living room were chuckling when Joe caught Robert's eye. 'She's got a saying for everything, has my Ada.' He spoke with pride in his voice. 'I'd be lost without her.'

Robert said he would stay on for a while to keep Ada and Joe company, so after loving farewells Abbie walked with Nigel to pick up his car which had been left parked on the main road. 'It's been a great day, hasn't it?'

Abbie skipped a few steps to keep up with her brother's long legs. 'Wonderful! I enjoyed it far more with Grandma and Granda than I would have done with anyone else. They were so delighted with everything they saw, it was a pleasure just to be with them.'

'That's the way I felt, and we'll have to take them out again soon.' They reached the car and Nigel opened the passenger door for Abbie, then he walked round to the driver's side and slid in behind the wheel. 'I'll park the car in Knowsley Road and we'll walk to Milly's.'

'Why would you do that?' Abbie asked, her voice high with surprise.

'I don't want Bobby to see it in case he thinks I'm a big-head. I'll tell him in a week or so, when our friendship is on a firm footing.'

'But that's ridiculous! A car isn't going to come between friends. If it did, then he wouldn't be worth having as a friend. He won't think much of you if he finds out from someone else, and I wouldn't blame him. Anyway, if I know Bobby Neary, he wouldn't turn a hair if you appeared driving a blinking horse and carriage.'

'I wouldn't like him to think I'm a snob, Abbie, or that I've only got in touch with him after all these years just to show off.'

'Nigel, we might be better off than his family, but that's all. We're just the same as we've always been, we haven't changed.' She put a hand on his arm. 'A true friend won't care whether you're rich or poor. But he will care if he finds out you haven't been honest with him.'

They were nearly at Balfour Road now and Nigel slowed down. 'You really think I should tell him?'

'Ye gods, Nigel, it's not a sin to have a car! I bet Bobby will be made up and ask you to take him for a run.'

His sister seemed so sure, Nigel turned into Balfour Road and stopped outside the Jamiesons' house. 'What time shall I pick you up?'

'Not too late. It's my first day at the college tomorrow and I want to have a good night's sleep and wake with a clear head. Shall we say ten o'clock, 'cos it's a fair run from here to Mossley Hill?'

'I'll say hello to the Jamiesons later, then.' Nigel got out of the car and locked the doors. 'I'll walk over to Bobby's.'

'Bring him with you when you call so me and Milly can say hello.' Abbie lifted the knocker and rapped twice. 'Good luck.'

As Nigel crossed to the opposite side of the road he slipped the car keys into his pocket. The Nearys lived about ten houses up and the short walk was one he'd made hundreds of times when he was a young boy.

The door opened before he had time to knock. 'I've been watching out for yer,' Bobby said, pulling the door to behind him. 'I forgot to tell yer me dad died two years ago and I didn't want yer asking after him and upsetting me mam.'

'Oh, I am sorry, Bobby. I'll be careful what I say.'

'Come on in, me mam's dying to see yer.' He pushed the door wide open and called, 'He's here, Mam – late as usual! He always was too ruddy slow to catch cold.'

'That's a nice way to greet an old mate.' Rose Neary drew Nigel to her. 'It's nice to see yer, lad, and ye're very welcome.' She was a small, thin woman, her hair more white than the blonde Nigel remembered. But her blue eyes still held the old twinkle and hint of mischief. 'Sit down and I'll put the kettle on.'

Nigel lifted a hand. 'No, thanks, Mrs Neary, me and Abbie have just come from my grandma's and she made tea for us.'

'Where's Abbie now?'

'At the Jamiesons', probably talking fifteen to the dozen with Milly. Like me and Bobby, they've got a lot of catching up to do.'

'Ah, I'd love to see her,' Rose said. 'She was a right happy, bonny lass was your Abbie. Next time ye're down, fetch her to see me.'

'I'll do that, Mrs Neary, I promise.' Nigel noticed the worry lines and his heart went out to her. She used to yell at him and Bobby if they did anything naughty, and would think nothing of giving them a clout around the ears or chasing them down the road waving a sweeping brush in her hand. But she'd been generous with her affection, giving him hugs and kisses that he didn't get off his own mother. He couldn't not mention her husband, the man she'd idolised. 'I was very shocked, and sorry to hear about your husband. It must have been terrible for you.'

Her blue eyes clouded over for a second. 'I still haven't got over it, lad, there's not an hour goes by I don't think of him. And I'd never have got through it without Bobby here, he's been a pillar of strength.'

'Ah, go on, Mam!' Bobby looked bashful. 'I did what I could, and that wasn't much. To hear you talk anyone would think I was Hercules.'

'Take no notice of him, Nigel, he's a real good son to his mam. We had a struggle at first trying to make ends meet, with Bobby on lousy wages and me doing a couple of cleaning jobs. We managed, though, and now he's turned twenty-one and gone on a man's wage, things are a lot easier.'

'Ay, you must be nearly twenty-one, Nige.' Bobby wanted to change the subject before his mam got too upset. 'I think your birthday was a few weeks after mine?'

'Two days ago, actually.'

Bobby's cheeky grin appeared. 'Me mam bought me a pair of shoes for mine, and I got a shirt off me nan. What did you get?'

Nigel sighed inwardly, wishing he was as outgoing as his sister. She would handle this with a smile on her face and a joke on her lips. 'I told our Abbie I wasn't going to tell you and I got a right tongue-lashing. She said if you were a true friend you wouldn't worry whether I was rich or poor. So if you laugh or take the mickey out of me, I'll set her on to you.'

'Holy suffering ducks, Nige, what's the big mystery? What

the heck did yer get for yer birthday? That's all I asked, just a simple question.'

'I got a car.'

For about ten seconds Bobby and his mother didn't move or speak, they were like statues. Then laughter erupted and Bobby held his tummy as he rocked. 'Ooh, yer mean one of those things with four wheels? Ay, yer'd better send your Abbie down to batter me 'cos I can't help laughing at your face!'

'What's wrong with my face?'

'Well, I'll tell yer what, mate, if I'd got a car for me birthday I wouldn't be looking as miserable as a wet week. I'd be out there polishing it up and swanking in front of the neighbours. So where is this car yer seem to be ashamed of?'

'It's parked outside the Jamiesons', and I am not ashamed of it. It's just that I was worried you'd think I'd turned up out of the blue just to show off.'

It was Rose who answered. 'No, lad, he would never think that. He came home from Balfour Hall the other night and not once did he mention the word dance. He was so full of seeing you again he could talk of nothing else. He won't be envious of your car, he'll be made up for yer.'

'What d'yer mean, Mam, I won't be envious?' Her son's face was deadpan except for his eyes which were alive with humour. 'Of course I'll be flippin' envious! Unless, that is, he takes me for a ride in it.'

Nigel smiled. Abbie had been right, a friend is a friend no matter what. 'I'd love to take you for a spin, Mr Neary.'

With a howl of joy, Bobby slipped into his jacket. 'Come on, then, what are yer waiting for?'

'I'm sorry my visit is so short, Mrs Neary, but your son is very impatient.' Nigel bent to kiss her cheek. 'I'll see you again soon.' Then he hurried after his friend who was running as though he had wings on his heels.

'Oh boy, it's a beauty.' Bobby ran a hand over the bonnet. 'Smooth as silk and I can see me face in it. Not that anyone would buy a car just to see their face in when they can get a mirror for tuppence. Unless they were as good-looking as me, then they might think it was worth buying one.'

Nigel unlocked the passenger door and held it open. 'At your service.' And the happy smile he got in return heartened him. As he walked around the car he remembered Abbie's words. 'We're just the same as we've always been, we haven't changed.' And neither had Bobby Neary.

Chapter Twelve

Bobby was like a young boy in his enthusiasm. 'Ay, this is the gear, Nige! Who taught yer how to drive?'

'My dad taught me in his car a couple of years ago. Mind you, for the first month he wouldn't let me off the path. While I wanted to get out on the roads, he made me learn how to change gear, all the hand signals and what happens when you press the clutch. He bought me several books with illustrations on all parts of the engine, and after giving me a few days to study them, he would sit me down and ask me questions. I thought it was a waste of time, and that I'd learn as I went on, but I'm glad now he was quite strict about it. While I won't say I know a car inside out, I think if it ever broke down I'd be able to find the fault.'

'Well, I'll say this much, ye're a good driver.' Bobby was watching every move with interest. 'One of these days I'll learn to drive. That's when me boat comes in of course, and I've got a few bob in me pocket.'

'I'll teach you if you like. Down the country lanes where there's no traffic.'

'Go way! Yer wouldn't, would yer?'

'If you'd like me to, yes, of course I will. But none of your mad capers, though, that's something you've got to understand. Driving is a serious business because you could kill someone by taking your eyes off the road and acting daft. And don't expect to be able to drive overnight, either, because that won't happen.'

'I might act daft and I might look daft, but I promise yer

Nige,' Bobby tapped the side of his head, 'I'm not daft up here. Since my dad died I've had to grow up quick. I never thought about how me mam managed for money before because with me dad's wages coming in, and my few bob, we seemed to be having things easy. I didn't care how much the rent was, what a loaf or pound of sugar cost, or how often the gas-meter needed a penny. Then in the space of a week all that changed.'

Nigel checked in his rearview and side mirror before pulling into the kerb. He was too interested in what his friend was saying to concentrate on driving. 'Go on, tell me about it.'

'Well, the money me dad was due from work all went on the funeral. And the week after, me mam was at her wit's end trying to scrape the rent money together. That's all she could think of, paying the rent to keep a roof over our heads. I suggested moving to a smaller, cheaper house, but she was crying that all her memories were in that house and while she was there me dad would always be with her. It was a terrible time. We went hungry most days, and couldn't afford to have a fire in the grate. That's when I grew up, Nige, when I could see me mam fading before me eyes. I didn't mind going to work on an empty tummy, or being cold, but I did worry about me mam. My boss was good, he gave me a few hours' overtime every week, and then me mam got a cleaning job. We were still living from hand to mouth, but we were paying the rent and we weren't starving. New clothes were a thing of the past, like, and many a time I've had holes in me socks and shoes. Then me mam got a bit stronger and took on another cleaning job and that extra money kept the wolf from the door.' Bobby pulled a sorrowful face. 'I'm a cheerful sod, aren't I? Yer take me for a ride in yer new car and all I do is moan.'

'I want to hear what your life's been like, Bobby, and I don't think you're moaning, you're just telling the truth. We were best mates when we were kids, and I hope we still are. And if you can't talk to your best mate, who can you talk to?'

'Ye're the first one I've ever talked to about the rough time we had. In fact, the neighbours probably thought I didn't give a damn about me dad dying and me mam out of her mind with worry. Yer see, I went around with a smile on me face because it's the only way I could cope. But I was crying inside, believe me, my heart was raw with grief.' Bobby shook his head at the memories. 'It's funny how life can be a bed of roses one minute, then hell the next. I had to grow up so quick it was a shock to me system. No more tanners for the pictures or to go dancing, no more pennies for the tram, it was shanks's pony everywhere. And worst of all, no father to laugh and joke with, and talk about work. I didn't appreciate it at the time, but my dad was a ruddy good mate to me.'

There was a crack in Bobby's voice and Nigel realised what an effort it was for his friend to relive those hard times. Perhaps a cigarette would help calm his nerves. 'Do you smoke, Bobby?'

'Not heavy, like, but I do smoke. Why?'

Nigel reached into his pocket and brought out his packet of Turkish cigarettes. 'Would you like one of these?'

'Oh God, aren't they the ones that stink?'

'They're all I've got, so it's Hobson's choice. Once you get used to them they're not so bad.' Nigel held his lighter to the flat cigarette in Bobby's mouth and grinned when he saw the nose wrinkle in disgust. 'Throw it away if you don't like it. The smell does take some getting used to, I admit. My dad's face has the same expression on it when I light up.'

'Nah, I'll smoke it,' Bobby said, grimacing as he puffed up. 'I mean, I'm going to get your smoke up me nose, anyway!'

Nigel took a puff of his own cigarette, leaned an elbow on the steering wheel and said softly, 'Do you feel like finishing what you were telling me, or would you rather not?'

'There's not much more to tell. It was a case of scrimping and scraping, with no enjoyment in life at all. But when I was twenty I got a shilling rise in me wages, and although I didn't want to take it off her, me mam insisted I keep that shilling so

I could go dancing again. She said a young lad was entitled to some pleasure, and as we'd never had the shilling before, we'd never miss it. She's a cracker is my mam, and honest to God, Nige, I love the bones of her. Yer know from when we were kids and she used to have a go at us, that she's got a big mouth. But her heart is twice as big.'

'Have you had any girlfriends?'

'One or two before me dad died, but none since 'cos I couldn't afford one. And even though life will be easier for us now, with me on full pay and me mam keeping her jobs on until we straighten ourselves out, I've never met a girl I could fall for.'

Nigel raised his brows. 'Not even Milly Jamieson?'

Bobby blushed. 'Nah, she's a good mate is Milly, and a smashing dancer, but that's as far as it goes. I've no intention of getting serious with any girl for a long time 'cos I've got me mam to think of. She's lost one man in her life, I don't think she should lose another, not for a while.'

'Things happen that we have no control over, Bobby; none of us know what the future holds. But I'm quite sure everything will work out well for you, and for your mother. And I'm glad you've filled me in on the ten years of your life I missed.' Nigel turned the key in the ignition. 'I asked if you wanted a ride in the car, and we've only come from Seaforth to Orrell Park. Do you want to turn back or carry on for a while?'

'Ay, hang about, Nige! What about the ten years I didn't see you? I know nothing about you, except yer got this car for yer flippin' birthday.'

'Until very recently, Bobby, my life was useless and boring. I will tell you about it sometime, but not tonight. Perhaps when I take you out for a driving lesson. How would that suit you?'

'Yer really meant that about teaching me, then?'

'I certainly did. I'd enjoy it.'

Bobby's face was a picture of happiness as he rubbed his hands together. 'That's the gear, that, Nige! If I learned to drive I could try for a driver's job at Owen Peck's, where I work. They have vans and lorries to deliver the orders for wood, and drivers get about ten bob a week more than the labourers. Ooh, I'd be quids in – a millionaire!'

Nigel grinned. 'You could afford to take Milly out one night.'

'Will yer knock it off over Milly! I've told yer, she's just a good mate.' He tilted his head and, a cheeky grin on his face, asked, 'Where was she going tonight with your Abbie?'

'I thought she was just a good mate?'

'She is! I'm just nosy, that's all.'

'They were staying in to have a good chinwag as far as I know. I'm supposed to be picking Abbie up at ten o'clock, and as it's a quarter to now, I think we should head back home.'

'I'll come in with yer, just to say hello. And don't yer be making anything of that, Nige, 'cos as I said, she's just a good mate.'

'Well, look what the cat dragged in!' Milly opened the door to the two men. 'I wasn't expecting you, Bobby Neary. I hope yer haven't been leading Nigel astray?' She stood aside to let them pass. 'The family are in the kitchen, as usual.'

Bobby's smile covered everyone. 'Yer haven't brought yer daughter up proper, Mrs Jamieson. She's got no manners at all. In fact, our cat's got more manners.'

Beryl grinned. 'I didn't know yer had a cat, Bobby.'

'We haven't. But next door has, and I'm adopting it for the next five minutes so I can compare it to your daughter's manners.' He winked at Milly's father. 'She nearly barred me path, yer know, Mr Jamieson. And that black moggy what I've adopted for five minutes – well, she wouldn't do that. She might hiss and spit, but she'd never bar me.'

Beryl went along with him. 'That's not like our Milly, she's usually very well-mannered. Why don't yer apologise, Milly, 'cos I think yer've hurt his feelings.'

Milly bent her knee to curtsy. 'I'm very sorry Mr Neary, I

wouldn't hurt yer feelings for the world.' Then she burst out laughing. 'Feelings! What feelings! That cat he's just adopted has got more feelings than him. And she's better-looking.'

Nigel was watching Bobby's face for a sign that Milly meant more to him than just a mate. But no, he couldn't see any spark between the two. Then again, they weren't likely to let anything show in front of her parents. And anyway, who was he to judge when he'd never had a real girlfriend? The only ones he'd ever met were girls singled out by Victoria for him to escort to a ball or dinner. All that was going to change now, though; he was going to be his own man in future.

'How about a cuppa before yer go, Nigel?' Beryl asked. 'Won't take a minute to make.'

'I think Abbie wants to have an early night in bed, Mrs Jamieson. She's got a big day ahead of her.'

'So she's been telling us,' Bill said. 'Standing on her own two feet and making her way in the world, eh?'

Bobby scratched his cheek as he looked at his friend. 'Haven't you got a big day ahead of yer, Nige?'

'Not as big as Abbie's. But I do have to be in work for eight o'clock.'

Abbie rested her chin on a curled fist as she studied Bobby. He'd always been full of life and on the go, but tonight he seemed brighter than usual. She'd even go as far as to say he was in a state of agitation. His eyes were shining, he was making wide sweeping movements with his arms, and his body reminded her of a coiled spring ready to shoot out and surprise someone. 'What's wrong, Bobby, has that blinking moggy got your tongue?'

'Yer could say that, Abbie.' He gave her a quick smile before turning to her brother and holding out his hands as though in prayer. 'Are yer going to tell them, Nige, or not?'

'What would you like me to tell them?'

'Look, yer've forgotten already! Not half-an-hour ago, did you, or did you not, promise to teach me to drive a motor vehicle?'

'Yes, I did promise, and no, I have not forgotten. If Tuesday doesn't interfere with your dancing routine, I will pick you up at half seven and we shall away to the country lanes where you will not be able to wreak havoc on another car or someone's garden wall.'

'Ooh, ye're not half trusting, aren't yer, Nigel?' This came from Kenny, sixteen years of age and the baby of the family. 'It's not another car or someone's garden wall yer should be worrying about, it's yer own car. He's as mad as a hatter, is Bobby, a real dare-devil.'

'Children should be seen and not heard, so you keep out of it,' Bobby told him, wagging a finger and trying to look fierce. 'Anyway, I'm returning the favour by teaching Nige to dance.'

Abbie quickly turned surprised eyes on her brother. Surely he wouldn't have agreed to that when they'd already discussed going to private lessons so as to surprise their friends? But she could see that Nigel was even more surprised than she was. 'Ah, now, that was never mentioned. Your driving lessons take priority, then we'll worry about my dancing.'

'Anything you say, mate,' Bobby said, giving everyone the benefit of his grin. 'Ay, he doesn't half speak posh, doesn't he?'

Milly, thinking Abbie was included in his talking posh statement, quickly went on the offensive. 'He doesn't speak posh, he speaks English as it should be spoken. As we all would if we weren't too flaming lazy to bother.'

'Yes, Miss.' Bobby looked suitably chastised. 'I'll tell yer what, when he's teaching me to drive, I'll be crafty and use it to polish up me English as well. Then, if yer like, Milly, at no cost to yerself, I'll teach you how to speak posh.'

Milly knew when she was licked and joined in the laughter. She might have known she'd never get one over on Bobby Neary. You could get yourself all het up and call him fit to burn, but all the time you were shouting and going red in the face, he'd be standing with a grin on his handsome face, and his blue eyes would be shining with mischief. In fact, he seemed to enjoy getting you wound up, so there didn't seem much point in wasting your breath, really.

'I think we should be going, Abbie,' Nigel said. 'Otherwise it'll be midnight before you get to bed, and you did say you wanted a clear head in the morning.'

'Ah, aren't yer going to see me home?' Bobby put on a little boy lost expression. 'It's dark out, yer know.'

'Sorry, but no can do. I have to get my little sister home.'

'Never mind, Milly will see me home safe, won't yer, Milly?'

'Some hope you've got!' the girl told him.

His shoulders drooping and his bottom lip quivering, Bobby made one last appeal. 'You'll walk me home, won't yer, Mr Jamieson? Yer see, me mam doesn't like me being out in the dark on me own.'

As Nigel was to say to his sister on the drive home, 'It doesn't matter if you can't find anything to talk about when you're with Bobby, 'cos he never stops. You could sit with your mouth closed all night and I don't think he'd even notice.'

'Yes, he's hilarious.' Abbie was still chuckling. 'But I have a feeling there's a serious side to him that he never lets anyone see.'

'You're right. Life hasn't been all milk and honey for Bobby and his mother, they've had a couple of rough years. But they're over the worst now, and I think it's made a better man of him. Behind the laughter and jokes, there's someone who is kind, caring and strong in spirit.'

'I agree,' Abbie said, squeezing his arm. 'You've got yourself a very good mate. And so have I.'

Agnes was leaning on her elbows staring down at the piece of paper in front of her. 'I don't know who she thinks she is! She'll be wearing a bleedin' tiara next, and expect us to curtsy.'

'Some hope she's got,' Kitty said, her legs swinging back to kick the seat of her chair. 'I'd be damned if I'd curtsy to the likes of her, the stuck-up cow.'

'Did Miss Victoria say how many people she's inviting to this dinner party?' Pete asked. 'Is it a big do, or just a few friends?'

Agnes raised her brows and looked down her nose. 'These are her exact words: "A few very select friends, Agnes. People who are used to the finest foods. And that is precisely what I will expect from you." Honest, I felt like clocking her one.'

Jessie was round-eyed. She'd been asked to stay behind the night of the dinner party to help serve, and she was nervous enough without it being piled on. But she couldn't help asking, just to make sure, 'How many courses did yer say, Aggie?'

'Seven including the coffee, sunshine. And of course the whisky and wine will be flowing all night.'

'How in the name of God anyone can eat seven courses is beyond me,' Kitty said. 'If yer ask me, they're greedy buggers.'

'Read the menu again, Aggie,' Pete asked. 'Just so I can tell the missus while we're eating our stew tonight.'

'I'll read what she's asked for, but I'm not saying that's what she'll get. She's written down two starters until she can make up her mind. One is poached egg on a bed of spinach, the other is soup. Then comes the fish course. That is definitely poached salmon in a dill sauce. The main meal is pheasant, plus all the vegetables and spuds. The dessert is a flaky pastry apple pie with fresh cream, followed by a selection of cheeses from Cooper's. After that comes the truffles she's expecting me to make. And they finish off with coffee.'

'I hate to show me ignorance, queen, but what the bleedin' hell arc truffles?'

'They're small soft chocolates flavoured with rum.'

'Ah, ay, queen, ye're not having us on, are yer? You can't make them!'

'I can, sunshine, but whether I will is another matter. I mean, how do they expect me to cook and bake all these, and serve on table? I did tell Miss Victoria I only had one pair of hands, but she didn't take no notice. She looked at me as much as to say, don't be making tiresome excuses, grow some more hands if necessary.'

'Why the hell did yer tell her yer could make these truffle things?' Kitty pulled a face. 'Ye're a fool to yerself, queen, that's what yer are.'

Agnes gazed across at the little woman. Their break was nearly over and they hadn't had one decent laugh. And that would never do. So after a quick think, she said, 'Well, it was like this, yer see, sunshine. When Miss Victoria mentioned truffles, I inadvertently let it slip that I could make them.'

Kitty's legs stopped swinging and her mouth stopped chewing on the cheese butty. Her eyes slid to Jessie and Pete to see if they were as in the dark as she was. But she could read nothing from their faces. 'How did yer say yer let it slip, queen?'

'Inadvertently, sunshine. I could have bit me tongue off after I'd said it.'

'And what does that inadly word mean?'

'It means I made a mistake, sunshine – have yer never heard the word before?'

Pete and Jessie kept their eyes straight ahead. Neither of them had heard the word before, but they knew Agnes was playing a joke on the cleaner and they weren't going to interfere. I mean, why stop something they knew would end in laughter.

Kitty was leaning as far across the table as she could manage. Her eyes like slits, she said, 'No, I haven't bleedin' well heard the word before, and neither have you. And d'yer know why? 'Cos there's no such word.'

'There is too! Just because you've never heard of it doesn't mean a thing, 'cos ye're pig ignorant, that's what.'

'OK, smart arse! Spell it for me.'

'I can't spell it off the top of me head,' Agnes objected, not thinking it would have got this far. 'I'd need to write it down, but I've got no paper handy. Pete, you've always got a scrap of paper in yer overall pocket, you write it down for us, there's a good lad.'

214

Pete's jaw dropped. 'Aggie, I can't even say the word, never mind write it down. You must have gone to a different school to us.'

'Are you saying there's no such word, as well?'

'I'm not saying no such thing! It's just that I've never heard of it, that's all.'

'Right, you ignorant lot, I'll show yer whether there's such a word.' Aggie was making her way to the dresser as she spoke. 'I'll write the ruddy thing down for yer and yer can look in the dictionary when yer get home.'

'Seeing as we don't possess a dictionary, queen, we'll take your word for it. But write it down and I'll show Alf what a clever woman yer are.'

Armed with paper and pencil, Agnes flexed her arms. Saying the word over and over in her head, she began to write, praying if she didn't get it dead right, no one would know the difference. Then with a flourish, she passed the paper over to Kitty. 'There yer are, sunshine, show that to your feller. Thirteen letters in that word, if yer'd like to count.'

Kitty stared at the paper for a few seconds, then folded it and put it in her overall pocket. 'I'm not doubting yer, queen, and I'm sure my Alf won't, 'cos he's as ignorant as me.' Her thin face puckered, she scratched her head before pushing her chair back. Jerking her head at Jessie, she said, 'Come on, queen, back to the grind.' They were at the door when she turned. 'I've had some cleaning jobs in me time, Aggie, but not one where I got a bleedin' education thrown in. Yer'll be charging me to come to work, soon.'

The cleaner sent Jessie to finish off upstairs while she started in the hall. She was polishing the ornate settle when the front door opened and Robert came in. 'I've come back for some papers I forgot to take with me.' He smiled at the little woman who looked much better than she had a few weeks ago. The extra half-a-crown a week was obviously helping, plus the extra food Agnes was allowed to give her. 'I'll not be two ticks.'

'Mr Robert, can I have a word with yer?'

'Of course you can. Here, or in the study?'

'In the study if yer don't mind. It's nothing important, just a joke between me and Aggie that I'd like yer advice on.'

Once in the study, Robert closed the door. 'What are the pair of you up to now?'

'It's this word what Aggie used, and I'd never heard of it. Of course she said I was pig ignorant and wrote it down for me. Pete had never heard of it either, so unless she's having us on, he's as thick as me.' Kitty took the paper from her pocket and passed it over. 'That's the word, and it's got thirteen letters in it.'

Robert was chuckling as he gazed at the writing. 'Inadvertently! She's more than a pretty face, is Agnes.'

'So she wasn't pulling me leg, Mr Robert?'

Robert tweaked the end of his nose to try and stem the laughter. 'Oh, I think she probably was to begin with, Kitty. After all, it's hardly a word one would throw into a conversation. But it is a word, and she's spelt it correctly.'

Kitty's face dropped. Then she had an idea. Mr Robert liked a joke as well as the next man, so he wouldn't mind her asking. 'I don't suppose yer know any other words with thirteen letters in, do yer, Mr Robert? Just so I can get me own back.'

'Oh, I think so, but give me a minute.' Robert was thinking the kitchen was the only happy room in the house. Then he snapped his fingers. 'I can go one better than thirteen letters. But a word is no good unless you know where it fits into a conversation.'

'I'll know if you tell me, Mr Robert.'

Robert pulled his chair away from his desk and sat down. 'I'll print it, so it's easier for you to learn how to pronounce it.' Using one of his own letterheads, he printed the word 'incomprehensible'. His face beaming, he handed the paper over. 'There are sixteen letters in that word, Kitty, but for it to have any effect on Agnes you must learn to say it correctly.'

216

'Excuse me language, Mr Robert, but bloody hell! I'll never get me tongue round that.'

'Yes, you will. Look, put the paper on the desk and we'll go over it.' With the end of his fountain pen, he broke the word into syllables and repeated it slowly over and over again. 'Now you try, Kitty, and don't be nervous.'

Five minutes later the cleaner was able to say the word without looking at the paper. Her face aglow with pride, she said with a laugh, 'Now all I need to know is what it means.'

'It means something you can't understand. For instance, I might say I find it incomprehensible that widows receive so little money. Or that some children have to go bare-foot because their parents can't afford to buy them shoes.'

'Oh, I get it! I know just the sentence to put it in. Just you wait, Aggie Weatherby, yer in for the shock of yer life. Thanks, Mr Robert, ye're a pal.'

'There's a catch I'm afraid, Kitty. I want you to do it now so I can stand outside the kitchen and listen. It should be a good laugh.'

Agnes was peeling potatoes when Kitty came into the kitchen. 'Don't tell me yer've finished yer work so quick? Yer can't have done a very good job.'

'I haven't started yet. I've got something to say to yer.' Speaking clearly and slowly, Kitty said, 'I find it incomprehensible that yer didn't say right out that yer weren't going to do those bleedin' truffles.'

Robert wasn't satisfied with listening, so he crept into the kitchen. And when he saw Agnes and Kitty with their arms around each other, shaking with laughter, he crept out again, not wanting to intrude on their pleasure. The scene heartened him and put him in an optimistic mood for the day. And when he was having lunch in a small café with Nigel and Jeff, he repeated the whole episode to them, every word and every action. And if the two ladies had known they were responsible for three grown men having smiles on their faces all day, they would have been delighted.

Victoria's dinner party was also the topic of conversation in a drawing room several miles away across the city, where Charles faced his mother. 'Just this once, Mother, I promise,' he pleaded. 'Surely a few hours isn't going to have a detrimental effect on your health.'

'Charles, you should have refused the invitation immediately.' Annabel Chisholm was most displeased. 'You know I have little time for Victoria or her mother. The rest of the Dennison family I get along with very well, but Victoria is such a dreadful snob – and that mother of hers is insufferable! In fact, I can't tolerate either of them. So please thank them for the invitation and say it is with regret your father and I will not be able to attend.'

'Oh, come on, Mother, just this once to please me. I have turned down several invitations on your behalf, I can't continue to do so.' Charles was used to getting his own way and knew he would eventually wear his mother down. She in turn, would coax his father. 'Please, Mother, for my sake? I promise I'll never ask again.'

Annabel studied the son she adored. He wasn't without faults, as she and her husband knew to their cost, but normally she didn't have the heart to refuse him anything. In this case, though, she was going to tread carefully for his sake. 'Charles, your intentions towards Victoria are not serious, are they?'

'Of course not, Mother! I have been seeing a lot of her lately because she is quite good company and always looks immaculate to take anywhere. But I have no intention of settling down for a few years yet.'

'Then you must make your position clear to her. And I think it would be a good idea to put an end to the relationship completely. Victoria is not the sort of girl I would welcome as a daughter-in-law. I can't find it in my heart to warm towards her. She is so arrogant, cold and humourless. And as for her mother, well, words fail me. I think the woman lives in her own dream world. Your father could buy and sell the Dennisons ten times over, yet Edwina and her daughter treat us like the poor relations. Both of them are suffering from delusions of grandeur, and I think you would be wise to walk away before you get in too deep. I am looking forward to having grand-children in the not too distant future, and I would be very disappointed, and concerned, if Victoria Dennison was their mother. It's because I love you so much, my darling, and want you to have a happy life, that I am advising you to steer clear of her.'

'I intend to, Mother. That has been in my mind for weeks now. But I can't end our association overnight, or she'd be ringing up and making a nuisance of herself. So it was my intention to attend the dinner party, and then gradually stop seeing her.' In his mind he was thinking of the first-class hotel, the bottle of champagne, the bed and the virgin. They came first, then the farewell.

'I hope you are not saying that just to persuade your father and me to attend this wretched party? I would be very angry, Charles, if I thought that were the case.'

'Cross my heart, Mother. If you come to the party, I promise that a week or two later, Victoria Dennison will be a thing of the past.'

'If that is so, my darling, then you can accept the invitation. Your father and I will suffer the insufferable.'

Chapter Thirteen

Robert took his seat at the dining table and after a cordial greeting to his family, he smiled at his youngest daughter. 'Well, my dear, how did your first day go? Was it very hectic or did you sail through it?'

Abbie pulled a face. 'Not so much hectic, Dad, as terrifying. I've just been telling Nigel about it. Everyone, teachers and students, were all very nice and friendly, but I don't think I'll ever get the hang of shorthand. It's really complicated, with different-shaped squiggles like curves and dashes which represent a word, or even several words. Fortunately everyone in the class was a raw beginner, so I wasn't the only one to feel stupid. According to the teacher, Miss Harrison, after the first week or so it will all start to make sense and we'll wonder why we were so afraid.'

Edwina clicked her tongue on the roof of her mouth and muttered, 'It will just be a complete waste of time.'

Robert sighed. Why couldn't the woman give her daughter some encouragement instead of putting her down. He was stung into saying, 'Wasting time is something you will know a lot about, Edwina. You have had plenty of practice.'

'That's not fair, Father.' Victoria had that supercilious look on her face. 'What you said was very hurtful and most uncalled for.'

'Oh, and how have you spent your day, Victoria? Have you been very busy?'

'Mother and I have been shopping, and to the hairdresser's. One has to keep up appearances. Also, I've spent an hour with

Agnes, going over the menu for the dinner party.'

Nigel, always at her beck and call until recently, was wondering why he hadn't broken free from her years ago. And when he turned there was a look on his face akin to pity. 'You really have had a tiring day.'

'Sarcasm, Nigel dear?' Victoria raised her brows. 'I shouldn't try it if I were you, you're still in the infant stage.'

'Yes, but I'm growing quickly and learning fast.'

Robert banged an open palm on the table. 'That is quite enough. I will not have petty squabbles at the dining table. And in future, when I'm talking to one member of the family, I will not tolerate interference from another.' His chest heaving in a deep sigh, he turned once again to Abbie. 'Back to your day, my dear. Was it all spent on learning these squiggles?'

'Oh no, the afternoon was given over to typing.' The atmosphere in the room was hardly conducive to laughter, but Abbie couldn't hold it back and it ricocheted from the four walls. 'I was hopeless at that, as well. We had to type "the quick brown fox jumped over the lazy dog" because that has every letter of the alphabet in it. It took ages to find each letter, but I plodded on, like everyone else, just using one finger. The teacher in that class is Miss Pye, and she told us to sit and look at the keyboard and try to memorise where the letters were. It's a good job all the others in the class were as slow as me, otherwise I'd have curled up with embarrassment.'

'Did you get any homework?'

'Not yet, but apparently we will in a couple of weeks when we've mastered enough shorthand signs to write short sentences. I can't practise typing because I haven't got a typewriter.'

'That's no problem, I'll buy you one. And to give you a bit more confidence, there are two girls in our Liverpool office who went to night-school to learn shorthand. I was talking to one of them today and she said it was weeks before the signs made sense to her. But you should see the speed with which she can write now. While I'm dictating a letter her hand just flies across the paper. So have as much faith in yourself as I have in you, my dear, and all will be well.'

There was a light tap on the door, and then Jessie came through ahead of Agnes. 'You should have left by now, Jessie, surely?' Robert was surprised to see the young girl. 'I hope your parents won't be worried about you.'

'Oh no, Mr Robert, I told them I'd be late. Yer see, Aggie wants me to get used to waiting on table so I can help her for Miss Victoria's dinner party.'

'Agnes will wait on the table herself,' Victoria said. 'I want everything to be just right.'

Robert sat back in his chair and rested his chin on a curled fist. Looking at the housekeeper's set face he knew there was trouble brewing, but this was one argument he had no intention of joining. Agnes was more than capable of sticking up for herself and it was only right that she be allowed to answer the person who had spoken of her as if she was a slave to be ordered around at will. So he decided to let things take their course. He didn't have long to wait.

The entrée tonight was salmon, served with one of Agnes's own recipe sauces. The fish looked delicious set on a silver oblong tray and decorated with sprigs of parsley. Without showing any of the anger that was raging within her, Agnes placed the tray in the centre of the table and stood back for a second to admire her handiwork. Then, satisfied, she dusted her hands together before looking down at Victoria.

'See them, Miss Victoria,' she held up her two hands, 'same number as I had last night when I asked how yer expected me to bake, cook, serve, wait on table and see to the washing up, all on me own. Oh, and we mustn't forget that in the middle of seeing to all this, I've got to get meself all dressed up like a dog's dinner. I know that's what yer'd expect of me, 'cos everything has to be perfect, doesn't it, Miss Victoria, to impress yer friends. So while you won't have to lift a finger or get yer own hands dirty, I'm the muggins who has to make sure we don't let the side down.'

The housekeeper's hands were now on her hips, a sure sign she meant business. 'Seven courses of mouthwatering dishes, yer said, and pastry that must melt in the mouth. All made, prepared and served by just one person. It's not a housekeeper yer want, Miss Victoria, it's a bleedin' magician. And as I ain't a magician, unless I can have Jessie here to give me a hand, I'm afraid ye're going to have to find some other silly sod to take over from me. Give them the menu and then watch them run for the nearest bleedin' door.'

There was complete silence as Agnes squared her shoulders, threw out her ample bosom and reached for Jessie's hand. 'Come on, sunshine, before there's no arse left in the potato pan.'

As soon as the door closed, Victoria jumped to her feet and leaned her palms on the table. She was absolutely livid. 'How could you sit there, Father, and allow me to be spoken to in such a way by a servant?'

'Because that is the way you deserve to be spoken to. In fact, I think under the circumstances, Agnes let you off very lightly.'

'Well, I don't intend to let her get away with it. I shall give her a piece of my mind and remind her of her position.' Victoria was striding purposefully towards the door, her lips a thin red line, when Robert's voice brought her to a halt.

'Then I hope you won't be too upset about having to cancel the dinner party. Another insult by you and Agnes will tell you in no uncertain terms where to go to.'

'She can't be allowed to get away with it, and I intend to have very strong words with her. No matter what happens I won't have to cancel the dinner party, for I'll bring in outside caterers.'

'I presume you have the money to do this?' Robert asked. 'Because I can assure you I will not pay one penny to outside caterers when we have the best housekeeper and cook in the whole of Liverpool. Apart from being excellent in her job, Agnes is also a very fine person, and should be treated with

224

respect.' He waved his hand towards the door. 'You have your strong words with her, but bear in mind what the consequences could be.'

Her hand on the door knob, Victoria could feel the eyes of her family boring into her back. And the longer she hesitated the less sure she was of herself. To save face with her family she should carry out her threat and march to the kitchen. But caution told her there was a lot at stake, so it would be foolish to antagonise Agnes further. The most important event in her life right now was the dinner party. It had to go ahead, so she could persuade Charles and his parents that she was the perfect hostess, and would be an asset to a man who moved in the very best social circles.

All these thoughts ran around Victoria's head in a matter of seconds. If she handled it properly, she wouldn't appear to lose face. 'I'll be seeing her later about the menu, I'll have words with her then.' Her hand fell from the door knob and she returned to the table. 'Would you like me to serve the fish, Father?'

'Edwina, perhaps you would prefer to serve?'

To show she was standing full square behind her eldest daughter, Edwina declined. 'No, I think Victoria is quite capable.'

Robert didn't miss the exchange of glances between Abbie and Nigel. Like himself, they were probably asking themselves why their mother and sister were so different in nature to themselves. He'd been asking himself this for years, but it was a question he could not find an answer to.

Robert had taken time out from the office that afternoon to visit the jewellers and pick up the locket he'd bought for Maureen. He was gazing at the two names he'd had engraved on the back of it when there was a light tap on the door. Quickly putting it back in the box, he opened a drawer in his desk and slipped it inside. 'Come in.'

Abbie's face appeared around the door. 'Are you busy, Dad,

or have you got five minutes? I didn't want to say anything at dinner because of the tension in the air after Victoria's rudeness to Agnes.'

'Come in, dear, I'm not busy. I was spending time wondering why some people are nice, and some are not. I'd had a perfectly happy day, starting off with Agnes and Kitty letting me in on one of their pranks which had me laughing all day. And when I repeated it to Nigel and Jeff, their lives were also made brighter because of these two women who have very little in the way of material possessions. But what they do have they are more than willing to share.'

'Tell me what they did, Dad, I could do with a laugh.'

It was easy for Robert to take off the two women; all he had to do was go back to his roots. And he soon had Abbie chuckling. Then he pushed his chair back. 'This is the best bit, and I'll have to stand up to do it justice.' Lacing his hands across his tummy he craned his neck as though talking to someone much taller. ' "I find it *incomprehensible* that yer didn't say right out that yer weren't going to do those bleedin' truffles." '

Abbie rocked with laughter. 'Oh Dad, aren't they priceless? Wouldn't the world be a much better place if everyone was like them? It goes to show that you don't need money to be happy.'

'Agnes is probably feeling pretty rotten right now, and I wouldn't blame her. She works very hard, is excellent at her job, yet gets little praise. So how about you and I going to the kitchen and cheering her up with our impersonations?'

'Oh yes, I'd love that! Can I go and get Nigel, so he can have a laugh? It would show Agnes that we love and appreciate her. And anyway, what I came to see you about concerns him, so it's two birds with one stone.'

'Run along then, while I pour a glass of whisky as a peace offering.'

Agnes had just sat down after washing the mountain of dishes and pans, when Robert and his two children came in.

'If ye're after anything to eat, yer can get it yerselves 'cos I'm bushed,' she snapped.

Robert and his daughter had rehearsed what they would say. Now, with a hand behind his back holding the glass of whisky, he said, 'No, nothing like that, Agnes. I inadvertently put some important papers down and for the life of me I can't think where.'

A bell was starting to ring in the housekeeper's head, but it was so low she didn't pay much attention to it. 'Well, I haven't seen them, Mr Robert.'

Abbie came to stand in front of her. 'I find it incomprehensible that yer don't know where the bleedin' things are.'

The first part of Agnes to shake, was her bosom. This was followed by her tummy, then rip-roaring laughter. 'So yer heard about it, did yer?'

'Heard *and* saw, Agnes,' Robert beamed. 'I was outside the kitchen door when Kitty came in, then I popped my head around to find the pair of you hanging on to each other and laughing your socks off.'

'Well, if yer can't have a laugh, yer may as well die off, Mr Robert. And yer must admit it was bloody funny. That Kitty Higgins is a godsend, believe me. I can be up to me neck in work, or in a blazing temper over something, but it just takes one smile from her and I forget me work and temper. But I'll tell yer something, and it's gospel. If it weren't for Kitty, and you three living in this house, I'd be long gone. I know I shouldn't say it 'cos ye're her father, but that Miss Victoria needs a bloody good hiding.'

'I'm not going to excuse her, Agnes, she's old enough to make her own apologies. And I know you are well able to stick up for your rights. But if the time ever comes when I think you are unable to, that's when I'll step in.' Robert brought his hand around with a flourish. 'This whisky is not in place of an apology, Agnes, it's for giving us all such a good laugh today. And that includes Jeff, who was in stitches.'

'Dad, we all were,' Nigel said. 'We were laughing so much

all the people in the café were laughing too, even though they hadn't a clue what was going on.'

Agnes lifted the glass. 'Given with a good heart, and accepted with a good heart. God bless yer, Mr Robert.'

'By the way, Agnes, just out of curiosity. Who would you say the winner was today? You or Kitty?'

'Good heavens, we don't have no winners or losers! Kitty wins one day, I win the next. Mind you, I can't see me winning tomorrow, there were sixteen bleedin' letters in that word yer gave her. That's going to take some beating.'

'I'll put my thinking cap on, Agnes, and see what I can come up with.'

'I will too!' Nigel offered. 'I'll have a look through the dictionary and write down any I find. But as you say, Agnes, sixteen letters is going to be hard to beat.'

The housekeeper took a sip of whisky, then a sly smile crept across her face. 'Make a word up, Mr Nigel. Kitty won't know the difference.'

'You wouldn't do that to her, would you?' Robert put on a stern look. 'That would be cheating, Agnes Weatherby.'

'Nah, I was only kidding. I wouldn't do that to Kitty, she's me mate.'

Abbie put her arm across the housekeeper's shoulders. 'We're your mates, too, Agnes, don't forget. And because you're like one of the family, I'm going to let you into a secret. I told you that Nigel and I had met up with our old schoolfriends, didn't I? Well, they go dancing and they pulled our legs when we told them we couldn't dance. So we're going to have lessons and take them by surprise one night.'

'Oh, that's good, Miss Abbie! I used to dance when I was your age, but the old legs wouldn't be up to it now.'

'Old! Listen to me, Agnes,' Robert said. 'You're a few years younger than me, so if you're old I must be ancient!'

'We'll put your legs to the test, Agnes, when we've had a few lessons. I'll waltz you round the kitchen until you're dizzy.'

'I'll take yer up on that, Mr Nigel. When do yer start these lessons?'

It was Abbie who answered. 'We don't know yet. But in college today I got friendly with a girl who told me she went to a dancing school in Queens Drive. It's run by a man and wife, and they also give private tuition.'

Robert chucked her under the chin. 'So it wasn't only squiggles you learned today, eh? Do you know where on Queens Drive the school is?'

'I've done better than that, Dad, I've got a phone number. The girl at college had it written in her diary and she gave it to me.'

'Then go and ring now to book a lesson!'

'I was going to ask you to do it, Dad, because I'd go all shy and wouldn't know what to say. So will you be an angel and ring for me?'

'On one condition. While Nigel is waltzing Agnes around the kitchen floor, I will have the pleasure of being your partner.'

Abbie was delighted. 'It's a deal.'

'Come along then, let's book your first lesson.' Robert laid a hand on the housekeeper's arm. 'I'll see you later, Agnes.'

Abbie ran on ahead while Nigel brought up the rear. 'Don't make it for tomorrow night, Dad, because I've promised to give Bobby a driving lesson.'

The housekeeper watched the door close on them. The tide was turning for those three people, and it wasn't before time. Miss Abbie had always been a free spirit, but her enthusiasm for life had been kept in check by those two miserable, conniving women who were at that moment sitting in the drawing room probably pulling some poor soul to pieces. Mr Nigel had broken through the chains that had bound him to them, and was working towards living like any normal twenty-one-year-old. He'd grown closer to his father, too, which was a good thing. Abbie had always been her father's daughter and never ceased to show her love for him.

Now Mr Nigel was beginning to show the same love.

A picture that had caused her much sadness over the last few weeks, flashed through the housekeeper's mind. It was the dressing-room off the main bedroom. And in that dressing-room was the single bed she made up each day, and hadn't mentioned to a living soul, even Kitty. That a man who gave so much to so many should be reduced to this by a wife who was cold and unloving, just wasn't fair. If ever a man needed love it was Mr Robert.

Agnes lifted her glass to the closed door. 'To my family. May God bless them.'

In the study, Robert put the telephone back on the hook and turned a smiling face to his two children. 'Wednesday night, a quarter to seven, for a one-hour lesson. It's the only time they could manage because the dancing school opens at eight. Their name is Ross and as both husband and wife are teachers you will each have your own partner. Oh, the fee will be one and sixpence each.'

'Oh Dad, you really are wonderful and I love you to bits.'

'Yes, jolly good, Dad.' Nigel's face showed he was apprehensive already. 'I hope I don't make a fool of myself. I have tried once or twice, when I've been to a ball with Victoria and her friends, but I was so clumsy I trod all over my partners' feet.'

'Nigel!' Abbie scolded. 'We are not to have any change of heart or doubts. This is something we have to be positive about, otherwise what will Milly and Bobby have to say? I'm determined to be at least as good as Milly, nothing else will satisfy me. So be strong and firm with yourself. Keep saying over and over that if Bobby can do it, so can you.'

'Now you two are sorted out, would you think it rude if I asked you to leave? I've brought a few letters home from the office which I want time to read thoroughly before sending a reply.' Robert was suddenly feeling the need to have some time on his own. The locket had brought thoughts of Maureen and he wanted to be alone with those thoughts. 'I'll see you later at suppertime.'

'Yes, OK, Dad.' Abbie linked her arm through her brother's and as they left the room she was saying, 'We'll have to get proper dancing shoes tomorrow.'

Robert waited a while before opening the drawer and taking out the black square box with the name *Boodle & Dunthorne* written in gold on the lid. He stared at it for several minutes picturing the dear, beloved face of the woman he hoped would like his gift and wear it always around her neck so he was forever in her thoughts. Then he opened the box and took out the locket. Rubbing a finger gently over the names engraved on the back, his longing to see Maureen was so deep it was like a pain in his heart. Only when he was in her company did he feel like a man who was loved. Oh, he was loved by the children, and many other people, but it was a different kind of love. On the night, all those years ago, when his wife had rejected him, the look of repulsion on her face as she did so had stripped him of his pride. He'd felt worthless; a man whose wife couldn't even bear him to touch her. And it had taken a long time to regain his self-esteem. He'd been a man in his thirties, with red blood running through his veins, a man of passion. But he would never force himself on his wife, his pride wouldn't allow him to do that. So twice, in desperation, he had sought the services of a prostitute. He knew many of the men who were respectable members of his club had a mistress or visited the homes of prostitutes, and he thought he could live with that. But he couldn't, he found it degrading.

Robert took off his jacket and hung it on the back of his chair. Then he undid the studs at the front and back of his collar and breathed a sigh of relief at the freedom to move his neck without the collar rubbing away at it. Then he sat down, stretched his legs out under the desk and allowed his thoughts to wander. He so looked forward to his monthly visit to Maureen's, but lately he was finding it wasn't enough. Every day something would crop up and he'd think, I'll have to tell her about this, or I wish I could ask her advice on that. She was his soulmate, and he needed to be with her more. And if he was, who would he be hurting? Not his wife, certainly, because there were times when she looked at him with such hatred it frightened him. She wouldn't care if he died and she never had to set eyes on him again.

Robert leaned his elbows on the desk, and covering his face with both hands, he let out a long sigh. Whatever happened, whatever he did, Edwina had brought it on herself. Every man needed the arms of a woman to hold him, and her lips to kiss him. A woman whose eyes would tell of her feelings for him, as they sat on the couch holding hands. A woman who made him feel a complete man again, and would give him the contentment he desperately longed for. And for him, that woman was Maureen, who he knew returned his feelings. They'd been discreet for the sake of respectability, but what nonsense it was to waste so many years for fear of what other people thought.

His resolve strengthened, Robert dropped his hands, placed the locket back in the box and returned it to the drawer. Then he reached for a sheet of notepaper from the wooden stand and laid it down in front of him. He didn't have to think about what to write, he knew. He would be calling at Maureen's on Thursday night about seven. She wasn't to worry, there was nothing wrong, he just had a desire to see her. He then folded the letter and put it in an envelope and sealed it down. But he didn't address it, for fear of prying eyes. He would do that tomorrow just before posting it.

When Agnes knocked with his last cup of tea of the day, she found him sitting in his chair in his shirt sleeves, with his thumbs hooked on to his maroon braces. His jacket was draped over the back of the chair and his collar and tie were lying on the desk. 'My goodness, Mr Robert, ye're looking very free and easy tonight. Yer look like a man who's shed his cares one by one. It's a good job I didn't come later when yer might have had even less on!'

232

Robert grinned. 'Had that happened, which is very unlikely, Agnes, I would have been more embarrassed than you. I admit my clothes are in a state of disarray, but as I'm comfortable, why worry? This study is my bolt-hole, away from yapping tongues and conversations spiked with spite and sarcasm. And in that comment I do not include Nigel or Abbie.'

'You do what yer like, Mr Robert, it's your bleedin' house.' The housekeeper tried to sit on the edge of the desk but her bottom kept sliding off, so she gave it up as bad job and settled for leaning against it. 'I've a little bit of news for yer. Miss Victoria came to see me, and although it wasn't an outright apology, it's the nearest anyone will ever get from her. In fact, in a roundabout way, she practically said we were all at fault except her! We had misconstrued her words. Of course she didn't expect me to see to the whole dinner party on my own, and we were all fools to have thought that was what she meant. Anyway, she'll be happy for Jessie to help serve at table and she'll leave everything in my capable hands.'

'There was never any doubt about the outcome, Agnes – this party seems to mean quite a lot to her. I can't for the life of me think why, but then my eldest daughter is a mystery to me in many ways. Did you come to an agreement, then?'

'Not much point in doing otherwise. It's a waste of time trying to talk sense with Miss Victoria, it's like water off a duck's back. She has a way of looking through yer, as though ye're not there at all. I've got to say she gets on me wick sometimes, but we've all got our faults, I suppose. It's just that she's got more than others.' The housekeeper's eyes fell on the letter propped up by the ink-well. 'D'yer want me to post that for yer tomorrow, Mr Robert?'

'No thank you, Agnes, I need to root the address out first. You poppy off to your room and put your feet up. You work a very long day and you need to rest.'

Agnes was about to say he could do with getting some rest, too, when she reminded herself of the situation. He seldom went into the drawing room these days, preferring the study, even though there wasn't the same comfort. And that single bed upstairs was far too small for a man of his size, he couldn't possibly get a good night's sleep. How long did he think he could keep that up for? 'Why don't yer bring one of the armchairs out of the drawing room into here, Mr Robert? If ye're going to work here, yer may as well do it in comfort.'

Robert caught and held her eyes. He was well aware that she knew he and Edwina were no longer even sleeping in the same bed, and he was more than grateful that the housekeeper had never, by word or deed, mentioned it. He also knew that his affairs were safe in her hands; she would never discuss them with others. Even Kitty, her closest friend. 'I'll sort myself out eventually, Agnes, have no fear. But your concern for me is very much appreciated, I want you to know that. You are a good friend to me.'

'It's easy to be that, Mr Robert, 'cos ye're one of life's gentlemen. And the best boss I've ever had.' Agnes straightened herself and smoothed down the front of her overall. 'But just 'cos I like yer doesn't mean I won't try and beat yer at dancing. You just wait until Mr Nigel takes me for a waltz, yer won't believe yer eyes.'

'Are you that good, Agnes?'

'I bet I'm the best baby elephant yer ever saw dancing. All I'm short of is a trunk.'

'Come now, Agnes, I bet you dance like a ballerina.' Robert stretched his arms over his head. 'I think I'll drink my tea, smoke a cigar and then have a stroll in the garden. I have a slight headache and the fresh air will do me good.'

'I'll leave yer in peace, then. Goodnight and God bless, Mr Robert.'

'Goodnight and God bless, Agnes.'

Robert saw the lights go out in the drawing room and looked at his watch. He'd wait for half an hour, to give Edwina time to prepare for bed, and hopefully be asleep before he went up. He had no appetite for any verbal exchange with his wife because it served no purpose and would most certainly bring back his headache. So to while away the time he opened the evening paper, seeking articles he might have missed earlier.

However, he might just as well have gone upstairs, because Edwina was sitting up in bed waiting for him. As soon as he opened the door, she switched on her bedside lamp. He inclined his head, feeling the need to acknowledge her presence, then walked towards the dressing-room.

'I've been waiting for you,' Edwina said, bedclothes up to her chin. 'I wish to talk to you.'

'Can't it wait until tomorrow? I really am very tired.'

'No, it can't! I'm very angry that you never take Victoria's side in an argument. You barely speak to her, yet seem to have plenty of time for Nigel and Abbie. You make it very clear that they are your favourites, but if you were a good father you would treat all your children alike.'

'If I ever thought Victoria was in the right, then I would most certainly take her side. But unfortunately, to my mind she is never in the right. She seems to be under the impression we were all put on this earth solely for her benefit, and should bend to her will. And you are the one who has encouraged her to be so. You talk of favourites, Edwina, but Victoria has always been your favourite; she can do no wrong in your eyes. You couldn't give a toss for Nigel and Abbie, and never have.' He turned once more towards the dressing-room door. 'And now you've said what you wished to say, I'll bid you goodnight.'

'There is another matter I would like to discuss with you. I would like you to return to sleeping in this bed. You are giving the servants something to talk about, and I imagine our neighbours are all aware of your peculiar sleeping arrangements.'

Robert closed his eyes and took a deep breath. Had this woman no sense or feeling? She wanted him in her bed, not because he was her husband whose rightful place was by her side, but because she was afraid of what the neighbours might say. He wouldn't be allowed to touch her, but he should be there to stop people talking about them. Not that he would want to touch her; even the thought turned his stomach.

'You really are quite mad, Edwina. How would the neighbours know what our sleeping arrangements are? And would my sleeping in your bed really be a lesser evil than being a topic of conversation in the neighbourhood?'

'Agnes makes that bed up every morning so is well aware of what is going on. And she is as thick as thieves with that Tilly Woods, next door's housekeeper. You can't tell me they haven't had a good gossip about it.'

'I'm not going to tell you what Agnes or anyone else talks about because I don't know. I do happen to have more faith in her than you do, though, and I believe she is beyond tittle-tattle. But one thing I do know, and I'm very sure of it: I will never again sleep in the same bed as you. You may bear my name, Edwina, but in my mind you are no longer my wife. You chose the path you wanted to walk down, and I have no desire to join you on that path. Our marriage is a sham, so why pretend otherwise? I regret the chains that bind us, and if it was possible, I would break them. Now, I'll say goodnight.'

Robert didn't look back as he closed the dressing-room door behind him.

Chapter Fourteen

Edwina was awake early the next morning, having tossed and turned all night as her mind ranted against her husband. Why did he still feel it necessary to mingle with the working class, and behave like them at times? Couldn't he have learned to move with the wealth they now had and leave the past behind? As she herself had learned to do. Never for one second did it occur to her that without the husband she had now come to detest, they would still be living in the two-up, two-down in Seaforth.

The sound of a car engine starting up had her sliding her legs over the side of the bed and hurrying to the window. Nigel's car was the first out of the gates, followed by Robert's. It was a sight that heightened the rage boiling within her. Thanks to her husband, her son had changed so much he barely spoke to her. And why did they have to go out at this ungodly hour every day as if they had to clock on at a job where someone else was boss? The family owned the firm, for heaven's sake! It was ridiculous for them to get there the same time as the employees. There was no one to tell them what they could or could not do. They could take the day off without having to explain themselves to a soul. But no, her husband preferred to think of himself as a worker, rather than the boss.

Edwina stood by the window for a while, her head heavy with dark thoughts. Rubbing a hand across her forehead, she blamed her husband for her sleepless night. Life in the house would be perfect but for him; he was the blot on her landscape. He didn't even care what people thought of them, or whether the whole road knew they no longer shared the same bed. This showed that while his bank balance had moved on, his mind had stayed in the gutter.

A movement at the gate had Edwina pulling the net curtain back. It was Abbie, swinging the briefcase Robert had bought her for her birthday. That was another black mark against her husband. Her youngest daughter would soon be made to toe the line if he wasn't here. The very idea of one of the Dennison girls going out to work was unthinkable. How could she expect to catch a rich husband when she was a working girl? She should have been made to go to finishing school for a year, then seek a man who would make her a suitable husband, as her sister had. Victoria was practically engaged to Charles Chisholm, the most eligible bachelor in the city. He was a marvellous catch, and when it was known he was getting engaged to Victoria Dennison, there would be a lot of disappointed mothers.

Edwina turned from the window, rubbing her temples. She needed something to dispel the headache, otherwise it would linger all day. Intending to pull the heavy cord which would summon Agnes, she was halfway across the room when she changed her mind. It would pay her to be extra nice to the housekeeper, to worm her way into her good books. And a few words dropped as to why her husband was sleeping in the dressing-room might put an end to any gossip already in circulation. So slipping on a dressing gown, she made her way down the stairs to the kitchen.

Kitty and Jessie were sitting at the table with Agnes, having their morning cuppa, when the kitchen door opened and Edwina entered. The two cleaners became rigid; both were terrified of the woman who could reduce them to tears with her sarcastic and cruel tongue. And they wouldn't dare answer back for fear of losing their job.

'Is this what you get paid for?' Edwina was looking for someone to vent her anger on and these two useless excuses for human beings were ideal. 'I'll thank you to get out of my sight before I send you packing.'

Chairs were being pushed back when Agnes lifted her hand. 'Stay where you are.' She pointed to the clock on the wall. 'They aren't supposed to start until eight o'clock, Miss Edwina, and as yer can see, there's another six minutes to go.'

Taken aback, Edwina floundered. 'I have a splitting headache and am in no mood to argue. But make sure they are off those chairs and hard at work in five minutes. Now, Agnes, I would like you to mix a headache powder and bring it to my room.'

'Right away, Miss Edwina. And if I were you I'd lie down with the curtains closed for an hour, until ye're feeling better.'

With a curt nod, Edwina stalked out of the room. She left behind her a lot of ill-feeling. 'Did yer ever know anyone like her?' The housekeeper was blazing. 'The bloody airs and graces she puts on, anyone would think she was royalty.'

'She's a stuck-up cow, that's what she is,' Kitty said shakily. 'But she's the one with the bleedin' money and we're the poor sods who have to take anything she wants to throw at us. Nobody ever said life was fair, queen, 'cos it ruddy well ain't.' Sighing, she got to her feet. 'Come on, girl, let's get cracking in case the queer one decides to keep an eye on us. It's a pity it's only a headache she's got and not an upset tummy what keeps her running to the lavvy all day.'

Jessie's head was nodding fast in agreement. 'If I was ever given three wishes, I know what the first one would be. I'd change places with her for a day and see how she likes being treated the way she treats us. I wouldn't half put her through it. I'd make her work until the sweat was pouring off her.'

Agnes chuckled. 'Posh people don't sweat, sunshine, they perspire. Anyway, I'd better get the drink up to her otherwise it'll give her something else to moan about. Long bloody string of misery, that's what she is.' As she mixed the headache powder in a glass of warm water, the housekeeper muttered, 'I wonder if she took lessons in being miserable? If she did, her teacher deserves a medal for doing such a good job. I've never

in me life known anyone as bad-tempered or as bloomin'
cantankerous as her.'

It was as she was climbing the stairs that Agnes began to
acquire a temper of her own. She was the one who was
supposed to supervise the staff, to tell them what to do and
make sure they did it properly. Miss Edwina was undermining
her position by sticking her nose in where it wasn't wanted.

This was the thought in the housekeeper's head as she
knocked on the bedroom door before entering. 'Yer drink,
Miss Edwina, and I'd suggest yer get it down yer while it's still
warm 'cos it's more effective then.' She stood in front of the
woman waiting for her to drink the sedative before airing her
complaint. Best if everyone knew the rules so there was no
misunderstanding. The kitchen was her domain and she did
not welcome interference. But to her surprise, Edwina made
no attempt to put the glass to her lips.

'I was in the wrong downstairs, Agnes, and I can only
apologise. I've been plagued with dreadful headaches for
weeks now and I'm not getting a decent night's sleep, which is
making me bad-tempered.' The lies had been well rehearsed.
'I'm so restless at night, Robert has taken to sleeping in the
dressing-room. But then you know that, as you make up his
bed each day. I'm so glad it was decided that you should take
care of our bedroom, and not the cleaners. I would hate them
to misconstrue the situation and spread false rumours.'

The expression on Agnes's face didn't change, but in her
head she was coming up with all sorts of names that would
apply to the woman facing her. Liar came top of the list,
followed by bad-minded, crafty, and polished. She must think
I was born yesterday, if she expects me to believe that little
gem of a lie, she thought. Well, two can play at that game. 'I
thought it must be something like that, Miss Edwina, 'cos Mr
Robert isn't daft enough to sleep on that small bed unless he's
got a good reason.'

Edwina's eyes narrowed. Did she detect a note of sarcasm?
No, the housekeeper's face was that of an innocent baby. 'I

keep reminding him that he needs his sleep, and I've tried every way I know to get him back into the big bed. But to no avail. He gets very irritated with my tossing and turning.'

'I can sympathise with that; there's nothing worse than someone twitching when ye're trying to sleep.' This came from a woman who had never slept in the same bed as another person since she was a very small girl, when her mother used to let her into the big bed for a cuddle when her father had left for work. 'Let's hope yer headaches come to an end pretty soon, eh?'

'I'm sure they will, Agnes, and I thank you for being so understanding.'

'I'll leave yer to your drink now and hope it does the trick.' Agnes made to move away, paused, then stepped back. 'Miss Edwina, I do keep an eye on the cleaners, yer know. I was under the impression that was part of my job. And I thought yer were satisfied with my work. But when yer complain, as yer did before, it's really me ye're ticking off and I find it unfair and very hurtful. The running of the house is my responsibility and when yer have a complaint I would ask that yer come to me with it, not Kitty or Jessie. If they have two people telling them what to do it will be very confusing for them and their work will suffer.'

'I understand, Agnes, and I have said I was in the wrong. It's these confounded headaches that are causing me to be short-tempered.'

'All the more reason to hope they come to an end pretty soon, then.' The housekeeper would like to have said she must have had the headaches continuously for ten years because she had never been anything else but miserable and short-tempered. But the woman wasn't worth wasting any more of her breath on. 'I'll see to breakfast for you and Miss Victoria now, I can hear her moving about.' When she got to the door she couldn't resist asking, 'Will you be wanting a full breakfast? I mean, I was wondering whether yer'd have any appetite with having such a bad headache?'

'I want a full breakfast served, Agnes. Never let it be said I allowed standards to slip because of a headache.'

The housekeeper closed the bedroom door behind her and putting a finger inside her white mobcap, she scratched her head. The woman was completely mad. No getting away from it, she was tuppence short of a shilling. There'd only be two people for breakfast in that ruddy big dining room, but she had to go through the whole rigmarole of silver serving dishes and enough food to feed a big family. A waste of good ingredients, just so a woman who lived in a different world to everyone else, could keep up the standards. Well, if that's what she wanted, that's what she'd get. But the food that was over wasn't going to go in the midden, that was a dead cert.

Looking around for a sign of the cleaner, Agnes grinned when she caught sight of Kitty's feet and bottom sticking out of Miss Abbie's room and moving in and out as she brushed the carpet with a small stiff brush. Mr Robert had bought them one of the new-fangled vacuum cleaners, but the little woman was terrified of it. She said when she switched it on it ran away with her. So she and Jessie switched rooms every day so that each room got vacuumed every other day. The young girl loved the machine, she was like a child with a new toy.

Agnes kept her voice low because Miss Victoria's room was next door. 'Kitty!'

The cleaner sat back on her heels. 'Yes, queen?'

'Don't spend the day worrying about the menu for you and Alf's dinner tonight, 'cos it's all sorted. Ye're having bacon, sausage, kidneys, mushrooms and tomatoes.'

Kitty's mouth gaped. 'Go 'way, queen! Yer not having me on, I hope, 'cos me mouth is watering now at the thought.'

'Scout's honour, sunshine. All courtesy of Miss Edwina. Mind you, she doesn't know it, but what the eye don't see, the heart don't grieve after.'

'Ay, that's the gear, that is, queen! I'll work with a vengeance now and I won't say one bad word against you-know-who. Not

242

out loud anyhow. What goes on in me head is a different matter 'cos it's got a mind of its own.'

The housekeeper put a finger to her lips. 'Silence is golden, sunshine.'

'I get yer, queen, and yer can rely on me. After all, it's me and my Alf what's going to eat like toffs tonight.'

'It's like working for two different families in this house.' It was the half-past ten tea break and Agnes was holding forth at the kitchen table. 'Seven o'clock I'm serving breakfast to Mr Robert, Mr Nigel and Miss Abbie. They eat in here, insist on me having me breakfast with them, and we have a ruddy good laugh. Bacon, egg and toast, that's all. No messing with fancy dishes or three knives and forks each, they eat with the kitchen crockery and cutlery. Just one big happy family, and I'm privileged to be treated like one of them.' She put down her cup, knowing her temperature was going to rise and she didn't want to risk any spillage. 'Then, an hour after they leave, I've got to put me different hat on and wait on Tilly Mint and Tilly Flop. Nothing but the best for them. We mustn't let the standard fall because there's only two of them, so it's silver service and the lot.'

'I've often wondered,' Pete said, stroking his chin thoughtfully, 'whether the Missus is all there on top?'

'Well, wonder no more, lad!' Kitty grinned as she punched him playfully on his arm. ''Cos she's as mad as a bleedin' hatter.'

Now the gardener had a very dry sense of humour; you could never tell by his face whether he was having you on. 'Yer know, I could have sworn it was the March hare that was mad, not the hatter.'

Kitty opened her mouth wide and rolled her eyes. 'Does it make any bleedin' difference who it was, as long as they were as mad as Tilly Mint?'

Agnes loved to see the cleaner's face when it became animated. The eyes flashed, the lips pursed then changed to a straight line, and the forehead rose and fell. 'D'yer mean Tilly Mint, or Tilly Flop, sunshine?'

'Don't you bleedin' well start, Aggie Weatherby, or I'll clock yer one. Whether I mean Mint or Flop, they're both crazy as coots.'

'Right, seeing as we've got that settled to everyone's satisfaction, let's move on to a more pleasant subject. I asked if I could tell yer this, so don't be thinking I'm telling tales out of school 'cos I'm not.' Agnes picked up her cup and held it between her chubby hands. No chance of spilling any when she wasn't likely to be waving her arms around in excitement. 'Mr Nigel and Miss Abbie are going for dancing lessons. They're having their first one tomorrow night. And Mr Nigel has promised he'll waltz me around the kitchen as soon as he's learned a few steps.'

'Ay, there's not half a lot of changes going on here, isn't there?' Kitty wriggled to the edge of the chair so her feet could touch the floor. 'You see it all, queen, 'cos ye're here all the time. We have to rely on you to tell us what's happening, so come on, we haven't got all day, spill the beans.'

'There's certainly changes in the two youngsters. In a matter of weeks, Mr Nigel has turned from a boy to a man. He's more talkative and much more carefree. And he's got a good sense of humour.'

'Ye're right, Aggie,' Pete said. 'The best thing that's happened to him is starting work. He's out all day, away from the two women who used to run his life for him.'

The housekeeper nodded. 'My sentiments entirely, Pete. They had him in their clutches all right, treated him like a lap-dog. But he's broke away and they'll never get him back. Him and Miss Abbie have taken up with their old school-friends again, and they don't live in posh houses like this, they're ordinary working-class folk. And that's where the dancing lessons come in. Mr Nigel's friend is called Bobby, and he likes to go jazzing every night. Same as Milly, who's Miss Abbie's friend. So, not to be outdone, our two are going for private lessons to surprise them.'

Jessie, her pretty face alight, said, 'My mam said I can go to a dance when I'm older. So if Mr Nigel teaches you, Aggie, you can teach me.'

'I can teach yer, queen! Just watch this.' Kitty jumped to her feet and made for the space in the kitchen where she could demonstrate. Lifting her skirts, she began to sing 'I'm Only a Bird in a Gilded Cage, a Beautiful Sight to See.' She swayed from side to side as she sang, her skirt held wide. Then she began to twirl to the tune, and much to the delight of everyone, she didn't only have a sweet voice, she could dance as well. Her old scruffy clothes and worn out boots took nothing away from her performance. If she'd been dressed in a beautiful ballgown she couldn't have delighted her audience more. And when she came to a stop, they gave her a well-deserved round of applause.

Jessie clapped her hands before rushing to hug the woman who had surprised and delighted her. 'That was lovely, Kitty! Oh, you are clever.'

Pete nodded in agreement. 'Turn-up for the book, that was. I would never have believed it if I hadn't seen it with me own eyes. Yer've got the voice of an angel and the grace of one of those swans on the lake in Sefton Park.'

'Ye're a dark horse, sunshine,' Agnes nodded. 'I've known yer for five years and that's the first time I've heard yer sing or seen yer dance. I think you could teach Mr Nigel, save him spending money out on private lessons.'

Kitty was flushed with the praise. 'Not much call for dancing or singing, is there, queen? The only place yer can even have a laugh is here, in the kitchen. The rest of the house is so quiet it's like a bleedin' cemetery. Most of the time the only sound I can hear is me own breathing, and even then I keep expecting a voice to come behind me telling me to stop making so much noise.'

'I wish Mr Robert had been here to see yer,' Agnes said. 'He would really have enjoyed it. In fact, I wouldn't have put it past him to ask yer if he could partner yer.'

'Aye, and pigs might fly, queen. But I enjoy dancing, and me and my Alf often move the chairs back in the living room and have a twirl. He's a good dancer, is my husband.'

'Ah, well, we've had a few surprises today!' The house-keeper glanced at the clock. 'It's nearly time to break it up. But another little bit of news before yer go. Mr Nigel is taking his friend Bobby out in the car tonight, and he's going to teach him to drive. So what with dancing lessons, and driving lessons, we should have plenty to talk about. Things are definitely looking up in the Dennison residence and I'm delighted.'

'I could probably give the lad driving lessons.' There was mischief written on Kitty's face. 'My Alf is always saying I drive him up the wall.'

'If yer don't get back to work, the three of yer, I know someone who'll be driving yer down the path, and telling yer not to bother to come back again. So scram!'

'God, ye're a bleedin' slave-driver, Aggie Weatherby. I'll not be entertaining yer again with me singing and dancing, if that's all the thanks I get.' The little woman got to her feet and jerked her head at Jessie. 'Come on, queen, I know when I'm not wanted. Honest, there's just no pleasing some people.'

'I'll sell tickets next time yer give a performance, sunshine! Tilly from next door would come, and the housekeeper from twenty-six. I might as well make a few coppers out of yer talents if I can.'

'Cheeky bugger!' Kitty pushed Jessie through the door, muttering, 'She's that bleedin' tight she'd pinch the eye out of yer head and then come back for the socket.'

Nigel was feeling very happy and contented as he stopped outside the Jamiesons' house. He'd enjoyed his day at work, knowing he was making good progress and pleasing his father and Jeff. Now he was looking forward to giving his old friend a driving lesson. He knew Bobby would pretend to act daft,

246

like he always did, but Nigel was determined to make a driver of him so he would stand a chance of getting himself a better job. And right now he'd be like a cat on hot bricks waiting for him.

Abbie pushed herself off the passenger seat and turned to talk through the open door. 'What time will you be picking me up, Nigel?'

'Are you and Milly going out, or are you staying in for a gossip?'

'We're going to the pictures. The Broadway I think, to see *Devil and the Deep*. Gary Cooper and Tallulah Bankhead are in it, so it should be good. But I'll be glad when we've had a few dancing lessons because I know Milly would much rather be going dancing. I can't expect her to give it up just because I've come on the scene.'

'No, I feel the same about Bobby. But we have our first lesson tomorrow, so at least we've made a start. And you never know, we might turn out to be good at it.'

'I hope so.' As Abbie stood up she saw a familiar figure hurrying towards them. 'Oh, aye, here comes trouble.' She said it loud enough for Bobby to hear. 'I don't fancy being you, Nigel, because this one will probably end up wrapping the car around a tree.'

Bobby was rubbing his hands and grinning broadly. He hadn't closed his eyes in bed last night, his tummy was doing cartwheels. And in work today the men had been telling him to put a sock in it because they were fed up hearing about the ruddy driving lesson. But he wasn't about to tell Abbie that. 'No, yer've got it wrong there, girl. During the first lesson I run into a brick wall. Wrapping a car around a tree takes experience, so that'll be during lesson two or three. That's if Nige isn't a nervous wreck after tonight.' He sounded more cocky than he felt. 'I think I'm going to take to it like a duck to water, though. I have every confidence in meself.'

Abbie moved away so Bobby could slip into the passenger seat. 'I hope you're right. Anyway, you'll both have a good laugh if nothing else.' She closed the car door and grinned at them through the window. 'Enjoy yourselves and take care.'

'Where are we going, Nige?'

'Somewhere quiet and not too far away. I want to get you started while it's still light so that only gives us just over an hour.' Nigel backed into a side street, then turned the car towards Knowsley Road. 'There's a few fields and lanes near the Old Roan, so we'll head for there.'

Bobby was watching every hand and foot movement. There seemed to be an awful lot to do. What with keeping one hand on the steering wheel and changing gear with the other, and working a foot at the same time, it wasn't going to be a doddle. But if other men could master it, there was no reason why he couldn't. And it would improve his job prospects no end. He was only a labourer now, and he thought that's what he would always be, until his old friend came on the scene. Now his heart was fired with hope and ambition. 'It looks very complicated, Nige. Was there ever a time when yer thought yer'd never get the hang of it?'

'There were many times,' Nigel laughed. 'I'd have given it up as a bad job except for my dad. He was so patient with me, I only kept on because I didn't want to disappoint him. And then one night everything slotted into place. I could change gear smoothly when I wanted to slow down, and when I took my foot off the accelerator the car didn't shudder and jump forward like a kangaroo. I didn't know who was the happiest, me or my dad. We sat in the car in this lane in Halsall somewhere, and we laughed our heads off. Then when we got home I went through to the kitchen, full of myself, lifted Agnes off her feet and spun her around. Honest, anyone would think I was the first person in the world to learn to drive a car.'

'Who's Agnes?'

'She's our housekeeper.'

Bobby's eyes were wide. 'Yer've got a housekeeper?'

Nigel didn't give himself time to think. If Bobby was going to be his friend it was only fair to be honest with him. 'Yes, and we've also got a gardener called Pete, and two cleaners, Kitty and Jessie.'

'Excuse me language, but bloody hell, Nige! What are yer doing with the likes of me?'

'Well, there's two reasons, really. Firstly, you're a friend I've missed in the last ten years and am delighted to have back as a friend. Secondly, what I'm doing with you now, hopefully, is teach you to drive.' Nigel stopped the car in a lane with fields either side. Then he turned to face Bobby. 'We might as well get this sorted out, and then forget it. Everything our family has in the way of money and possessions, is down to the hard work of my father. Apart from him, not one of us has ever earned a penny. Until a few weeks ago, I had never done a hand's turn in my life. That is not something I'm proud of, but it's the truth. But I am not a snob, and neither is my father or Abbie. Do you remember Jeff, who works for my dad?'

'Yeah, I remember him. He used to give us a penny for sweets.'

'Well, I count him among my friends, along with the housekeeper, the cleaners and the gardener. In fact, Agnes is far more than a housekeeper, she's more like a mother to me and Abbie. Any problems, it's her we run to.'

'I notice yer never mentioned yer mam, or Victoria. Why is that?'

'I told you the other night that I would one day sit down and tell you what my life has been like for the last ten years. We can't do it tonight if you are ever going to get behind this steering wheel. But I promise I will tell you, the good and the bad. One thing I will say, though, is that I was very much at home in your house last week, and I am very much at home with you. Now, if it puts you off that my father has worked hard and made a lot of money, then it's not me who's the snob, it's you, Bobby Neary.'

'I'm not a flipping snob. Neither am I put off.' As Bobby gazed at his friend, he realised there had been sadness in his life. Perhaps there still was, because after all money can't buy you everything. Him and his mam had had a rough time, but the worst of their troubles were over. Unless he was very much mistaken, Nigel's were not. 'Listen, mate, are yer going to give me this driving lesson or not? It'll be time to put the light out and go to sleep if yer don't get a move on.'

Nigel grinned. 'OK, let's swap over and I'll show yer where everything is and what it does.' When they'd exchanged places, he said, 'Just look at the dashboard and familiarise yourself with it, then the pedals, gearstick and handbrake. Ask any questions you want, don't be afraid of being thought thick. Don't forget I've been through it myself and know how you feel. The books my dad bought me are in the glove compartment, you can take them home with you and read them from cover to cover. There's illustrations, as well, so spend as much time as you can trying to understand what does what, how and why. Then next time we come out I might even let you switch the engine on.'

'So there's going to be a next time?'

'Of course there is, on Thursday, if that suits you. Unless you chicken out, that is.'

'Blimey! First I'm a snob, now I'm a chicken!' Bobby's cheeky grin came into play. 'Ay, I know a chicken what was a snob. Me mam bought it last Christmas, and it was such a snob it crossed its legs and wouldn't open them to let me mam stuff it. She tried everything, even wrestled with it on the kitchen floor, but couldn't get it to budge. That chicken was determined she wasn't going to get her hand up its backside. She had quite a battle with the ruddy thing, calling it every name under the sun, but she had to give up in the end and stuff it from the neck down.'

Nigel's head fell back and he roared with laughter as he conjured up the imaginary scene as described by Bobby. Mrs Neary had a large vocabulary of swear-words, and the air would have been blue. That's if it had really happened, of course.

'You're incorrigible, d'you know that?'

'Ay, listen, mate, it's going to be hard enough learning how this car works without worrying about you using words the length of our road. So come on, what's this?'

'That is the gearstick.' Nigel was laughing inside. It seemed he was going to be getting a lesson at the same time as Bobby. A lesson on facing adversity by laughing when there was nothing to laugh at. Showing the world a happy face when you were worried sick about the mother you loved. He could be crying inside, but Bobby Neary's pride was too strong to allow this to show. Nigel knew his friend was a stronger, more forceful and outspoken character than he was, but he intended to catch up with him. He couldn't wish for a better role model.

'I'm only picking Abbie up, I won't be staying. Just a quick hello and goodbye.'

'Still, I'll come in with yer,' Bobby said. 'Like yer said, just to say hello and goodbye. Except they'd think I was losing me marbles if I said goodbye instead of ta-ra.'

Nigel's eyes slid sideways, but his friend's face gave nothing away. Yet he must have a reason for wanting to call in at the Jamiesons' this time of night, especially just for a few minutes. 'Are you sure you've not got a soft spot for Milly?'

'I've told yer, Nige, I'm not getting serious with any girl for a few years. Milly's a good mate, a good dancer, but that's it.'

'But what if the Jamiesons don't want visitors this time of night? It is quite late, Bobby, and we might not be welcome.'

'Nah!' Bobby's hand lifted the knocker and rapped twice. 'The Jamiesons are not like that. They make everyone welcome.'

The door was opened by Milly, who had heard Bobby's words. 'We make most people welcome, Robert Neary, but there are times when we draw the line. For instance we wouldn't welcome drunks, or tramps.'

'That's all right, then.' Bobby pushed past her. 'If I wasn't welcome, yer wouldn't have called me by me Sunday name.'

'Come in, boys,' Beryl called. 'And let us know how yer got on.'

'There yer are, yer see.' Bobby put his face close to Milly's and stuck out his tongue. 'Yer mam's glad to see us, anyway.' He whistled as he walked towards the back room, leaving Nigel to shrug his shoulders.

'I did tell him it was too late to call on people, but he wouldn't have it.'

'Oh, aye, he thinks everyone loves him, does Bobby.' Milly lowered her voice. 'Not to worry, Nigel, 'cos he's always welcome in this house. In fact, he'd be made welcome in every house in the road. He's a really good bloke.'

'Yes, I know.' Nigel followed her into the kitchen to where Bobby was standing in the middle of the room with his hands going quicker than his mouth.

'And I was just turning the corner when this feller stepped off the kerb, right in the path of the car, and if I hadn't had me wits about me, and slammed the brake on, I'd have run over him for sure. Nigel's face was as white as a sheet, I thought he was going to pass out.'

'Bobby Neary, you're the biggest liar on God's earth,' Abbie said, trying to keep a straight face. 'How d'you think them all up?'

'It's easy to make lies up. I started, oh, about thirteen years ago. I had a good teacher, though, and that helped. It was a kid who lived in this road then, and she couldn't half come up with some whoppers. She used to go crying to her mam saying I'd pulled her hair, when I hadn't even touched her. Not that I'm saying I wouldn't have done if she hadn't been a better runner than me.'

Abbie remembered the times she'd been out of breath running from this boy. He used to pinch the ribbon from her hair, and tease her to come and get it. 'I never snitched on you to my mother, and you're the only person I know who could stand there and tell such bare-faced lies.'

Nigel went one better. 'He's the only person I know who can nearly run over a bloke with a stationary car!'

Bobby waited for the laughter to die down, then he spread out his hands. 'See, two snitches in one family. Yer can't help feeling sorry for them.'

Chapter Fifteen

Abbie was sitting on the padded stool in front of her dressing table, when Nigel came in. 'You're not ready yet, are you?' she asked, dismayed. 'I'll be another quarter of an hour.'

'No, I'm not ready. I've just been down to ask Agnes to keep our dinner back until half-past eight.' Nigel looked uneasy. 'I really think we should tell Mother, don't you? We can't cut her out of our lives completely, it wouldn't be fair.'

'I have been thinking about that.' Abbie met his eyes in the dressing-table mirror. 'I can't say I fancy it because she's bound to have something to say which will take the pleasure out of our evening, she always has. But you're right – she is our mother and we can't cut her out of our lives. Shall we go along to her room now, and get it over with?'

Her brother looked relieved. 'You'll come with me, then?'

'Of course I will.' Abbie put down the silver-backed brush she'd been using on her hair. 'We haven't got a lot of time, you know, so don't let her keep us talking.'

Edwina looked surprised when she saw the children, but there was no smile of pleasure or friendly greeting. 'This is most unusual, is it something urgent?'

'No, nothing like that, Mother.' Nigel found she still had the power to make him feel small and worthless. 'Abbie and I won't be having our dinner at half-past seven, we've asked Agnes to keep it until we get home. We thought we should tell you.'

Edwina's distaste could be seen in her raised brows and thin lips pressed in a straight line. 'Really, this is no good; we can't be changing mealtimes and disrupting the running of the house just on someone's whim. We sit down for our dinner at seven-thirty and I will not tolerate any interruption in the routine. So you must alter your arrangements, and I'll expect to see you at the dining table at the usual time.'

'I'm sorry, Mother, but it's not possible to change the time of our appointment,' Abbie said. 'We would have chosen a later time if we'd been given the choice.'

'In that case, ring up to cancel the appointment and ask for one at a more convenient time. It is bad enough that you and your father have taken it upon yourselves to have an early breakfast, upsetting the whole routine here, but under no circumstances will I allow you to do the same for our evening meal. A house this size has to be run in an orderly manner, otherwise chaos will prevail and the high service I expect, and you take for granted, will cease to exist.' She waved her hand as a sign of dismissal. 'Go now, and do what you have to do.'

'Mother, I am not cancelling the appointment.' Abbie stood her ground. 'I'm not in the habit of letting people down at the last minute.'

'I feel the same, Mother,' Nigel said. 'I'm sorry if it upsets you, but neither of us are inclined to change our mind.'

With two of her children standing before her openly defying her, Edwina's nostrils flared with anger. This was the work of her husband; they would never have dared do this a few months ago. 'And where, pray, is this appointment that is more important to you than obeying your own mother?'

Nigel felt like curling up in a corner. His mother had always been able, with a look or a sneer, to make him feel worthless. And she was doing it now. But this time he had to stand up to her or he'd never be able to call himself a man. 'Abbie and I are going to a dancing academy for private lessons. Tonight is the first lesson and a quarter to seven was the only time we could be fitted in.'

Edwina folded her arms and snorted. 'I might have known that once your father took you to Seaforth, he would encourage you to become like the people he is so fond of. I had hoped you were intelligent enough to realise we have come a long way up the social ladder since the days he so loves to talk about, and it isn't practical that in our position we should associate with the working classes. But as you seem intent on learning to dance, presumably to visit these common dance halls, then I can only believe you have no ambition to get on in life – unlike your sister, Victoria, who is about to become engaged to one of the most influential men in the city. What a pity you don't take a leaf out of her book, and not your father's.'

Abbie could feel herself boiling inside with anger. How dare her mother stand there and belittle her husband when he was the one who had given them everything they had. But when she glanced at Nigel, he gave a slight shake of the head, indicating he would prefer her not to say what was in her heart and her head.

'Mother, I have no intention of standing here listening to you castigating Father.' Nigel straightened his shoulders and stood tall, bringing to mind the picture of that lonely, single bed. That the man they all owed so much to should not even have the comfort of a decent bed, never mind the love of his wife, made him more angry than he'd ever been. Looking at his mother's stern face now, he knew she was incapable of loving anyone, be they husband or children. All she cared about was money and the position she thought it gave her in society. And it was at that moment he understood fully what his father had had to endure for many, many years. Locked in a loveless marriage, yet never complaining. 'I was stupid enough to think you might be interested in what your children were doing, even be pleased that we were beginning to enjoy life. But as that is not the case, I think it best if Abbie and I leave now before too much is said. We will, of course, be keeping our appointment at the dancing academy. Come along Abbie, we don't want to be late.'

He cupped his sister's elbow and walked with her to her room. Once there he closed the door and leaned back against it. 'I found no pleasure in speaking to my mother like that. But I'm not going to let her ruin my life, as she's ruined Father's.'

'Nigel, I am so proud of you! You were absolutely brilliant! I wanted to scream at her, the way she was talking about our Dad. Why does she always have to pull him down? She treats him no better than she would the milkman or the coalman. But screaming wouldn't have achieved anything, only one almighty row. You were so cool, you carried the situation off beautifully. She'll lead us a dog's life from now on, but I don't care, because that's the way she's always treated me, anyway.'

'We'll talk about it later, Abbie, there isn't time now. I'll finish getting myself ready then give you a knock.' His hand on the door handle, he asked, 'Did you get a chance to buy dance shoes?'

She shook her head. 'We only get an hour's dinner break, and I'd never have made it into town and back in that time. What about you?'

'Same here. I didn't like asking for extra time off, the rest of the staff would think it was favouritism. So Mr and Mrs Ross are going to think we're a fine pair turning up without dance shoes. Still, I suppose light leather shoes will do just as well, even if they don't look the part.'

Abbie waited until he was halfway out of the door, then making her voice gruff, she tried to imitate Bobby. 'Hey, Nige!'

As she had hoped, there was a smile on her brother's face when he turned. 'The voice isn't quite right, but a very good attempt.'

'I'll work on it while you're getting ready. I just wanted you to know I love you.'

'I love you, too!'

Nigel was tying the laces of the light beige soft kid shoes, when he paused. Love wasn't a word used much in this house except for Abbie and his father. His sister was always open with her feelings and didn't care who heard when she told her father she loved him. But he could not remember a time when his mother or Victoria had used the word, and neither of them encouraged an endearment or even a hug. He hadn't thought it unusual because most of his adult life had been spent in their company, but the events of the past few weeks had opened up a floodgate of memories. Especially seeing his Granda and Grandma again. Each night in bed, staring at the ceiling, he remembered more and more. They had showered him with love when he was a child. He didn't go short of hugs and kisses then. His Grandma used to hold him tight and say, 'I love the bones of yer, sweetheart, and I'd eat yer if I could.'

A tap on the door had Nigel hurrying to open it. 'I'm ready, Abbie. As ready as I'll ever be, that is. I just hope I don't make a fool of myself.'

'Don't you dare! What have I told you about being positive?' Abbie asked, as they made their way down the stairs. 'I promise you that when we get home, we'll have learned enough steps to practise the waltz in front of Agnes. If we can't, then I'm going to leave it to you to explain to her why we're too thick to learn to put one foot in front of the other.'

'I hope we're not that bad!'

'We better hadn't be, because I've made up my mind to go dancing with Milly in a few weeks.' She chuckled as she ran out of the front door. 'We'll have to find a dance hall where they only play waltzes.'

Robert pushed his plate back and folded his napkin. The atmosphere was so tense it hadn't made for an enjoyable meal. He didn't bother asking why, he guessed his wife had found out about the dancing lessons and he wasn't about to enter into a war of words. His fobwatch told him it was a quarter past eight and Nigel and Abbie should be home any minute. He was eager to find out how they'd fared, so decided to have his coffee in the kitchen, which would be the first place they made for. And Agnes didn't object to the smell of his cigar. 'If you'll excuse me, I'll have my coffee in the study.'

He could feel two pairs of eyes boring into his back as he crossed the room, and knew as soon as the door closed behind him he would be the subject of two vitriolic tongues. Still, he was used to it by now and it didn't have the power to hurt him. Anger him, yes, but not hurt. And while they were talking about him they were leaving someone else alone.

'They're not back yet, then, Agnes?' Robert pulled one of the big wooden kitchen chairs out from the table. 'I can't wait to hear how they got on.'

'Mr Nigel's car went past the side window just as you came in.' Agnes dried her hands and grinned at him. 'They'll be coming through that door any minute.'

The words were barely out of her mouth when the door burst open and the two youngsters came in, eyes shining and big grins on their faces. Abbie made a bee-line for her father and threw her arms around him. 'Dad, it's been brilliant! Mr and Mrs Ross are so nice, I didn't feel a bit nervous.'

When Robert gazed into her deep brown eyes, it was like looking into the mirror when he was shaving and his eyes stared back at him. 'The thing is, my dear, did you learn anything?'

'Oh, yes! Mr Ross was my partner and his wife was with Nigel. We were only walking at first, so we could see their feet, and it was just one, two, three, over and over. Those are the basic steps for a waltz, and they were dead easy.'

Agnes caught Nigel's eye. 'Come and give us a hug, sunshine, and tell us all about it.'

'If I told you the truth, you'd think I was bragging.'

Abbie had plonked herself on her father's knee. 'If you don't brag, then I will. Tell them what Mr and Mrs Ross said, Nigel, and don't be so bashful.'

'They said we did very well considering it was our first lesson. And they also said we will make good dancers because we've got rhythm and loose body movements.'

'Let's show them what we've learned, Nigel.' Abbie jumped

to her feet. 'Come on, I know we're not experts but we can manage a few steps. Dad and Agnes won't laugh at us, so don't be shy.'

'I made a promise to Agnes that she'd be the first one I danced with, and I can't break my promise. So if she doesn't mind taking a chance on me standing on her toes occasionally, I'm game if she is.'

'Then you'll be my partner, Dad.' Abbie pulled Robert to his feet. 'If you pick it up, we might even take you dancing with us one night.'

Robert looked across at Agnes and winked. There were very few people their age who hadn't danced sometime in their lives, even if it was only at parties. But not for the world would he burst the bubble that was making his children so happy. Particularly Nigel, who was only just beginning to find out what he'd been missing. 'I know, let's all sing "After the Ball Was Over", so we've something to dance in time to.'

So it came about that when Edwina entered the kitchen, intending to ask why coffee had not yet been served, she found her husband dancing with Abbie and her son dancing with the housekeeper. And all four of them were singing. To say she was not best pleased would be putting it mildly. She was so filled with anger she could barely get the words out. 'Coffee, Agnes, immediately!' With a withering look she stormed out of the kitchen.

'Oh dear, I'm in for it now,' Agnes said. Then she grinned. 'And just when I was beginning to enjoy meself.'

'It's my fault,' Abbie groaned. 'I'll take the coffee through and explain to Mother that it was my idea.'

'Indeed not!' The housekeeper moved fast. The tray was set with silver coffee pot, sugar basin and jug of hot milk. 'I had it ready to take in when you arrived. It's only a few minutes late, nothing to lose her rag over.' With that she picked up the tray, squared her shoulders and stuck her nose in the air. 'I'll be back in five minutes and see to your dinner.'

'If anything is said, Agnes, refer my wife to me.'

261

'Don't worry, Mr Robert, I'm quite capable of looking after meself.'

But Agnes was not prepared for the onslaught that hit her as soon as she entered the dining room. Edwina got to her feet and leaned her clenched fists on the table. 'What on earth are you thinking of, allowing dancing and singing in the kitchen? Kindly remember it is your place of work, not a place for such common carryings on.'

Then Victoria, fired up by her mother's tirade, joined in. 'When will you get it into your head that you are a servant here, not a member of the family. You get paid to work, and it would do you well to remember that if you wish to keep your job here.'

The housekeeper put the tray in the middle of the table before even looking at either of the women. She was telling herself to do as Mr Robert said, and refer them to him. But it wasn't in her nature to stand and be insulted without answering back. And although she was as mad as hell at the injustice, she kept her voice low. 'Miss Edwina, and Miss Victoria, I would remind you that I start work at six o'clock every morning, Sunday included. The kitchen is my domain, and as long as I do the job I am paid to do, to your satisfaction, I am entitled to some time to meself and a laugh and a joke doesn't do no harm. I might as well die off if I can't get some pleasure out of life. D'yer expect me to work right through until yer've been served yer supper at ten o'clock, and then wash the dishes before I retire to my room? Working non-stop for nearly seventeen hours? If that is what yer expect from a house-keeper, then yer can find a replacement for me. I'm not going to work those hours and be treated like a dog's-body. I will leave at the weekend, if that suits yer. It will give yer a few days to find a replacement.'

Without waiting for a response, Agnes turned and left the room. With her head held high, she maintained her dignity. But once outside the dining-room door she slumped against the wall, tears threatening to spill. She didn't mind getting told off if it was justified, but having a laugh in the kitchen after working nearly fifteen hours didn't call for being spoken to as though she was a slave. And there were other things that added up to her feeling more sad and miserable than she'd felt for a long time. Those two women she'd just left, with faces that could turn milk sour, should have been in the kitchen with them to join in the jollity. Particularly Miss Edwina – you'd think she'd be interested and want to share in her children's pleasure. Most mothers would, but then again, Miss Edwina wasn't like a mother, more like a bad-tempered, hard-hearted headmistress. That's one job she would be good at and take great delight in. She certainly had the face for it. She'd love the power of having a cane in her hand, ready to come down on any poor child caught whispering to the girl sitting at the next desk.

Agnes moved away from the wall. They'd be wondering in the kitchen what was keeping her. She wouldn't tell them what had been said, not tonight. They'd been robbed of some of their pleasure, she wouldn't take any more away from them. She'd wait until she got to bed before deciding her future.

Three faces turned to her when she entered the kitchen. 'Well, Agnes, did you get a dressing down?'

'Everything's all right, Mr Robert, just a storm in a teacup.' Agnes busied herself by the large gas range. 'I'll see to your dinners now, Mr Nigel and Miss Abbie. Are yer eating it in the dining room?'

'If we're not in your way, Agnes, we'd rather eat out here,' Nigel said. 'It's much more homely, and Abbie and I are going to have one more little practice before bedtime.'

'Ye're welcome in here, yer know that.' Without making any eye-contact, the housekeeper covered her hands with a tea-towel before taking dishes from the oven. 'I'll see to the youngsters first, Mr Robert, they must be starving. Then I'll make a fresh pot of coffee for yer.'

'No hurry, Agnes, I'm not going to die of thirst.' Robert's elbows were on the table and he had his chin cupped in a hand. There's something not quite right here, he thought. He'd known the housekeeper too long not to recognise signs that said she wasn't the happy person she'd been fifteen minutes ago. The slumped shoulders, the missing smile and the lack of eye-contact were enough to set his mind working. She said everything was all right, just a storm in a teacup, but he found that hard to believe. Nigel and Abbie were busy talking, so he was able to study the movements of the woman he'd grown very fond of over the years. When things were rough, he always knew Agnes was there with her sympathetic ears. His port in a storm.

The longer Robert sat there studying her, the more convinced he became that something was amiss. Agnes had never gone so long without speaking, she usually nattered the whole time. And then he saw her chest heave and her lips pucker as though blowing out a sigh. 'I'm just going to get my cigar case, Agnes, I've left it in the study.'

'Shall I go, Dad?' Nigel offered.

'No, thank you, son. Agnes is just about to put your plates on the table. I'll only be away a few minutes.'

Robert had his hand on the knob of the dining-room door when he heard raised voices inside. It sounded as though his wife and eldest daughter were exchanging sharp words. Well, there was no point in eavesdropping when he could possibly have sharp words of his own to contribute.

Silence fell when Robert entered the room. But he noticed both women were agitated and after one guilty look at each other, they fixed their eyes on the wall opposite. Pulling out a chair, he sat down. 'Now, Agnes tells me everything is all right, but why do I have a feeling she is not telling the truth? Enlighten me, if you will.'

'The problem is, Agnes forgets she is a servant here, and not a member of the family.' Edwina threw a dark glance at her daughter. 'When I suggested the kitchen was not the place for dancing and singing, she took umbrage and told us to find another housekeeper as she would be leaving at the weekend.

She can be so childish at times, like a little girl who doesn't like being told when she's been naughty.'

'I would like to hear the conversation word for word, please. And Victoria, I want to know what part you played in this.'

'I've told you what happened,' Edwina said, her anger distorting her face into ugliness. 'What more do you want? Or do you think I am lying?'

'I don't think, Edwina, I know! Now, word for word, from both of you. And I suggest you don't try to play it down as though it was all Agnes's fault, because I intend asking her. And as she appears to be more truthful than you, and has a better memory, you can rest assured I will find out exactly what was said.'

Edwina gave a very watered-down version of her verbal attack on the housekeeper, making it sound as though she was only being reasonable and there was no call for Agnes to take the stance she did. But Victoria brazened it out and repeated everything word for word. Then she stared hard at her father, as though daring him to do his damnedest because what she'd said needed saying. And for good measure, to add fuel to the flames, she added, 'Every servant should know their place.'

'Oh, Agnes is very well aware of her place. It is you, and your mother, who seem to have trouble remembering your place. I was the one who suggested a moment of jollification to celebrate Nigel and Abbie's first dancing lesson, not Agnes. So why did you not have words with me, Edwina? You could have voiced your displeasure as soon as you entered the kitchen. But you didn't, because you knew you would be told how petty and ridiculous your objections were. So you waited for an easier target on which to spill out your venom. Well, let me now set the record straight. If I choose to dance with my daughter, and my son wishes to dance with the housekeeper, then who is to say this is not allowed? Certainly not you two, whose only contribution to the well-being of this house is misery and unpleasantness.'

Robert was beside himself with anger. That an incident so

innocent and spontaneous could cause such a fuss, and result in a decent woman being so humiliated she handed in her notice, was beyond his comprehension. And as he faced his wife and eldest daughter, it flashed through his mind that he didn't even like them. The thought frightened and saddened him, but he felt no guilt. He had tried his level best over the years to bridge the gap that he knew was opening up between them. He had given them everything they desired, but it had never been appreciated. They had mistaken his kindness for weakness. 'You have gone too far tonight, in accusing and degrading an innocent woman; you have crossed the boundary of decent behaviour. It happens so often, there are times I think your sanity is in question. But that is another matter. The matter in hand has to be dealt with immediately, and this is what I have decided. As you both seem to object to the way I wish this house to be run, I believe you would be much happier away from here. So I am prepared to buy a small house for you to live in. There will be no servants, but I will furnish it comfortably and give you an allowance to live on. If this does not meet with your approval, there is an alternative. You can go along now, to the kitchen, and apologise to Agnes. Not a half-hearted, don't-really-mean-it apology, but one where you beg her forgiveness and ask her to reconsider and stay on as housekeeper. If she refuses, then it's back to the first option. I will purchase a small house for you, where you will only have each other to insult and order about. You see, if Agnes leaves because of you, there is no way I will allow you to stay. I wouldn't want to live in the same house as you, wouldn't want to have to see your faces every day, knowing you have ruined the life of a decent woman.'

Robert got to his feet. He knew the housekeeper would be sick with worry right now, hurt and distressed that she was having to leave the house that had been her home for so long, when she hadn't done anything wrong. And he didn't want her to worry one moment longer than was necessary. 'You have five minutes to decide what you want to do.'

Edwina stood up so quickly her chair toppled over backwards. 'You can't throw your wife and daughter out, it's preposterous! Your name would be blackened across the city, you would be shunned by all decent people.'

'What would you know about decent people? You judge a person by the size of their house, the number of servants they have and their wealth. Well, let me tell you that riches do not automatically make a person honourable. A labourer, earning fifteen shillings a week to keep a family on, is as likely to be a decent person as someone with a fat bank balance. So being shunned by your decent people wouldn't worry me one iota.' Robert took a handkerchief from his pocket and wiped his brow. 'You have five minutes to decide. I'll be in the study.'

'Mother, I have no intention of going on bended knee to a servant.' Victoria was pacing the floor, her arms folded across her tummy. 'You started it, so it's your place to try and smooth things over.'

Edwina didn't see it that way. 'Victoria, you had far more to say to Agnes than I did. But laying blame isn't going to get us anywhere. This is a very serious situation, and I hope you realise just how serious. Your father means every word he says, and we could find ourselves in a small two-up, two-down in one of the rough areas of the city.'

'He wouldn't dare!'

'Will you stand still and listen to me!' Edwina so seldom raised her voice to her eldest daughter it brought Victoria to a halt. 'It would be very unwise to cross him in this. If we can't persuade Agnes to stay, he will carry out his threat, believe me.'

Mother and daughter faced each other. They were so alike in looks, with permanently haughty expressions and eyes that never smiled. Victoria had youth on her side and would be considered, at first glance, to be a really good-looking girl. But it would be safe to say that in years to come, she would end up not only resembling her mother in looks, but would also have her cold and humourless nature. 'Then for heaven's sake, let's say we're sorry and get it over with.'

'I'll ring for Agnes and have her come here, because Nigel and Abigail may still be in the kitchen. But before I do, I have to stress that this apology has to look and sound as though we mean it. There's a lot at stake, Victoria, so we can't afford to lose. Your dinner party would have to be cancelled for a start, and that is only a minor consideration. What your father has in store for us, if we fail, is far worse.' Edwina touched her daughter's arm. 'For both our sakes, I ask that if we have to beg, then so be it.'

'Oh dear.' Victoria's hand fluttered. 'Charles is coming tomorrow afternoon and I'm practically certain it's to tell me his parents will be coming to the dinner. However will I face him if I have to cancel?'

'If we play our cards right, it shouldn't be necessary.' Edwina walked over to the bell rope and tugged. 'Don't forget we should both appear suitably contrite.'

Agnes was having a cup of coffee with Nigel and Abbie when the bell rang. 'It's the dining room, I'd better go and see what they want.'

'Stay where you are, Agnes,' Nigel said. 'I'll go.'

The housekeeper put her cup down. She felt more like flying than facing those two women again, but she wasn't about to get the two children mixed up in any unpleasantness. They'd find out soon enough what was going on, but not tonight. 'No, I'd better go. Perhaps Mr Robert has decided to have his coffee in there.'

Agnes stopped outside the dining-room door and took a deep breath. She knew Mr Robert wouldn't be in there, just as she knew she was going to get an apology that would mean as little to her as it did to the two women who would give it. They thought they could treat her like dirt one minute, say they were sorry the next, then expect things to go back to normal. Until the next time they felt like throwing their weight around.

Well, it wouldn't work this time, she'd had a bellyful of them. But she was still employed here until Saturday, and she would carry out her duties until she walked out of the front door with all her belongings in a case and canvas bag.

'Sit down, Agnes,' Edwina said, waving her hand to a chair. 'Victoria and I would like to have a word with you.'

The housekeeper put her hands on the carved back of the chair and said, 'I'd rather stand, Miss Edwina.'

This put Edwina at a disadvantage, having to look up to the housekeeper, but she was in no position to argue. 'Victoria and I want to apologise, most sincerely, for our rude behaviour earlier. We were in the wrong, and we are very sorry. Am I correct in saying this, Victoria?'

'Oh, absolutely, Mother! I feel quite awful about it, and I do beg you to accept our most heartfelt apologies and forget about the whole miserable incident. And, of course, we have no intention of letting you leave, Agnes, we value you too much.'

The two women waited for Agnes to speak, and when she didn't, they both looked flustered and ill-at-ease. Seconds ticked away, and still there was silence. In the end, Edwina was forced into saying, 'Will you kindly accept our apologies, Agnes, please?'

'I'm sorry, but my mind is made up and I'm not about to change it. I'm sick to death of complaints from the pair of yer and I'm not taking any more. If it was an isolated incident, I might accept that yer were sorry. But it wasn't a one-off, and I don't think ye're a bit sorry. I've put up with yer shenanigans because of Mr Robert and the two children, but I've had it up to here.' Agnes put her hand flat on the top of her head. 'I don't have to put up with the likes of you, and I won't be sorry when I never have to set eyes on yer again. When Saturday comes, yer won't see me heels for the dust.' With that, she swung around and left the room.

'Well, what impudence!' Victoria felt completely vindicated by the housekeeper's reaction. 'I'm sure if Father had witnessed

269

that, he would realise it is not us who are in the wrong. We must tell him immediately.'

'Don't expect any sympathy from that quarter, because you won't get any,' Edwina warned. 'The situation for us is quite serious and I really don't know how we can rectify it if Agnes won't co-operate. There is little we can do.'

'There is one thing we can do,' Victoria said, a cunning look in her eyes and a supercilious curl to her upper lip. 'We have an ace card in our hand and I propose we use it forthwith.'

Edwina leaned forward. 'If you have something in mind, out with it quickly, for we are running out of time. What is the ace card you speak of?'

'Abigail. She and Agnes dote on each other, and if she knew what was in the offing, it would break her heart. She would, without doubt, go running to the kitchen crying her eyes out and begging Agnes not to leave. Abigail is the one person who could bring about a change of heart, and in so doing, would solve our problems.'

'Would all this happen quickly enough, though? Your father gave us five minutes and we have long gone past that time.'

'Then I suggest we move with haste. Abigail should be in her room by now, I will have words with her. They won't be the truth, of course, but by the time she is told what really happened, her tears will have done the trick. And you can have a word with Father, telling him how we grovelled, and that Agnes is considering her position. He is not stupid, he won't believe you, but it will buy us some time.'

This didn't appeal to Edwina. 'I would prefer to be the one to speak to Abigail, if you don't mind. As you well know, your father and I haven't been on the best of terms for many years.'

Victoria nodded, well aware of the situation between her parents. She fully agreed with, and supported her mother, finding the very thought of sexual intimacy distasteful. She was prepared to put up with Charles's roving hands, and would even allow him further liberties if it led to him proposing, but once they were married it would be a different proposition.

270

He could seek his carnal pleasures elsewhere. 'All right, Mother, you talk to Abigail. But don't forget she's our last hope, so it's important you choose your words with care. It's also important that she believes you. I'll deal with Father.'

Chapter Sixteen

Robert looked up from his desk when Victoria entered the study. She hadn't knocked and he opened his mouth to say it was polite to knock before bursting into a room, but he left the words unspoken. It would have been a waste of time, anyway, because his eldest daughter thought it was her right to do as she pleased. 'What can I do for you?'

'I came to tell you that Mother and I have apologised to Agnes and she is going to reconsider. I have no doubt that she will change her mind about leaving.'

Robert knew this wasn't true as he had made several journeys to the kitchen to make sure the housekeeper wasn't upset. So he knew exactly what had been said. However, he wanted to see what lengths his wife and daughter would go to, to dig themselves out of the hole they were in. 'Right, now you have told me, would you leave me to get on with what I was doing? Please close the door after you.'

Victoria was clenching her fists so tight her long painted nails were digging into the palms of her hands. He was dismissing her as though she was a child, and the urge to punch his face was strong. But she had the presence of mind to stay calm and walked out of the study, closing the door quietly behind her. He hadn't even asked her what had been said – nothing! It was as if he wasn't interested. She stood at the bottom of the stairs, looking up, and wondered whether to join her mother in Abigail's room. But even though she was consumed with curiosity, she told herself it would be better if they didn't appear too eager. So she made her way to the dining room to await her mother.

Edwina was taken by surprise to find Nigel sitting on the side of Abigail's bed, deep in conversation with his sister. This wasn't what she was expecting at all, and for a brief second she thought of making an excuse and leaving. But she couldn't afford to put it off until tomorrow, there was no time to spare. So, with her arms hanging stiffly by her sides, she walked across to the thick padded stool in front of the dressing table, and sat down. 'I have some news which, I'm sorry to say, will upset you. It has certainly upset Victoria and myself – we are absolutely devastated.'

Nigel leaned forward and rested his elbows on his knees. 'What is it, Mother?'

'I'm afraid Agnes has given in her notice. She's leaving on Saturday.'

A cry came from Abbie. 'Oh, no, she can't do that!' The tears were quick in coming. 'She can't leave us, I won't let her. I love her!'

'I know you do, and I have tried to talk her around, but she won't take any notice.' Edwina was delighted to see Abbie's reaction. The tears were just what was needed. 'She won't listen to me or Victoria, but she may listen to you.'

Abbie immediately ran for the door, but Nigel was off the bed like a shot and stopped her in her tracks. 'I'll come down with you, Abbie, but I want to ask Mother a few questions first. Come and sit next to me.'

As she watched her son lead his sister back to sit on the bed, his arm around her shoulders, Edwina cursed him to all eternity. If he hadn't been here, Abigail would have rushed downstairs, tears flowing, without asking a single question.

'What brought this about, Mother?' Nigel asked quietly, his eyes unwavering. 'Leaving certainly wasn't on Agnes's mind an hour ago, so something drastic must have happened since. Have you had a row with her?'

'It wasn't a row, and I think she's making a mountain out of a molehill. I merely said I didn't think the kitchen was the place for singing and dancing.'

Nigel squeezed his sister's shoulder for comfort, before asking, 'Where is the place for singing and dancing, Mother? I can't think of anywhere in this house where you would allow it. If a person laughs, it brings a scowl to your face, never mind singing. But to tell Agnes off for something that Abbie and I were responsible for, is wicked.'

'I did not tell her off!' Edwina didn't like having the tables turned on her and she could feel her temper beginning to surface. 'I have told you what happened and that's all there is to it.'

'You don't have to open your mouth to make your displeasure known, it's written all over your face. I should know, I've been a victim of it often enough. Many is the time you've made me cringe, Mother, but not any more. Nothing you say will have any effect on me in future; you no longer have the power to hurt or humiliate me. And I don't blame Agnes for wanting to leave – I wouldn't want to work for you either.'

'Don't say that, Nigel,' Abbie wailed. 'I'll be so unhappy if she leaves because I do love her. She's been like a mother to me.'

He stood up and held out his hand. 'Come on, let's go down and see her. Would you like to come with us, Mother, so we can hear both sides of the story?'

'How dare you suggest I might be lying.' Facing the housekeeper, or her husband, was something Edwina couldn't cope with right now. She deeply regretted what she'd said to Agnes, and wished she could take the words back. Not because she felt she was in the wrong, or was sorry for what she'd said, but because it had all back-fired on her. And the consequences didn't bear thinking about. 'I never thought the day would come when a child of mine preferred to believe the words of a servant, rather than their own mother.'

'Come along, Abbie, let's go.' Hand in hand, brother and sister walked down the stairs, followed by their mother. When they reached the bottom they turned to the left, towards the kitchen, while Edwina made for the dining room.

Agnes was sitting at the table peeling potatoes ready for the next day, when she heard the door open. Then Abbie was running towards her, her cries loud, and the housekeeper threw the knife down and jumped to her feet. 'There, there now.' Her motherly arms holding the girl close to her bosom, she rocked slowly. 'Come on now, sunshine, don't cry. Tears will spoil that pretty face of yours.'

Nigel looked on, feeling helpless. He didn't blame Agnes for leaving, no one with any pride would put up with his mother's insults for ever. But he didn't want her to leave; the house wouldn't be the same without her. Besides, it was all so unfair!

'Come on now, sunshine.' Agnes held the girl away from her and gazed into the deep brown eyes, now blurred with tears. 'Blow yer nose, like a good girl, while I clear the table and we can sit and have a talk.'

'Just tell me you're not leaving, Agnes, please?'

'Look, ye're giving yerself the hiccups.' Agnes cupped the tearstained face between her hands. 'Now stop crying and sit down. Mr Nigel has kindly cleared the table for me, so all I have to do is bring the kettle to the boil and we'll have a cuppa in no time.'

'I'll see to the tea, you sit down,' Nigel said, turning up the gas under the large, iron kettle. 'You've done enough running around after this family for one day, and precious little thanks you've got for it.'

'I'm the housekeeper here until Saturday, Mr Nigel, and I'll not let me standards slip before then. But because yer twisted me arm, I'll let yer make the tea.'

Abbie pulled her chair as close as she could. 'You're not really leaving, are you? You've just had a falling out with Mother, that's all, isn't it?'

The housekeeper, whose own eyes were red-rimmed with crying, shook her head. 'Not this time, Miss Abbie, I'm afraid.

They can't treat people like dirt and expect yer to forget all about it. I don't want to leave, believe me, but there comes a time when a person says enough is enough, and that time has come for me.'

Nigel set a teapot and three cups down on the table. 'We'll manage without a saucer, it'll save washing up.' Then he sat facing the women. 'We've heard Mother's version of what happened, now we'd like to hear yours, Agnes. That's if it's not too painful.'

'I've shed me tears, Mr Nigel, a bucketful of them. Likely as not there'll be many more when the time comes to walk out of the door, but right now I'm in control. I don't want you falling out with your mother, though, not through me. So believe what she tells yer, sunshine, it'll make life a lot easier for yer.'

Nigel knew the housekeeper wouldn't say anything that would set them against their mother, so a direct question wasn't going to get an answer – unless it was asked in a roundabout way. 'I can't understand why this row was so different from the others you've had. And heaven knows you've had plenty to put up with, Agnes, we all know that. As usual you were getting blamed for something that wasn't your fault, and you have every right to be angry. But you know what a dreadful snob Mother is, and you usually take what she says with a pinch of salt. What is so different this time?'

'It wasn't what Miss Edwina said, though it was uncalled-for and she had a bleedin' cheek. I'd have got over that all right – water off a duck's back. It was what Miss Victoria said that I couldn't take.' Agnes's voice cracked a little.

'Surely you wouldn't let Victoria upset you, Agnes – you know she's an even bigger snob than Mother, and she's just not worth it. What on earth did she say that made you give in your notice? After all, your leaving affects me and Abbie, and we don't want you to leave. To us, you are one of the family.'

'To you, perhaps, Mr Nigel, but not to Miss Victoria. Her words will be imprinted on my mind forever. "When will you get it into your head that you are a servant here, not a member of the family". That's what she said, and it hurt. Yer see, I know I'm not one of the family, really, but ye're the only family I've got. Mr Robert, and you two, I couldn't love yer more if I was one of yer.' Agnes thought there were no more tears left, but she could feel a lump in her throat and took a mouthful of tea to try and move it. She could see tears rolling unchecked down Abbie's face and that brought more pain. 'Wouldn't yer think that after ten years, some sort of bond would have been formed between Miss Edwina, Victoria and meself? Not love, but respect, understanding and friendship? I don't think that would be asking too much, but apparently I'm wrong.'

'But we love you, Agnes,' Abbie sobbed. 'Doesn't that count for anything? Won't you stay on for us, please?'

The housekeeper reached for her hand and held it tight. 'I won't be going out of yer life, sunshine, I'll come and see yer on me days off. I'll always keep in touch, see how ye're getting on, and any boys yer start going out with will have to meet with my approval.'

'I can't believe this is happening,' Nigel said. He was deeply upset. 'It's like a nightmare. Has Dad been along to see you?'

'He's been in and out like a Jack-in-the-box to make sure I'm all right. He's hurt, upset and very angry. I'm heartily sorry for him, but if I gave in now, the same thing will happen in a week or two and we'd be going through this all over again.'

'But where will you go?' Abbie asked. 'You can't just walk out with nowhere to go.'

'That's the least of me worries, Miss Abbie. I can find a job tomorrow, no problem. My main worry is leaving you two and Mr Robert. No matter where I go to work, it's not going to be the same as here. This is where my heart is. And another worry I've got is, what will happen to Kitty? She won't last five minutes with me not here. There are two people in this house who treat her like scum, and without me to protect her, they'll have her out in two shakes of a lamb's tail. And without this job, her and her husband will starve. She's a cracking little worker, and one of me best mates. No matter how down in the dumps I've been, Kitty can always bring a smile to me face. A little ray of sunshine, that's what she is. What's going to happen to her now?'

'I could say I'll make sure Kitty keeps her job, and that she's treated properly,' Nigel said. 'But that would mean I accept you're leaving here on Saturday, and I'm not going to do that. Not without a fight. You're the only mother Abbie and I have known for the last ten years, and we're not going to lose you if we can help it. What do you say, Abbie?'

His sister sniffed up before agreeing. 'I'll do anything to keep Agnes here, Nigel, but I feel so helpless. What can we do?'

'I'm going to have a word with Dad – I can't see him just accepting this. You stay and keep Agnes company, help her peel the potatoes.'

Nigel turned after closing the kitchen door behind him to find himself face to face with his mother. 'Well?' Edwina said. 'Is she staying on?'

Nigel closed his eyes. After all the trouble and heartache this woman had caused, she was still on her high horse. No remorse, no sadness. 'She? Who is "she", Mother?'

Edwina tutted. 'Really, Nigel, you know who I mean. Is she leaving or staying?'

'Why don't you go and ask her, if you are so interested?' She was standing directly in front of him, barring his way, so he side-stepped round her. 'Now, excuse me.'

He rapped on the study door and walked in, to find his father sitting with his head in his hands. 'I'm sorry to interrupt, Dad, I know you must be feeling dreadful. As, indeed, do Abbie and myself. But I feel I can't just sit and do nothing, not when so much is at stake. I can't get it through my head that Agnes is leaving because she got the blame for something she didn't even do. It's totally unbelievable! Surely there's something we can do to stop this farce?'

'Sit down, son.' Robert pointed to the chair on the opposite side of the desk. 'I've been doing some serious thinking, and I have come up with a decision that will affect the whole family. It is something I have thought about many times over the last ten years, but always pushed it to the back of my mind. So while Agnes has nothing to do with the decision I've made, what happened here today brought it to a head. You might hate me for what I am going to do, and that would make me very sad. But I can no longer live in a house where there is no warmth, no laughter and certainly, heaven forbid, no dancing: where two of the inhabitants of the house live in a totally unreal world. I'm in my mid-forties, still a relatively young man, and I want some happiness in what life I have left. For that reason, I have decided to divorce your mother.' Robert searched his son's face for signs of anger or dislike, but there were none. 'I'm sorry, son, I really am, but I can't carry on living an empty, cold life. I am only human, and I need affection and love. Both of these I have been starved of for far too long. There are many things you don't know, but now is not the time to tell. One day, perhaps, then you'll understand.'

'I know, Dad,' Nigel said quietly. 'I don't blame you, and will stand beside you all the way. Mother has asked for it in more ways than one. Perhaps I shouldn't say it about the woman who brought me into the world, but it is the truth. She is impossible to live with, and impossible to love. Unfortunately, Victoria is the same.'

Robert breathed a sigh of relief. 'I have been sitting here, my mind in a whirl, dreading what your reaction would be. I'd be broken-hearted if you and Abbie turned against me, because I do love you both very much.'

'Dad, I understand, and I know Abbie will, too! No man should be expected to put up with what you have. I'm surprised you didn't do it years ago.'

'I don't want you to mention this to Abbie, or anyone, until I've been to see my solicitor tomorrow. When I've been made aware of the ins and outs, I'll tell your mother before anyone else. I owe her that much.'

'Would this make a difference to Agnes leaving? Oh, I do hope so, Dad, because over the years she's really cared for me and Abbie. If she hadn't been here, there'd have been no one to run to when we were in trouble. No one to bandage our cuts, heal our wounds or listen to our worries. No one to hug us and kiss us goodnight. We owe a lot to her, Dad, and neither of us will ever forget that.'

'I'll have a good talk to Agnes tonight. Not about the divorce, that wouldn't be fair on your mother, but I think I can tell her enough to stop her from leaving. You can rest assured that I will do anything to keep her here, where she is loved and needed.'

'Will you be telling Mother tomorrow night?'

'I have an appointment tomorrow night, so I won't be coming home for dinner. If my solicitor can see me in the morning, then I'll come straight home and speak with your mother, and Victoria. It's an unpleasant task, and one I'm not looking forward to. So the sooner I get it over with, the sooner the weight is lifted from my shoulders.'

'Abbie and I are going to Seaforth tomorrow night. We're going to visit Grandma and Granda, then Abbie's seeing Milly and I'm taking Bobby for his second driving lesson. So Abbie will be the last one to know the news.'

'A day or two won't make any difference. If I can persuade Agnes to change her mind, that should make your sister happy. Then I'll pick the right moment to sit and have a talk to her.'

'Will I see you in the office tomorrow?'

'I'll go in at the usual time, and ring the solicitor from there. If he can see me in the morning, all well and good. I'll come straight home from his office and face the music. I don't think your mother will take the news calmly, so I could be here for a while. If that happens, I won't have time to go back to the office because, as I said, I have an appointment. Now, if you'll coax Abbie to go up to her room, I'd like to have a chat with Agnes. If all goes as I'm hoping it will, I'll let you both know tonight. That should ease your minds and enable you to have a good night's sleep.' As Nigel was turning the knob on the door, Robert added, 'Thank you for being so understanding. It's nice to know I have someone to talk to, man to man.'

'I'm sorry it's taken me so long to grow up, Dad. But I have now, and I'll always be here for you.'

'Yer've no need to keep coming in to see if I'm all right, Mr Robert. Yer've got more to do with yer time than worry about me.'

'I'm not the only one worrying about you, Agnes Weatherby, my two children are worrying themselves sick. And after we've had a little chat, I want to be able to climb those stairs to tell them this is your home now, and for the rest of your life.'

'Ah, we're not going through all that again, Mr Robert, are we? Every time we talk, I'm reminded about leaving, and then I'm reduced to bleedin' tears.'

'Well, we'll have no more bleedin' tears tonight, if you don't mind. I just want to ask you a question or two, and that's not enough to cry over, surely?'

'Oh, go on, then, what d'yer want to know?'

'Serious, Agnes?'

'Serious, Mr Robert.'

'My first question is simple. If you didn't have to take any orders from my wife or Victoria, would you stay on?'

'That's a bloody stupid question, if yer'll excuse me language. How can I stay on and not take orders from the boss?'

'Say she, or they, weren't the boss any more, then you wouldn't need to take orders from them, would you?'

'Either I'm not thinking straight, or you're not making sense, Mr Robert. They're yer wife and daughter, and I'm only the ruddy housekeeper! If I don't have to take orders from them, what do I do? Tell them to sling their flaming hook?'

'Do you trust me, Agnes?'

'Of course I do! Except when ye're talking in bleedin' riddles.'

'I can't tell you too much tonight, but if I said that in the not too distant future, you would not have to take orders from my wife, or Victoria, would you believe me?'

The housekeeper caught his eyes. 'I haven't caused no trouble with you and Miss Edwina, have I? That wasn't my intention, to come between man and wife, and if I have I'm very sorry.'

'Anything I do, Agnes, has not been brought about by you, and that's the truth. Do you think I have a happy life? Do you think my wife is loving and caring towards me?'

That brought a quick response. 'No, I bleedin' well don't! She's got a man in a million and doesn't know she's born. Ye're too good for her, she doesn't deserve yer. I might be talking out of turn, but yer did ask me and I'm not telling no lies.'

'Then all I'll say, Agnes, is don't look for another post. Because come Saturday morning, you aren't going anywhere.' Robert lowered his head to smile into her face. 'This is yer bleedin' home, all right? Understand?'

'No, I don't bleedin' understand, Mr Robert. But I'll tell yer something for nothing. Wild horses wouldn't drag me out of that door on Saturday, now. I'll be staying out of bloody curiosity. So put that in yer ruddy pipe and smoke it.'

'You drive a hard bargain, Agnes Weatherby. But I ask you to be patient with me. I may have some news of importance tomorrow, or at the latest, on Friday. In the meanwhile, if you hear any screaming and shouting, or things being thrown around, take no notice. It will be my wife taking revenge on me for putting her in her place, at long last.'

'Ooh, er! Now that does sound exciting, I must say. Before I go to bed I'd better check we have plenty of lint and bandages, to dress the wounded soldiers. But I don't want no blood spilt, mind, 'cos it's the very devil to wash out.'

'I'm very good at ducking, Agnes, so have no fear.' Robert waved to her from the door, before making his way upstairs to see his children. The housekeeper appeared to have calmed down now, and in agreeing to stay on, she had lightened his burden a little. But nagging away at the back of his mind was how he would get through tomorrow, when faced with the combined fury of his wife and Victoria. He found the prospect daunting, knowing they both had vicious tongues and tempers. He also believed they were capable of using physical violence to get their own way. But no matter what they resorted to, they wouldn't get him to change his mind, on that he was determined. And no matter what, he would get through the ordeal by reminding himself that at the end of it, he would be going to Chester. There, in Maureen's arms, he would find the comfort and companionship his heart and mind craved.

Abbie sat at the kitchen table the next morning taking her time with her breakfast. Her father and Nigel had left for work, but she dawdled, wanting to spend as much time as she could with the housekeeper. 'If you'd gone, Agnes, I would have gone with you.'

'That would have been a bit awkward, sunshine, wouldn't it? I couldn't have taken yer in me case 'cos it's too small.' Agnes turned from the stove to stroke the rich dark hair. 'So it's just as well I'm not going, isn't it? Besides, yer wouldn't want to leave yer dad, or Mr Nigel, would yer?'

Abbie giggled. 'No, I'd have had to bring them along, too!'

The housekeeper heard voices outside and put a finger to her lips. 'Not a word.'

'Good morning, Aggie.' Kitty stopped in her tracks when she saw who was sitting at the table. 'Good morning, Miss Abbie.'

'Good morning to you, Kitty, and to you, Jessie. What's the weather like outside?'

'Fair to middling, Miss.' Kitty thought for a few seconds,

then said, 'I don't think yer'll need yer fleecy lined ones on, it's not that cold.'

'That's enough out of you, Kitty Higgins,' Agnes said, removing Abbie's cup and plate. 'And it's time you were on yer way, young lady, or yer'll be late.'

'There yer are,' Kitty said, nodding her head. 'She's told two of us off in one go. Naggy Aggie, that's what we'll have to call her.' The little woman stood on tip-toe to hang her coat on the hook behind the door. 'Why the bleedin' hell they had to put the hook so high up I'll never know. Must have been a giant what done it.'

'Watch your language, please, we have company.' The housekeeper turned her head to hide a smile. 'Miss Abbie isn't used to hearing swear words.'

'Yes, I am! I hear you swear, Agnes, and my Grandma knows a lot of swear words.'

'Does she, queen?' The cleaner's pixie-like face beamed and her eyes shone. All signs of a joke to come. 'Will yer ask her to write them down for me, queen, so I can keep up with me mate, Aggie Weatherby? Sometimes the air's blue in this kitchen with her carry-on, and I get so embarrassed I don't know where to put me face. Words I've never heard of in me life, and I couldn't tell yer what they mean if yer paid me! I had a very sheltered upbringing, and my old mother, God rest her soul, would turn in her grave if she knew the riff-raff I was mixing with.' Kitty glanced at the housekeeper. 'I could have used a bigger word than mixing, but it's slipped me mind. It was ass . . . something or other.'

Agnes was really enjoying herself. This was just what she needed after the awful day yesterday. 'I think the word yer want is associating, sunshine.'

Kitty beamed. 'How many letters in that, queen?'

The housekeeper counted them off on her fingers. 'Eleven.'

'She's not half clever, my mate, it's not only swear words she knows. Anyway, queen, would yer tell yer Grandma I'd be beholden to her if she'd write all the swear words down

285

for me, so I can finish me education?'

'Miss Abbie would be better employed going on her way and bringing her own education up-to-date. So, come on, sunshine, poppy off. If yer have to wait for a tram, yer'll be late for yer first class.'

'I'm going, I'm going, I'm going! I don't feel like it this morning, but needs must when the devil drives.' As she rose from her chair, Abbie smiled at Jessie who was always very quiet when a member of the family was present. 'Are you settling down in your job, Jessie?'

'Oh, yes, Miss.' A lovely smile came with a curtsy. 'Aggie and Kitty take good care of me, and I really like it.'

Abbie looked at Kitty who had mischief written all over her. 'Are you always so happy, Kitty?'

'No point in being otherwise, queen, 'cos yer won't get many friends if yer walk around with a miserable gob on yer. Take Naggy Aggie here, she hasn't got a friend in the world, and it's all down to the miserable clock on her. All day long I'm telling her jokes to try and make her smile, but I might as well talk to the wall.'

The housekeeper clapped her hands together before jerking her thumb towards the back door. 'Will yer get going Miss Abbie, so I can give these two a cup of tea before they start work?'

'I know when I'm not wanted.' The girl picked up her briefcase and as she was passing, she kissed the housekeeper on the cheek. 'I'll see you tonight, Agnes.'

'You will, sunshine, and you take care how yer go.'

It was nine o'clock and Agnes was filling the breakfast serving dishes when Victoria flounced into the kitchen. She was wearing a floor-length pink satin dressing-gown, tied at the waist, and the matching mules on her feet were adorned with feathers. 'Agnes, Mr Charles is calling about ten o'clock, and I would like Jessie to change into her maid's uniform to open the door to him. She would look far more efficient, don't you think?'

'Whatever you say, Miss Victoria.' She's brazen, she is, thought Agnes. The trouble she caused yesterday and now she was acting as though it had never happened. 'Was there anything else?'

For a brief moment, Victoria was taken off-guard by the abrupt question. She'd been hoping to build up some dialogue to try and gauge the housekeeper's mood. Something that would give an indication as to whether she still intended to leave on Saturday, or whether Abbie had been able to talk her round. But bold as she was, the stern face gazing unblinkingly at her told her clearly she didn't stand a snowball's chance in hell of finding anything out. 'Will you see Jessie looks presentable, then, Agnes?'

'As you wish, Miss Victoria.'

Her lack of subservience began to grate on Victoria's nerves. This woman was getting paid to do her bidding, and should show more respect. Tossing her head, she said, 'Oh, and keep Kitty out of the way, will you. She looks like a bag of old rags.'

That was something Agnes was not prepared to stand and take. Not about her mate, Kitty, who, as a person, made ten of this arrogant young upstart. 'Shall I stay out of sight as well, Miss Victoria? Yer see, Mr Robert bought us all new uniforms last week, so if Kitty looks like a bag of old rags, it follows that I must look the same. Oh, my uniform isn't black, but it would be stupid to put white on Kitty when she's on her hands and knees scrubbing floors and cleaning up the waste left lying around by the family.'

'I really don't have time to stand chatting when Mr Charles will be here in an hour and I still have to dress and eat breakfast. Just make sure that both my orders are carried out to my satisfaction, Agnes.' When she reached the door, she called over her shoulder, 'Mr Charles will expect refreshment – make sure it is to his liking.'

The housekeeper didn't know how she kept her mouth closed, except that it was with great difficulty. That was one

287

young lady who deserved to be taken down a peg or two, and given a ruddy good hiding into the bargain. Agnes wasn't that keen on Mr Charles, he had a wandering eye and was too sweet to be wholesome, but she felt sorry for him if he intended to tie himself to Miss Victoria for life. No one deserved that sort of fate.

The housekeeper carried the tray through to the dining room and spread the covered dishes out on the sideboard. There was no sign of Miss Edwina or Victoria, so she went in search of Jessie. And when told she was to wear the frilly lace cap and apron, the young girl's pretty face lit up. 'Can I get changed now, Aggie?'

'No, there's plenty of time. You finish Miss Abbie's room, then come down. Now where will I find Kitty?'

'Someone taking my name in vain, are they?' Kitty came out of Nigel's room and began to act the goat by using a feather duster as a sword. Thrusting, ducking and diving, she advanced towards the housekeeper and brandished the feather duster under her nose. 'Yer money or yer life.'

'Ye're tickling me nose, sunshine.'

'Better than tickling yer fancy, queen! Now hand yer money over, or else.'

'It'll have to be or else, 'cos I haven't got no money. And you'll have no job if Tilly Mint or Tilly Flop come out and find yer acting daft. I only wanted to see yer to say we'll have our break from a quarter past ten this morning. That's an extra fifteen minutes.'

'How come, queen? Has someone died and we're having a little service for them, out of respect, I mean? If I'd known I'd have picked a few flowers out of the garden when Pete had his back turned.'

'I thought I had a good imagination, sunshine, but you beat me hollow. No, Mr Charles is calling at ten, Jessie is to open the door to him in her new outfit, and then the ladies will be entertaining for at least an hour. Which means we can take it easy. That's not to say the jobs don't get done properly, 'cos

288

I'll be checking. It just means working a bit faster so we have a longer break.'

A door opposite to where they were standing opened, and out came Victoria. 'Is this all you have to do with your time, gossip?'

'I was just passing on your orders, Miss Victoria,' Agnes told her with the innocence of a baby. 'But we all know what's expected of us now, so I'll get back to me kitchen and the dirty dishes. Jessie, I'll see you when yer've finished in Miss Abbie's room.' Chuckling silently, the housekeeper walked down the stairs behind Victoria. With a bit of luck Mr Charles might propose today, and wouldn't that be the best news ever? Not for Mr Charles, like, but that was his worry.

'Do I look all right, Aggie?' Jessie's emotions were very mixed. She was happy and proud, but also terrified. 'I hope I don't say nothing wrong.'

'All yer have to do, sunshine, is open the door, smile, give a little bob, and say "Good morning, Mr Charles." If he has a hat, you take it from him and lay it on the table in the middle of the hall. Then you walk in front of him to the drawing room, open the door and announce him. When he's in the room, you close the door quietly and come along here to tell me how yer got on. And when they ring for refreshments, you can help me serve those. Yer might as well get the wear out of the uniform while yer can, sunshine.'

'I've never met this Mr Charles, is he kind?'

'Yes, he's very friendly, so you've no problems. Now turn around so I can get a good look at yer.' The flawless beauty of this fresh-faced young girl never failed to strike Agnes. And the innocence in her eyes added to the beauty. 'Yer look grand, sunshine, I bet yer mam would be proud of yer.'

'Ooh, there's the bell, Aggie, are yer sure I look all right?'

'Yer look lovely, just don't forget to smile.' Agnes patted her bottom. 'You'll be fine.'

Kitty was on her hands and knees on the landing polishing

the spindles of the staircase, when the bell rang. With a smile on her face, she sat back on her heels and waited for Jessie's big moment. She watched the girl walk towards the front door, and she looked so pretty, the cleaner couldn't have felt more proud if she'd been her own daughter.

'Good morning, Mr Charles.' Jessie kept the smile on her face and did a little bob, even though her whole body was shaking with nerves. 'Can I take your hat?'

Charles Chisholm was speechless for a few seconds. He'd never seen anyone so lovely in his life. 'Well, well, who do we have here?' He held on to his hat and stood in front of Jessie to bar her way.

'My name's Jessie, sir, and I'm a junior maid.' The girl's face reddened and she stared down at her shoes. 'Can I take your hat, now, please?'

Charles put a finger under her chin and raised her face. 'You are a very pretty girl, why haven't I seen you before? I'll have to come more often if you are to open the door to me.'

Kitty, hidden away on the landing, looked on with mounting horror. Jessie's head was being propped up by Charles's finger, and she was forced to look him in the face. Kitty could almost smell the young girl's fear and embarrassment. If he doesn't stop, the cleaner thought, I'm going to tell Aggie and I don't care whether Miss Victoria likes it or not.

'How old are you, Jessie?' Charles asked, his face getting closer. 'You're quite the prettiest thing I've ever seen in a long time.'

That does it, thought Kitty, the poor girl looks terrified. Someone's got to put a stop to it before he goes too far. These rich people think they can do what they like with servants. He won't see me if I slip down the stairs, he's got his back to me and is too interested in Jessie to hear me. With her hands holding up her skirt, the cleaner tip-toed down the stairs and headed for the kitchen.

'Mother is looking for a new junior, Jessie.' Charles had a liking for young girls, and this beauty was like a rose-bud waiting to burst into full bloom. Young and innocent, the perfect combination. 'Would you like to come and work in my home? I'd make sure you were well looked after.' His face was within inches of hers when he felt himself being pulled around and away from the now crying girl.

'No, she wouldn't, Mr Charles, she's quite happy where she is.' Agnes nodded to Jessie. 'Go into the kitchen, sunshine and I'll make yer a cup of tea when I've shown Mr Charles into the drawing room.'

Charles had the grace to blush. 'I can see myself in, Agnes, you don't have to bother.'

The housekeeper flashed him a dark look but didn't answer. She strode to the drawing room and threw open the door. 'Mr Charles to see you, Miss Victoria.'

With a sickly sweet smile, Victoria crossed the floor and held out both hands. 'Charles, darling, how lovely to see you.' She leaned forward for a peck on the cheek, then looked past him to the housekeeper. 'Agnes, I thought I left instructions for Jessie to open the door. Why did you take it upon yourself to disobey?'

'Oh, I didn't disobey, Miss Victoria,' Agnes said breezily. 'But I'll leave it to Mr Charles to explain what happened while I see to yer refreshments.'

Chapter Seventeen

Robert stepped from the building in Dale Street and walked towards his parked car. He'd been to see his solicitor, George Mellor, and had gone through the most harrowing and embarrassing two hours of his life which had left him completely drained. George had been his solicitor for over ten years now, and they were on friendly terms. But that didn't make answering personal questions any easier. Such as having to admit it was seventeen years since he and Edwina had lived together as man and wife. That had him squirming in his chair. But as the solicitor had said, many questions had to be asked, and the truth had to be told if he was petitioning for a divorce.

Robert lowered himself into the driving seat, but didn't start the engine. He needed a few quiet minutes to sort things out in his mind before facing Edwina, and where better than the solitude of his car where there would be no interruptions? He wasn't looking forward to the task ahead, and thought a stiff whisky wouldn't go amiss. But while that would give him Dutch courage, it wouldn't leave him with a clear head.

The familiar clip-clop of a horse's hooves had Robert turning to gaze out of the window. And the sight of a horse pulling a heavily laden cart took him back over the years. He'd come a long way since the days of his horse and cart, but he'd been a damn sight happier then than he was now. Sitting on the front seat of the cart, with Jeff next to him, and furniture piled high at the back, they might not have appreciated it then, but life was good. Not much money, but a firm friendship that had never wavered, and lots of laughter. It would all have been so different if he'd had a loving wife standing beside him through the years, proud of his achievements and proud of their children. He envied Jeff, who had a wonderful, happy marriage. A loving wife to go home to every night, and children who adored him.

Robert sighed and switched the engine on. It was too late to go back to the office, the staff would be on their lunch hour, so he'd go straight home and ask Agnes to make him a bite to eat before facing the inevitable show-down with his wife. There'd be ranting and raving, he knew that, but nothing would make him change his mind. He'd made his decision and would stand firm on it. And there was something to keep him going through the storm. The safe, warm haven of Maureen's arms.

'Hello, Mr Robert.' There was surprise in the housekeeper's voice when Robert walked into her kitchen. 'I wasn't expecting you.'

'I couldn't tell you because I didn't know myself what was happening. I completed my business earlier than I thought, and as I wanted to have a word with my wife, I decided to throw myself on your mercy for some lunch.'

'Miss Edwina and Miss Victoria are in the dining room now, if yer want to eat with them. There's enough food for yer.'

'No, a sandwich out here would be fine, if I won't be in your way. I'll be having a hot meal later this evening.'

'What'll it be then? Cheese, beef or ham?'

'How about one of each? They say variety is the spice of life, and I could certainly do with some spice in my life.'

Agnes bustled to the larder and came out with a plate in each hand. One was bearing a piece of beef, the other ham. 'Mr Charles was here earlier, to see Miss Victoria.'

'That should have pleased her. It was probably about the confounded dinner party she insists upon having. I think she's set her sights on Charles and I don't know who to feel most sorry for, him or her.'

After the little episode with Charles Chisholm this morning, which left young Jessie crying her eyes out and refusing to leave the kitchen until he'd gone, Agnes thought him and Miss Victoria deserved each other. But there was no point in repeating it to Mr Robert, he had enough to contend with. Unless his daughter tried to make trouble for poor Jessie, that was. If she was daft enough to do that, then the whole sorry tale would come out, putting her boyfriend in a very bad light. 'I'd say it was much of a muchness, Mr Robert. Six of one and half-a-dozen of the other. Then again, there's not many of us what don't have faults.' Under her breath she muttered, 'It's just that some are bleedin' worse than others.'

'Have Kitty and Pete had their lunch break?'

'Yeah, ages ago. It's nearly time for their afternoon cuppa, when we'll all be entertained by Kitty. She's a bloody hero, Mr Robert, honest.' As she talked, the housekeeper was cutting and buttering bread. 'As yer well know, her and Alf have got sweet Fanny Adams, but yer never hear a complaint out of her. She's always got a smile on her face, and can turn anything into a joke. She can't half sing, too, she's got a smashing voice. Pete reckons she's good enough to be on the stage.'

'We'll have to have a party one night, then, and she can be the star. A real knees-up jars-out, Agnes – remember those days?'

'I certainly do!' The housekeeper put a plate of sandwiches in front of him. 'Yer could have the time of yer life on just one bottle of milk stout. Mind you, my mother used to say yer don't need drink to enjoy yerself.'

'When I get my life sorted out, we'll have an old-fashioned party. Kitty can bring Alf, Pete his wife, and Tilly your mate from next door can come. Nigel and Abbie can invite their friends, and I have a friend of my own who would be delighted to come.' Robert looked up at the housekeeper and pulled a face. 'Wishful thinking at the moment, Agnes, but it will

295

happen some time in the future. Can you put up with me until then?'

She nodded. 'Of course I can. What a daft bleedin' question to ask! Now get that tea down yer before it goes stiff. What time is Miss Edwina expecting yer?'

'She's not expecting me, Agnes, nor is she expecting the news I bring. But I've made up my mind that my life has to change, I need more out of it than I'm getting. So I have decided on a course of action which will suit me, but will make my wife very angry. What it is, you will find out in the next day or two.'

'Yer don't have to tell me yer business, Mr Robert, I don't expect that. As long as I know ye're happy, that's good enough for me.'

'I consider you a very dear friend, Agnes, and you have a right to know what is happening in the house and to the members of the family. You haven't always been well treated or appreciated by certain members, I'm sad to say, but I have always held you in high regard. And I don't need to tell you that Nigel and Abbie love you dearly.'

'They're the children I never had, Mr Robert, but that's all I'm saying, 'cos otherwise I'll be crying buckets again.'

Robert wiped his mouth on the napkin Agnes had placed by the side of his plate. 'When I've spoken with my wife, I'll go upstairs to wash and change. Then I'm off to see a very dear friend.' He pushed back his chair. 'I presume my wife and daughter will be in the drawing room now?'

Agnes nodded. 'Ring if yer want me.'

Robert stood outside the drawing room, straightened his tie and took a deep breath. The sooner this was over, the better. He could hear the voice of his daughter and, by the tone, she sounded excited. Probably because of the visit by Charles Chisholm. He knocked and opened the door. 'Good afternoon, ladies. I wonder if you would be kind enough to leave me alone with your mother, Victoria. I wish to speak with her.'

'Why can't you say what you've got to say in front of me?' Victoria's eyes were hard under her raised brows, and she spoke to her father as though he was someone beneath her. 'Surely I can hear what you have to say?'

'Don't you dare take that attitude towards me! How dare you!' Robert's anger was overriding his nerves. 'I asked you to leave the room, now I am *telling* you! I wish to speak to your mother in private, so please leave us alone – now!'

'I prefer her to stay,' Edwina said icily. 'I have no wish to be alone in the room with you.'

Robert gazed from one woman to the other. They are both quite mad, he thought. Like mother, like daughter. 'If this is your wish, I will make what I have to say as brief as possible.' He stood in front of the fireplace, his feet apart, his thumb hooked in the pocket of his waistcoat. 'I am tired of living a lie, married to a woman who is my wife in name only. So I have been to see my solicitor this morning and asked him to start divorce proceedings.'

There was complete silence until his words sank in, then the two women looked at each other with smirks on their faces. 'If your intention was to frighten me, then you've failed miserably,' Edwina said. 'You can't divorce me, you have no grounds.'

'You must think we're complete idiots, Father, if you expect us to fall for that.' Victoria was on her feet, a stiffened finger pointing at Robert. 'So you just walked into the solicitor's office and said you wanted a divorce. What a load of poppycock! You need grounds for a divorce, and I'm quite sure Mother hasn't committed adultery.'

Robert in turn pointed a finger at his daughter. 'You will sit down, right now, d'you hear me? And you will take no part in this discussion at all. Open your mouth once more, and I will forcibly eject you from this room.' Breathing heavily with temper, he faced his wife. 'You do need grounds for divorce, yes, and I have them in abundance. Not adultery, just the opposite, in fact. A divorce can be obtained where a wife refuses her husband his conjugal rights. And since it is seventeen years since you allowed me those rights, then according to my solicitor I have ample grounds for divorcing you.'

That is when all hell broke loose. 'You mean you discussed our private affairs with a complete stranger?' Edwina was pummelling his chest with clenched fists and screaming, 'How dare you! How dare you! You swine, you!'

Victoria was white with anger. She wasn't worried about her mother now, but what a stigma divorce would be on the family. How could she look her friends in the face when they found out? So her screams were mingling with Edwina's. 'What sort of a father would do that to his family? Think of the disgrace! I hate you, I hate you!'

Kitty, who could hear the screams, ran to the kitchen. 'Aggie, there's murder going on in the drawing room, the screams are something shocking. Someone must be getting a hiding, the racket they're making.'

Agnes threw the dishcloth into the sink and dried her hands. 'I don't know what it's about, sunshine, but I think Mr Robert was expecting a fight. He told me last night if I heard screaming and shouting, not to take any notice.'

The cleaner shook her head. 'It sounds bad to me, queen, like the two women are tearing him to pieces. Yer know what bad buggers they are, they'd think nothing of scratching his eyes out if he upset them.'

A picture of Mr Robert flashed through the housekeeper's mind and there was blood running down his handsome face. That was enough to send her running. 'You wait here, Kitty, don't follow or we'll only make it worse.'

When Agnes burst into the drawing room, it was to see Robert making no attempt to protect himself from the blows that were being rained on him. You can carry being a gentleman too far, she thought. He could fell them in one swoop if he had a mind to. No one had heard her come in because of the racket, so she called at the top of her voice,

'What the hell is going on here? Call yerselves ladies, do yer? That's a laugh, I've seen down-and-outs behaving better than you. Now stop it this minute, yer should be ashamed of yerselves.'

Victoria turned on her. 'Get back to the kitchen where you belong, and keep your nose out of our affairs.'

'Listen to me, young lady. I stopped taking orders from you yesterday, so don't waste yer breath. Mr Robert is too much of a gentleman to lay a finger on a woman, but I'd be in me element giving you a good hiding. It's something I've been itching to do for ten years now, 'cos ye're completely out of control.' Agnes glared from mother to daughter, almost daring them to start something. But neither said a word. 'Mr Robert, there's a cup of tea poured out for yer in the kitchen.'

'I'll be along in a minute, Agnes, thank you. I just want a few more words with my wife and daughter.' He waited until the housekeeper had left, then pointed to the two empty chairs. 'Sit down, please, and listen. Nothing on God's earth will make me change my mind about divorce. I intend going through with it, come what may. I believe I am entitled to a better life than I've had since Abbie was born. I love Nigel and Abbie very much, but unfortunately I can't say the same about you two. Neither of you have ever done anything to deserve my love or respect. A few days ago, I offered to buy you a small house where the two of you could live in comfort. The offer is still open. I could make you take it, if I so choose, because in this country a man is head of the family and, rightly or wrongly, the law is on his side if he wishes to turf people out on to the streets. You may wish to think this over, and I will give you the time to do so. But in the meanwhile, you do not order the staff around in the way you have been doing. You ask them to do a chore for you, you do not order them. And in case you don't know the difference, what I have just said to you is an order.' The faces of his wife and daughter spoke volumes, but their lips stayed silent. 'I am now going to have my cup of tea, then get washed and changed for an appointment I have this evening.' With that he left a room where you could have heard a pin drop. But the silence didn't last for long.

'This is all very distressing, Mother,' Victoria said. 'I hope the subject of divorce is not mentioned at the dinner party. It could ruin my chances with Charles.'

'Providing you are allowed to have the dinner party, there will be no occasion to mention it. Robert certainly won't, he'd be too ashamed.'

'He can't stop me having it, I won't let him! I have been trying to gee Charles along into proposing, and I thought if the party was a huge success, as I intend it to be, it could be the very thing to make him pop the question. He keeps telling me I'm the only girl for him, but seems shy about popping the question. So it's vital, Mother, that the dreadful word divorce is not even whispered.' Victoria's eyes were hard and calculating. 'You must take responsibility for this happening, you know, Mother. Surely you could have let Father have his wicked way with you once in a while, and suffered in silence? Five minutes of your time every couple of months would have prevented this catastrophe.'

'I couldn't bring myself to let him touch me. The thought of his hands on me makes me feel physically sick. But I have been an excellent wife to him in every other way. Why could he not seek his pleasures elsewhere, as I'm sure many men do. In fact, I would be very surprised if he hasn't.'

'You would have a hard job proving that, Mother, and degrade yourself in the process.' Victoria thought her mother very naive. When she got married, she would be far more in control. 'I'm hoping to be married from this house, with Father forking out for a wedding which will be the talk of the town. So let's not rock the boat too much for now.'

'Robert!' Maureen's beaming smile and tender eyes told of her joy. 'It's lovely to see you. I've been so excited since I got your letter, like a young girl waiting for her first date.'

As he held her close, Robert could feel the pressure easing from his mind. Her arms were so warm and comforting he sighed with contentment. 'You've no idea what it means to me to see and hold you, my dear. My life has been dreadful since I last saw you, especially today which has been a nightmare.'

Maureen kissed his cheek before taking his hat and hanging it on the hallstand. Then she took his hand and led him through to the living room. 'Do you want to talk first, or eat?'

'I would very much like to talk first, I have so much to tell you.' Robert drew her down on to the couch and put his arm around her. 'Before I burden you with my worries and woes, though, I want to tell you that this once-a-month visit is a thing of the past. I must see you far more often, Maureen, I need you in my life.'

She smiled and squeezed his hand. 'Oh, how the neighbours will talk if they see your car here more frequently. I'll be labelled a woman of ill-repute.'

'Will that worry you?' When she shook her head, he said, 'Last time I was here I asked you if you would marry me if I was a free man. You made me so happy when you said you would. Do you still feel the same?'

'Yes, I'd marry you tomorrow if it were possible.'

'It won't be possible tomorrow, my darling Maureen, but it will be in the future. But let me start at the beginning instead of the end.'

Nigel was driving Abbie and himself down to Seaforth when he had an idea. 'What about taking Milly and Bobby to see Grandma and Granda for half an hour? I don't think they get many visitors and it would be a change for them.'

'I think that's a marvellous idea. They'd have a good laugh with Bobby, the way he's always acting the goat.'

'He might act the goat, Abbie, but he's far from being daft. Him and his mother have had a rough time.' He went on to tell her how Bobby's father had died, and how grim things had been with hardly any money coming in. How his friend had

had to grow up overnight, from boy to man. 'It's only now he's finished serving his time that things are a little better for him and his mother. He's a good bloke, and a good son, that's why I have a lot of admiration for him. And I'll help him all I can, like teaching him to drive.'

Abbie expressed her surprise. 'Fancy Milly not telling me all this. Because he's always joking, you'd think he didn't have a care in the world.'

'Don't let on I've told you, he's got a lot of pride and he'd hate to think we feel sorry for him.' Nigel turned into Balfour Road. 'You ask Milly if she feels like going to Grandma's, while I go for Bobby. It'll only be for half an hour, though, because I've promised my mate another driving lesson.' He chuckled. 'He gets as far as switching the engine on tonight.'

Ten minutes later the youngsters were on their way, happy to be in each other's company. 'Ay, does yer Gran know we're coming?' Bobby asked, sitting in the front passenger seat and feeling like a million dollars. He was hoping they'd pass someone he knew, so he could wave to them and show off. 'They mightn't feel like company.'

'You don't know my Grandma and Granda,' Abbie laughed. 'They'll be made up. You'll love them. They're so cuddly, I could eat them.'

'Yer better hadn't do that tonight, yer'll put me off me driving lesson. And don't yer think that's carrying things a bit too far?' Bobby asked. 'I mean, I love my Nan, but I wouldn't want her on me plate at dinner-time.'

'Yer wouldn't know the difference if yer put a dollop of HP sauce on it.' Milly kept her face straight. 'That's what the cannibals do. If they don't like HP they use tomato sauce.'

'I'm glad to say we've arrived.' Nigel parked the car close to the pavement. 'The conversation was getting a little too grisly for my delicate stomach.' He saw his Grandma looking through the window and waved. 'I bet she'll dash around tidying up before she opens the door.'

And he wasn't far wrong. Ada pushed the evening paper

under a cushion on the couch while telling her husband to give the hearth a quick brush over with the little stiff brush hanging on the companion set. 'They've brought friends with them, so make yerself presentable while I open the door.'

Joe chuckled. 'We've sat around twiddling our thumbs all day, now it's suddenly a mad rush! The house is as clean as a whistle, sweetheart, yer could eat off the floor. I don't know what ye're worrying about.'

'Well, being a man, yer wouldn't, would yer? The dirt could be meeting yer at the door, but yer wouldn't see it.' Ada patted his cheek, a twinkle in her eye. 'There's a button undone on yer shirt, sweetheart, be a good boy and fasten it.' Then with a smile that held all the love she had for him, she made her way to the front door.

'We've brought our friends to see you, Grandma,' Abbie said. 'They're both quite mad, so don't be surprised at anything they do.'

'When you get to our age, sweetheart, there's very little left in life to surprise us.' Ada kissed and hugged her grandchildren, then extended the greeting to Milly and Bobby. 'Yer friends are always welcome here, yer know that.'

Joe was standing in front of the fireplace when they all trooped in, and his wife went to stand beside him. 'This handsome man is my husband, Joe. Fifty years we've been wed, and never a cross word between us.' The twinkle was back in her eyes but her face was deadpan when she said crossly, 'I thought I told yer to fasten the button on yer shirt, Joe, so why haven't yer? Honest to God, yer'd be going round half-naked if I wasn't here to keep yer in order.'

Joe's lined face split into a grin. 'I love it when yer shout at me, sweetheart. That's if it's only in fun, like. I'd run like hell if I thought yer meant it.'

Bobby looked at the two old folk and knew what Abbie had meant about them being cuddly. You couldn't help but fall for the two of them. 'Ay, Abbie, I'll have yer Granda with HP, and you can have tomato sauce with yer Grandma.'

Ada looked puzzled. 'What's this about sauces? I haven't got no dinner for yer 'cos how was I to know yer wanted one?'

'Take no notice of him, Grandma,' Nigel said. 'My mate has a warped sense of humour. It all started with Abbie saying she loved you so much she could eat you.'

'I'm not taking the blame for that, Nige! It wasn't me what said yer Gran would be tasty with HP sauce, it was Milly.'

'That's right, blame me!' Milly punched him hard on his arm. 'Yer always were a clat-tale, Bobby Neary.'

He grinned into her face. 'And you always wanted what somebody else had. Ye're jealous now because there's only two of them and they're both spoken for. And before yer say it, no, yer can't have my Nan, with or without sauce.'

'Before there's any bother, and yer come to blows, I'd just like to say something.' Ada was in her seventh heaven when her grandchildren came, and now they'd brought their friends it was an added pleasure. 'Me and Joe haven't been separated for the last fifty years, and we're not going to start now. We will insist upon being on the same plate, cuddled up to each other, with a bleedin' big dollop of tomato sauce.'

When the laughter had died down, Milly said, 'You're lovely, both of yer. But I don't know yer name and it's a bit awkward. What can me and Bobby call yer?'

'Well, I'm Joe, and my dear wife is Ada.'

'We can't call you that, it would be disrespectful and me mam would clip me over the ears if she heard me. But it would be nice if we could call you Uncle Joe and Auntie Ada. Would you think us cheeky if we did that?'

'We'd be highly delighted, wouldn't we, Ada?'

'Pleased as Punch.' And indeed, Ada was. When they had company it gave her and Joe something to talk about later, when they were alone. Gave them more interest, like. 'Now I'll put the kettle on for a cuppa. Do yer all take milk?'

'Hang on a minute, Grandma,' Nigel said. 'Bobby's learning to drive and I'm taking him out for an hour. We were going to go somewhere in the country, but there's plenty of quiet streets around here that would do. So if the girls will stay on until we get back, me and Bobby could have a cuppa, then run them home. Unless you had something planned, Abbie?'

'No, we hadn't planned anything,' Abbie said. 'But Milly's told me I'm going to a dance next week whether I like it or not. She'll drag me there if necessary.'

'I was going to have a word with yer about that, Nige,' Bobby said. 'If you can teach me to drive, I can teach you to dance. That's fair, isn't it?'

'But I thought—' Ada caught Abbie's warning glance and cursed herself. The private dancing lessons were to be a surprise, and she'd nearly let the cat out of the bag. So she was stuck in the middle of a sentence and had to think quick. 'Are you and Milly courting, Bobby?'

He let out a loud guffaw. 'Give me a break, Auntie Ada, I've got more sense than that. She's a proper bossy-boots, is Milly, I'd never get a word in!'

'You cheeky beggar!' Milly pretended to be highly indignant. 'Anyone that went out with you would want their bumps feeling. I'm looking for a handsome lad with money in his pockets.'

'Now I'm not trying to sell meself, but they don't come more handsome than me, and right now I've got three shillings and sixpence in me pocket.' He winked at Ada. 'Many a girl would swoon for a handsome lad with three and a tanner in their pocket, don't yer think, Auntie Ada?'

'I would. If it wasn't for my Joe here, I'd swoon real good.'

'When you two have stopped insulting each other, I'd like to ask my brother something.' Abbie knew that what she was going to say would knock the wind out of Bobby's sails. 'Can't me and Milly come with you, Nigel? We could sit in the back seat and we'd be so quiet you wouldn't know we were there.'

'What?' Bobby looked horrified. 'I don't want an audience when I'm making a fool of meself. Oh no, Abbie, over my dead body.'

'That can be arranged.' Milly wouldn't have gone in the car

with them if they'd agreed. It wouldn't be fair on the lad, they'd make him nervous. 'What's your favourite sauce?'

Nigel was chuckling when he took hold of Bobby's arm. 'This could go on all night, so let's make a move. Give us an hour and a half, Grandma.'

The girls were having a game of cards with Ada and Joe, when the car horn sounded. The cards were lowered face down on to the table, and they all moved to the window. There were shrieks of surprise when they saw Bobby behind the wheel, grinning like a Cheshire cat. Then came a mad scramble for the door, but youth gave way to age, and it was Joe and Ada who reached the car first.

'I've just driven the car up the street.' Bobby was so excited he couldn't get his words out quick enough. 'Honest to God, ask Nige! All on me own, and I haven't knocked no one over, or run into a lamp-post.' Like a child with a new toy, he couldn't stop himself talking. 'Mind you, that dog was nearly a goner. If I hadn't remembered where the brake was, he'd have had it.'

His excitement had rubbed off on Nigel. 'I can't believe it myself. He's picked it up a lot quicker than I did. Not that I'd let him out on the main road yet, but another couple of lessons, a lot of practice, and he'll be fine.'

'Can Milly and I get in the back, and he can drive us to the very top of the street?' Abbie asked. 'Go on, Nige.'

'I'm sorry,' Bobby said, through the open window, 'but if I drive to the top, I'd have to turn around to come back again. And I'm not that clever yet.'

'I'm glad for yer, son,' Ada said. 'Yer'll be able to take yer mam out for a run.'

'Only one thing wrong with that, Auntie Ada.' Bobby's shoulders were shaking with laughter. 'I haven't got a car. Mind you, that needn't stop me taking me mam out for a run, but she's not too good on her feet, so I'd end up giving her a piggy-back.'

Joe bent down and said softly, 'Yer will have a car one day, son, I know yer will. And then yer'll be able to take yer mam out. And yer girlfriend, when yer get one.'

'When I'm saying me prayers tonight, Uncle Joe, which do yer think I should pray for? A girl or a car?'

'Well, let's put it like this. I'd definitely say pray for the girl if yer could be sure of getting one as good as my Ada.'

'Nah, I'd probably end up getting one with a face like the back of a tram, and a bottom to match. So I'll stick with the car. At least yer get a key with a car, so yer can turn it off if yer get fed up with the noise. Yer don't get a key with a girl.'

'Ye're a bleedin' hero, you are, son.' Ada was really taken with Bobby and was glad Nigel had such a good, down-to-earth lad for a friend. 'Now will yer come in and get this cup of tea we've been waiting for? I'm spitting ruddy feathers.'

'I hope we're good enough to go dancing on Monday, now we've promised,' Abbie said as they were driving home. 'I'd hate to make a fool of myself.'

'We've got a lesson tomorrow night, one on Saturday afternoon and another on Sunday. If we haven't learned enough by then to give a good account of ourselves, we never will.'

'Are we going to tell Milly and Bobby we've taken lessons? They'll think it funny that all of a sudden we can dance, after telling them we couldn't.'

'Yes, we'll tell them.' Nigel began to chuckle. 'But only after we've surprised them. I can't wait to see the look on Bobby's face.'

'I've got mixed feelings about that, Nigel. He was so happy tonight, and so grateful to you for giving him driving lessons, he might think we've been underhanded. It's almost like saying we don't need him to teach us anything. If I was in his place, I think I'd be hurt.'

Nigel was thoughtful for a while, then he said, 'You're right, Abbie. I hadn't thought of it that way. It would look as though we were showing off, bragging that we could afford to take private lessons, and didn't need him. What we could do, is go to the lesson we've booked for tomorrow night, then when it's over, go through to the dancing class. And the same on Saturday. It wouldn't sound so bad saying we've been to dancing classes.'

'That's an idea! I like Bobby, and wouldn't like him to think we were making a fool out of him. And did you notice that Grandma and Granda took a real shine to him? When I was in the kitchen, helping Grandma with the tea, she said, "He's a cracker, he is. A lad after me own heart".'

'He's a character, all right. He can turn anything into a laugh. Tonight I was showing him how and when to change gear, how to use the clutch so the car didn't jump forward, and all the time he had me in stitches. He talks so much, you think he's not taking anything in, but I soon found out how wrong I was. When I suggested he try and drive the car a short distance, just far enough to get the speed up to change gear, he did it perfectly. In the end, he was driving so well I let him get into top gear, and it was as smooth as a driver who'd been driving for years. A bit more practice on the roads and he'll be able to take a car out on his own.'

Abbie giggled and lowered her voice to a growl. 'Only one thing wrong with that, Nige, I haven't got a car.'

Nigel turned his head to smile at his sister. 'I've reached the opinion that if Bobby wants anything bad enough, he'll get it. Unless it's Milly, of course – she'd give him a run for his money.'

'According to her, there's definitely nothing between them. They're just very good friends. Which is a pity because they'd make a fine couple. Milly would make a good wife.'

'Who knows who would make a good wife or husband?' Nigel was thinking of his parents. They must have thought they were made for each other, yet look how that marriage had turned out. And how would his sister take the news that they were to divorce? 'You have to live with a person to really know them.'

'Yes, you and I have seen a good example of that.' Abbie folded her hands in her lap, and brother and sister lapsed into a silence that lasted until they reached home.

'You poor darling, you really are having a bad time.' Maureen ran a finger down his cheek. 'And none of it is your fault, so you have no cause to feel bad about it. I have never really criticised your wife before because I didn't think it was my place. But she is a very silly woman not to have appreciated how well-off she was.'

'I've told Nigel about the divorce, but I haven't had the chance to talk to Abbie yet. Then I'll have to break it to Ada and Joe, my mother- and father-in-law. I don't believe they'll think badly of me for it, they know I haven't had an easy life with their daughter. The fact that she's been absent from their lives for the last seventeen years speaks for itself. I have never gone into depth with them regarding the state of affairs between me and Edwina, because I didn't want to upset them. And I certainly won't do it now. But I am of the firm opinion that my wife is mentally disturbed. It's the only conclusion I can reach which would explain her strange behaviour.'

'What will happen now? Will you buy a house for her and Victoria?'

'I'll let the dust settle first. I'm certainly not going to force them to leave quickly. I'll give them time to consider, and even choose a house themselves. Victoria is giving a dinner party next week, so I won't do anything until after that.' Robert pulled her closer. 'I feel tons better after talking to you. I know I have no right to use you, but there's no one else I can unburden myself to – at least, no one I feel comfortable talking to, who understands as you do. That's why I need to know I can see you more often. If it meets with your approval, I would like to call at least once a week.' He was heartened by her nod. 'And in time, would you be prepared to leave this house to come to me?'

'You know my views, Robert. I would never be your

mistress. I love you dearly, but I would not live with you if there was no ring on my finger. My conscience would not allow me to live in sin.'

'I wouldn't ask, or expect you to. I just want you to tell me you will be my wife when I am a free man. Your promise alone, my dear, dear Maureen, would help me through whatever time we have to wait.'

'You have my promise, Robert. You see, my love is as great as yours.'

Chapter Eighteen

'I've told yer about that nosy cow what lives opposite to me, haven't I? Ivy Simpson her name is, her husband's Derek and she's got a son of seventeen called Danny.' Kitty was swinging her legs under the chair and talking through a mouthful of cheese sandwich. 'Everyone in the street has got her decked, she knows everything what goes on in the neighbourhood. Sometimes she knows about things before they bleedin' happen!'

'What's she been up to this time, sunshine?' Agnes, like Pete and Jessie, was ready for a piece of gossip, it brightened the day. 'She's not having it off with the coalman, is she?'

'Nah, she's too ugly to get a feller. Unless they put a bag over her head, or took her down a dark entry. But she thinks everybody else is. Not all with the coalman, like, she's got her beady eyes on the milkman and the rentman. According to her, they're all having it off with the woman who lives next door-but-one to me. Now Josie, that's the woman's name, she's younger than most of us and hasn't been married very long. Nice-looking woman, too.' Kitty reached for another sandwich and began to chew. 'I think that's why Ivy Simpson picks on her 'cos she's jealous. Anyway, this Ivy was in the corner shop one day and was telling everyone who cared to listen, that she'd seen the milkman slipping in next door-but-one after he'd finished his round. She's a real troublemaker, and I'll show yer how she talks.' The cleaner put down her sandwich and stood up. 'She's twice my size, so use yer imagination.' Folding her arms, and hitching up an imaginary large bosom,

311

Kitty pursed her lips and nodded her head as though she knew something they'd all be amazed at. 'This is what she said to the women in the corner shop. "Three times I saw the milkman going in there last week and he was there over an hour 'cos I timed him. Brazen hussy, that's what she is. Someone should tell her husband, 'cos if she has a baby, ten to one it won't be his. And not content with the milkman, she's having it off with the bleedin' rentman! We all pay him at the door, but not her, oh no, he's invited in. And he's there long enough to be up to no good".'

'Someone should tell this Josie what's being said behind her back,' Agnes said. 'It could get back to her husband and if he believed it, it would cause trouble.'

'Oh, the neighbours have sorted it out.' Kitty took her seat and picked up her sandwich. 'That's what I was starting to tell yer.'

Agnes gasped. 'D'yer mean all that was just a warm-up to what ye're going to tell us? In the name of God, sunshine, we'll be here all day!'

'No we won't, if yer listen quick.'

Jessie giggled, thinking that was really funny, but Pete, in his slow controlled voice, said, 'We can only listen as quick as you talk, Kitty.'

'It's you what's slow on the uptake, Pete, so get yer brain moving 'cos my tongue will be going fifteen to the bleedin' dozen. I'll finish this tale if it kills me.' She glanced across at the housekeeper. 'All right, queen?'

'Go ahead, sunshine, but it had better be good.'

'First I'll give yer a quick run-down on the nosy sod what lives opposite. She spends the whole day standing on her step or peeping through her curtains. Her window is facing ours and she can see right through. I bet she could tell me how many times my Alf goes down the yard to the lavvy. Anyway, the neighbours decided to teach her a lesson, and this is what they did. They told Josie what had been said about her, the milkman and the rentman. And then they told the men. They were all blazing at first, wanted to go and choke her. But they thought of a better way to get their own back. So yesterday, the milkman called on Josie about two o'clock, and they did no more than draw the front-room curtains over! Well, yer can imagine what this did to nosy Ivy! She stood on the front step hopping from one foot to the other, waiting for one of the neighbours to pass so she could have a good gossip. But everyone in the street was in on it, and not one came out of their houses. She was still standing on the step when Dave, Josie's husband, came walking up on his way home from his six-to-two shift. Everyone was behind their curtains, watching what was going on, and they said she nearly fell over herself to get to Dave before he knocked. They couldn't hear what was said, but they found out afterwards. Nosy poke said, "I think yer should know that there's something fishy going on between yer wife and the milkman. He's been here a few afternoons this week, he's here now, and look, they've got the curtains drawn so no one can see in. There's dirty work going on, and you have a right to know." Dave, all innocent like, said, "Oh dear, what can they be up to? Would yer come in with me, in case I lose my temper and kill him?".'

Kitty gazed at the three people who were hanging on to her every word. 'Ay, it's not half exciting, isn't it?'

'Get on with it, buggerlugs,' Agnes said. 'And if this is one of yer jokes, so help me, I'll swing for yer.'

'Now would I do that to you, me best mate? Too bloody true I would!' Kitty held up her hand. 'Only kidding, queen, only kidding. Yer'll like the next part, it's dead funny.' Her eyes sparkling, she asked, 'Is there another cup of tea in the pot?'

Agnes put her hand on top of the teapot. 'Yer'll get nothing until yer've finished this very long tale. I've been patient with yer, sunshine, but don't push me too far.'

'Right, queen!' Kitty leaned her elbows on the table and cupped her face. 'Yer can imagine Ivy being over the moon, being invited in to see murder committed. She practically

313

pushed Dave out of the way to get in the house first. And what did they find? Josie was setting the table and Jerry, the milkman, was in the kitchen fitting new shelves on the wall. Apparently he's a friend of Dave's, and he'd offered to come an hour each afternoon, as a favour, to whitewash the kitchen and fit new shelves. Of course Ivy didn't want to believe them, so she was soft enough to say if that's all they were up to, why had they drawn the curtains. Josie didn't answer her, but Dave did, he wiped the floor with her. Said if he heard she'd even used his wife's name again, he'd be over like a shot. He wouldn't hit a woman, but he'd knock hell out of her husband and he in turn could do what he liked to punish her. He escorted her to the door, and as she was stepping down on to the pavement, he said, "Oh, the rentman comes here for a cup of tea to drink with the sandwiches his wife gives him. I'll see him meself next week 'cos I'll be on afternoon shift, so I'll tell him ye're keeping an eye on him. Now bugger off, and don't even look sideways at my wife, ever again".'

'My God, sunshine, yer didn't half stretch that story out. I could have told it in half the time.'

'Shall I tell yer about the pregnant woman in half the time, then, queen?'

'What pregnant woman?'

'The one in our street!'

'What about the pregnant woman in your street? She didn't have the same milkman as Josie, did she?'

'If ye're going to be sarky, queen, I won't bother telling yer about her.'

'Good!' Agnes rubbed a finger in circles on the fat on her elbows. Then curiosity got the better of her. She'd never rest if she didn't find out. 'What happened to the pregnant woman?'

But Kitty wasn't going to be won over so easily. 'No, yer wouldn't be interested, queen, even if I did tell it quick.'

Agnes banged her clenched fist on the table so hard, it had the cups rattling in the saucers. 'Tell me about the ruddy pregnant woman, sunshine, or I'll come round this table and throttle the living daylights out of yer.'

'Keep yer hair on, queen, it won't do yer heart no good getting excited like that.' Kitty was really enjoying herself and intended to milk the situation for all it was worth. Pushing her cup across the table, she said, 'Pour me a cup of tea out, Aggie, 'cos me throat's dry with all the talking.'

Pete and Jessie watched with interest. They knew Agnes and Kitty would never fall out so there was no fear of a real fight. By the time the end of their break came, they'd all go about their work laughing their heads off.

Agnes narrowed her lips into a straight line and flared her nostrils. 'This had better be good, sunshine, or you and me are going to come to fisticuffs.' She pushed the refilled cup back across the table. 'Now, about this pregnant woman.'

The cleaner laced her fingers and formed a protective wall around the cup so it couldn't be whipped away from her. 'Well, she wasn't really pregnant, queen, not really.'

'How d'yer mean, not really? She was either in the puddin' club, or she wasn't. It's not something yer can be half-hearted about.'

'Well, it's like this, queen. Her name's Alma, and her husband goes away to sea. He's away sometimes for as long as six months. Anyway, didn't the bold Ivy pick on Alma. Said she had a fancy man what called to see her two or three times a week when her husband was away. Well, it got back to Alma and she decided to give the bad-minded so-and-so something to talk about. So she started to put things down her knickers to make her look as though she was in the family way. Every week or two she added a bit more, and Ivy Simpson was having a field day. She was telling everyone that the husband had been away five and a half months, and she was certain of that because she'd seen him going down the street with his sailor's bag slung over his shoulder. A Wednesday it was, ten o'clock in the morning. Now, wasn't he in for a shock when he came home to find his wife four months' pregnant with another feller's baby. But it was her what was in for a shock, and made

315

to look a fool in front of the whole neighbourhood. Alma's husband came home, and of course Ivy was expecting there to be murder. She actually stood outside their front door waiting for the fireworks to go off. Can yer imagine her disappointment when Alma came out on her husband's arm, all lovely and slim? It was such a shock to Ivy's system, she didn't speak to a soul for weeks. But once people stopped laughing every time they saw her, she was back to her old tricks.'

'There's someone like her in every street, and they all get their come-uppance eventually.' Agnes pointed to the clock. 'Time we were all back at work. I think I told yer Mr Charles is calling about eleven, didn't I?'

Jessie's hand flew to her mouth. 'Ooh, I don't have to open the door to him, do I, Aggie?'

'No, you stay out of sight on the landing, I'll open the door to him. And what a big let-down that'll be, if he's expecting a beautiful young girl. Serves him bleedin' well right.'

Kitty pushed her chair back under the table, then did a little jig. 'If yer want to give him a bigger let-down, let me open the door to him. He'll think he's at the wrong house.'

'I think he's at the wrong house anyway, sunshine, 'cos God alone knows what he sees in Miss Victoria. With his money, he could have anyone he wanted. Still, if yer can believe all the gossip yer hear, he might be a big catch money-wise, but that's about all. He hasn't got the best of reputations. Fond of married women, apparently.' The housekeeper suddenly remembered young Jessie, and joking apart, that sort of talk was not for young ears. 'Go on about yer business, and I'll see yer later.'

'Mother, when Charles arrives, do you think we could have some time on our own? Say after fifteen minutes, you remember something you have to do? Be discreet, of course, so it doesn't appear obvious.'

'Yes, of course, dear. I'll stay for a short while out of politeness, then say I have a letter to write.' Edwina was almost

316

as eager as her daughter for Charles to propose. What a feather in her cap it would be. And how she would laugh in Robert's face. 'This is an unexpected visit, isn't it?'

'I was supposed to be going out for a meal with him this evening, but when he rang before, he said his father was away for the day on business, so he was taking advantage of his absence by allowing himself a few hours off.' Victoria's usually sullen face was looking as near to being happy as it ever would. 'I think it's a good sign, don't you, Mother? He would hardly take time away from the office if he wasn't really keen.'

'I agree, my dear, it certainly looks promising.'

'If he does propose, do you know what I shall take great pleasure in doing? Telling Father, and seeing the surprise on his face. I'll have no need of the "small, but comfortable" house he intends to pack us off to. And I will relish every word when I tell him so.'

'I would suggest caution there, Victoria, until you have an engagement ring on your finger. If things don't turn out as you wish, and indeed as I wish, we would be at the mercy of your father. And if we push him too far, he could make life difficult by cutting our allowance. He has been generous with us, as you must admit, but all that could change.'

'Oh, I feel quite confident about Charles. If he weren't smitten, he'd spend the few hours he has free at his club, not with me.'

Edwina cocked an ear and lifted her hand. 'There's the bell now.'

Victoria crossed to the huge mirror over the marble fireplace and patted her hair into place. 'Do I look all right, Mother?'

'You look lovely, dear. Blue is definitely your best colour, it brings out the colour of your eyes. Charles is bound to be dazzled.'

There was a knock on the door and then Agnes appeared. 'Mr Charles to see yer, Miss Victoria.'

317

Passing the housekeeper as though she wasn't there, Victoria held her hands out to Charles. 'How lovely of you to surprise me like this.' She lifted her face for a kiss. 'I was delighted when you phoned.'

Charles shook hands with Edwina before sitting down. 'Why sit in a stuffy office when I can enjoy the company of two beautiful ladies?'

'I shan't be staying long,' Edwina smiled sweetly. 'I have a letter I must write today. But first I must enquire after your parents. I do hope they are both well?'

'Both enjoying good health, I'm glad to say.' Charles stretched his legs and crossed them at the ankles. As always, he was immaculately dressed in a suit of the finest cloth. The Paisley-patterned cravat around his neck was kept in place with a gold pin, in the centre of which was a large diamond, and his highly polished shoes peeped from below light grey spats. 'They're looking forward to the dinner party on Thursday.'

There were three people in the room, and each one of them would lie for their own ends. As Charles had just done. His parents were dreading Thursday, as they had no love for the two women he was now being over-polite with. But like everything in his life, Charles would have no compunction about lying to get what he wanted. His whole purpose in coming here today was to get something he badly wanted.

'If you'll excuse me, I'll leave you now.' Edwina gave him the benefit of one of her sickly sweet smiles. 'I'll ask Agnes to bring refreshments in fifteen minutes.'

'No, don't do that, Mother.' Victoria didn't want the housekeeper barging in at an inopportune moment. 'I'll ring when I need her.'

When Edwina was safely out of the room, Charles moved over to the chaise longue. He patted the space beside him, and said, 'Come and sit next to me, my sweet.'

Her hopes riding high, Victoria did as she was bid. 'It is so good to have you here, my darling. It was a lovely surprise to

318

hear your voice on the telephone. I felt a tingle run right down my spine. That's the effect you have on me, my love.'

'You are having that same effect on me right now, my sweet. I came because I felt I had to see you.' He pulled her close and put his arms around her. 'I need you and want you so much, you're driving me mad with desire.'

'Charles, restrain yourself.' Victoria wasn't embarrassed, though, she saw his ardour as a sign that he was coming round to realising he wanted her for his wife. And to fan the flames of his ardour, she lifted her long skirt before crossing her shapely legs. She knew she had a good figure and she intended to use it for her own ends. Hence the very low neckline on the dress she'd changed into after his telephone call.

'How can I when you look so ravishing?' Charles ran a hand up to her thigh. 'I want to make passionate love to you, right now.'

'Really, Charles, what would Mother say if she walked back into the room? I would die of embarrassment.'

'Don't worry, my sweet, I do have some control over my emotions. At least I do when I know that very soon I'll be rewarded for my patience.' He smiled when he saw her look of puzzlement. 'Remember, darling, a room in the best hotel and a bottle of champagne? You're surely not going back on your word?'

'I thought we were going to discuss that after the dinner party? I really do have a lot on my mind as everything must be perfect for your parents. I want them to see that your girlfriend is a very capable hostess.'

'I'm sure they know that, my sweet.' Charles had come with a very definite plan in mind and he was a man used to getting his own way. 'And knowing you would be too busy to discuss our arrangement, I went ahead and booked a room in the Adelphi Hotel for Wednesday night.'

'But I couldn't – that's the night before the dinner party! You should have consulted me first, Charles, then I could have told you to leave it until the following week.'

'I couldn't wait until the following week, my sweet. You have tantalised and teased me for too long, and my desire is overwhelming me.'

'But you still haven't made a commitment to me, Charles, and this places me in a very awkward situation. You really are asking a lot of me.'

'My darling Victoria, you really don't expect me to buy the goods without seeing them first, do you? If you buy a new hat, I'm sure you always try it on before making a purchase.'

'Am I to be compared with buying a new hat? Really, Charles, such talk does you no credit, and humiliates me.'

'It was spoken in jest, my sweet. I didn't think for one moment that you would take me seriously.' Charles ran his finger down her neck to the swell of breasts so lavishly on display. 'I wouldn't upset you for the world. And after all, if my memory serves me right, the room in a first-class hotel, and a bottle of champagne were your idea. Which of course I was more than willing to agree to. But it now seems that you were leading me on, with no thought of fulfilling your promise.'

'I was not leading you on, and I never go back on a promise.' This wasn't going the way Victoria had hoped. She had to be very careful how she handled the matter or she could lose him altogether. She was under no illusion about his motives, never had been, but if that's what it took to snare him, then she would do whatever he wanted. 'I'll agree to do as you ask, my darling, because I want to please you. But I need a little back in return. And that is the assurance that I am truly your only girlfriend and your intentions are honourable.'

Charles didn't care what he promised her, he was always making promises to women and hardly ever kept them. But he had to appear sincere, and that was something he was also good at. So he managed a hurt look on his handsome face. 'Honourable! Are you questioning my honour, Victoria?'

'No, of course not. It was the wrong word to use and I apologise. But a lady does like to be petted and pampered,

Charles, and have sweet nothings whispered in her ears.' He was winning hands down, Victoria told herself, and she had to come out of this meeting with something. So she held the side of her face close to his, and said, 'There is my ear, my darling, now tell me what you know I am longing to hear.'

It was all getting very tedious for a man who could bed as many women as he had time for. But he'd done a lot of bragging to his friends about being the first man to take Victoria, and he wasn't about to lose face. Several bets had been laid on his success or failure. He had no intention of failing. So, pulling on the lobe of her ear, he whispered huskily, 'You are my one and only girlfriend and I think you are adorable.'

Victoria kept her sigh of relief silent. 'We'll have a good talk about the future after the dinner party. I do want things to go off well because I need your parents' approval. Do you know if they like me, Charles?'

But he wasn't going to go down that path. So he veered smilingly away from the question. 'You clever little minx, you! Not so shy and innocent as you would have me believe, are you?'

Victoria was perplexed, but pleased that he looked so happy. 'What have I said that is so clever, my darling?'

He put a finger under her chin and raised her face so their eyes were meeting. 'By saying we will talk after the dinner party, you insinuated that there will be little talking going on in the hotel bedroom on Wednesday. And you are quite right, my sweet, because we will have far more exciting things to do. I intend to make you very happy, and I know you will please and satisfy me.' He kissed the tip of her nose. 'You are going to please me, aren't you, Victoria?'

How could she refuse when she had him, as she thought, in the palm of her hand. 'It is my intention to both please and satisfy you. But as you know, I have never been to bed with a man before so I have had no experience. You must help me, Charles.'

He was gloating inside. It was her inexperience that was the attraction. Most of the women he went with had had dozens of lovers and the thrill was missing. Victoria was a virgin, and it would all be new to her. How he would enjoy teaching her how to pander to his insatiable appetite for sexual acts that were different from the normal. 'You need have no fear, my sweet. I will make sure that a couple of glasses of champagne are drunk to help you relax, and I can promise you you will enjoy the experience.' He took out his gold fobwatch and gave a sigh. 'Now, I really must get back to the office. And although I hate to disappoint you, there is a strong possibility I won't be able to make it tonight. It depends upon what time my father gets back. He receives many business calls at home in the evenings, and in his absence I'm expected to take over. It's bad luck, and jolly boring, but business comes first I'm afraid. If I'm not here by eight o'clock, you'll know I can't make it. I'll be thinking of you, though, and counting the minutes until I pick you up at seven-thirty on Wednesday night. Don't have dinner here, we'll have it in the Adelphi before retiring to our room, where a bottle of champagne will be waiting for us.'

'You aren't expecting me to stay the night, are you? I mean, what would I tell Mother?'

Charles shook his head, anxious to be off now he'd successfully accomplished his mission. 'I'll have you home before midnight, so tell her I'm taking you to a party at a friend's house.' He kissed her hand, then her cheek. 'Goodbye, my sweet, and keep me in your thoughts. If I can't make it tonight, I'll see you Wednesday.'

'Shall I ring you tonight, to see if you're free?'

'No, don't do that, my father likes the line left open in case he needs to call.' That was the last thing Charles wanted. If she rang, his father would probably answer the telephone because he wasn't away on business at all. And if she asked for him, he wouldn't be there. He had an appointment with a very rich widow who was very free with her favours. And in gratitude for his services, she showered him with expensive

322

presents. 'Make my excuses to your mother for not saying goodbye, but I really must be on my way. Don't bother to come to the door with me, I'll see myself out.'

'Mother will be furious that you haven't had any refreshment.'

'Who needs food and drink, my sweet, when I can feast my eyes on you?'

As Charles made his way to where his car was parked, a little nagging voice in his head was telling him he'd have trouble shaking Victoria off when the time came. But he answered the voice by saying he'd never had any trouble ditching girls before. He lived dangerously, he knew that, but he loved the excitement of it. He'd only been in real trouble once, and that was when he was seventeen. The junior maid he'd made pregnant was only fourteen, and his father had paid the girl's father handsomely for his silence. It had taught Charles a lesson, though, and that was to stick to married women, or girls who slept around.

When Bobby opened the door to Nigel, he had his dance shoes tucked under his arm, his hair was slicked back and he was grinning from ear to ear. 'Are yer coming in to say hello to me mam, Nige, or are yer eager to be off?'

'Bring him in for a minute,' Rose called. 'Because you're dance mad, doesn't mean yer can forget about being polite.'

'Hello, Mrs Neary.' Nigel had a bag under his arm which he passed over to her with a smile. 'I've brought you a few chocolates. I wasn't sure what you liked, so I chose Cadbury's because they are my favourites.'

'I thought they were yer dance shoes,' Bobby said, scratching his head but taking care not to dislodge any hairs. 'Yer can't go to a dance without proper shoes.'

Nigel couldn't answer right away because Rose was hugging and kissing him. 'Ta, lad, that's real kind of yer. It's years since anyone bought me a box of chocolates. In fact I've never

323

had one as big as this – it must have cost yer a bleedin' fortune.'

'Mam, will yer let Nige speak, please? Where's yer dancing shoes?'

'Your mother first, Bobby, so be patient.' Nigel kissed the cheek of the woman who brought back many happy memories. Memories of being young and rebellious as boys often are, and clips around the ear for answering back. But also memories of always being welcome in this house, and the warmth, the sharing and friendship. 'They didn't cost me a bleedin' fortune, Mrs Neary, but even if they had, you would be worth every penny. But don't expect a box every week, my wages don't run to that with having the car to fork out for.'

'Ye're a good lad, Nigel, and yer always have been. Even when yer were giving cheek yer always did it in a nice way.'

'Ah, but what about when we used to knock on your door and then run like the devil? You never did catch us with the sweeping brush, did you?'

'Oh, I could have done, lad. The trouble was, by the time I caught up with yer, I'd have had no bleedin' breath left to wallop yer one.'

'I hate to interrupt this very interesting conversation, but I thought yer came down to go to Balfour Hall, Nige. The way things are going, we'll just be in time for the interval waltz.' Bobby wasn't one for giving compliments, he always felt uncomfortable. But he was made-up about the box of chocolates, 'cos he loved his mam and would give her the world if he could. 'And about these dancing shoes, haven't yer got none?'

'Abbie has them. I said we'd call for her and Milly.' Then Nigel, as arranged with his sister, said casually, 'And you'll be happy to know we won't disgrace you because we've been to a dancing class a couple of times since we last saw you. Not that we'll be up to your high standard, that'll take years, but at least we won't be raw beginners.'

'I'll pass judgement after I've seen yer on the dance-floor.

324

I'm not taking any chances with your Abbie until I've seen her perform. After all, I've got me reputation to consider.'

'You big-headed bugger!' Rose said, head shaking, but love in her eyes for the son who had given her a reason for living. 'I hope when yer finally decide she's good enough for yer, she tells yer to go and jump off the Pier Head.'

'Don't wait up for me then, Mam, 'cos if I have to swim home, it's a long way from the Pier Head to Seaforth. Especially for someone who can't swim.'

'Can't swim!' Nigel's voice was high with surprise. 'Of course you can swim, we used to go to Waterloo Sands when we were younger.'

Bobby looked shame-faced. 'Yeah, but yer never saw me swimming, did yer? Oh, I used to splash about and get me cossie wet, but me feet never left the ground. To tell yer the truth, Nige, I'm terrified of water.'

Rose chuckled. 'Even when it comes out of the bleedin' tap! Haven't yer ever noticed he's got a permanent tide-mark round his neck?'

There came a loud banging on the door, and Nigel pulled a face. 'This will be Abbie and Milly. They must have got fed up waiting.'

Bobby hurried along the hall, shouting, 'We haven't got cloth ears, there's no need to knock the flippin' door down.'

'Well, what's keeping yer?' Milly asked. 'We've wasted two dances waiting for you two. I wanted to go on, but Abbie wouldn't go without her brother.'

'It's his fault we're late. I'm beginning to think it's me mam he's come to see, not me.'

Nigel's head appeared over Bobby's shoulder. 'What's all the fuss about? I've only been here five minutes. It isn't polite to rush in and out of someone's house. But I'm ready now, so shall we make a move?'

Bobby was pulling the door closed behind him when his mother shouted, 'Have yer got yer swimming costume with yer?'

He grinned. 'No, I've decided me best bet is not to ask Abbie for a dance. I'll see yer, Mam, ta-ra!'

'Oh, aye,' Abbie said. 'What was all that in aid of?'

'It was me mam's idea of a joke.' Bobby fell into step with Nigel, behind the two girls. 'She said if I asked yer to dance, she hoped yer'd tell me to jump off the Pier Head.'

'Why would I do that?'

'That's a daft question,' Milly laughed, squeezing her friend's arm. 'That's what most people would like him to do.' She began to walk faster. 'Come on, it'll be time to come home before we get there. All the best-looking fellers will have been taken by now.'

'They won't, yer know, because we're not there yet,' Bobby called after them. 'Watch the girls make a dive when me and Nige walk in.'

Milly, her face aglow with laughter, shouted back, 'Yeah, a dive for the cloakroom!'

Nigel grabbed his friend's arm and practically lifted him off his feet. 'Come on, we can't let them pay for themselves!'

'Of course we can.' Bobby shook his head. 'Yer've got a lot to learn, Nige. Yer don't pay for a girl unless ye're going out with her. Otherwise they start getting ideas.'

'They're not just any girls, Bobby, it's my sister and her friend. I'd feel terrible if we let them pay for themselves.'

'OK, yer talked me into it.' Bobby took to his heels, calling over his shoulder, 'Hurry up, mate, ye're not half slow.'

They caught up with the two girls just before they reached Balfour Hall, and were inside the building before Abbie and Milly knew what was happening. 'I'm paying for meself,' Milly said, standing in the lobby with her tuppence entrance money in her hand. 'Don't take the money off them, George.'

'Too late, Milly, I've already taken it, and given them the tickets.' The doorman shrugged his shoulders. 'You pay next time, that's fair.'

The girl reluctantly agreed. 'But that doesn't mean I have to dance every dance with yer, Bobby Neary.'

'Chance would be a fine thing, Milly Jamieson. Yer don't think me fans would let me spend the whole night with one girl? There'd be a mutiny.'

'I won't have any worries about who I dance with,' Abbie said, butterflies in her tummy. 'I'll be sticking like glue to Nigel.'

Bobby and Milly spoke as one. 'Oh, no you won't!' Then they looked at each other and burst out laughing. 'That's the first time we've ever agreed on anything,' Milly said. 'We must be getting old, Bobby.'

'Speak for yerself, I have no intention of ever growing old. Me body might, like, 'cos I can't do nothing about that. But I'm going to stay young at heart.'

'Can I suggest we venture into the dance hall?' Nigel asked. 'Because all we're doing here is growing old.'

They all trooped into the hall where couples were dancing to the tune of a foxtrot, and found two empty chairs where they changed into their dancing shoes. 'Will our things be all right if we leave them under the chairs?' Abbie asked. 'Not that there's much in my handbag to pinch, anyway.'

'Yeah, no one will touch them.' Bobby held out his hand to Milly. 'Come on, we may as well finish this dance off.'

Nigel looked at his sister. 'Are you game?'

She nodded. 'I'd rather make a fool of myself with you, than Bobby. I'm dreading him asking me to dance. I think I'd faint.'

But once on the floor, she relaxed and found herself going through the steps Mr Ross had taught her. And when the dance was over, both she and her brother were pleased with their performance. 'I think we did very well, don't you, Nigel?'

'Remarkably well! But we have to remember we've only ever danced with each other; we might not do so well with a stranger.'

Coming up behind them, Bobby said, 'I heard that, Nige, and I don't think yer've got anything to worry about. Yer did fine considering ye're only just learning. I noticed ye're a bit

327

stiff on the spins, but yer can practise those in our house.'

Nigel chortled. 'Abbie as well? You see, she's the only one I can dance with.'

'She's no need to come to our house, I'll teach her here.' He held out his hand. 'Come on, Abbie, it's a waltz.' Although the girl looked terrified, there was no way she was going to let Bobby Neary get the better of her, so she allowed herself to be led away. And Milly roared with laughter when she heard him saying, 'I don't mind if yer stand on me feet, Abbie, but would yer try and keep off the little toe on me left foot, 'cos I've got a corn and it doesn't half give me gyp.'

'He's a flipping scream, he is.'

Nigel was busy taking his courage in both hands. 'I won't blame you if you say no, Milly, but would you like to dance?'

She did a little curtsy. 'Thank you for asking, kind sir, I would be delighted. And don't worry, I don't have any corns.'

Abbie was concentrating hard, trying to follow Bobby's footwork. One of these days she'd be able to dance as well as he did, and then she'd show him what for. She was so busy keeping up with him, she didn't realise he was speaking to her until he squeezed her hand. 'Relax, Abbie, and let your body go limp.'

When she met his eyes, she felt her heart miss a beat and her tummy did a somersault. She couldn't understand why, but he appeared to be staring at her with a far-away look in his eyes. The silence seemed to last for ever, but in the end she pulled herself together. 'Your body can only go limp if you're in a faint, Bobby.'

'Oh, don't faint on me, please, 'cos your Nige would kill me. Couldn't yer just go into a half-faint, like?' They were walking around the room now which wasn't like Bobby at all. He wouldn't waste time walking when he could be dancing. 'We're coming to a corner now, so when I tell yer, spin around.'

'Which way?'

'Which way? Yer've got me there.' He screwed up his eyes. 'Let's see now, if I turn to the right, that means you're turning left.' His face split into a grin. 'I'll tell yer what. Seeing as ye're me mate's sister, I'll let yer stand on me toes so yer've got to go the same way as me.'

'What about the little toe on your left foot?'

'Ye're getting very personal now, talking about me little toe. I'm surprised at yer, Abbie Dennison.'

They were laughing so much they did the spin without either of them realising they had performed it perfectly. And they were still giggling when they walked off the floor.

'How did yer get on, Nige?'

'I think you should be asking Milly that. I enjoyed it, but it wasn't my feet being trodden on.'

'He didn't step on my feet once, take no notice of him,' Milly said. 'He did really well.'

For the rest of the evening they swapped partners for each dance. Except when it was an excuse-me, then they didn't see much of Bobby because the girls all made a bee-line for him. And much to her amazement and horror, a tall, dark, handsome boy excused Abbie in a quickstep when she was dancing with Bobby. He wasn't very happy about it, and asked the boy if he had any corns.

'No, I haven't got no corns.' The boy was tugging Abbie towards him. 'What's it got to do with you, anyway?'

'It's got nothing to do with me, mate, whether yer've got corns or not. But Miranda here, she likes a boy with corns.'

'Is that your name, Miranda?' the boy asked when he finally prised Abbie loose. 'It's an unusual name.'

Abbie couldn't speak or she'd have burst out laughing, so she just nodded. And after a few spins around the dance-floor, the record came to an end and she was able to join her friends.

Milly couldn't contain herself. 'Oh dear, oh dear, Miranda!'

Nigel thought it hilarious. 'Where on earth did you get that name from, Bobby? I've never heard it before.'

'That's nothing,' Abbie told them, through hiccups brought on by laughter. 'He asked the poor lad if he had corns!'

* * *

They were driving home when Nigel said, 'That's the happiest, and most enjoyable time I've had since we moved away from Balfour Road. It made me wonder if we wouldn't have been better staying there.'

'I've thought that many times. But we really didn't have much say in the matter, did we? Anyway, none of us knew the way things would turn out. Especially Father, he thought he was doing the best thing for his family.' Abbie had been told by her father about the divorce. He had sat her down in the study and quietly told her what he had set in motion. 'I feel really sorry for him because he's put up with Mother for years without complaining. And while I know it's a terrible thing to say, I don't feel sorry for her. In fact, I have no feelings for her at all. She's never been a real mother, not like Milly's or Bobby's. I'm eighteen years of age and cannot remember ever having been kissed by her. That isn't natural.'

Nigel took her back to a happier subject. 'So you enjoyed yourself tonight?'

'Oh, yes, my tummy's still sore from laughing. I had a marvellous time and can't wait for Wednesday.'

'Same here. But I'm seeing Bobby tomorrow night for another driving lesson.'

Chapter Nineteen

'There's none so queer as folk, is there?' Agnes had her hands wrapped around her cup and there was a look of resignation on her face. 'Miss Edwina is the only one eating at seven-thirty tonight, but she insists on everything being set as though the whole family were present. Silver serving dishes – the lot.'

'How come she's the only one in?' Kitty asked. 'Where's everybody else going?'

'Well, it's Mr Robert's day for Chester, then he said he's going straight on to the club to dine with friends. Mr Charles is taking Miss Victoria to a party somewhere, and it's dance night again for Mr Nigel and Miss Abbie. They're having their meal as soon as they come in from work.'

'It's ridiculous you having to set that big dining table just for the Missus,' Pete said, with a look of disgust on his face. 'Yer'd think she'd have more sense.'

'She hasn't got no bleedin' sense, so how can she have more?' Kitty's legs were swinging faster to match her feelings. 'Wouldn't yer think she'd let yer have an easy night with the others all going out? The miserable cow!'

'Oh, yer haven't heard the best yet,' Agnes told them. 'I've got to get dolled up in me lace hat and pinny, as well! "We mustn't lower our standards." That's what Miss Edwina said to me. "I insist upon keeping to a routine, otherwise there'd soon be a deterioration in the running of the house. And that I will not allow".'

'I'll stay behind tonight, Aggie, and give yer a hand,' Jessie said. 'I could wash the dishes for yer, and yer'd be finished in half the time.'

'That's good of yer, sunshine, but I can manage. Don't forget, yer'll be very late tomorrow night. It's the dinner party and we'll be rushed off our feet. I know Miss Edwina's a bloody nuisance, and a bit not right in the head. I mean, fancy sitting in state in the dining room, all on her own, talking to four bleedin' walls! But if that's what she wants, if it keeps her happy, then she can have it. But she's getting her supper at a quarter to ten whether she likes it or not, 'cos I'm going next door to spend an hour with Tilly. I've got to keep up with all her news.'

'She's got a good boss, hasn't she, queen? Not a pain in the arse like ours. I mean, she wouldn't be asked to set a table for five when there's only one person going to eat, would she? Not bleedin' likely she wouldn't.'

'Yeah, she's got a good boss, sunshine, but then so have we. Yer won't get a better boss than Mr Robert, no matter where yer go.'

Kitty nodded in agreement. She had cause to know how good her boss was. There was no more walking to work for her now, not since he gave her the half-a-crown a week rise. And he always asked Aggie to make sure there was food for her to take home every night. But the cleaner had to voice the truth, as she saw it. 'He's a cracker, is Mr Robert, I'll grant yer that, queen. But still, it's a pity about his bleedin' wife.'

'I dunno, she doesn't get me down so much now.' Not a word would cross the housekeeper's lips about Robert's private life. What was told to her was in confidence, and that's how it would stay. 'There's been a big change here in the last couple of weeks which you probably wouldn't notice as much as me. And it's mostly down to the two youngest children. They are full of life, and seeing their happiness has made Mr Robert happy. Breakfast-time now is the best part of the day for me, because the four of us never stop laughing. The biggest surprise is Mr Nigel, he has altered beyond recognition. This friend of his, Bobby, can take the thanks for that, and I can't wait to meet him 'cos he sounds a real funny character. Mr Nigel took him for another driving lesson last night, and we were all in stitches at the things he got up to. Not that he's too daft to learn to drive, but the sayings he comes out with.'

'Tell us some of them, queen, so we can have a laugh.'

'I can't think of any of them off the top of me head, sunshine, but I'll see if I can remember some of them to give yer a laugh at dinner-time.'

'I hope yer do, queen, 'cos yer've already let me down once this morning.' Kitty put on her hard-done-by look. 'I was really hurt when yer said breakfast-time is the best part of the day for yer. I mean, it doesn't say much for us three, does it?'

'Ah, well, yer see, I don't count you three when I'm talking, 'cos ye're me very best mates, aren't yer? I'm with yer all day, and ye're like family to me. And nobody can make me laugh more than you, sunshine; ye're me very own laughter-maker.'

'That's nice of yer, queen, 'cos if haven't got you, I haven't got no one.'

'You've got me, Kitty,' Jessie piped up. 'I'm yer friend, and I think ye're the funniest person I've ever met in me whole life.'

Kitty's grin couldn't have been wider. It wasn't often she got compliments, except off her Alf, of course, so she treasured them. She glanced down the table to where Pete sat. He had his head down and was deep in thought. 'Ay, buggerlugs, can't yer hear me getting praised to high heaven? Yer might at least agree with them.'

'I'm sorry, Kitty, I wasn't listening. I can't get over the Missus making Aggie set a table for five people when she's the only one having dinner. There's something wrong with the woman.'

It was Agnes who answered. 'The way I see it, Pete, we have three happy, normal members of this family, and two who are not quite with it, like. They live in a world of their own. Miss Victoria is her mother all over. Self first, last and always. If yer were dying of thirst they wouldn't give yer a drink. And if yer fainted at their feet, they'd just step over yer. And when yer came round, they'd tell yer off for daring to faint on their carpet. Sometimes I don't know whether to laugh at them or cry me bleedin' eyes out.'

'Ay, Aggie, d'yer think this Charles feller will marry Miss Victoria? That would be a blessing, wouldn't it? At least we'd be shut of her.'

'He'd be signing his own death warrant if he married her. Not that I've much time for him, like, but at least yer get a smile out of him, which is more than yer get out of her. She really thinks she's someone special, who just has to sit and order people around. For example, yesterday lunch-time, she spilt a drop of tea on the table. All she had to do was mop it up with her napkin, but no, she wouldn't lower herself to do something so menial, she had to ring for me. And she doesn't ask me to wipe it up, she points a finger and says, "Clear that, Agnes". Never a please, thank you or by-your-leave. And that is the way she always is. Talk about a cut above the rest, that's what Miss Victoria thinks she is. And God help any man who marries her 'cos he'll be letting himself in for a life of hell.' The housekeeper put down her cup, clasped her two hands together and cast her eyes to the ceiling. 'Please God, I don't mean no harm, but if You do find someone daft enough to marry her, will You make sure he's got a whip in his hand, 'cos he'll need one.'

'Ay, queen, while yer were at it, yer should have asked for someone with the patience of a saint, 'cos he'll need that as well.'

'I don't like asking for too much all at once, sunshine, it looks greedy. But next time I'm saying a little prayer, I won't forget to mention about the patience.'

'And will yer tell Him not to take His time about it, 'cos our patience is running out.'

Once again the housekeeper's eyes were raised to the ceiling. 'Dear God, take no notice of what we say, we're not laughing at You, but with You. We know You must have a sense of humour 'cos You put people like Kitty on this earth to make people laugh and be happy.'

'That was nice, that, queen, real lady-like yer sounded. And thanks for putting in a good word for me. I'll re – er . . . recop – recup – oh, blow it, I'll return the favour when I say me prayers tonight.'

'The word yer were looking for, sunshine, was reciprocate.'

'Thanks, queen, I'll do that as well.'

Victoria looked at the people sitting near their table in the restaurant, and there was a look of disdain on her face. Why, would be hard to understand, because all the women were very expensively dressed, as were their companions. No one dined at the Adelphi unless they had a healthy bank balance. But even to a few acquaintances who smiled and waved, she merely inclined her head. Charles didn't miss this haughty gesture and thought what a dull bore she was. But another thing he didn't miss were the admiring glances of the men when he'd led Victoria into the restaurant. What she lacked in some things, she more than made up for in looks. Especially her figure, which was shown off to perfection in the deep lilac dress she was wearing – low-cut at the neck and nipped-in at the waist. If only she had a bit more life in her, smiled occasionally as though she meant it and had a sense of fun, he might even consider marrying her. But she had none of those qualities, and to tell the truth he was always bored stiff in her company. He didn't intend to be bored tonight, though, that was for sure.

'More wine, my sweet?'

'Really, Charles, you'll have me drunk. It doesn't take much to get me tipsy, but I'm sure that's not your intention.'

'Of course not, my lovely,' Charles lowered his voice as he refilled his glass. 'I want you to be very alert when we retire to our room. Your passion will be helped by a bottle of the finest champagne served in this establishment.'

Victoria wasn't in the least shy or embarrassed by his reference to what was to follow. She wasn't looking forward to the actual deed, where his hands would no doubt be all over her body, but while she might find it distasteful, she certainly would not be embarrassed. But her favour wouldn't come cheaply. For his couple of hours of fun, she expected nothing less in return than a proposal. Perhaps not tonight, but in the very near future. And she would work to that end.

'You spoil me, Charles.' She flirted with him across the table. 'And I can't resist falling for your charms.' Her eyelids fluttering, she asked softly, 'I hope I am having the same effect on you, my love?'

'Oh, absolutely! So much so, my sweet, I can wait no longer. I suggest we dispense with coffee and retire to our room.'

Determined that he should find her so irresistible tonight he would give some indication that he wanted her in his life permanently, Victoria said coyly, 'My, you are eager, Charles.'

'Never more so, my sweet.' They made a striking couple as he cupped her elbow and escorted her from the room, and many heads turned their way. Victoria noticed this and was delighted. And when they entered the lift to go to the suite Charles had booked on the second floor, she was in very high spirits.

'The meal was very enjoyable, my dear, thank you.' Robert was sitting on the couch when Maureen came through from the kitchen. 'Leave the dishes for a while and come and sit next to me.' He was pleased to see she was wearing the locket he'd bought, which she had been delighted with, and said she would wear every day.

Sitting beside him Maureen reached for his hand. 'It's lovely to see you again so soon, almost as if we were courting.'

'Which is what we are, my dear. I intend to court you until the day I am a free man, and then I'll be proud to ask you to be my wife. I hope we can marry as soon as possible after my divorce comes through. Would you want a big wedding, or a quiet service in a register office with just our closest family and friends attending?'

'A quiet wedding would suit me fine. I'm too old to want a big fussy affair. And as I don't have any family, and very few friends, the church would be noticeably empty my side, and full yours.'

'Would you like to know how many family and friends I have? I believe you'll be surprised at the people I regard as my real friends. My family would consist of Nigel and Abbie, plus my mother and father-in-law, whom I look upon as my own parents. Then, closest to me, is Jeff and his family. I'm hoping Jeff will be my best man because we've been friends for so many years. They are the ones I would like present at the service. But I would like to have the wedding reception in my home, with all my friends there.'

Maureen lowered her head, and her voice held a trace of sadness. 'I don't even have anyone to act as my maid of honour.'

Robert put his arm across her shoulders. 'Oh, you will, my darling, you will. Long before that day arrives you will have met Nigel and Abbie, and all my friends. And you will learn to love them as much as I love them.'

'I'm longing to meet your children, but a little apprehensive. What if they don't like me?'

'How could they not like you? How could they not adore you, as I do? They don't even know of your existence yet, except for Jeff, and I think it too soon to tell them. I'm hoping my wife and Victoria will be living elsewhere in the next month or so, and when they are gone I will not only mention you, I will take you to my home to meet Nigel and Abbie, and the staff whom I regard as friends – Agnes, Kitty, Pete and Jessie. You have heard me talk so much about each and every one of them, they won't feel like strangers to you.'

'I wish this was all going to happen soon, Robert, I want so much to be part of your life. I'm grateful for the last three years, they've meant a lot to me. But now I know our friendship is able to move on, I want more. To be able to walk down the street with you without worrying about neighbours peering through their windows. To link your arm, to show we are more than just friends. That's what I want now, Robert, and it can't come quickly enough.'

'Give me time to sort out my affairs, my dear, and then we can do the things you would like to do. When Edwina moves out, we will be officially separated and the divorce well in hand. Then I can introduce you as someone I intend to marry, and you will have no cause for either embarrassment or guilt.'

'I'll probably be shy at first, Robert, because I've led a very quiet life since my parents died. Certainly I've had no social life. So I'll be relying on you to be standing next to me when I meet the people who are important to you.' Maureen suddenly giggled. 'Anyone would think I was a shrinking violet, wouldn't they? And I'm not really, 'cos you can't be shy working in a shop. Customers expect a pleasant face behind the counter, and the chance for a good natter.'

'I have an advantage that you don't have, my dear, in that I know my friends. And you would fit in with them very well. After all, I was a stranger to you the day I knocked on your door, and that was only because you were given charge of selling the contents of the house next door. I remember you were a little withdrawn at first, but we were soon enjoying a conversation.' He raised her hand to his lips and kissed it. 'It was fate which brought us together, and I often think what I would have missed if the family of the deceased had chosen someone else to oversee the sale. How bleak my life would be now if you were not part of it. I dread the thought.'

'Robert, I have gone over the events of that day hundreds of times. I remember almost every word spoken. I never thought I'd see you again, and as you had told me you were married, I was angry with myself for wishing for the impossible. But I couldn't get you out of my mind, even though I told myself I was a scarlet woman, wanting someone who belonged to another. Then when you called the following week, I was so happy to see you I could not bring myself to send you away.'

'Our patience will be rewarded one day,' Robert told her. 'We may have to wait up to two years, but at least we have a future to look forward to. And never again will there be a month between our meetings. I'll be coming at least twice a week, if that meets with your approval?'

'Need you ask?' Maureen snuggled up to him. 'Your every wish is my command, my very dearest, darling Robert.'

'Ay, ye're looking very nice tonight, Milly.' Bobby tilted his head as he gave his verdict on the pretty blue dress with its frilled neck and cuffs, and nipped-in waist. 'Yer'll have all the lads after yer.'

Milly blushed. 'Does that mean I don't look nice other nights?'

'Trust you to take the huff. I pass yer a compliment and yer get sarky with me.'

'That's because I don't trust you to pay me a compliment without there being a joke behind it. So come on, what's wrong with the dress?'

'I don't think Bobby was pulling your leg, Milly,' Nigel said. 'You do look very pretty, the dress and colour suit you.'

Milly put her hands to her cheeks. 'Now I've gone all red, and it's your fault, Bobby Neary.'

'I knew it would be, it always is. Ye're the only girl I know who gets a cob on 'cos someone tells them they look nice! I'll keep me mouth shut in future, even if yer look a sight. I won't even tell yer yer've got a ruddy big hole in the heel of yer stocking.'

Milly lifted one leg, then the other. 'I haven't got a hole in me stocking.'

'I never said yer did! What I said was, *if* yer had a hole I wouldn't tell yer.' Bobby appealed to Abbie. 'Do you carry on like this when someone pays yer a compliment?'

'I don't know, why don't you try me?'

He eyed her up and down. 'Yeah, you look all right, Abbie.'

'All right? Is that the best you can do, Bobby Neary – all right?'

'I'm not going to say yer look nice, 'cos look at the trouble I got into with Milly. Anyway, yer always look – er – all right, Abbie.'

'What would yer do with him?' Milly asked. 'He's best left alone.'

'They've just started a tango, Milly, so do yer want to dance with me, or not?' Bobby asked. 'Yer can always leave me alone when it's over. In fact, if yer like, I'll go and stand in a corner in between dances, all on me own.'

'Yeah, OK.' Milly winked at Abbie. 'But if yer hand's not clean, don't put in on me back, 'cos yer'll dirty me new dress that I bought from TJs for two and eleven.'

Bobby was leading her on to the dance-floor when he said, 'Aye, all right. D'yer mean the dress I'm not supposed to say yer look nice in?'

Nigel grinned at his sister. 'I'm blowed if I can make those two out. One minute I think they've got a crush on each other, the next I believe Bobby when he says they're just mates. What do you think?'

'Like you, I'm undecided. They're a good match, both as crazy as each other. But whether there's romance in the offing, I wouldn't know.' Abbie raised her brows. 'Are you going to ask me for this dance, Nigel, or do I have to ask you? Between you and Bobby, I'm going to end up with an inferiority complex.'

The next dance was an 'excuse me' foxtrot, and the two men swapped partners. Before Bobby put his hand on Abbie's back, he said, 'Yer don't have to worry if yer got this dress at TJs for two an' eleven, me hands are clean.'

They'd only gone once around the dance-floor when Bobby felt a hand on his arm and a voice said, 'Excuse me.' He turned to find the same bloke who had excused Abbie last week, and he wasn't best pleased. 'This is getting to be personal now. Go and excuse one of the other girls, there's plenty of them.'

Bobby was a big lad, but this bloke towered over him. 'This is an excuse me, and I want to dance with Miranda. So will you unhand her, please?'

Abbie could see Bobby's shoulders shake, and knew he was going to laugh. And she had a feeling this bloke, who was quite good-looking, wouldn't take kindly to being laughed at. A picture flashed before her eyes of a blow being thrown, and Bobby lying flat on his back on the dance-floor. So she pulled herself free, whispering, 'I'll see you later.'

'Is he yer regular boyfriend, Miranda?' the boy asked as he swept her along. He was a very experienced dancer, and Abbie was hard put to keep up with him. 'He seems to think he owns yer.'

Should she tell him her name wasn't Miranda? That was the question burning in Abbie's mind. If she told him it was only Bobby being playful, he might think he'd been made a fool of. 'No, he's not my regular boyfriend, just a very good friend.'

'How about coming to the pictures with me one night, then? My name's Eric, by the way, and anyone here will tell you I'm a decent enough lad. So how about it?'

Before Abbie had time to think, she was being excused again, by Bobby. And as Eric walked away, he said, 'Think about it, Miranda, and let me know later.'

'Think about what, Miranda?' Bobby asked with a chuckle, twirling her around and around, his movements flowing with the tempo. 'And what will yer let him know later?'

'I'll tell you when the dance is over, but you haven't half dropped me in it. If I tell him my name's not Miranda, and you were only kidding, he'll probably clock you one.'

'Who, Eric Leyland? Nah, there's no harm in Eric, he's all talk.'

'Ye gods and little fishes! Just listen to yourself, Bobby

341

Neary. There's no one breathing who can talk more than you do. Anyway, do you mean to tell me you know this boy?'

'Of course I do, so does Nige. We were in the same class at school.'

'Well, why the heck did you treat him as though you'd never seen him in your life before? And another thing, he didn't mention he knew you.'

'He wouldn't if he was trying to cop off with yer, would he? And from the sound of things that was what he was trying to do.'

By the time the dance came to an end, Abbie didn't know whether to laugh or cry. It was all right for Bobby to joke about it, but she was the one who had to face the lad if he asked her for a dance. 'Nigel, do you know a boy called Eric?'

'The boy who just excused you? Yes, he went to our school, why?'

'Because he's asked me for a date, and he thinks my name's Miranda.'

'He's asked yer for a date!' Bobby's voice was high with surprise. 'The cheeky devil! I'll have to have words with him.'

'You will not, you've caused enough trouble as it is.' Abbie looked to her brother for help. 'What am I supposed to say, Nigel? Shall I tell him we were having a joke and gave each other funny names?'

'Don't worry about that,' Milly laughed. 'If he's asked yer for a date, he won't be worried what yer name is.'

'What did you tell him, Abbie?' Nigel asked.

'I didn't tell him anything, because soft lad here cut in on us. I'm not worried about him asking for a date, I can talk my way out of that, it's the name I'm worried about.'

'Why would yer talk yer way out of it? He's a nice lad, is Eric,' Milly said. 'It wouldn't do you any harm to go out with him one night. I know many girls who'd give their right arm to be asked out by him.'

'It's rather a long way from here to Mossley Hill, though.' Nigel was wondering what his dad would say in this situation.

But his sister was eighteen, after all, not a child. 'Still, you must make up your own mind.'

'But she doesn't know the lad from Adam!' Bobby said. 'He could be Frankenstein for all she knows, or a werewolf. She could go in the Broadway one night, all hale and hearty, and come out with two bite-marks on her neck and not a drop of blood left.'

'If I didn't have a drop of blood left in my body, yer daft nit, I'd hardly be able to walk out of the Broadway, would I? And anyway, don't you be talking about me as if I'm not here.'

'If yer go out with him, yer won't be here, will yer? That would only leave Milly for me and Nigel to share. We'd be tearing her from limb to limb, and she wouldn't like that at all. Especially if she's wearing her TJs two and eleven dress what I haven't got to say she looks nice in.'

'I'm afraid you haven't any time left to decide, Abbie, because Eric is on his way over for this dance,' Nigel said. 'But don't be talked into anything you're not sure about. After all, we'll be here again on Friday night, you'll see him then.'

'Hello, Nigel,' Eric said, after smiling at Abbie. 'I thought it was you the other night, but I wasn't sure. Nice to see yer again.' He held out his hand, saying, 'Can I have this dance, please, Miranda?'

Oh, I can't keep this up, Abbie thought, we're making a fool of the lad. 'Yes, you can have this dance, but I'd like to clear something up first. The four of us were having a joke last week, changing our names to ones which were out of the ordinary. I chose Miranda, but my name is really Abigail, or Abbie for short. Bobby here picked the best of the lot though, he had us calling him Jasper.'

Eric looked at the dumbstruck Bobby, and burst out laughing. 'That's a good one that, Bobby, and it doesn't half suit yer. It matches yer blue eyes.' Still laughing he led Abbie onto the dance-floor. 'Jasper! Oh, he'll never hear the last of that, I'll pull his leg soft.'

'That would be a very mean thing to do,' Abbie told him,

although she thought herself clever to have pulled such a fantastic name out of the blue. 'After all, it was a game between the four of us, and I only told you because I couldn't let you go on calling me Miranda.'

'OK, if you say yer'll come out with me one night, I promise I won't make fun of him. How about that?'

'I think the best way to stop you making fun of a friend of mine, is to let you join the club. Would you like me to choose a name for you, Eric?'

When he smiled down at her, Abbie noticed he had nice blue eyes and a set of strong, white, even teeth. 'Go on, then,' he said. 'Anything for a laugh.'

'How about Jeremiah? I think that's a beauty.'

'It's only a joke, isn't it? I mean, I'd be a laughing stock if that got around.'

Abbie smiled. 'Of course it's only a joke! And anyone who can't take a joke is not worth bothering with.'

Eric thought this over. 'Yeah, I agree. But if that Bobby Neary spreads it around, I'll break his flaming neck for him.'

'He can hardly do that, can he? Not with a name like Jasper.'

'Yeah, it's a good one, that.' Eric was a natural dancer, and easy to follow. His hand firm on her back, he guided Abbie through intricate steps she didn't think she'd ever master. 'Now, how about this date we were talking about?'

'You were talking about it, Eric, I haven't said a word. I don't have many nights free because I go to commercial college and have homework to do. But I'll be here on Friday night with the gang, so you could ask me for a few dances and we can get to know each other. I haven't dated a lot, you see, so I'm new at the game.'

Eric had to be satisfied with that. She hadn't turned him down flat, that was something. 'I'll look forward to it. Now, what do I call you? Miranda or Abbie?'

'Oh, Abbie, please. The Miranda joke was wearing a bit thin. Mind you, I've no one to blame but myself – I chose the name.'

At the end of the dance, Eric walked her back to her companions. He nodded pleasantly, then made his way over to his mates. Milly was filled with curiosity. 'Well, how did yer get on? Have yer made a date with him?'

Abbie shook her head. 'No. I said I'd see him here on Friday, that's all.'

'Well, if he thinks he can split our foursome up, he's got another think coming.' Bobby's nodding head added stress to his statement. 'And if I hear him even think the name Jasper I'll crack him one, then put you across me knee, Abigail Dennison.'

'Oh, I've sorted that out. I said he could join our gang if he'd let me give him a daft name. So it won't be Eric asking me for a dance on Friday, it'll be Jeremiah.'

There were hoots of laughter, then Bobby said, 'Nice one, Abbie. But I'll still knock his block off if he touches my arm again in an excuse me.'

'I wouldn't worry too much,' Abbie told him. 'He probably thinks I've got a screw loose now, thanks to you, and he'll steer clear. He'll look for a girl who doesn't want to change his name from a good sensible name like Eric, to a high-falutin one like Jeremiah.'

Yet Nigel couldn't help but notice that for the rest of the night, Eric's eyes followed Abbie around. He was a nice enough lad, but his sister had never been out on her own with a boy before, and Nigel felt protective towards her. He couldn't tell her what to do, though, she had a mind of her own. His best bet was a talk with his dad.

Charles lounged on the side of the bed, his open dressing-gown revealing his naked body. He had a glass of champagne in one hand and a cigar in the other. He was still feeling high after the thrill of making passionate love to Victoria, who was lying naked in the middle of the bed as rigid as a post. She had attempted to get dressed as soon as his ardour had been satisfied, but he'd stopped her, thinking he might as well get as much as he could from the evening. His eyes ran over her naked figure, a figure that would fire any man's senses. She hadn't enjoyed being made love to, he knew that. But instead of putting him off, it heightened the thrill for him. She hadn't resisted, she'd allowed him to do as he wished, but had taken no active part herself. He remembered the young parlour maid he'd raped, she'd been a virgin, too. But it had been a hurried affair, fumbling in a passageway with long skirts and drawers while the young girl put up a lot of resistance. It was something he could brag about to his friends, but it wasn't as thrilling as he had made out. Certainly not as enjoyable as tonight, where he'd been able to have his way without fear of being caught.

'I'd like to get dressed now, Charles.' Victoria had hated the last hour, finding it degrading and humiliating. It had been quite painful, too, in the beginning. This seemed to have been lost on Charles, who ignored her cry and kept on thrusting like a man possessed. When they were married she would suggest he took a mistress. This was not the time to mention that, though, so she mustered a smile. 'Did you hear me, darling?'

'Yes, my sweet, but I don't want the pleasure to end yet. I could feast my eyes on your naked beauty for ever.' He ran a finger down over her breasts and stomach, then slid it between her legs as his heartbeats increased and his breathing became heavy. 'I must possess you again, my lovely, or my head will burst.'

'No, Charles, please! It really is time we were going. Don't forget, I have the dinner party tomorrow night and I need my beauty sleep. I want to look my best for your parents.' Victoria could feel his hot breath on her shoulder and began to panic. 'Please, Charles, I beg you. I would feel so ashamed if I became pregnant.'

'I have told you, my sweet, that a virgin does not become pregnant the first time she has intercourse.' No amount of pleading would have got through to Charles, he was now at the point of no return. He slipped off the dressing-gown he'd

346

found hanging behind the door in the bathroom, and flung it on the floor. 'Only a man made of stone could resist you, and I'm not made of stone.' He covered her body, and was fired with a passion that blurred his vision and his senses. Everything was blotted from his mind, except the need to satisfy his desire. He took Victoria with a roughness and savagery that had her biting on her lip to keep the screams back. And when his passion was exhausted he rolled away from her and lay on his back, breathing heavily as he gazed up at the ceiling. There were no sweet words or caresses for Victoria now; he had achieved what he'd set out to do.

Glancing sideways at him, Victoria told herself she had paid a high price tonight. And she vowed that Charles would be made to pay an even higher one.

Chapter Twenty

'You seem very pale and tired this morning, dear,' Edwina said, looking across the breakfast-table to where her daughter was sitting. 'Were you very late getting home?'

'Yes, it was after midnight.' Victoria felt absolutely drained. She was sore all over, even had bruises on the inside of her legs. It was fortunate that no one could see them. Last night in the Adelphi had been a nightmare which she'd relived a hundred times as she'd tossed and turned in her bed, unable to sleep. Charles had behaved like an animal and she didn't know how she was going to look him in the face again. She could quite understand why her mother refused to go through such degradation with her father. The law might demand that the wife perform her wifely duties, but no decent woman would allow herself to be used as she was last night. No wonder there were so many prostitutes on the streets, and so many houses of ill-repute. And she had suffered further humiliation as they were leaving the hotel just after half eleven. There was the indignity of passing the liveried porter who hastened to escort her to the revolving door. His face had been impassive when Charles slipped a silver coin into his hand, saying, 'We have decided not to stay the night, my good man.' You could tell by the porter's face he knew they had no intention of staying the night, that the room was only booked with one purpose in mind. The absence of a portmanteau was enough to tell him that. And when he said, 'I understand, sir,' he said it in such a way as to suggest he really did understand. Oh, how humiliating that had been. But what had happened

349

hadn't altered her resolve to marry Charles. In fact, it had made her more determined. He may have acted like an animal, but he was an animal with the riches she craved.

'I do have a headache, Mother, and think I should lie down for an hour with a shade over my eyes. Once I've made sure Agnes has everything under control for the dinner party, I shall retire to my room and rest.'

'Did you have an enjoyable evening?' Edwina was eager for news. She had her own plan for the future, but that rested on her daughter's marriage into the Chisholm family. 'Any progress with Charles, d'you think?'

'So many questions, Mother! Yes, the evening was pleasant enough, but with having guests tonight I would have preferred to decline the invitation. However, Charles wouldn't hear of it.' There was defiance in the set of Victoria's jaw. Nothing would put her off the path she had chosen to take. So lies took over from the truth. In fact, lies and the truth were all one to her. What she said was what she wanted to hear. 'It was neither the time nor the place for serious conversation as Charles is a very popular man, and we had little time on our own. But yes, I think we progress a little further with each meeting.'

'Have you not thought to ask him directly what his intentions are?' Edwina asked, her interest being purely selfish. Why was her daughter allowing things to move so slowly? 'I would have thought that after your father's ultimatum you would have been keen to jog him along. If he were to propose, then I'm sure Robert would allow us to stay in this house until after the wedding. Indeed, as father of the bride it would be his duty to lead you down the aisle, and be responsible for all the expenses.'

Victoria ground her teeth together. She couldn't afford to upset her mother because she was her only source of cash when her monthly allowance ran out. But why was she being so tiresome, on this of all days? 'No, Mother, I have not asked him outright, that would be most unladylike. And it would not have the desired effect, as Charles is a law unto himself. He will do as he wishes, and in his own time.' She folded the heavy linen napkin and placed it on her plate. 'I really couldn't eat any more, I have no appetite. So if you will excuse me, Mother, I will go along to the kitchen and spend some time with Agnes. I want to go over the menu with her to make sure she is preparing every course as I requested. This is one time I can't have her replacing something I've asked for, with something she finds easier to make. Everything has to be perfect tonight, for a lot hinges on the Chisholms having an enjoyable evening, with the best food eaten in good company.'

'I'm sure Agnes won't let you down, dear. Her food will be compared favourably with anything the Chisholms' or the Thompson-Brownes' cooks could offer.'

'I intend to make sure that is so, Mother. I shall be checking on her at intervals all afternoon. I am leaving nothing to chance.'

'Miss Victoria, everything is in hand.' Agnes was thinking how ridiculous it was to worry so much about a ruddy dinner party. Particularly when it kept you awake all night as it must have done to the young woman facing her who looked dead beat. 'I started at six o'clock this morning and made the desserts. There will be a choice of two which I think will go down very well. If yer look in the larder yer'll see I have made pastry cups, which I will later fill with strawberries and cream. I've also made trifles because I know Mr Charles is very partial to them. Then there are two dozen fancy cakes which I will decorate this afternoon, plus twelve of the chocolate boxes you asked for. So all the little fiddling things are done and I'll start on the potatoes and vegetables when the staff have had their morning break. Oh, and Pete is attending to the flowers.'

'Can we go through the menu again, Agnes, to set my mind at rest. Everything must go smoothly, it is very important.'

Agnes told herself to leave the swearing until later. But Miss Victoria was really getting on her wick. Talk about teaching your grandmother to milk ducks wasn't in it. There would only be eight at the dinner party, and she'd catered for up to twenty in her time. She could serve eight standing on her ruddy head. 'Oxtail soup to start, and surely you can smell that simmering away on the stove now. Then poached salmon steaks in my own special sauce. And I promise they will be a delight to the tongue. The main meal is pheasant for them what like it, and prime leg of pork for them what don't. So, as yer can see, Miss Victoria, I'm doing everything yer asked me to.'

'Except for the truffles, Agnes. You know, the chocolate shapes you make filled with Turkish Delight and ginger.' Victoria could see this didn't please the housekeeper, so she resorted to flattery. 'You do them so beautifully, Agnes, and the last time you made them they were a huge success with the guests.'

'That's as maybe, but they take ages to make and yer need plenty of time on yer hands. They're not something yer can rush 'cos they're so fiddly.' Agnes was telling herself to keep calm, but it was very difficult. Especially when the person asking for all this couldn't even boil a flaming egg! 'I'll see how I'm off for time, Miss Victoria, but I can't promise.'

'Oh, please, Agnes, I'll be eternally grateful to you.'

'It's the time, Miss Victoria. I haven't any Turkish Delight in, or ginger. That would mean sending Jessie out for it, and she really can't be spared.'

That was only a minor problem for someone who spent their life giving orders. 'Ring Coopers and ask them to deliver what you need.'

'I wouldn't have the nerve to ask them to come this distance for such a small order. They'd think I had a ruddy cheek.'

'Nonsense! I'll ring them myself.' With that, Victoria flounced out of the room leaving the housekeeper so mad she was practically breathing fire.

Agnes was still sitting at the kitchen table when the cleaners came through a few minutes later. Kitty was carrying a huge bucket with a mop standing up in it, and each time it banged against her leg she groaned. 'This bloody thing weighs heavier than me! I don't know why the hell Miss Edwina won't allow us to empty the ruddy water down the lavvy upstairs, save carting it all the way down here to the outside grid. She'd soon change her tune if she was the one carrying the bleedin' thing.'

Jessie, her arms full of the bedding she'd stripped off Abbie's bed, told her, 'I said I'd carry the bucket, Kitty, but yer wouldn't have it.'

The little woman gave her a cheeky grin. 'If I'd let you carry it, queen, I'd have had nothing to moan about, would I? And yer can't beat a good moan in the mornings, it sets me up for the day. Even though me bleedin' legs will be black and blue.' Kitty noticed the housekeeper sitting with her chin resting in her hands and a none-too-happy expression on her face. 'What's the matter with you, queen, have yer looked in the mirror and didn't like what yer saw?'

'I'm not in the mood for jokes, sunshine, so don't expect me to burst me sides laughing.'

'Ah, what's wrong, Aggie?' The bucket was immediately lowered to the floor and Kitty was about to make her way over to her friend when the door was flung open and Victoria marched in.

'You will have the ginger and Turkish Delight before lunch-time, Agnes, so you have no excuse for not making the truffles.' Victoria had turned to leave the kitchen when she spun around again. 'Oh, as you said, they wouldn't deliver a small order at such short notice, so I suggested they could bring the weekly order. They soon changed their tune then.'

The housekeeper gaped. 'How can they bring an order when I haven't even made it out yet? I give them the order over the telephone on Friday morning and they deliver the same day. So if they don't know what I want, they can hardly deliver it.'

'Oh, that's all right.' Victoria waved a hand in the air as if to say there were ways of getting what you want, and she had proved it. 'I merely told them to repeat last week's order.'

Kitty and Jessie were wide-eyed as Agnes jumped to her feet and sent her chair toppling over backwards. 'Yer had no right to do that, Miss Victoria. I'm the one who knows what is needed in this kitchen.' Resting her clenched fists on the table, the housekeeper looked as angry as she felt. 'One week in every month I order enough tea, sugar and other dried goods, to last a month. They were all on last week's order, which means we'll get the same this week. I'm going to have enough dried goods to last nearly two months.'

'So what? It's food that will keep, isn't it?'

'What do I tell Mr Robert when he's handed another big bill? I'm not taking the blame for it, so you can tell him.'

Victoria could see the cleaners listening to every word, and she didn't intend the housekeeper to get the better of her. 'Father will pay the bill without even noticing. After all, he has no reason not to trust you, or has he?'

'Ye're going too far, Miss Victoria, so I suggest yer leave the kitchen before I say or do something we'll both regret. I'm responsible for the buying of food and all cleaning utensils, and I make sure that everything is accounted for. And when the bill comes with the order today, I'll make sure Mr Robert knows how it came about. All because yer wanted fancy chocolates for yer fine friends. And ye're always the same, selfish to the core. Yer think yer can have everything yer want, and it's to hell with everybody else. Well, yer friends haven't got the chocolates yet, and who's to say if they ever will?' Agnes bent to stand the chair upright. 'Now leave the kitchen, please, Miss Victoria, because we've got work to do.'

The change in Victoria's attitude was nothing short of miraculous. 'I'll tell Father about the delivery, Agnes, I'll take full responsibility. So please say you'll make the truffles? Please?'

'I'll see how my day goes, Miss Victoria, and that's all I'm prepared to say. It's not often that people question my honesty, and I'll not forget that.'

354

'I didn't mean it, Agnes, really I didn't. It was said in the heat of the moment, and I regretted the words as soon as they left my mouth.'

'Yer should think before yer speak, because yer tongue spits out venom. And yer should think before yer take it upon yerself to do a job that is rightly mine.' The housekeeper turned her head to where the cleaners were standing like statues. 'Empty the bucket, Kitty, while I make the tea for our break. Jessie, you throw that bedding in the laundry room and then go down the garden and give Pete a shout.'

They went about their business as though she wasn't there, so Victoria had no option but to leave the kitchen. She stood outside for a few seconds, wondering whether to ask her mother to have words with Agnes, but decided against it. It wouldn't help, not with the mood the housekeeper was in. In fact, if she was pushed too far, she might even refuse to have anything to do with the dinner party. And what would they do then? So, with her head pounding and her body sore and weary, she climbed the stairs to her room. There, she drew the curtains before throwing herself on the bed, where she cried with frustration at not getting her own way and being misunderstood by everyone.

'Ye're not going to make those truffle things for her, are yer?' Kitty asked, her face contorted in disgust. 'I'm buggered if I would, the cheeky sod.'

'If I do them, sunshine, it won't be for her, it'll be for my reputation. I don't want her blackening my name with the guests, because talk travels. I'm not blowing me own trumpet, but I am noted as being one of the best housekeepers and cooks in the city and I don't want me name tarnished. Miss Victoria will get her dinner party and it will be a fine affair. Everything will be perfect, I'll make sure of that. But I won't be doing it for her, it'll be for meself. And for Mr Robert. I wouldn't let him down.'

'She's just like her mother, yer know,' Pete said. 'She gets something in her head and thinks yer can just pluck it out of thin air. In the middle of winter, the Missus will ask me to pick some roses for the table. And when I explain it isn't the time of year for roses, she tuts and gives me a look that says it's my fault, then asks for carnations! And this is after she's walked the full length of the garden, where anyone with half an eye could see there weren't any flowers in bloom. And never so much as a please, thank you, or kiss my backside! As for a smile, well, that's out of the question and I've stopped expecting one. But for someone who makes out she was born with a silver spoon in her mouth, it's downright ignorant.'

'The house never seems to be short of flowers, so where d'yer get them from?' Kitty asked, taking advantage of the fact Pete was being talkative. Sometimes he'd sit at the table and not open his mouth. Mind you, you could understand that, he was the only man with three chattering females.

'The Missus orders them from a nursery where they have flowers all the year round grown in hot-houses. They don't come cheap, I can tell yer. But it's only what yer can expect because the bloke has to keep the hot-houses warm twenty-four hours a day. That's where the flowers for tonight are coming from, and they'll be costing Mr Robert a pretty penny 'cos she's ordered three dozen red roses, three dozen pink carnations and two dozen of those huge blooms what have a bigger head than I've got.'

'Bloody hell! All this for eight people.' Agnes shook her head in disgust. 'She throws money around as though it's going out of fashion.'

'It's a sin when there's people starving,' Kitty said. 'What they're paying for flowers just for a bleedin' dinner party, would keep a family for a whole week.'

'What gets me, is that it's all done to impress their toffee-nosed friends,' Agnes said. 'They're always trying to impress, but tonight seems to be extra special. I think they're going all out to charm Mr Charles into proposing.'

Jessie, who had taken a great dislike to Charles Chisholm,

pulled a face. 'Ugh, he's horrible, he is. Is Miss Victoria really going to marry him?'

'She's hoping so, sunshine. And I say a prayer every night that he'll pop the question and we can all celebrate. The day that young lady walks out of this house for good, I'll put the bleedin' flags out.'

'Ay, Aggie, don't the Red Indians make some sort of love potion?' Kitty was back to swinging her legs. 'I've seen them on the pictures, and they give this drink to the girl they fancy and when she's drunk it, she falls head over heels in love with him. She can't stand the sight of him before, but she's all over him after she's drunk this stuff. So it must be good. Wouldn't it be great if yer knew what they put in it and yer could stick some in those truffle things.'

The housekeeper saw the funny side and rocked with laughter. 'Ooh, I can just see it in me head. Everyone eats the truffles, so I could be going into the dining room to collect the dirty dishes, all innocent, like, 'cos me mind is innocent, and I'd scream me head off when I saw four couples all over each other on the floor.' The table was pushed back an inch as her tummy shook and everyone reached out quickly to save their tea from spilling over. 'Oh dear, oh dear, oh dear! That really has tickled me fancy. Have any of yer ever met Mrs Thompson-Browne?'

'No, queen, I haven't,' Kitty said. 'There's not much chance of them allowing me out there if they have visitors. I might lower the tone of the place, yer see.'

'Well, I know Pete and Jessie have never met her, so I'll tell yer what amused me about the love potion. We think Miss Victoria is a snob, but she can't hold a candle to either of the Thompson-Brownes. She – her name's Bernice – has got huge buck teeth which are always on show 'cos she can't close her mouth over them. She's the type what can't speak without waving their hands about, and she talks so far back yer have to go in the next room to hear her. And her husband – David Thompson-Browne – he has one of those haw-haw laughs that sound like a donkey, and he wears a monocle in his right eye which falls out every time he straightens his face. What effect a love potion would have on those two, I dread to think.'

Agnes's imagination was running riot and she lay her head, face down, on to her folded hands. 'I'll be all right in a minute,' she spluttered, 'when I get me breath back.'

'Take yer time, queen, we're just glad to see yer happy again. Yer'll have to forgive us if we don't seem to appreciate how funny it is, but yer have the advantage of knowing the people ye're talking about, and we don't.'

The housekeeper lifted her face to show the tears of laughter were still running. 'Well, yer all know Miss Edwina, so use yer imagination and picture her throwing herself at Mr Robert in a frenzy of passion.'

Kitty chuckled. 'Me imagination is not that good, queen.'

'Nor mine,' Pete said.

Jessie meanwhile sat quietly saying nothing, thinking this wasn't a conversation for fourteen-year-old girls, even though she couldn't quite understand what they found so funny anyway.

'Perhaps this love potion isn't a good idea after all, queen,' Kitty said. 'I mean, it's like putting arsenic in a steak and kidney pie, isn't it? There's only one person yer want to kill, but yer end up having to kill the lot.'

Now this is something I can understand, thought Jessie, feeling very pleased with herself. 'Kitty, yer could always make a small pie for the person yer wanted to kill, and the others wouldn't come to no harm eating the big one.'

Kitty met Agnes's eyes across the table and they silently agreed they wouldn't embarrass the girl by laughing out loud, they'd wait until later. 'Yer've got a point there, queen, but don't yer think the one what got the small pie put in front of him would be suspicious?'

Her pretty face was set in concentration for a few seconds while Jessie gave this some thought. Then she said, 'I don't think so, Kitty. If I got a small pie all to meself, I'd think I was very lucky.'

'Yer wouldn't be very lucky if it had arsenic in it, would yer, sunshine?' When Agnes glanced at the clock and saw their break had stretched to half an hour she jumped to her feet. 'Oh, my God, will yer just look at the time! Today of all days, when I've got so much to do.'

Three chairs were scraped back sharply, and Pete was out of the back door before they knew it. 'We'll get cracking on the dining room, queen, and we'll give it such a good going-over it'll think it must be its birthday.'

'All right, sunshine, I'll get going in here. I want everything ready early, so I'm not running round like a blue-arsed fly at the last minute.'

'Have yer made up yer mind about the truffles, yet?'

'No, I'm still thinking about it.' The housekeeper hadn't made up her mind, but she was weakening. After all, her reputation was at stake and she wanted to prove she was still the best cook in Liverpool.

'Had a busy day, have you, Agnes?' Robert was pulling his gloves off as he came through the side door. 'You look quite flustered.'

'Yer could say I've been busy, Mr Robert, yeah. And it'll get a damn sight busier before the day's over. Still, it doesn't happen often, thank God.'

'Have you had any help?'

'Kitty and Jessie have been brilliant. The house is shining from top to bottom.' She gave him a broad grin. 'If yer see any guests flicking their cigar ash on the floor, or leaving glasses on a polished surface, give them a go-along for me, will yer?'

'That's one way of livening up a dull party. To tell you the truth, Agnes, I can't stand these stuffy dinner parties, they bore me stiff.' He glanced into the larder. 'Where are Kitty and Jessie?'

'Jessie's up in my room putting on her best uniform. Honest, Mr Robert, she's so excited about getting dolled up, she's like a child with a new toy. And as for Kitty, well she offered to stay on until after the party so she could wash the dishes after each course. But I was frightened Alf would worry about her, so I sent her home to let him know. She should be back any minute.'

'She's a good mate, isn't she?'

'The best, Mr Robert, the best. And I'll be glad of her help tonight, 'cos it'll be hard going with just Jessie to help. She a willing girl, and she's quick, but she's not used to waiting on and I'll need eyes in the back of me head watching her. Still, yer can't put an old head on young shoulders, can yer? Miss Victoria seems keen for this party to be extra special, so we'll all do the best we can.'

Robert could see the beads of sweat on the housekeeper's forehead, and couldn't help thinking that this woman would flog herself to death tonight, while the one who was keen for the party to be extra special, would sit back and be waited on. And at the end of it, there wouldn't even be a thank you. 'I'd better go and bathe, or I'll not be ready when the guests arrive.' He put his hand on Agnes's arm and squeezed. 'You can only do so much, remember that. It's no good killing yourself for a stupid party.'

The housekeeper was watching his retreating back when the side door opened and Kitty skipped in. 'Permission granted and I'm reporting for duty.' She rubbed her thin hands together. 'Alf said to keep him one of yer famous truffles if there's any over.'

'I've already put a couple away for you, and for Jessie. There wouldn't be any over, no matter how many I put out. I've even known people to put them in their bag to take home with them.'

'Go 'way! That's something I'd expect from the likes of me, queen, but not from toffs. They've got plenty of money, why can't they buy their own instead of pinching?'

'You cheeky beggar! Yer can't buy truffles as good as the ones I make. They're in a class of their own, even though I do say so meself. Just place them in the middle of yer tongue,

360

close yer mouth, and after two seconds yer'll think ye're floating on a cloud.'

'Ye're a clever bugger, Aggie, I'll say that for yer. On top of all yer scullery skills, ye're a ruddy poet!'

Agnes bit on her bottom lip. Here she was, with so many things on her mind, like making sure the meat was cooking as it should, the vegetables were simmering on a low light, the salmon was ready to poach while the guests were on their starters, and the fresh cream had to be whipped for the cakes and trifles. Yet in the midst of all this, little Kitty had the knack of making her smile. 'What did yer say I was, sunshine, besides being a poet?'

'Well, I said yer were a clever bugger, queen. Then I said yer were known all over for yer scullery skills.' The cleaner narrowed her eyes. 'It was a compliment, in case yer don't know.'

'I'd take it as one if I knew what it meant. Yer wouldn't by any chance mean me culinary skills, would yer?'

'That's what I said, queen!'

'Yer did not! Yer said scullery skills!'

'You fussy bugger! I was near enough, wasn't I?'

They both turned when a quiet voice asked, 'Do I look all right?'

The young girl was a picture of innocence and beauty. Her blonde hair had been combed upwards and held in place with hair grips so it wouldn't slip down under the white lace cap. Her blue eyes were like a summer sky, and her skin flawless. 'All right doesn't do yer justice, sunshine, yer look beautiful.'

'Yer certainly do, queen, like a film star. Yer'll have all the men flirting with yer.'

Jessie was clasping and unclasping her hands. She was really looking forward to tonight because she'd never seen a dinner party. But there was one blot on her horizon. 'Aggie, yer won't let me be on me own with Mr Charles, will yer?'

'There's no way yer'll be on yer own with him, there'll be too many other people there. And I'll keep me eyes open, 'don't you worry. I can't see how it would happen, but if it did, tonight or any other time, then all yer've got to do is open yer mouth and scream yer head off.'

'That's good advice, queen, and you remember it.' Kitty raised a questioning brow at Agnes. 'Isn't it time yer were getting yerself ready, queen? Just tell me what to keep me eye on and go and titivate yerself up.'

'All the time and titivating in the world wouldn't make me look like Jessie here,' Agnes muttered as her wide hips swayed towards the door. 'Only a miracle would do that.'

'Aren't yer forgetting something?' Kitty called after her. 'Beauty is in the eye of the beholder, queen, and yer'll always look beautiful to me.'

'How's it going in there?' Kitty, her sleeves rolled up to her elbows, was standing on a milking stool in front of the sink, her arms covered in soap suds. They were in her hair, too, where she'd rubbed an arm over her forehead which was dripping with sweat. 'Are they enjoying themselves?'

'They seem to be. As yer can see, all the plates are as clean as a whistle so the food is going down well. And I'm beginning to think Miss Victoria painted that smile on her face 'cos it's been there since the Chisholms arrived.'

'They don't half use plenty of dishes, don't they?' Kitty looked comical standing on the stool slaving away at the stack of dishes that seemed neverending. She no sooner got one stack out of the way than another took its place. She reminded the housekeeper of a small Cinderella who wasn't allowed to go to the ball. 'What the bleedin' hell do they do with them all? Me and my Alf use one each, why can't they?'

'Ah, well, we're dealing with monied people here, yer see, sunshine. They need a side plate with each course and special knives and forks for everything. None of yer common as muck carry-on here!'

Kitty chuckled. 'They can't lick their plates, eh?'

Agnes threw her hands in the air. 'Lick their plates! Oh, horror of horrors!'

'They don't know what they're missing, queen. Then again, I don't think the toffs enjoy life as much as us common-as-muck folk.'

'Ye're right there, sunshine. If yer heard the way they talk, it's enough to make yer sick. All la-de-dah, like. That Thompson-Browne is the funniest, with the side of his face all skew-whiff trying to keep the monocle in place. And every now and again this horse laugh comes, followed by his loud voice, "Oh, I say, old chap." I think he's bleedin' hilarious.'

'Is Mr Robert enjoying himself?'

'It's hard to tell, sunshine. He gets on well with old Mr Chisholm, and I'd say they were the only two normal people in that room. Mr Charles will never be half the man his father is.'

'How's Jessie making out?'

'All right, so far. I don't think she can believe her eyes, or her ears. I'll send her down with the next lot of dishes and she can tell yer herself. What she won't tell yer, though, is that for all their finery, she knocks the other women into a cocked hat for looks.' Agnes touched the lace cap to make sure it was straight, then smoothed down her apron. 'I'll see yer later, sunshine.'

Ten minutes later Jessie came in bearing a tray laden with dirty dishes. After laying the tray down carefully on the table, she turned to face Kitty, and her whole being was alive with excitement. 'Oh, yer should see them, Kitty, they look like film stars. I've never seen nothing like their dresses in all me life. And they've got their hair all done fancy, and bands around their foreheads with little feathers sticking up at the side.'

Kitty gaped. 'Not Miss Edwina, surely?'

'No, not her or Mrs Chisholm. They've both got beautiful dresses on and yer can't see their necks for jewellery, but they haven't got no bands around their heads. They'd look a bit daft at their age, wouldn't they?'

'Yeah, I suppose ye're right, queen.' Kitty stepped down from the stool and wiped her hands on her pinny. 'I'm going to sit for five minutes 'cos me feet are killing me. So come on, what else are the ladies wearing?'

'They could open a shop with all the necklaces, bracelets and rings they've got on. Oh, and their shoes, Kitty, they've got very thin straps and great big high heels.' Jessie closed her eyes. 'What else is there now? Oh yeah, their faces are painted with rouge, powder and thick lipstick. And they've got that much scent on, yer can smell it all over the house.'

'And what about the men?' Kitty asked, trying to get a picture of it all in her mind. 'What are they wearing?'

'I think Aggie said they were dinner suits, with white shirts and bow ties. Mr Robert looks very handsome, and although I don't like Mr Charles, he looks handsome, as well. Miss Victoria is all over him, touching his arm and smiling up into his face. She's not half throwing herself at him, and my mam has told me a girl should never run after a feller 'cos he won't think much of her if she does.'

'Your mam is right, queen, no self-respecting girl would chase after a feller. But for all our sakes, I hope Miss Victoria catches him.' Kitty sighed as she got to her feet. 'I'll make a start on these dishes and you'd better go and see if Aggie needs yer for anything.'

'She'll be pleased, will Aggie, because everyone is saying how delicious the food is. Mrs Chisholm even said if she's ever looking for a job, there's one waiting for her in their house. She was smiling when she said it, but yer could tell she meant it.'

'Aggie's not leaving here,' Kitty said, once again standing on top of the stool. 'I won't let her, 'cos she's me mate and we're sticking together.'

It was half-past ten when Agnes came to collect the coffee cups. These were the last of the dishes and the guests would now be retiring to the drawing room for brandy and liqueurs.

Jessie came close on the housekeeper's heels and Robert raised his brows in concern. 'It's very late for you, Jessie, your mother will be worrying. I'm sure Agnes can manage on her own now most of the dishes are washed, so I'll run you home.'

'There's no need to disturb yourself, Robert,' Charles said, rising from his chair. 'I'll gladly take the young lady home.'

'No, Charles.' Victoria laid a hand on his arm. 'The girl gets a tram home every night, and tonight is no exception. She really is quite capable.'

'I will run her and Kitty home.' Robert waved a hand to silence any objection. 'It's late and I will not have them walking the streets in the dark.'

George Chisholm nodded in agreement. 'Quite right, Robert, there's some strange people around at this time of night.' His smile covered the housekeeper and Jessie. 'You have both served us well this evening and you have our thanks. And the food, Agnes, as my dear wife has said, was fit for a king.'

The Thompson-Brownes added their praise before Robert gestured to Jessie. 'I'll give you five minutes to change into your outdoor clothes, then I'll take you and Kitty home.'

After seeing the guests were comfortably settled in the drawing room with full glasses, Robert made his way to the kitchen. There he was surprised to see Nigel and Abbie chatting away to the housekeeper and cleaners. 'Where on earth have you two been?'

'We thought Agnes would have enough to do without worrying about us, so we went for a meal after work,' Nigel told him. 'Then as you know, I was taking Bobby for a driving lesson.'

Robert gazed at his daughter. 'And you, my dear, have you been to Milly's?'

She grinned mischievously. 'Yes, and we both sat in the back of the car while Bobby had his lesson. He wasn't very keen on the idea, mind you, and me and Milly weren't very

365

popular to start with. But when he saw we weren't going to budge out of the car, it was a case of either putting up with us or going without a lesson. We won in the end, because he really does want to be able to drive to enhance his job prospects. And he's coming on well, isn't he, Nigel?'

Her brother grinned. 'He's so good, I let him drive us to Grandma's. And anyone would think he'd driven hundreds of miles, he was so pleased with himself.'

'How are Ada and Joe?'

'They're fine. We stayed for a hour with them, then Bobby drove us back to Balfour Road. King of the Road, he calls himself now.'

'Dad, we've done nothing but laugh the whole night,' Abbie said. 'Bobby had us in stitches he's so funny. Grandma and Granda were doubled up, tears running down their cheeks. He doesn't half cheer people up, and we've had a smashing night.'

I wish I could say the same thing, Robert thought but didn't say. The empty chatter of the last three hours had really got on his nerves. Apart from George and Annabel Chisholm, not one of the others had an ounce of intelligent conversation in their heads. Fashion, hairstyles, shoes and the odd bit of bitchiness about some of their friends, that's all they had in their empty heads. He actually felt pity for them because they missed so much in life.

Robert sighed. 'Come on, I'll get you and Jessie home, Kitty. And thanks for helping out tonight, I really do appreciate it.'

'I'll run them home, Dad,' Nigel offered. 'There's no need for you to leave your guests.'

'No thank you, son, I've had three hours of our guests, and that is enough for anyone who is of sound mind. I'll be glad of the break and some fresh air.'

Agnes came through from the larder with two bags and a plate. She held the bags high. 'Mr Robert, I'm giving Kitty and Jessie some of the left-overs. It's only a few truffles and cakes for now, but I'll be giving them some of the meat and what-not tomorrow night. That's all right with you, isn't it?'

'Of course it is, you don't need my permission. Now come along, Jessie, and you, Kitty, it's been a long day for both of you.'

The housekeeper waited until they were out of the door before setting the plate on the table. She grinned when she saw the look of joy on the faces of Nigel and Abbie. 'I've saved these truffles specially for you 'cos I know they're yer favourites, and you're my favourites.'

Chapter Twenty-One

'Thank you for an enjoyable evening.' Annabel Chisholm offered the tips of her fingers in a handshake. 'We must have you over to ours some time.' The words were spoken in a matter-of-fact voice that would have told most people they weren't to be taken seriously. But as usual, Victoria heard what she wanted to hear.

'Oh, you're too kind,' she gushed, as she had been doing all through the evening. 'I'd be delighted and will look forward to it with great anticipation.' Her eyes were bright as she watched Annabel rest a hand on her husband's arm to help steady her as she negotiated the three deep steps in heels that were far too high for a woman of her age. She approves of me, Victoria told herself, her spirits soaring. Tonight has clinched it. The dinner party had been a huge success, with Agnes excelling herself with food so delicious it would have pleased the most discerning of palates.

Victoria was surprised to see Charles standing in front of her. 'You're not leaving yet, are you, darling? We haven't had a minute to ourselves and I do so want to talk to you.'

'I'm sorry, my sweet, but I have no choice. You see, Father thought it unnecessary to bring two cars, and as it is unwise to argue with him, I came in his. I am, therefore, forced to travel back with them.' He pecked her cheek. 'Anyway, I am feeling rather tired as last night was rather hectic, don't you agree?'

Victoria blushed and glanced around to see if her father was still standing near. He'd come out to see their guests off, but he must have returned to the drawing room. 'Charles, my family are under the impression I went to a party with you last night, so please be careful what you say.' She tapped his cheek quite firmly with a stiffened finger. 'I think you are really very naughty to leave me now, you must have known I would want some time alone with you.'

'I'll make it up to you, my sweet,' Charles said lightly. 'My father is very generous with me so I never go against him if I can help it. And anyway, I thought it not unreasonable of him to expect me to travel in the car with him and Mother. We were, after all, coming to the same house.' His arm around her waist, he pulled her close and whispered, 'I'll ring you tomorrow, my sweet, I promise.'

'Charles!' There was authority in the voice which said that George Chisholm was used to being obeyed immediately. 'Your mother and I are waiting.'

'Coming, Father!' After another quick peck, Charles made a hasty departure, calling over his shoulder, 'I'll telephone tomorrow.'

Victoria closed the door and leaned against it. She had taken it for granted that Charles would want to stay behind and spend some time with her, and was disappointed it hadn't worked out that way. Surely his father should have understood that a young courting couple needed to be alone, even if only to kiss each other goodnight. Still, as Charles had implied, his father was the one with the money, and she agreed it would be foolish to fall out of favour with him. And although it was a disappointment in as much as she was hoping for a definite seal to be put on their relationship, it didn't alter the fact the evening had been a huge success. And as Mrs Chisholm had intimated she would be invited to their house in the near future, it must mean it was clear to her that her son's intentions towards Victoria were serious.

Edwina was waiting for her daughter, her expectations high. Standing in front of the fireplace, her fingers laced in front of her, she showed surprise when Victoria closed the door behind her. 'Where's Charles?'

'He came in his father's car, so he went home with them.' Victoria glanced quickly around the large room. 'Has Father gone to bed?'

'I presume so. I haven't seen him since he went to the door with you. He must have gone straight upstairs.'

'Then let us sit for a while and have a chat.' Victoria waved her mother to a chair. 'I think everything went off very well, don't you?'

'Extremely well. Agnes surpassed herself and is to be congratulated. You really must thank her in the morning.'

A hand was waved in the air. 'I'll leave that to you, Mother, you're better at it than I am. You see, I can't see the point in thanking someone for doing something they are being paid to do. I think it is totally unnecessary.'

'We may need her help again, so it's best to keep on the right side of her. I'll have a word with her in the morning. The Chisholms were very impressed with the meal, and the large variety of dishes they had to choose from. As Annabel said, they have a good cook but her confectionery isn't anywhere near Agnes's standard.' Edwina wasn't fashion-conscious and all her dresses were the same style. Long sleeves, high neck and completely straight. The one she was wearing tonight was deep purple, and if it weren't for the long string of pearls around her neck, the word to describe her would have been drab. But for once, her colourless face was animated. 'Has Charles given any indication, yet?'

'We had no time alone, Mother! But I think Mrs Chisholm is beginning to realise we are quite serious about each other. She said I must go to their house soon. I think that tells us the way her mind is working. With regards to her husband, I really wouldn't know because he's not an easy man to talk to. He can be quite brusque at times.'

'That's just his manner, dear. He's used to dealing with businessmen and is noted for having an astute mind. He was born into money, and inherited a good business from his father. But from what I've heard, the company is now worth

371

twice what it was when he took over.'

'Charles said his father is very generous with him, but he implied he wouldn't like to cross him. And watching him tonight, I can see that anyone crossing George Chisholm would do so at their peril.'

'Robert gets on very well with him. Perhaps that's one avenue you could explore.'

'Definitely not!' Victoria shook her head so vigorously a lock of hair freed itself from a clip and fell down over her forehead. 'I refuse to ask any favour from my father, and I forbid you to discuss my affairs with him. Charles is to telephone me tomorrow and will no doubt arrange to take me for a run in his car after dinner. I can get a lot out of him when we're alone, and I'll work on setting a date to go to his home. I have a feeling his parents have a big influence on him, so I must go out of my way to please them.' She stood up and stretched her arms high. 'I'm very tired. I slept little last night, and today has been so long and wearisome. I'll see you in the morning, Mother, goodnight.'

'I'll be up directly, I must first turn out the lights. Good-night, my dear.'

'Can we have our dinner early tonight, Agnes, out here?' Nigel asked. 'Abbie and I are going dancing.'

'Of course yer can. I'll have it ready at half-six for yer.'

'I'll have mine the same time, Agnes.' Robert couldn't bear the thought of spending the evening in the drawing room with his wife and Victoria. He'd been so ashamed of them last night, the way they'd practically grovelled to the Chisholms. Particularly his daughter, she really was going too far in her pursuit of Charles. If she was hoping to worm her way into their good books, she was going the wrong way about it. George Chisholm was a straight-talking man, in business and socially. And he expected no less from those he associated with. He wouldn't be won over by the insincere charm and flattery displayed last night. 'I might go on to my club for a

372

few hours, or even go to Seaforth to see Ada and Joe.'

'Come to the dance with us, Dad,' Nigel said, giving his sister a cheeky grin. 'You can meet Jeremiah, the bloke who's got his eye on Abbie.'

'Nigel, will you pass the toast and shut up, please?' Abbie shook her head, sending her dark curls bouncing. 'His name's Eric, Dad, and he seems a nice boy. But he hasn't got his eye on me, he just asked me for a dance.'

'And he asked you for a date,' Nigel reminded her. Then when he saw she was embarrassed, he said, 'He's a lad who used to go to our school, Dad, and he is all right.'

'I don't think you should go out on a date with a boy you've only had one dance with, my dear,' Robert said. 'Even if Nigel does think he's all right.'

'I won't be making a date with him, Dad, I'm happy going out with Milly. But I'm eighteen now, I've got to go out with a boy some time.'

'Yer can bring him here first, Miss Abbie,' Agnes said. 'So I can give him the once-over. We can't have yer going out with any Tom, Dick or Harry.'

'I'll make a note of that, Agnes.' Abbie reached down to the briefcase at her feet and brought out a piece of paper. 'Can I borrow your fountain pen, Dad?'

Smiling, Robert unclipped the pen from his top pocket, took the top off and passed it over. 'Take care, it's my favourite pen.'

Abbie was shaking inside with laughter as she stuck her tongue out of the corner of her mouth and began to write slowly. 'Any boy, unless his name is Tom, Dick or Harry.'

'Yer've forgotten something, sunshine.'

'What's that, Agnes?'

'No Jeremiahs, either. I couldn't be doing with getting me tongue around that all the time, it would do me bleedin' head in.'

Robert pushed back his chair and stood up. 'We'd better be making a move. But I've got an idea, Abbie, and it's just to set my mind at rest. If you do meet a boy whom you like enough to go out with, and he's from the Bootle or Seaforth area, get him to call at your Grandma's for you. She's a good judge of character, is Ada, and if she is satisfied he's good enough for you, I'll be very happy.'

'Gosh, Dad, I'm not going to marry the first bloke who comes along! And Eric only asked me to go to the pictures with him, he didn't ask me to elope.'

'Still and all, it's best to do as yer father says, sunshine, 'cos yer never know.'

'Agnes, I've got Nigel and Bobby looking out for me now, and soon it'll be me Grandma and Granda, and you! I'll never get a boyfriend if they have to pass the test with all of you. They'll run a mile from me.'

'We'd better all start running now if we don't want to be late.' Robert slipped his arms into his coat. 'The trouble is, Agnes, my dear, you make us so comfortable in the mornings we don't want to move.'

'Yer going to move now because I'm going to chase yer.' The housekeeper began to collect the plates from the table. 'Mr Robert, yer did say I could give the left-overs away to Kitty and Jessie, didn't yer?'

'Yes, anything you do is fine by me.' Robert was following his children out of the side door when Agnes called him back

'Did Miss Victoria say anything to yer about the order from Coopers?'

'No, what order?'

'I'll tell yer tonight, it's not important. You be on yer way.' The housekeeper went about her work without the energy or the inclination. She was tired after the busy day yesterday, and she was back in the kitchen at six this morning. But it wasn't really the tiredness that was making her feel down in the dumps, it was the ingratitude of Victoria. She'd promised to tell her father it was she who had telephoned Coopers and asked for a repeat order, and she hadn't. She'd got everything she asked for regarding the blasted dinner party, but she couldn't even keep that little promise. Selfish to the bloody core, she was. Now it was left to the housekeeper to present the bill that came with the order yesterday.

Agnes put the plug in the sink and carried the heavy iron kettle over from the stove. As she watched the steaming water pouring from the spout, she told herself that no matter how much Victoria begged, she would never serve at another dinner party in this house. Let the stuck-up snob find some other muggins to do it.

'I'm paying for meself,' Milly said, with a look of determination on her pretty face. 'It's not fair that you two should pay every time.'

'We called for you to bring you to the dance, Milly, and that makes a difference,' Nigel told her. 'When you call for a girl, you don't expect her to pay for herself.'

'Quite right.' Bobby nodded in agreement. 'You two go in and me and Nige will sort the finances out.'

'Come on, Milly.' Abbie took hold of her friend's arm. 'If they want to throw their money about, that's their look-out.' As she pulled open the door to the dance hall, they could hear the strains of a waltz and she began to hum. 'Mmm, my favourite.'

'Here, I'll pay for Abbie.' Bobby held out his hand and offered a threepenny bit and a penny coin. 'You pay for Milly.'

Nigel handed over eightpence to the man on the door. 'It doesn't make much difference who pays for whom, does it?'

'Ah well, there's method in me madness, yer see, Nige. If that Eric keeps asking Abbie for dances, I can tell him I brought her and he can get lost.'

Nigel looked horrified. 'You can't do that! Abbie would die of embarrassment.' He studied his friend's face for any sign he was acting daft, but there wasn't one. 'You wouldn't happen to have a soft spot for my sister, would you?'

'Nah, yer know me for girls, Nige, they're just mates to me. I'd be lost without them, like, 'cos I'd look a right drip dancing on me own. But that's about it. Time to think of courting and settling down in a couple of years' time.'

'In that case, why are you so interested in whether Eric asks Abbie to dance?' Nigel pushed the main doors open. 'He's not doing you any harm because there's plenty of girls falling over themselves for the privilege of dancing with you.'

'It's not that, mate, I'm not that petty. I just think we should keep an eye on yer sister 'cos she's a long way from home. Some of the lads that come here are a bit tough, and she's not used to that.'

'You don't know my sister very well, or you'd soon realise she's more than able to look after herself. You try getting one over on her and you'll soon find out.' Nigel heard the tutting and saw the look of disgust. 'What is it?'

'I told yer, didn't I? Just look, there he is, the queer feller dancing with Abbie. He didn't waste much time, did he?'

Nigel chuckled. 'We've both been left on the shelf, Bobby, because Milly is up dancing as well.'

'We might just as well have come on our own and saved ourselves tuppence. Not that I'm tight with me money, like, just careful.' Bobby slapped his friend on the back. 'Come on, Nige, take yer pick from the bevy of beauties just waiting for us. I'll take that blonde over there, the one in the blue dress, and you take her friend in the green.'

Nigel hung back. He wasn't sure enough of himself to ask a stranger to dance, he'd prefer to wait for his sister or Milly. But Bobby wasn't having any of that. 'Come on, mate.' He gripped Nigel's arm tight and frogmarched him across the dance-floor, weaving between dancers with determination. He stopped in front of a blonde girl in a blue dress, and a brunette dressed in green, both of whom were waiting in anticipation.

On the dance-floor, Eric was trying to persuade Abbie. He had slowed down so he could look into her face. 'Have yer thought any more about coming to the pictures with me one night? We'd just go local, and I'd have yer home early.'

'I don't live around here, I live the other side of Liverpool.

But my Grandma and Granda live in Arthur Street, do you know it?'

'Yeah, it's just down the road from here. But what's that got to do with me taking you to the pictures? Unless yer want me to take yer Grandma and Granda as well?'

Abbie's infectious laugh rang out. 'You'd probably have more fun with them than you would with me, they're great!' She saw Bobby watching them and waved. 'I just meant that if I did go out with you one night, you could call for me at my Grandma's.'

'Now it's beginning to look hopeful.' His spirits high, Eric spun her around and around. 'So, when can I have the honour of escorting you to the Gainsborough or the Broadway?'

'My dad said he didn't think I should go out on a date with a boy I've only had one dance with. He worries about me, you see.'

'I can understand that, but it's not as though I'm a total stranger, is it? I went to school with your brother and Bobby Neary, and I live in the next street to the Nearys.' His white teeth flashed when he grinned down at her. 'Shall I tell yer something, Abbie? I've never in me life had so much trouble trying to date a girl.'

'Well, I'll let you know later. You see, Nigel runs me down here, so I'll have to find out what nights he's coming next week.'

'Has Nigel got a car, then?' When she nodded he looked impressed. 'He must be doing well for himself – good for him!'

'He works for my dad. You must remember he's in the removal business because the vans were always outside our house when we lived in Balfour Road.'

'Yeah, I remember. And I know he's still in business because I often see the vans around. I even noticed when the *Dennisons* became *Dennison and Son*. So yer see, Abbie, yer might not know much about me, but I know quite a bit about you.'

The dance came to an end and he walked with her to where

Milly was standing with the two boys. 'I'll be back for another dance,' he promised.

'Give someone else a chance first, will yer, mate?' Bobby said. 'Come back after the interval.'

'Bobby! Don't be so rude!' Abbie could feel the colour mounting her cheeks. 'He doesn't mean anything, Eric, it's his idea of a joke.'

'There's one thing I know about Neary's jokes, Abbie, and that is they are not funny.' With that Eric walked away with a grin on his face.

Abbie looked bewildered. 'What's got into everyone? First Bobby's rude to Eric when there was no need for it, then Eric's rude back. I'll be frightened to open me mouth if this carries on.'

'Don't worry, me and Leyland won't come to blows. He can be dead sarky, though.' Bobby didn't seem the least bit put out. He had that mischievous look on his face when he asked, 'Why do you laugh at me jokes, Abbie? Is it just because yer think I expect yer to laugh?'

'I can't laugh to order, Bobby, it wouldn't come out right. No, I laugh because I think you're dead funny.'

'And me!' Milly was quick to come to the defence of a friend. 'I think ye're always ruddy hilarious.'

'Right. So let's see if we can solve this mystery. I'll be Sherlock Holmes, and you, Nige, can be Dr Watson. Now I'll start off with meself, shall I? Well, I must think me jokes are funny, otherwise I wouldn't come out with them. And you two dear girls, you both profess to find them funny.' Bobby struck up a stance that had his friends in stitches. His eyes were narrowed, he had a pretend pipe in one hand, and he took on a thoughtful pose. 'Now the strange thing about this case, Dr Watson, is that Eric's views are at odds with ours. What conclusion do you come to, old chap?'

'There's only one conclusion I can come to, Mr Holmes. And it is that Mr Eric Leyland has no sense of humour.'

'Well thought out, Watson. I knew you wouldn't let me down.'

'Ye're getting us all as daft as yerself.' Milly tilted her head at Nigel. 'Are yer going to ask me to dance, Dr Watson?'

'With pleasure, Milly.'

'And where's your manners, Bobby Neary?' Abbie was hoping Eric wouldn't come now and spoil things. She was beginning to feel a bit guilty about splitting the foursome up. Perhaps it would be best if she had second thoughts about making a date. 'You shouldn't keep a lady waiting, it just isn't done in the best of circles.'

Bobby grinned and put his arm around her waist. 'Oh, I say, is that right, Miss Dennison? Then I mustn't let the side down, eh?'

Abbie was partnering her brother for the next dance, and her eyes happened to light on Eric dancing with a very pretty girl with auburn hair. They seemed to know each other very well, too, as they were laughing and chattering away. 'I think Eric is a bit of a flirt, don't you?'

'What makes you say that?' Nigel asked. 'He doesn't strike me as being a flirt.'

'Well, he's asked me again for a date, but look at the way he's chatting that girl up. He seems to fancy his chances.'

When Nigel's roving eye picked out Eric and his partner, he burst out laughing. 'Don't you notice anything unusual about them?'

Abbie shook her head. 'Only that they're very friendly.'

'I should hope they would be. They're brother and sister! I'm surprised you didn't notice the resemblance.'

Abbie felt foolish. She must have sounded as though she cared about Eric dancing and chatting with another girl. 'I can see they look alike, now. She's very pretty.'

'Yes, she is. If I remember correctly, her name is Doreen. There's only about a year difference in their ages, so she would have been in a higher class at school than you. I'm surprised to see her here, I would have thought she'd be courting by now. She's certainly very attractive so it can't be for want of opportunities.'

Abbie pulled slightly away from him so she could look into his face. 'Why don't you ask her for a dance? I dare you to, Nigel.'

He surprised her by saying, 'I might just do that. The next time Eric asks you to dance, as long as Bobby's with Milly, so she won't be left in the lurch, I think I'll take the plunge. I can't keep on just dancing with my sister and her friend, lovely and all as they are.'

'What d'you think I should say when he asks me about going out with him? I put him off by saying I had to wait until you were coming down here so you could give me a lift. But I did say I would ask you what nights you were coming next week. I didn't know what else to say because I didn't like turning him down flat. I quite like him, but then I don't know much about him and I'd be tongue-tied for something to talk about. What should I do, Nigel?'

'That's entirely up to you, Abbie. No one can make up your mind for you, especially Bobby, because he's pulling your leg. Him and Eric get on quite well, actually. So it's up to you. If you like Eric, then make a date with him. If you're not that keen, then don't. You can't go out with someone just because you're too soft-hearted to refuse.'

Abbie had faltered in her steps and had to concentrate on getting back into line with her brother. Then she asked, 'Are you telling me that Bobby Neary is quite friendly with Eric, and is just putting on an act? And the same with Eric?' When Nigel nodded, her lips pursed. 'Right, I think they both need to be taken down a peg or two, and I'll think of a way to do it.'

'That's easy.' Her brother smiled. 'Make a date with Eric! That would dent Bobby's ego. And if you didn't want to go out with Eric again, that would take *him* down a peg or two.'

'But why should Bobby worry about who I go out with? Except for breaking up the foursome. But it's bound to break up sometime, isn't it? It can't go on for ever. You could meet a girl you like, or Milly could meet a boy. It needn't stop us coming here on the nights we weren't dating. I wouldn't want to drift away from Milly now I've found her again, I want her to be my friend for life. But we both need other friends, and so do you and Bobby.'

'You just talked me into it, Abbie. I'll definitely ask Doreen to dance at the first opportunity.'

'This doesn't mean I'm not going to find some way of getting my own back on Bobby and Eric, though. They've both had a laugh at my expense and I intend to teach them a lesson. I don't know how, but I will do so by the end of the night. But I do need a bit of help from you, Nigel, because I need to know what nights you will be coming down next week. I can't get here without you.'

'As long as you don't involve me in your nefarious plans, Abbie. I couldn't knowingly help you make a fool of Bobby, or Eric for that matter. So apart from driving you down here, which I'll be doing anyway, I beg you not to tell me what you are up to.'

Abbie grinned. 'We'll be coming here next Monday, so that's out. But how about Tuesday, when you take Bobby for his lesson? Would you drop me off at Grandma's then?'

'I'll drop you off before I pick Bobby up, but more than that I do not want to know, Abbie, so please don't involve me.'

'I wouldn't dream of it, dear brother.' Her mind was working overtime. She'd find some way of putting both Bobby and Eric on the spot. They weren't going to have a laugh at her expense and get away with it. Mind you, she had to admit they had fooled her, and it was funny. Still, she'd show them they weren't the only ones who could play pranks.

The next dance was a foxtrot, and a 'gentleman's excuse me', and turned out to be hilarious. Bobby was dancing with Abbie, and Nigel with Milly. And when Bobby first felt a tap on his shoulder he turned with a scowl on his face thinking it would be Eric. However, his scowl turned to a look of surprise when he saw a lad with ginger hair and a face covered in freckles, smiling at him and holding his hand out to Abbie. There was little he could do but give in gracefully until the pair had circled the floor twice, when he claimed her back. They'd hardly got into step before Eric appeared and again Abbie was taken from him. She was dizzy by this time, trying to keep up with different styles of dancing, so she didn't notice Bobby standing on the edge of the dance-floor with a look of grim determination on his face. And next to him stood Nigel, who had been parted from Milly.

'It's a conspiracy, this is, Nige. They're ganging up on us.'

'Hardly a conspiracy, Bobby, it is an excuse me. And both girls are very pretty so we can expect competition.'

'They're not getting away with it. I started the dance with her, and I'll finish it.' With that, Bobby weaved his way through the dancing couples and his tap on Eric's arm was more of a prod. 'I'll take my partner back now, if yer don't mind.'

Eric grinned. 'I'll see yer later, Abbie.'

'He will if I've got any feet left,' Abbie groaned. 'I'm only a learner, I can't keep up with all the different steps. Every one of my toes has been trodden on.'

'Not by me they haven't. I'm very careful with yer.'

'Well, I think I'll be sitting out the next dance, thanks, Bobby, to give my toes a rest.'

'It's the interval waltz next, yer can't sit that out. But yer will have fifteen minutes after that to rest yer feet.'

'They're talking to me, Bobby, and they're not too happy with me. In fact, my two big toes are asking me what I'm playing at.'

'Tell them I'll massage them in the interval, that should cheer them up.'

When Bobby grinned into her face, his eyes shining, Abbie's tummy did a flip. Just like it had one night last week. That's funny, she thought, I wonder what caused that?

Milly came off the dance-floor looking radiant. She'd danced with three good dancers and was in very high spirits.

'We did well there, Abbie. And two of my blokes asked me for a date.'

'Don't you be at it, Milly Jamieson,' Bobby said. 'We're having enough trouble trying to keep Abbie on the straight and narrow, without you starting.'

'Pardon me, but I can look after myself, thank you.'

'So can I!' Abbie was sitting down with her legs stretched out. Her toes really were sore, and she wouldn't be surprised if they were black and blue. 'I don't need a nanny.'

Bobby held out his hands and shrugged his shoulders. 'Did yer hear that, Nige? We're doing our level best to protect them and they're as good as telling us to get lost. D'yer know, I've even offered to get down on me knees and massage yer sister's feet for her. And all I get is a kick in the teeth.'

'You touch my feet, Bobby Neary, and a kick in the teeth is exactly what you will get. The very idea, indeed!'

'You couldn't have said a worse thing, Bobby,' Nigel said with a grin. 'She's very ticklish is my sister. Can't bear anyone to touch her feet.'

'Nor can I bear anyone to stand on them.' The strains of a waltz filled the air, and Abbie shook her head before anyone had a chance to ask. 'I'd have to be a sucker for punishment to get up for this, so you three go and enjoy yourselves while I suffer in silence.'

Bobby and Milly were off like a shot, while Nigel looked down at his sister. 'Are you sure you don't mind being left on your own? I'll stay with you if you like.'

'I'll be fine. You go and ask Eric's sister for a dance while you've got the chance.' When he hesitated, she said, 'Go on, Nigel, be daring.'

Abbie was still watching her brother's retreating back when Eric came and plonked himself in the chair next to her. 'You wouldn't be hiding from me, would yer?'

'It's my poor feet, they simply refuse to let me stand on them. They're not used to being trodden on, so I'm resting them until after the interval. But you don't have to sit with me, you go and find yourself a partner.'

'No, I'll sit with yer and we can arrange our date. Have yer asked Nigel what nights he'll be fetching yer down?'

Abbie didn't know she was going to say it until the words were out of her mouth. 'Tuesday night, and you can call to my Grandma's for me about eight o'clock.'

Eric's face lit up. 'That's smashing! I thought I was going to get the run-around again. Have yer thought about where yer'd like to go?'

She shook her head. 'Can we decide when you call for me? We'll know what's on at the flicks then, and if it's a film we want to see. Come a bit early, so yer can get to know me grandparents, they'd like that.'

'Right, that's settled then. But yer'll be here on Monday, won't yer?'

'I imagine so, but in case anything turns up to stop me, I'll definitely be in my Grandma's on Tuesday about a quarter to eight.'

Eric let out a cry of surprise and pointed a finger. 'Ay, look! Your Nigel is dancing with me sister Doreen.'

'What's wrong with that? You don't mind, do you?'

'Of course not. I'm just surprised he remembers her.'

'Yes, he pointed her out to me before. Does she come here often?'

'Only when she's had a falling-out with her boyfriend, which is every couple of weeks. They fight like cat and dog, and spend more time not speaking, than speaking. I've told our Doreen I don't know why she bothers, he's not worth it.'

'Ah well, you see, no one can control their heart. Their head may tell them all the sensible things to do, but the pull of the heart is stronger.'

'You sound as though ye're speaking from experience. Have yer had many boyfriends?'

Abbie told herself there was no point in telling lies. 'Have I heck! I've had no boyfriends and no experience. Green as a cabbage, really.'

384

Eric grinned. 'Ye're honest anyway, which makes a pleasant change. Most girls would never have admitted to that. I'm really looking forward to getting to know you, Abbie. Starting Tuesday, eh?'

Edwina looked at the clock for the umpteenth time. 'It's nine o'clock, it doesn't look as though Charles is going to telephone.'

Victoria was grinding her teeth together. She was on tenterhooks herself without having to watch her mother looking at the clock every ten seconds and telling her the time. 'Mother, I can see the clock, I do not need you to be constantly reminding me. Something must have cropped up to prevent Charles from ringing. Does it honestly matter so much?'

'But he promised faithfully, didn't he?' Edwina really didn't know when to draw the line. She couldn't see that her daughter was upset because she was too busy thinking only of herself. 'One would have thought he'd ring out of common courtesy, if nothing else, to say how much he and his parents had enjoyed the evening.'

'Mother, will you please not harp on it. I'm sure there's a perfectly simple reason why Charles has not been able to ring, and he'll tell me when he gets the opportunity.'

Edwina's eyes narrowed to slits. 'Why don't you ring him? What harm would there be in saying you were concerned about his well-being, as he hasn't contacted you as promised.'

'That would be going too far, Mother. I would not wish his parents to think I was throwing myself at him. They thanked me last night for the very enjoyable evening, one can't expect them, or Charles, to offer further praise. Things are moving more slowly than I would have wished, but they are moving. I feel quite confident our relationship is on a firm footing and I would not want to jeopardise that by appearing too pushy. If he doesn't telephone tonight, I'm quite sure he'll call tomorrow. So can we now change the subject, Mother, because I find it tiresome.'

Edwina picked up a fashion magazine and idly turned the pages. Her daughter could be very stubborn at times. She didn't seem to realise that her fishing line would have to be well baited to hook Charles Chisholm. She couldn't afford to miss chances, as she had tonight by not making what would be seen as a completely innocent telephone call from a young woman to a man who had been her close companion for months. But then, Victoria would never listen to advice, she would always follow her own instinct. It was to be hoped that in this instance her instinct was taking her down the right road.

Chapter Twenty-Two

It was Sunday when Charles finally telephoned, full of apologies that were insincere but which were music to Victoria's ears. Friday had been a long day as she'd waited within earshot of the telephone, longing to hear the familiar tinkle. And the day hadn't been helped by her mother's constant whining about how inconsiderate it was of Charles not to keep his promise. But if Friday had her a bag of nerves, Saturday was a nightmare. The day seemed to be endless, and as it wore on, so her nerves became more ragged as she saw all her hopes of marriage to one of the richest men in Liverpool, being dashed against the rocks. So on Sunday, when Agnes opened the drawing-room door to tell her Mr Charles was on the phone, although she rose slowly from her chair and walked with poise so as not to appear eager, her heart was racing and her hopes awakening. And she was prepared to believe any excuse he made about his two-day silence.

What Victoria didn't know, as she placed the telephone receiver to her ear, was that the telephone call was only being made because Charles feared she would ring his home and get him into hot water with his parents. They had told him in no uncertain terms, after the dinner party on Thursday, that they hoped he wasn't serious about the Dennison girl, as they thought her totally unsuitable as a wife and would not welcome her in their family. Knowing his lavish lifestyle was at risk if he displeased them, he chose to play along and insisted there was no prospect of him ever marrying Victoria. She was just a friend he took out for company. And he told himself it would be best to cut all ties with Victoria. But he knew her well enough to know if he tried to make a clean break now, she wouldn't take it quietly. Better to do it gradually so there was a minimum of fuss.

'When am I going to see you?' Victoria asked. 'You really are very naughty not to have telephoned before now when you knew how much I would be missing you.'

'It will have to be tomorrow, my sweet. Mother has a social engagement tonight and insists upon dragging me with her. And as I've told you, I am completely dependent on my parents for cash, so I have to do as I'm told and toddle along like a good little boy. I know it's a bind, but I'll make it up to you tomorrow, I promise. I'll pick you up about seven, we'll go for a meal, then a nice long run in the country. You'd enjoy that, my sweet, wouldn't you?'

Yes, thought Victoria, it would be better than nothing. But she had an idea in her head that would move matters a little faster. 'Why not suggest to your mother that it would please you if I could accompany you this evening? After all, I am your girlfriend.'

'Out of the question, my sweet. These events are planned several weeks ahead, and they will have catered for the number of guests who have been invited and accepted. An extra one would play havoc with the seating arrangements. But if it's any consolation to you, I won't enjoy it, they're such stuffy affairs. I would much rather be with you.' And so the lies went on and on. Except Charles didn't see them as lies. They were getting him out of an awkward situation, therefore they were a godsend. 'I will be thinking of you all the time, my sweet, and Monday can't come quick enough.'

'I suppose I'll have to be satisfied with that.' Victoria sighed. 'But it seems such a long way off, and I'm missing you so much.' Then she said something that sounded like a veiled threat and sent a shiver down his spine. 'Don't forget I gave in to your wishes regarding the Adelphi on Wednesday. I did something I would never have dreamed of doing for anyone else. I only did it because you had confirmed I was truly your girlfriend, and I did so want to please you. I showed how deeply I care for you, and I would expect you to be now more open in your regard for me.'

Oh God, Charles groaned inwardly, she's almost threatening blackmail. And because he knew she was capable of walking through anything that got in her way, he believed that is what she would do if pushed too far. 'Of course, my sweet, I intend to be very loving towards you. Both my lips and eyes will tell you how much I adore you. But as this can't be done over the telephone, it will have to wait until tomorrow. So be patient, my love, the hours may seem long but they will pass. And until we meet, you will never be out of my thoughts.' When he replaced the receiver on the cradle at the side of the telephone, Charles felt weak at the knees. He would have to tread carefully here. He'd been in many tough situations before, but none of the women involved had been as strong-willed as Victoria Dennison. Ending their association could take months, instead of weeks.

At the other end of the telephone, Victoria had no such fears as she replaced the receiver and went in search of her mother to tell her what had transpired. And for the first time in three days, she felt light in heart. She had heard the change in Charles's voice when she mentioned the Adelphi and it gave her food for thought. She knew now how to bring him to heel if he ever had the urge to wander off.

Agnes stretched between Mr Robert and Nigel to put the toast-rack on the table. There was still more bread being toasted on the grill so she leaned against the sink while waiting for it to be the golden-brown which was a favourite with the family. 'Miss Victoria told me last night that she won't be home for dinner this evening, she's dining out with Mr Charles. So what plans do you three have?'

'Abbie and I would like our dinner at half-six, please, Agnes,' Nigel said. 'And if you don't mind our company, we'll have it out here.'

The housekeeper was using her fingers to pick up the hot slices of toast and transferring them to the bread board. 'My God, they're hot. I nearly burnt me bleedin' fingers off. Serves me right for not using a fork.'

'I'll have my meal out here, too, Agnes, at the same time as the children,' Robert said. 'Then I've got a meeting with a friend.' A vision of Maureen flashed through his mind and the world seemed a better place knowing he'd be seeing her tonight.

'And Miss Abbie's going on her first date.' The housekeeper placed the extra toast on the table and sat down to start her own breakfast. 'Are yer excited, sunshine?'

'Not yet, but I will be a nervous wreck when the time comes.' Abbie gave a conspiratorial wink to her father. She'd told him what she had in mind for tonight, and he had passed the information on to her grandparents when he'd called there yesterday. But she hadn't told her brother, thinking that what he didn't know wouldn't hurt him. Besides, she might not be able to pull it off, and then she'd look foolish. She patted her hair now and grinned. 'Still, a girl's got to start sometime, and somewhere, hasn't she?'

'There's a first time for everything, sunshine, and it's what yer'll look back on as yer grow older. Yer first dance, first date and first kiss. And the first time yer heart misses a beat and yer tummy feels as though it's got birds flying around inside. That's when yer meet someone special and fall for them.'

Nigel didn't object to the first dance, or the first date, but talk of the first kiss was going too far for his kid sister. 'Agnes, they're only going to the pictures. She doesn't even know the lad very well, so I think he'd be very lucky to get as far as holding hands.'

Abbie took a fit of the giggles. There was no way she could see herself lifting her face for a kiss, like they did in films. And as for looking starry-eyed and soppy – well, she didn't think anyone would ever make her feel that way. 'What about you, Nigel? Isn't it about time you tasted all these goodies, like a first date, first kiss and missing heartbeats? Then you could tell me whether they're worth the effort.'

'There's no hurry, Abbie. As Bobby says, we've got a few years to enjoy ourselves yet, before we start thinking of courting and settling down.'

'Bobby will never settle down, he doesn't seem interested in girls at all.' Abbie wiped away a trickle of butter from her chin. 'He never chats them up, and he's far from being a flatterer.'

'There's a different side to him than you see, Abbie. Than anyone sees, really.' Nigel knew his friend wouldn't thank him for discussing his business, but he wanted to put the record straight for a lad who had taken on the responsibilities of a man when he was still only a boy. 'He won't let himself fall for anyone because he doesn't want to leave his mother on her own. He thinks the world of her, and apart from anything else, it's his wages keeping the house going. He's not a bit like he makes out, you know, it's all show. He's got a good head on his shoulders and wants to get on. That's why I hope he can get a better job when he's had more experience of driving.'

Nigel turned to his father to say, 'D'you know what I admire most about him, Dad? He doesn't envy anyone better off than himself. If I'd turned up the other week with no soles on my shoes, a torn jacket and holes in my trousers, I'd still have been welcomed with open arms. He doesn't care that my suits are expensive, or that I have a car. He treats me just the same as he did ten years ago. And I admire him for that.'

Robert, who never ceased to be surprised by the changes that were happening to his son, now knew who was helping with these changes. 'I'd like to get to know him better, Nigel, so why not drive him up here one night?'

Nigel shook his head. 'There's no chance of me doing that, Dad. If Mother saw him, she'd probably look down her nose and tell him to use the tradesmen's entrance. I'll not put him in a position where he could be insulted.'

'Things will change in the not-too-distant future, son, and

you and Abbie will be able to invite who you want, when you want. In fact, I was thinking only yesterday that Christmas would be a good time to bring all our friends together. I know it's over two months away, but it would be something to look forward to, and plan.'

Abbie had been feeling sad when her brother was talking about Bobby, sorry she'd ever said anything about him, even though she was only joking. But her father's words had cheered her up a little. 'Who were you thinking of inviting, Dad?'

'The list is long, my dear, and I'm afraid it might upset Agnes for the day if I were to tell you how long.'

The housekeeper sat forward, her face aglow. 'Would it hell! I'd be made up to have a proper party where we could have a sing-song. Come on, Mr Robert, tell us who's on yer list and it'll cheer me up for the day.'

Robert chuckled. 'Don't say you weren't warned. Top of the list is the children's grandparents, Ada and Joe. They're like a mam and dad to me, so they have priority over everyone. Then there's the Jamieson family, all of them. And Bobby and his mam. Oh, and I mustn't forget my best friend, Jeff and his family. And the friend I'm seeing tonight would be on the list.'

'Do we know this friend, Dad?' Nigel asked.

'No, but you soon will. And now we come to Kitty and her husband, Pete and his wife, and young Jessie if she would like to come.'

Agnes was beside herself with joy. 'Oh, it sounds marvellous, Mr Robert, and I think ye're a thorough gentleman for including the staff amongst yer friends. Wait until I tell Kitty, I bet she'll jig around this kitchen singing her head off.'

'I'd rather you didn't mention it yet, Agnes, because it is a long way off. But it will happen, I promise.'

Abbie had been counting on her fingers. 'Dad, that comes to about twenty-three if we count ourselves. And poor Agnes is the one who will have to cater for them.'

'Don't you worry about that, sunshine, it will be a labour

of love. And I'll have Kitty and Jessie to help, don't forget.'

'You will have plenty of help, Agnes,' Robert said, thinking everyone would know Maureen was part of his life by then and he just knew she would roll her sleeves up, like the housekeeper, and get stuck in.

Nigel pointed to the clock on the wall. 'Dad, look at the time. We're going to be late, and so is Abbie.'

'I don't think we'll get told off, do you?' Robert smiled, pleased with his son's diligence and the fact that he never used his position to take time off. 'I think you should run Abbie to the college, save her rushing if she misses a tram.'

The three were donning their coats when the back door opened and Kitty breezed in, followed by Jessie. 'Good morning, queen, it's quite nippy out.' The words were out of the cleaner's mouth before she realised the housekeeper wasn't alone. 'Oh, I'm sorry, Mr Robert, I didn't notice yer in time. Good morning to yer, and you Mr Nigel and Miss Abbie.' She couldn't keep the mischievous grin back. 'Ye're all late this morning, it'll be six strokes of the cane for yer.'

'I will insist upon being able to keep my gloves on, Kitty, if the teacher is smaller than I am. If not, I'll be a coward and grovel at his feet.'

'Tell him yer mam sent yer on a message, that's why ye're late.'

'Ah, but that would be a lie, Kitty.'

'Ah yes, Mr Robert, but in my book it beats the bleedin' cane any day.'

As the threesome left the kitchen laughing, they passed Jessie, who was giggling behind her hand and thinking it very brave of Kitty to talk to her boss like that. Mind you, he was a good boss and it was her lucky day when she got this job.

When Nigel dropped Abbie off outside their grandparents' house, he asked, 'Will you be back for half ten, if we call for you then?'

She nodded. 'Yes, I think so. If not, you can sit and talk to

Grandma and Granda while you're waiting.'

'Bobby will be with me, so we can have a game of cards with them to pass the time.' He began to drive away, shouting through the open window, 'Have a nice evening.'

'I will!' Abbie waved and turned to find her Grandma standing at the open front door. She smiled, flung her arms around the slight figure and gave her a kiss. 'It's lovely to see you, Grandma. My dad did tell you I was meeting a boy here, didn't he?'

'He did, sweetheart, and Joe's getting the playing cards out now.' Ada closed the door and followed her granddaughter into the living room. 'But are you sure your young man will go along with it?'

'He's not my young man, Grandma, I've never been out with him before.' Abbie saw Joe standing with his arms wide, and she walked into them. 'Mmm, you're a little love, Granda, and you grow more handsome every day.'

'What's all this about a young man, lass? Doesn't he think ye're going to the flicks?'

Abbie nodded. 'I know I should have more sense at eighteen, but I've never been out with a boy before and I know I'll end up not opening my mouth, and him thinking I'm as dull as ditchwater. So I thought if we stayed in and played cards, I could get to know him and feel more relaxed in his company.' She slipped her coat off and draped it over the arm of the couch. 'We'd better make a start because he'll be here any minute. Will you deal the cards, Granda, while I explain? You see, apart from the reason I've given you, which is the truth, I've got another little reason of my own which I'm not going to tell you until later. So shall we start the game so it all looks above board?'

They were ten minutes into the game when a knock came on the door. 'I'll go, Grandma, and don't let on if you hear me telling little fibs.'

Eric looked very smart in a suit that had just been pressed, a shirt that was pure white, a blue tie perfectly knotted under his Adam's apple, and a shine on his shoes you could see your face in. His hair was slicked back and his smile was wide. 'Are yer ready, Abbie?'

'Come in and meet my grandparents. We're halfway through a game of cards, so will you wait until we've finished the hand?'

'We'll have to look snappy if we don't want to miss the start of the big picture.'

'We won't be long.' Abbie closed the front door, then ushered him into the living room. 'These are my grandparents, Mr and Mrs Brady. Gramps, this is Eric.'

The old folk lowered their cards and greeted him warmly. 'It's nice to meet yer, son,' Joe said, shaking the lad's hand. 'And my, you are a big 'un, aren't yer?'

'And handsome with it.' Ada craned her neck to look up into his face. 'Yer welcome, sweetheart.'

Eric was pleased and flattered. 'Thank you, it's kind of you. And I promise I'll take good care of yer granddaughter.'

'We'd have finished the game but for me,' Abbie said, taking her seat. 'Like dancing, cards are new to me and I'm slow on the uptake. It takes me ages to know which card to throw down. Can you play rummy, Eric?'

'Yeah, we often have a game at home on a Sunday night. It's an easy game to learn, there's nothing to it, really.'

Abbie patted the wooden dining chair next to her. 'Come and sit here and you can help me out. Tell me if I'm picking the right card up, or throwing the wrong one away. Don't do it for me, though, or I'll never learn. Just a little bit of help, that's all I need.' She smiled across the table at the old folk who were wondering if her plan was going to work. And why she wanted it to, anyway. 'Perhaps one day I'll be good enough to beat these two cardsharks.'

'We haven't got long, Abbie,' Eric said. 'Or we'll miss the start of the big picture.'

'Yes, I know.' Then Abbie showed him her hand. 'It's my turn, so do I pick that ten of hearts up?'

Eric leaned closer until their heads were touching, and he found the experience very satisfying. 'You don't need it, so pick one off the pack.'

She picked the seven of diamonds and would have discarded it if he hadn't quickly stayed her hand. 'Don't throw that away, you need it.'

Her face the picture of innocence, Abbie asked, 'Why do I need it?'

'Because yer've got the six and eight!' Holding her hand was a very pleasant sensation and he kept a grip on it while he explained. 'Yer've got a run of three now, so you can put them down.'

'Oh yes, aren't you clever! But what do I do with the five cards I've got left?'

'You throw one away first, then wait for your turn.'

Ada and Joe were looking on with amusement. They didn't know what was going on in their granddaughter's mind, but whatever it was she seemed to be winning at it. If they didn't know better, they'd think she'd never played a game of cards in her life before.

When the game ended with Abbie winning, she was beside herself with excitement. At least she pretended to be. Clapping her hands and bouncing up and down on her chair, she heaped praise on Eric for being responsible for her success. And his chest expanded at least six inches. But he wasn't prepared for what she was to say next. 'Let's have another game, shall we? And you can tell me what to do again.'

'But we're already late for the big picture, Abbie.'

'Then we can go another night! Teach me how to play cards, please?'

The flattery, the big brown eyes and the angelic smile, did it. How could he refuse such a combination? And there was the promise of another night to go to the pictures. So Ada put the kettle on and brought out a plate of biscuits, all the while thinking what a crafty little so-and-so Abbie was. Considering she'd had no experience with boys, she was certainly doing very well for herself. But she was also doing her and Joe a favour, 'cos they were enjoying themselves. And once he felt more at home, Eric let himself go and proved he had a good sense of humour.

They were laughing and joking when the knock came on the door at a quarter to ten. 'I'll go,' Joe said. 'You shuffle the cards, Eric.'

Abbie listened with her ear cocked. And when Joe greeted his grandson, she waited to hear a second greeting. When it came, she let her breath out slowly and sat back in the chair.

Nigel entered the room first, and his brows shot up in surprise. 'I thought you were going to the pictures?'

'We were,' Eric told him, 'but your sister fancied a hand of cards and it got too late.'

Bobby poked his head over Nigel's shoulder. 'Don't tell me yer've spent the night playing cards, Leyland? It's not like you to waste a date by staying in.'

'We can do what we like, Bobby Neary,' Abbie answered him. 'We don't have to ask your permission. And we've really enjoyed ourselves, haven't we, Eric? He's taught me how to play rummy.'

Her brother kept his mouth closed. What was the use of making a liar out of Abbie by saying she didn't need to be taught, she already knew. He glanced at Ada and Joe, and could see the amusement in their eyes. They were enjoying themselves, anyway. 'Me and Bobby came early to have a game with you, Grandma. We weren't expecting Abbie to be back until half ten.'

'Well, sit down and make yerselves comfortable now ye're here. Shall I put the kettle on, or would yer like a game of cards, seeing as that's what yer've come early for?'

Abbie got in before her brother could answer. 'Yes, have a game with us, Nigel, the night is still young.'

'We haven't got enough chairs, sweetheart,' Joe said. 'We've got one in the bedroom, but it would still leave us one short.'

'We could manage.' Abbie wasn't going to be put off. 'I'll

397

sit on the arm of your fireside chair, I'll be fine. All we need is the chair from upstairs and I'm sure Nigel will oblige.'

She's very bossy tonight, her brother thought as he took the stairs two at a time. I've never known her to be like that before. And she was still giving orders when he came back with the round-backed wooden chair.

'You can have my seat, Bobby, and sit next to Eric.' If looks could kill she would have been a dead duck, but she pretended not to notice the scowl. 'I'll pull the fireside chair over and sit next to Granda, opposite to you.'

Ada was dying to laugh at the faces of the two boys. It would be hard to say which one was more put out by the way things were working out. And Bobby didn't help much by growling, 'I hope yer don't cheat, Leyland.'

'If I did cheat, I'd be that good at it yer wouldn't even notice.' This was the answer from the boy who had hoped he'd be sitting on the back row of the Broadway right now, holding Abbie's hand. Instead, he was holding a hand of cards.

Once they were all settled, Nigel was asking his Granda to cut the cards when Eric said, 'Why don't yer sit next to me, Abbie, and I can keep me eye on yer cards? Neary can sit over there.'

'No, I'll be all right,' Abbie told him with a smile. 'If I get stuck, I can ask Granda.'

The atmosphere livened up when the game got under way, with Bobby and Eric trying to outdo each other with jokes. Apart from laughing, Abbie had little to say for herself, but her eyes never left the two boys at the opposite side of the table. She was trying to find out if her feelings were the same for both of them. And she found the answer when Bobby was throwing a card away and he happened to catch her eyes. He stopped speaking for a few seconds, looked surprised, then his face split into a grin and he carried on with what he'd been saying. But when Abbie's heart missed a few beats and her tummy lurched, she knew why she only got these strange feelings when Bobby Neary was around. It was like Agnes

398

had said, only the housekeeper had been talking about two people falling for each other, not just one. And so far Bobby had shown no sign. Still, she had plenty of time to work on winning him. But in the meanwhile there was Eric to consider. The trick she'd played on him tonight was mean, and she felt guilty. He was a nice lad, and she liked him. But there was no point in leading him on when her heart lay elsewhere. She would go to the pictures with him one night, as promised, and tell him then that she had to spend some nights studying and really didn't have time for a regular boyfriend.

'I'm getting tired now, shall we call it a day?' Abbie stretched her arms over her head. 'It must be all the laughing we've done.'

'Nigel said I can drive back to Balfour Road, so I'll soon wake yer up. Yer'll be gripping the edge of yer seat as I speed along at thirty miles an hour.'

'I think I'll walk,' Eric said. 'I'm too young to die.'

'Take no notice of him, he's a good driver. And as it's my car, he certainly won't be driving at thirty miles an hour.'

As he was collecting the cards in, Bobby appealed to Ada. 'Isn't it terrible when yer mates don't trust yer, Mrs Brady? It's very hurtful and me heart's bleeding. I know it is 'cos the blood's dripping into me socks.'

'I know yer must be hurt, 'cos ye're a sensitive lad.' Ada looked suitably serious. 'Didn't I say to you the other night, Joe, that Bobby's a sensitive lad?'

'The very words yer used, sweetheart. "Bobby's a sensitive lad", that's what yer said.' Joe's chuckle was deep. 'I can't see it meself, like, but seeing as you and me agree on most things, I'm prepared to bow to your better judgement.'

As they were putting their coats on, Eric managed a word in Abbie's ear. 'What night are we going to the pictures?'

'Shall we make it tomorrow night?'

'But that's dance night!'

'I know, but I'm really going to have to spend some nights at home, doing homework. But you go to the dance if you want to, and we'll leave the pictures until another time.'

'No, tomorrow night will be fine. Shall I pick you up from here at a quarter to eight?'

Abbie noticed Bobby straining his ears. If he had any feelings for her, this should be causing pangs of jealousy. 'Yes, that's fine. The dance finishes more or less the same time as the pictures come out, so Nigel can pick me up outside Balfour Hall.'

'Will you two stop whispering and put a move on,' Bobby growled. 'It's bad manners to whisper in company, and even worse manners to keep yer chauffeur waiting. So get going before I put the fares up to tuppence.'

Charles had seemed very subdued during the meal, and even now, while they were driving along a country lane, he wasn't very talkative. 'You don't seem your usual happy, charming self, Charles. Is anything amiss?'

'I'm not exactly full of the joys of spring, my sweet, but it need not concern you. Father has decided, in his wisdom, that I do not take enough interest in the firm, and spend far too much time away from the office.'

'Does he have reason to complain?'

Charles tapped his fingers on the steering wheel, his face downcast. It was all an act for Victoria's benefit, to prepare her for seeing far less of him. 'I suppose he does, really, because he works quite hard himself. Each time I come to see you during the day, it means I'm out of the office. And he's beginning to lecture me on where my interests lie. He spends hours every evening in the study, pondering over accounts and other things, which I really don't have a clue about. And today he had me on the carpet about the lack of interest I show in a business that keeps me in luxury. He's right, of course, I should know the business inside out. And he's right to be concerned that if anything happened to him there would be no one to take control who had a knowledge of every aspect of the business. And there's quite a lot to learn, with the home market, imports, exports and so on. So in future, I am to take less time away from the office, and spend an hour or two each evening in the study with him, until I know the business inside out.'

Victoria was quiet for a few seconds, her mind divided into two camps. On the one hand she didn't like the idea of seeing less of Charles, but on the other hand his father had a point. And if she was hoping to become his wife, it would be in her interest to keep on the right side of the family. 'I think your father is right, of course, Charles. He is known in the city as being a very astute businessman, and I'm sure he'd be proud if you followed in his footsteps. I can't say I like the idea of seeing a lot less of you, but that is being selfish. After all, the end result would benefit both of us.'

Charles put a hand over hers and squeezed. 'How understanding you are, my sweet.' His eyes were gloating, but this she couldn't see. 'I am so lucky to have you, and I promise to visit every time I have a spare hour.' He pulled up at the side of the lane and took her in his arms. 'It won't be for ever, I'll work jolly hard, I promise.' Looking over her shoulder into the field opposite, he smiled. That had gone a lot easier than he expected. A few months of seeing each other perhaps just once a week, then breaking off shouldn't prove too difficult.

Victoria too was smiling. 'You will tell your father I didn't object when told our meetings were to be curtailed, won't you? I'm sure he'll appreciate the sacrifices I'm prepared to make for the good of the firm.'

So two people, each as scheming as the other, carried on with their journey. Charles thought his lies had given him a way out of the relationship, while Victoria firmly believed that the sacrifices she'd agreed to would not only bring Charles closer, but also his family and his wealth.

'You have told your family about me?' Maureen asked, surprise in her voice. 'I thought we agreed to leave it for a few months.'

Robert had his arm across her shoulders and he looked at her with tenderness. 'I haven't told them about you, my dear, only that I have a friend I would be inviting to the Christmas party we've talked about. A party for all the people who are dear to me, and have been for many years. People who I have never invited to my home because I knew Edwina would not make them welcome. Nigel did ask if he knew the friend I referred to and I said he didn't but soon would.' He saw a flicker of fear in her eyes and brought her hand to his lips. 'Don't look so frightened, my dear love, everything will be fine. I know Nigel and Abbie, and all my friends, will be delighted I have someone like you in my life. It is my hope that my wife and Victoria will soon find a house they think suitable, and that they will be out of my home in the next month. Then I will tell my two children about you, and take you to meet them. You will also meet Agnes, Kitty, Pete and Jessie. Then I'll give you a breather before introducing you to my friends.'

'It's a daunting prospect, Robert, and one that I would not even think about if I didn't love you enough to want to spend the rest of my life with you.'

'You won't have to go through it alone, my dear, I will be by your side at all times. In the years to come, through laughter and heartache, I will always be there for you.' When he smiled, Maureen thought how boyish he looked. 'If I tell you something, do you promise not to laugh or think me a foolish old man?'

'You are not an old man, Robert. You are a handsome man in the prime of his life and I think myself very fortunate to have met you. Now, what is it that you want to tell me?'

'After I'd known you for a while, and I began to have loving feelings towards you, I used to lie in bed each night and dream a little dream. It wasn't like a dream you have in your sleep, but a wideawake dream which I could enjoy then and every night after. All I had to do was close my eyes and conjure up a picture of you. And the times I spent dreaming were the happiest times of my life. I could forget the dreadful circumstances under which I was living, and pretend that you and I were married. You were living in my home, and sleeping in my bed. I just had to reach out to touch you, and you made my life complete.'

Maureen wiped away a tear with the back of her hand. 'I also went to bed every night and dreamed a little dream, Robert, and the dream was identical to yours. I never expected it to come true, though; it was just a lovely dream that brought you closer.'

Robert was touched. 'Our dreams will come true, my dearest darling, I promise. If I have to move heaven and earth, you will one day be my wife, and mother to Nigel and Abbie. And the promise I have just made, I intend to keep. Now, could I have a kiss, please, so I know this is *not* a dream?'

'I'm going to the pictures with Eric tomorrow night,' Abbie said, as they were driving home. 'But I won't make another date with him.'

'Why is that?' Nigel took his eyes off the road for a second. 'If you don't want to go out with him, why bother going tomorrow?'

'Because I played a dirty trick on him tonight, coaxing him to stay in and play cards. You see, I wanted to get to know him a bit, and see if I like him. But it was childish of me and not fair to him. So I'll go out with him tomorrow and tell him I haven't time for a regular boyfriend as I have a lot of homework to do.'

'But you only take half an hour to do your homework, so that's only an excuse.'

'It won't be after today. Dad told me this morning he'd ordered a typewriter to be delivered today, so I will be spending more time on homework. My speed at typing is hopeless, I'm way behind some of the others in the class. So I'll just go to Seaforth with you on dance nights, so I don't lose touch with Milly. Once the course is over, and providing I pass all the exams, I'll be able to see her more often and we can go further afield to dances.'

Nigel gave this some thought. 'He's a nice bloke, is Eric.'

'Yes, I know, but he's not the one for me, Nigel.'

Her brother gave this more thought. 'Oh, have you met anyone that just might be the one for you?'

'I think so, but I'm not going to tell you.'

Nigel grinned. 'It's Bobby, isn't it?'

Abbie twisted in her seat. 'I'm not telling you, and don't you dare say anything to Bobby Neary, or I'll never speak to you again.'

'My lips are sealed,' Nigel said, while thinking, The lady doth protest too much.

Chapter Twenty-Three

It was four weeks later, on a Sunday afternoon, when Nigel went in search of his sister. He found her sitting chatting to their father in his favourite spot in the bay window of the dining room. 'I wondered if you'd like to come for a run to Blackpool, Abbie? I'll be calling to Grandma's first and visiting with them for half an hour, then I thought I'd let Bobby drive to get more experience in traffic. It would be his first long journey and he'd learn more in that one run than he'd learn in a month running around the local streets.'

Abbie's mind was working as he spoke. There'd been no change in Bobby's attitude towards her, and she treated him as she always had. They laughed and joked with each other, but that was it. She still went to the dances three times a week, but the foursome was now a sixsome. Eric and his sister Doreen had joined their group. It wasn't a deliberate action, it just sort of happened. Eric still came over to ask her to dance, even though she'd refused to go out with him. Then he started to ask Milly for the odd dance, while Nigel partnered his sister and Bobby would dance with her. That's how it was every night, with the boys dancing with the girls in turn. And while she was dancing with Bobby, her body would be tingling all over, and she couldn't understand why he didn't sense it. But he didn't, he still treated her like his best friend's kid sister. 'Can Milly come?'

Nigel found himself blushing. 'If you want her to, but I mentioned it to Doreen at the dance last night and promised if we decided to go, I'd give her a knock to see if she wanted to come with us. But there was nothing definite arranged, so if you would prefer Milly to come instead, then there wouldn't be a problem.'

Robert tilted his head. 'I hear the name Doreen coming up quite often. Is she perhaps someone special, Nigel?'

'She's just a girl I dance with, Dad. You know of course that she's Eric's sister, and that's how I know her?'

'Mmm. I thought you were rather sweet on Milly so I'm behind with the goings-on of my children. Bring me up to date, please, so I don't put my foot in it.'

'I do like Milly, she's a nice girl and I'm fond of her. But I've a sneaking suspicion she and Eric are getting close. That's the way it looks to me. Wouldn't you agree, Abbie?'

'You could be right. But Milly and I tell each other everything and she hasn't said a dickie-bird about Eric.' Abbie jumped to her feet before her father delved into her love life – or lack of it. 'I'll go and get changed, Nigel. And I do get on well with Doreen, so I'll be quite happy for her to come.' With that she planted a kiss on her father's forehead and left the room.

Robert looked up at his son. 'Would I be bad-minded in thinking Abbie left in case I asked about her love life? She hasn't mentioned any boy since Eric.'

Nigel sat in the chair vacated by his sister. 'She'll kill me if she thinks I've said anything to you, so please don't repeat it. She'd deny it anyway, as she has to me. But I think she's got a soft spot for Bobby. When I asked her this, she really blew her top, so I've kept away from the subject since.'

'And how does Bobby feel about her?'

'I haven't asked him, Dad, and I don't think I should. He is a friend of mine, after all, and it would be very embarrassing for him if I asked how he felt about my sister. And Abbie would be mortified.'

'Yes, I can understand that.' Robert folded the Sunday paper he'd been reading when Abbie came in to talk to him, and he laid it on the side table. 'From what I've heard about Bobby

Neary from you and Abbie, I'd say he was quite a proud lad, would you?'

'Without a doubt. If he was dying of hunger, he'd be too proud to ask for food. That's the way he is.'

'So, I got the right impression.' Robert smiled. 'You go and get yourself ready or you'll have your sister on your back. Tell your Grandma and Granda I'll see them later this evening, and you enjoy your afternoon out in pleasant company. And tell young Bobby I said if he drives all the way to Blackpool and back, he can drive anywhere.'

Nigel chortled as he got to his feet. 'Dad, he's big-headed enough. A compliment like that and he wouldn't get his head in the car.'

'Would you have him any different?'

His son shook his head. 'No, Dad, I wouldn't change a hair on his big head.'

Robert bade his son goodbye, then opened up his newspaper. But although he looked at the words, he wasn't reading them. He was remembering himself at twenty-one years of age and thinking how much like young Bobby Neary he was then. Poor as a church mouse, but working like hell to make something of himself. And he'd been a proud lad, too!

'Are yer sure yer want to trust yer car with me, Nige?' Bobby asked. 'It's a long way to Blackpool and there's bound to be a lot of traffic on the roads.'

'Bobby, will you get in, please? If I didn't trust you, I wouldn't sit in the car with you, never mind let you drive it.'

'If it was my car, I wouldn't let me drive.'

Abbie, sitting on the back seat with Doreen, knocked on the window. 'For heaven's sake, Bobby Neary, will you stop talking and get in? If we're willing to trust our lives with you, why should it bother you?'

With a grin stretching from ear to ear, Bobby stuck his head through the open door. 'It's not your lives that are worrying me, it's me own life. I don't know whether to trust meself or not.'

Nigel gave him a push from behind. 'In you go, Neary! If at any time you feel you're tired, or not in control, then just shout out and we'll swap places.'

'On yer own head be it, Nige.' Bobby slid behind the steering wheel and turned to look at the girls. 'If yer get frightened back there, yer can come and sit on me knee.'

Doreen chuckled. She was a nice-looking girl with light mousy hair, deep blue eyes and white teeth that sparkled when she smiled. She also had a very slim figure and shapely legs. 'We'll be lucky if we get out of the street, never mind make it to Blackpool.'

As Bobby switched the ignition on, he tilted his head to look at Nigel. 'I told yer girls were nothing but a pain in the backside. We haven't even set off yet, and they're moaning already. It's the mouths that do it. God didn't do a bad job of the faces, I mean, credit where it's due, but He should never have put that hole under their noses.'

'By my reckoning, I've said twenty-six words since I got in the car, and Doreen's said sixteen,' Abbie piped up. 'What about yourself, Bobby Neary? Would you say you'd used a hundred, or more?'

Nigel turned in his seat. 'Don't encourage him, Abbie, please.'

'Ah, don't be mean!' Bobby said. 'I like it when Abbie encourages me.' He winked over his shoulder. 'She does it so nicely, better than anyone else I know.'

Little did he know, when he finally pulled away from the kerb, that his wink had caused Abbie's heart to lurch. And even if he didn't see her in the light she wanted him to see her in, she was happy to be in his company.

His hands gripping the steering wheel, and his eyes steady on the road, Bobby still managed to keep them amused with tales of his workmates. Some of them were so far-fetched no one really believed them to be true, but they were so funny, and brought so much laughter, who cared whether they were true or not? And when Nigel offered to take over the driving when they were halfway to their destination, Bobby flatly refused. 'I'll make it to Blackpool if it kills me,' he said. 'But I'll do me level best not to kill you as well. Not after yer've been good enough to let me drive yer car, Nige.'

And make it he did. With flying colours, Nigel said, as he suggested they park in one of the side roads as the wind was very strong coming in from the sea, and high waves were lashing over on the promenade. 'Yer picked a fine day for it, Nige,' Bobby said, making sure the handbrake was on. 'We'll get blown off our feet if we venture out there. And after me getting yer here safe and sound, I'd not take kindly to yer being drowned. In fact, I'd think yer were very inconsiderate and ungrateful.'

'The wind won't be so strong in the back streets,' Nigel said. 'And we need to stretch our legs. So we'll find a café, have something to eat and drink, then make our way back home because it's getting dark now.'

When the girls stepped out of the car they were almost blown off-balance and they put their arms around each other for support. After Nigel locked the car, he said, 'You look after Abbie, Bobby, and I'll see to Doreen. The wind will be at our backs so it won't be too bad.' He put his arm across Doreen's shoulders and led the way up the street.

'Come on.' Bobby pulled Abbie close. 'Girl of my dreams.'

She snuggled up for warmth, so there wasn't an inch between them. 'Flatterer.'

His answer was blown away in the wind, but although she couldn't be sure, she thought she heard a faint, 'It wasn't flattery.'

They found a small café and as soon as Nigel pushed the door open, the smell of fish and chips wafted up their nostrils. 'I couldn't resist that smell. I didn't think I was hungry but I realise I'm starving.' He saw an empty table, and when they were seated, he asked, 'Who's game for fish and chips?'

The girls nodded, glad to be out of the bitterly cold wind. 'They smell lovely, and I could do with warming up,' Doreen said. 'How about you, Abbie?'

'I'm all for it.' Abbie was rubbing her arms briskly. 'And could I have plenty of salt and vinegar on, please?'

Nigel gave the order to a waitress and asked if they could have a pot of tea for four to be going on with. And ten minutes later, warmed up inside, they were tucking into fish and chips that were delicious. 'This batter is the gear, just the way I like it,' Bobby said. 'As good as the chippy at the bottom of our street.'

Refreshed and warm, Nigel asked the waitress when she was clearing the table, if they could have another pot of tea. It was at this point the girls excused themselves to visit the ladies' room and repair the damage to their hair and make-up.

'We picked a lousy day to visit the seaside, Nige. It's not fit weather for man nor beast.'

'The object of the exercise was to let you have a long run in the car. And it's been good in that respect because you really did very well. I think I'll drive part way back, though, Bobby because this wind will be blowing the car from side to side. You can take over halfway if you want to get some practice driving in the dark.'

'Whatever you say is all right with me, Nige. We'll see how it goes, eh?'

Nigel picked up the spoon from his saucer and began to tap it lightly on the rim of the cup. 'I'd like to ask Doreen to come out with me one night, to the pictures, but I haven't got the nerve. I was wondering if you'd come and make up a foursome with Abbie.'

'Nah, yer know I don't get too friendly with girls, Nige, so I'd rather not if yer don't mind. I feel mean after yer've been so good to me, but no, I wouldn't want to do that.'

'But it's only with our Abbie – and only for the once. I wouldn't feel shy about asking Doreen after that.'

'No – sorry, mate.'

'What's the matter, don't you like my sister?'

'Of course I like her, how could anyone not like Abbie?'

'Well why, for heaven's sake?'

'Because taking a girl to the pictures is like being on a date, isn't it? And if a girl thinks it's a date, she'll expect yer to take her home and make another date. Then ye're hooked.'

'Abbie wouldn't expect that. She'd take it as a bit of fun. But I can't understand you refusing something as innocent as going to the pictures with a girl you've known nearly all your life and is like a sister to you.'

Bobby turned his head away, and it was so unusual for him not to look you in the eye when he was talking to you, Nigel listened with more than a little interest. 'Your Abbie doesn't feel a bit like a sister to me, that's the trouble.'

'I don't understand,' Nigel said, hoping he wasn't getting too hopeful too quickly. 'What's the trouble?'

'This is strictly between you and me, Nige, OK? If yer repeat one word then you and me will be out of touch with each other for another ten years.' Bobby leaned his elbows on the table and rested his chin on his clenched hands. Gone was the cocky lad who turned everything into a joke and pretended not to take anything seriously. 'Yes, I do like your Abbie, and not like a sister either, if yer know what I mean. But she doesn't want to bother with the likes of me, she wants a bloke who can give her the things she's used to. So it's no good starting something that I know wouldn't have a happy ending. Your Abbie might treat it like a bit of fun, but I wouldn't, and I'd end up being hurt and miserable.'

Nigel was sorry when he saw the girls coming through a door opposite; he would have liked to have continued the conversation and perhaps make Bobby see sense. 'They're here now, we'll talk about this some other time. I won't ask Doreen for a date, not tonight.' He pushed his chair back and stood up. 'Shall we make a start, girls? I'm driving halfway, then Bobby can take over if he wants to.'

* * *

411

It was ten o'clock when Robert got home. He was halfway up the stairs when he heard his name being called. When he turned it was to see Edwina standing in the hallway looking up at him. 'Did you call me?'

'Yes, I want to talk to you.'

'Can't it wait until I've hung my outdoor clothes up?'

'I think not. I have something of great importance to tell you. Please come to the drawing room immediately.'

Thinking it was news that she had found a house to suit her and Victoria, Robert ignored her curtness. He wouldn't have to put up with it for much longer. So placing his hat and gloves on the round mahogany table in the centre of the hall, he followed his wife. 'I'll leave my coat here for now,' he said, draping his overcoat over the arm of a chair. 'What is this important news?'

Edwina looked down at her clasped hands for a second, then met his eyes. 'Victoria is with child.'

Robert thought he hadn't heard right. 'I beg your pardon?'

'Your daughter is expecting a baby.' There was no emotion in the voice or on her face. It was a statement made in a matter-of-fact tone.

The colour drained from Robert's face. He could feel himself going light-headed and sat down in the nearest chair. 'Surely this is not true?'

'I would hardly tell a lie about something so serious. She is upstairs now, distressed beyond measure.'

Robert lowered his head. His wife never pulled anyone's leg, nor told a joke, because she had no humour in her. So he knew what she was saying was true. But, dear God, how could this have happened, and apart from his daughter, who else was involved? 'If this is true, who is the father?'

'It *is* true, and Charles Chisholm is the father of the child.' Again the words were spoken without emotion, and this brought on Robert's anger.

'You said Victoria was upstairs, distressed beyond measure. Surely you mean she's *ashamed* beyond measure? Because, by

412

God, she should be thoroughly ashamed of herself. And you seem to be taking it very calmly, Edwina. Do you have any idea of the scandal this will cause? The scandal will affect the whole family, not just her. Nigel and Abbie will be devastated, and I will have to face my colleagues and friends.'

'I might have known it would be your favourites you thought of first. But Victoria is your daughter, too. Have you no feelings for her?'

'She is twenty-three years of age, and she must take responsibility for the consequences of her actions. Not for one moment would I believe she was taken advantage of, because she wouldn't allow anyone to take advantage of her. So she went into this with her eyes wide open, and now must shoulder the burden of guilt and scandal.' Robert could feel beads of sweat on his forehead and reached into his pocket for a handkerchief. 'Has Charles Chisholm been informed?'

'Victoria phoned him this afternoon and he came immediately. He didn't want to believe it at first, but she told him if he didn't tell his parents, then she would.'

Robert shook his head as though bewildered by the turn of events. 'She is a scheming bitch, and although I have no time for Charles, I can feel pity for him now. She was determined to marry him, and this is the only way she could achieve it. And I know why you're not shedding any tears, because you wanted it as much as she did. Well, I think your high society friends will be turning their backs on you when this becomes public.'

'Charles will marry her. If they arrange a wedding quickly, no one will give a second thought when the baby is born.'

'D'you know, Edwina, I believe you are as wicked as your daughter, if not more so. If there is no wedding, and I can't see the Chisholms giving their consent, then the child will be born a bastard. And neither you nor your precious daughter will be able to hold your heads high again. I wouldn't pity you because you would be getting your just deserts. But I would

413

have pity for the poor innocent child who would have to live with the stigma all its life.'

It was almost as though he hadn't spoken, as Edwina ignored all he had said. 'Would you have a word with Victoria? I think she would like to ask you to intercede on her behalf with George and Annabel Chisholm.'

Robert held his head in his hands. He felt absolutely beaten. Just when he was getting a little happiness into his life, this bombshell had to fall. And he had no doubt that his eldest daughter did what she did to trap a man she thought rich enough to be worthy of her. And for that, the family name would be disgraced.

'I do not have the desire nor the stomach to face my daughter right now. I will eventually have to come to terms with it – if, in fact, it is true. But right now I feel the shame that Victoria should be feeling. And if the family name suffers, I will never forgive her.'

'No one need ever know.' Edwina's tone was flat, as though the subject had nothing to do with her. 'Both Victoria and I believe Charles will do the right thing by her. After all, he is hardly blameless.'

'I realise that. I believe there are three people who share the blame equally. Charles, whose reputation as a philanderer is common knowledge, Victoria for leading him on and allowing him to have his way with her, and yourself, Edwina. You are the one who brought our eldest daughter up to be an out-and-out snob, only interested in a person's status. And in this you certainly succeeded. But what a pity you didn't teach her how to say no to any sexual advances – something I remember you were extremely good at seventeen years ago.' Robert got to his feet and reached for his overcoat. 'I'm going up to bed now. Perhaps with a clearer head tomorrow, I will be able to face Victoria.'

'Will you please not discuss the situation with anyone until word comes from Charles. He has been persuaded by Victoria and myself, that the best solution to stop wagging tongues, would be to elope to Gretna Green.'

She's talking to me as if I were a child, Robert thought. Not once has it ever crossed her mind that it is through my hard work that she lives in this luxury. What a blind fool I was years ago not to have seen how she was changing, and put a stop to it. But it was too late now to be thinking about what might have been. 'You and your daughter are good at scheming, are you not? I think all this was planned, and if she can drag Charles to Gretna Green by the scruff of the neck, you both get what you've plotted for, without any of the scandal. Or so you think.'

Robert's shoulders were drooping and he felt he'd aged ten years. He wished he could close his eyes for a minute, then open them to find he'd been having a bad dream. 'Goodnight, Edwina, we'll talk further in the morning.' He got to the door and turned. 'I have been to visit your mother and father today. I wonder what they would think of a granddaughter who is too much of a snob to visit them, but is low enough in morals to have an illegitimate baby? I'm glad they don't know you or Victoria as you are now, because you would break their hearts.' With a weary sigh he left the room to climb the stairs slowly. And he passed Victoria's room without a glance.

'Have you gone quite mad?' Annabel Chisholm looked from her son to her husband. 'George, have you nothing to say? Please tell Charles that marrying the Dennison woman is quite out of the question. I just will not allow it.'

'We told him that weeks ago, dear, and he promised then he had no intention of marrying her. Unfortunately, our son can't resist taking his trousers down.'

'George, what a dreadful thing to say! And completely unhelpful.'

'You only see what you want to see, my dear, and only hear what you want to hear. He is your beloved son and can do no wrong. You view him through rose-coloured glasses. But the reality is far different. I am going to shock you, but that is the only way to bring you to your senses. I wonder if you realise that many of the women you invite here as friends, have been bedded by your son?'

Annabel's hand went to her throat. 'George, how can you say such a thing? Charles, tell your father that is not true.'

Charles, whose face was as white as a sheet, coughed before saying, 'I really don't think bringing all these things up is going to help the present situation, Father. In the circumstances, I would be glad of your help.'

George viewed his son through lowered lids. 'If she is pregnant, how can you be sure it is your child?'

'Oh, I'm very sure, Father, because Victoria was a virgin.'

Shaking his head in disgust, George asked, 'Was it to win a wager with your friends that you stole her virginity?'

'No!' Charles was going to admit to as little as possible. 'It was her idea that we book a room at the Adelphi, not mine.'

'Do you love her?'

Charles gave this some thought. He couldn't say he didn't even like her, his father would ask why he had taken her to bed if that were the case. Or, worse still, he'd accuse him of sleeping with anyone who wore knickers. 'I'm fond of her, yes, but whether it's love I really couldn't say.'

Annabel was rocking back and forth, crying with sadness that her beloved son was being treated like a villain, while all the time it was the Dennison bitch who'd brought him to this.

George glared at his wife. 'Weeping and wailing won't solve the problem, Annabel, so please stop making such a noise. I can't think clearly.' He turned to his son, whom he had never viewed through rose-coloured glasses. 'And what do you and Victoria intend to do?'

'I haven't agreed to any plans, I said I would be guided by you and Mother. But one suggestion from Victoria, which would stop wagging tongues and any scandal, would be to elope to Gretna Green.'

'And you really believe your friends and business colleagues are so naive they will think you are head-over-heels in love, and can't wait to be married properly in a church? Give them credit for some intelligence, Charles, for God's sake.'

'You don't have to marry this woman, Charles,' Annabel said in a tearful voice. 'Your father will give her a generous allowance for herself and the baby. She is as much to blame as you, so don't let her ruin your life.'

'Have you faced Robert Dennison yet?' George asked abruptly. 'What does he have to say about the mess you and his daughter are in?'

'He wasn't at home, so I didn't have a chance to talk to him.'

'Well, my suggestion is that we leave things until tomorrow before coming to any hasty decisions. I will ring Robert and meet with him in the morning.'

'Will I have to be present at the meeting, Father?'

George viewed his son with disgust. 'I don't think anything would be gained by you being present. You're good at creating problems, but when it comes to solving them, you haven't got the guts or the intelligence. Please leave your mother and I now, so we can each air our views. I will tell you tomorrow what decision we reach.'

'Come in, Robert.' George Chisholm waved to a chair on the opposite side of his desk. 'Sit down and I'll have my secretary bring us a pot of tea. Unless you would prefer a stiff whisky?'

'Need you ask, George?'

'I think we could both do with a double.' Charles's father entertained clients in his large, well-furnished office, and he kept an excellent supply of wines and spirits in the magnificent oak dresser that graced one of the walls. From a cupboard he produced a bottle of the finest Scotch whisky and poured a generous measure into two glasses. He handed one to Robert, then sat facing him. 'Well, what are your thoughts on the problem that has landed in our laps?'

Robert looked at the clear golden liquid and swirled it around in the glass. 'Do you want the truth, George, or would

417

you prefer I came cap in hand and made excuses?'

'The truth, of course, man. I would expect nothing less from you.'

Robert drank deeply before placing the glass on the desk. 'My opinion is that my daughter and your son deserve each other. Victoria is a scheming woman, and a first-class snob into the bargain, while Charles is a womanising philanderer who has played the field and finally got his fingers burnt.'

George's chuckle was hearty. He knew Bob Dennison was one man he would get the plain unvarnished truth from. It made a pleasant change from listening to his wife crying all night, that her son had been trapped and under no circumstances should he be saddled for the rest of his life for one little mistake. 'And do you think they should wed?'

Robert was uncompromising. He too had lain awake all night, and his thoughts had been with his two youngest children and Maureen. And as the night wore on, he had become determined that two foolish people, who were both out to satisfy themselves, were not going to spoil the happiness of the three people he loved most. 'Under any other circumstances, George, I would say they got themselves into this mess, let them decide how best to get out of it. But they are not the only ones to consider – there is also an innocent child. And I would not want any grandchild of mine to bear the stigma of being a bastard.'

This was something neither George nor his wife had considered. 'It would also be my grandchild, Robert, don't forget.'

'I am well aware of that, and you are entitled to your own views on the matter. But I had to make my personal feelings known. For myself, I have to be truthful on all counts. I do not think Charles and Victoria would make good parents, they are both too selfish and too vain. But even a bad father is better than no father.'

George took a while to consider this. Robert was right, of course; even Annabel would have to agree that their grandchild

418

should not be born out of wedlock. 'What about this idea of them eloping to Gretna Green? Are you in favour of it?'

'It won't stop tongues wagging in the long run, but at least they would be married and the child would bear the Chisholm name.'

For a year or so now, George had been hoping his wayward son would settle down and eventually produce not only a grandchild for he and Annabel to love, but also an heir to the business. 'I believe that is the best solution. I can't say I'm overjoyed that things have worked out like this, or that I would have chosen your daughter as a proper wife for Charles. But we can't turn the clock back so there's nothing to be gained by saying what we would have liked. Shall we agree, then, Robert, to urge them to elope to Scotland as soon as possible? I believe they have to be in residence in the area for a certain period before they will be allowed to marry.'

'There is another important detail we must discuss,' Robert said, 'and that is where they will live. I will not, under any circumstances, allow them to live under my roof.'

The Chisholms' home was nearly twice the size of the Dennisons', but George knew no building was large enough to house both Annabel and Victoria. Certainly not in the present circumstances. Perhaps when the baby was born his wife might be more tolerant. 'I agree that they should not live with either of us. I shall buy them a house which will serve until my son begins to earn enough to choose their own. As you are in the furniture business, would you be prepared to provide suitable furniture?'

Robert nodded, the knots in his tummy beginning to unwind. 'I will supply furniture, carpets and window drapes. Also ornaments, mirrors and paintings. And I will continue with Victoria's allowance for six months to enable them to settle in.' He emptied the glass before meeting and holding George's eyes. 'There is one more thing I would like to do, if you have no objection. I know my daughter will have no patience with a baby, and will soon tire of the novelty. So I would like to be the one to choose a nanny once the child is born. Someone kind, caring and loving. Three virtues sadly lacking in Victoria, which every child needs for a happy childhood. Would that meet with your approval?'

'I would be grateful. And now I think the things we have discussed should be passed on to the two people concerned without delay. As soon as you leave, I will instruct one of my men to seek out any houses on the market he feels suitable. With a bit of luck this sorry business could soon be behind us, with our children married and living in their own home. It could be achieved in a couple of weeks if a house became available that is in good condition. I presume you will have no problem supplying the furniture?'

'I could have all the furniture required in a day or two. It will be my choice, but that is unavoidable as I have no intention of asking Victoria to view that which I have in stock. She, and Charles, should consider themselves very lucky.'

'They won't have any choice in the residence, either, because that will be my choice. And I agree with you, they should consider themselves lucky. If they don't they can bore each other stiff with moans and complaints.' As Robert rose from his chair, George asked, 'By the way, is your wife upset about this whole sorry mess?'

Robert shook his head. 'I would say she is delighted, George. You see, Edwina is an even bigger snob than Victoria, and equally as cold-hearted. Her daughter marrying a Chisholm will delight her no end. She won't feel any shame that it is a shotgun wedding, for she wouldn't allow shame to discommode her.' He placed his bowler firmly on his head at the angle that was the most comfortable, and was pulling on his gloves when he remembered his manners. 'George, I want to thank you for making this interview as painless as possible.' He offered his hand and returned the strong handshake. 'I appreciate the stance you have taken.'

'Let me tell you something, Robert, that may ease your mind a little. Victoria was a virgin before my son got his hands on her. You could have come in here like a raging bull.'

Relaxed enough now to smile, Robert said, 'It's a good job we both know our children are not angels. Anyway, I'll go straight home now and pass on what we have decided. I would suggest that Charles should visit Victoria this afternoon and make arrangements for the journey to Scotland. The sooner it is over, the better.'

'Yes, that's one appointment I'll make sure he keeps. And Robert, I'll contact you as soon as a suitable house has been found. We'll keep in touch, eh?'

'Of course. None of this is our making, so there's no earthly reason why there should be a change in our friendship. Goodbye for now, George, or as my old mam used to say, ta-ra.'

Long after Robert left the office, George was still thinking of him. Asking himself how anyone as sound and honest as Robert Dennison had ended up with a wife and daughter who were cold-hearted, humourless and wicked. Then he remembered his own son wasn't exactly perfect. But at least he himself had a loving wife to snuggle up to in bed at night. He doubted Robert had even that.

Robert opened the drawing-room door and poked his head in. He ignored Victoria and nodded to his wife. 'I want to speak to you upstairs, Edwina, now!' He disappeared before she could protest, and there was little she could do but follow.

'Sit down, please, and listen to what I've got to say.' Robert quickly told what the outcome of his meeting with George had been. 'Charles will be here this afternoon and he and Victoria will make arrangements to travel to Gretna Green. They will need to stay there a few days before being married.'

There was a sly look on Edwina's face. It was working out just as she'd hoped. But she still wasn't satisfied. 'I want to view any house George Chisholm finds. It might not be suitable or to our taste. So would you inform him of my wishes, please.'

'You can go to hell, Edwina. Victoria will take what she's given and be grateful. And if you try to rock the boat I will guarantee George Chisholm will withdraw his offer and wash his hands of the whole affair. He'll pull the rug from under your feet, and rightly so.' Robert stared hard at his wife of twenty-five years. There was no emotion in his heart for her, not even pity. 'Am I to understand you will be moving out to live with Victoria?'

'Yes, of course I am. You don't think I'd stay here once she leaves, do you?'

'Oh, I hope not, Edwina. With the two of you gone, this house will become a proper home and I can't wait for the day. Now pass all the news on to your daughter, and warn her if she asks for more, she'll end up with nothing. And so will you.' He knew he was being childish but she'd hurt him so much over the years he couldn't resist adding, 'You could even end up back in Arthur Street. You remember Arthur Street, don't you, Edie? The street you were born in and where your mother and father still live?'

Chapter Twenty-Four

'Mr Nigel, yer father said when yer've hung yer clothes up, will yer go straight to the study, he wants a word with yer.' The housekeeper kept her back to him, stirring a pot with a huge wooden ladle. 'And Miss Abbie, she came in five minutes ago, so she'll beat yer to the study.'

Nigel raised his brows at her. 'Is it good news, Agnes?'

She pulled a face and shrugged her shoulders. It wasn't up to her to tell him the best news she'd had in years. Much as she'd like to shout it from the roof-tops. 'I wouldn't know, Mr Nigel, yer'll have to get yer skates on and find out.'

Nigel raced up the stairs, threw his coat and leather briefcase on the bed and was out of the room and back down the stairs in seconds. He knocked on the study door then poked his head in to see Abbie sitting facing their dad. She looked happy and was telling him how her typing speed had increased since he bought her the typewriter.

'Bragging again, are you?' Nigel closed the door behind him and sat on the edge of the desk. 'There'll be no stopping her soon, Dad, she'll be taking over from us.'

His sister smiled at him. 'That's the idea, brother dear. You'll have to watch yourself when I join the firm.'

'Can I ask you to be serious for a short while? I have something to tell you.' Robert didn't know of an easy way to tell them, only what was the truth. 'Your sister, Victoria, is marrying Charles Chisholm, and they've eloped to Scotland.'

There was a deadly silence for a few seconds, then Nigel studied his father's face to see if there was a hint he was pulling their legs. But he could read nothing from his expression. 'I don't think you're joking, are you, Dad?'

'It's hardly something I would joke about, son. No, they left this morning and will be away about ten days. When they return they will be man and wife.'

Abbie was leaning forward, her eyes wide. 'But why? Why didn't she tell us?'

'When people elope, Abbie, the general idea is not to tell anyone. But people who elope usually do so because their parents won't agree to the marriage.'

Nigel looked puzzled. 'I don't understand, Dad. Why couldn't they wait and have a proper wedding?'

'It was their choice,' Robert said. 'And ours is not to reason why. Your mother and I have known since Sunday, and of course Charles's parents were told at the same time. His father has instructed one of his managers to seek a suitable house for them, and indeed, this morning George rang me to say there are two available which we will both view tomorrow.'

'You mean Victoria will not be coming back to live here?' Abbie asked.

'If a suitable house is found for them, then no, Victoria will not be coming back here. George is buying them the house as a wedding present, and I have promised to furnish it. We hope to have everything finalised before their return.'

'Mother won't be too happy about that, will she?' Nigel said. 'She will miss Victoria very much.' He didn't say what was really in his mind, that the only one in the house their mother had any feelings for, was his older sister. 'Is she very upset?'

'On the contrary, your mother is delighted. You see, she is going to live with them.'

'I've got to say, Dad, I find it very odd.' Nigel couldn't believe what he was hearing was true. 'I didn't even think they were courting seriously. Victoria had designs on Charles, anyone could see that. But he is so fond of the women I thought it would be years before he finally decided to settle down.'

'Nigel, no one was more surprised than I.' Robert shook his head. 'No, that's not true, George and Annabel Chisholm were very surprised, to say the least. Still, it was Victoria's and Charles's choice, and they are the ones who will have to live together. Whether Charles realises he's taking on my wife as well, I don't know. But somehow I think that is one surprise still in store for him.'

'Have you no objection to Mother leaving?' Abbie asked in a low voice, not wanting her beloved father to be hurt. 'Did she ask if you would allow her to leave?'

'When has my wife ever asked my permission for anything? We haven't even been civil to each other for years. But I certainly have no objection to either her or Victoria leaving this house. To say otherwise would be hypocritical.'

'I understand, Dad,' Nigel said, a picture of that lonely single bed flashing before his eyes. 'Perhaps I shouldn't say it about my own mother and sister, but I believe this house will be a lot happier without them.'

'I'm not going to pretend, either,' Abbie admitted. 'There's been nothing normal about our lives for as long as I can remember. I haven't seen my friend Rowena since I left school as I've been afraid to invite her here because of Mother. And while I'm always made welcome at the Jamiesons', I couldn't be sure Milly would get the same welcome here. Even though Mother and Mrs Jamieson knew each other well when we were young and lived down there. And that's no way of living, is it, Dad, when you can't even invite your friends home? I don't know why Mother and Victoria are the way they are, but they've spoilt my life since we came to live here.'

'I know, my dear, and I blame myself for that. I should have put my foot down years ago. But in ten days' time, please God, you will be able to invite all your friends. I want to see your grandparents here so they can sit in the garden and enjoy Pete's labours. Milly, Bobby and their families you must invite whenever you like. And I can't forget my friend and colleague of many years, Jeff. He's only been here three or four times in the ten years we've lived here. He didn't have to tell me why he began to make excuses for not coming, I didn't need telling. You see, he knew your mother as Edie Brady, a nice-looking, happy girl who lived in the same street. He liked Edie Brady, but he couldn't stomach the Edwina Dennison she became. It will be a proud day for me when he and his family sit at my table. And I have another friend who has always lent me a sympathetic ear; they will always be welcome.'

Abbie jumped to her feet and put her arms around him. 'You're not upset, are you, Dad?'

'No, I am not upset. To tell the truth, I am relieved. I seem to have been living on a knife-edge for years, trying to keep the peace and holding back what I really wanted to say. I know now I was wrong. I should have been more masterful, protected you more and made sure you were living in the sort of happy environment all normal children should have and are entitled to. But you must have known your mother wasn't easy to live with. And I was so weary of the constant bickering and arguing, I threw myself into building up the business hoping the money I was bringing in would buy you the best, to make up for what was lacking in your lives. But all it brought was misery for you, and myself. And it went to your mother's head, unfortunately, taking her into a fantasy world of makebelieve. She refuses to admit she has ever been poor, and, sad to say, she had a willing ally in Victoria.'

'I'm glad they are both leaving,' Abbie said defiantly. She'd suffered their taunts and snide remarks for as long as she could remember, just because she didn't want to be as snobbish as they were. 'Nigel and I will have you all to ourselves and we'll spoil you rotten. You'll see, in another ten days, how happy we'll be.'

'I'm sure I will, my dear. And now the divorce is under way, your mother should be out of my life within the next eighteen months. Then I can put the past behind me and start again.'

'You'll find yourself someone nice, Dad, someone to make

426

you happy. You're a very handsome man, and the women will be after you.'

'I think not, Abbie, the days of courting are over for me. I need someone who loves me and will be there to listen to my ups and downs, who will be a good mother to you and Nigel and make our home a warm and cheerful place. A place and a woman we will be glad to come home to after a day's work. Then I'll be a happy and contented man.'

Nigel had only been half-listening to the conversation. He wasn't swallowing the story as Abbie was, being convinced there was more to the situation than met the eye. But he wasn't going to express his doubts to his father because no matter what the truth of the matter was, his dad was better off without either his mother or sister. 'Dad, does Agnes know?'

'Yes, of course she had to be told because of the meals, and Victoria's empty bedroom. Besides, I look on Agnes as a friend whom I know I can trust to confide in. Kitty and Jessie have also been told. I would love to have heard the conversation in the kitchen this morning – I bet the air was blue. But although they certainly had no reason to like your mother or sister, I bet things were said in fun, not malice.' Robert smiled. 'Now, poppy off and get ready for dinner.'

'You go, Abbie, I want a quick word with Dad. You wouldn't be interested, it's only about something that happened in work.'

Once his sister had closed the door behind her, Nigel looked at his father. 'It's nothing to do with work, Dad, I only said that to get Abbie out of the way. It's a personal thing I wanted to talk about, but if you've enough on your mind it will keep until another day.'

'Nonsense, I will always have time to listen to you. What is it?'

'It's about Bobby. I can't teach him any more now, he's an excellent driver. He'd been hoping his boss would promote him to a van driver, so he could earn better wages, but the man turned him down flat, saying he needed a driver skilled in heavy goods vehicles and he wasn't about to spend time and money on letting one of the drivers teach him. Bobby was so disappointed, Dad, and I wondered if you had any ideas?'

'You couldn't have picked a better time to ask, because I might have an opening for him in the next week or so. I'm waiting for the delivery of a new removal van, and the driver will need a second man to help with the furniture. There's no reason why he wouldn't allow Bobby at the wheel when he thought it convenient and safe.' When his son didn't agree right away, Robert asked, 'You don't think that would go down well with Bobby? Perhaps he'd prefer to stay on at Owen Peck's?'

Nigel pursed his lips and blew out a low whistle. 'This puts me in a very difficult position, I'm afraid. To do a good turn for two people I think the world of, I would have to betray their confidence. You see, each of them asked me not to repeat what they'd told me, and they might never forgive me if they found out.'

'If it's for their own good, of course they will! Anyway, I'm not likely to repeat what you tell me, am I? So who are the two people involved, and what has it got to do with Bobby getting a job as a driver?'

'Well, it's Bobby and Abbie. She likes Bobby a lot, Dad, but she said if I told anyone she wouldn't speak to me again. So to try and get them together, I asked Bobby if he'd make a foursome up to go to the pictures. Me with Doreen, him with Abbie. He turned me down flat, saying he didn't want to get serious with a girl. So I did a bit of probing, until in the end he told me the real reason he wouldn't go to the pictures with Abbie. He really likes her, you see, but he said she didn't want to bother with the likes of him because he could never give her what she's used to.' Nigel moved from the desk to the chair opposite his father. 'It's not often you see the serious side of him, but I did that night when he opened up his heart. He didn't want to start getting too near Abbie, because he'd be the one who would end up hurt and miserable.'

Robert was thoughtful as he tapped the end of his pen on

the desk. Perhaps it would be better if he stood aside and let things take their course. Then again, he could interfere in such a way no one would know. 'When I've said what I'm going to, Nigel, we will both forget this conversation ever took place. Agreed?'

'Yes, of course.'

'I know you're seeing Bobby tonight because it's dance night. So why don't you casually mention that I'm going in for a new van. Then you could say I'd be looking for a driver and a second man in the next week or so. Put the idea into his head then leave it up to him. If he's interested, he'll soon let you know. And as this conversation didn't take place, then he won't think there's been any conniving.'

'What would your feelings be, Dad, if it did come to pass that they fell in love with each other? Would you have any objection?'

'To Rose Neary's son becoming my son-in-law? I'd be absolutely delighted! But you will have to tread carefully, Nigel, because the last thing you want is to make Bobby feel as though you're doing him a favour. The lad has his pride, I wouldn't want to be party to it being broken.'

A grin spread across Nigel's face. 'Thanks, Dad, I'll do exactly as you say. Will you still be up when we get home, so I can tell you how it went?'

'I'll be late in myself, I'm going to see a friend.' Robert was going to Maureen's, and he had so much to tell her he knew it would be after midnight when he got home. 'Anyway, why not tell me over breakfast when Abbie's present? If she really likes him, we should keep her in the picture without appearing to do so.'

'I'll do that.' Nigel put a hand on each of the chair arms to push himself up. But there was something he really wanted to say first, so he stretched over to put a hand on his father's arm. 'It must have been a worrying few days for you, Dad, and your mind must be spinning. Yet you still made time to listen to me, and even offer to help. I want you to know I am very grateful.'

'Nigel, I have vowed to myself that I will spend the rest of my life making up to you and Abbie for the missing years of your childhood. Ten long years, and all my fault for not realising what was happening before it was too late. I will do all in my power to make it up to you. And before you go, is this Doreen a serious contender for your affections?'

Nigel blushed. 'I like her, Dad, we get on well together. But that is as far as we've progressed, so it's early days yet.'

Robert wagged his head from side to side, tutting. 'I don't know, all this intrigue going on behind my back. My two children involved in affairs of the heart and I know nothing about it! I can only excuse myself by saying I haven't been thinking straight lately, and walking around with my eyes closed. But that will all be rectified in the near future. While I will never interfere in your lives unless I think it right to do so, I want to be part of them.'

'You will be, I promise.' Nigel felt like hugging his father to show how much he loved him, but thought it unseemly in a man. 'I envy Abbie being a girl and able to kiss you. All I can say, Dad, is thank you.'

Robert waved a hand. 'Just let me know tomorrow whether thanks are in order. I hope they are.'

Nigel's chance came when he and Bobby were waiting for Doreen and Milly to come back from the cloakroom. Abbie was dancing with Eric, so the coast was clear. 'Did I tell you my dad was waiting delivery of a new van? It's not to replace one of the older ones, it's just that business is brisk and a new van is necessary.' He tried to sound very off-hand and it seemed to work as Bobby showed interest.

'Have you ever driven a van, Nige?'

'No, I'm afraid my job is mostly stuck in the office. I've often wanted to try, though, because I fancy it would give you a feeling of power, sitting so high up in the world. I might ask my dad if I can have a go sometime.'

'I'd give my right arm if I had the chance to drive one. I

430

can't see it, though, so it's just wishful thinking on my part.'

'Well, my dad will be looking for a driver and a second man in the next week or two, so why not apply for the job as second man?'

'What's a second man when he's out?'

'He helps with the furniture, but in most cases they also drive the van occasionally. That's in case the driver is ever off and they need someone to take over.'

Bobby's eyes were bright. 'And is yer dad going to interview men for the jobs?'

'Sometimes he does, sometimes one of the managers does it. I could find out a bit more about it if you're interested, Bobby. Would you like me to?'

His friend dropped his head to gaze down at his shoes. 'I don't think so, Nige, but thanks all the same. You asking yer dad for a job for me would put him in an awkward position. He might feel obliged to take me on because I'm a mate of yours, and I wouldn't want that.'

'You come up with some crazy notions sometimes, Bobby Neary, honestly! And you don't know my dad if you think that. If he thought you weren't right for the job, he wouldn't give it to you. The men handle some very expensive furniture, so he's very choosy who he takes on. If you'd prefer to stay on at Owen Peck's, then do so by all means. It was just an idea I had, with you saying you were keen to drive a van and earn better wages.'

This gave Bobby food for thought. 'There'd be other men interviewed for the job, so I wouldn't get preferential treatment?'

'My dad is a businessman, Bobby, and the best man would get the job. I'm beginning to feel sorry I mentioned it now, because if you didn't get taken on, it might make a difference to our friendship and I don't want that to happen.'

'Blimey, Nige! Yer said I didn't know yer dad very well, but you don't know me that well if that's what yer think. As if I'd fall out with yer 'cos I didn't get a flippin' job! There'd be no fear of that, mate.'

431

'So I'll make some enquiries, shall I?'

'Yeah, if yer will. But no special treatment, right? If I get the job it's got to be on me own merits, not because I happen to be yer mate.'

'I understand.' Nigel saw Doreen and Milly coming through the door and said, 'As soon as I find out when the interviews are, I'll let you know. And just to keep your driving up to scratch, I'll come down tomorrow night and we'll go for a run.'

Maureen was wide-eyed as she listened. Why did this man, who was so kind and caring, have so many troubles thrust upon him? And what a dreadful person his daughter Victoria must be, to bring shame upon the family. 'I'm so sorry for you, love. You really don't deserve all these terrible things that are happening to you. And you say your daughter expressed no shame or remorse for the situation she's got herself into?'

'I didn't mean to upset you, my dear, but because I intend you to be an important part of my life, it is only fair you know the whole truth. I have had no communication with Victoria, I couldn't bring myself to look into her face. But from my wife, I gather there is no shame nor remorse. Edwina herself is actually quite delighted that her daughter is to marry the son of one of the richest men in Liverpool. And, of course, it is something for which Victoria has been angling for many months. The reason for the hasty wedding seems not to bother them at all. And I have to say that Victoria and Charles are very suited to each other, both being selfish, arrogant and greedy. Not one word of sorrow nor regret has been uttered, at least not in my presence. It may have been different in the Chisholm house, as George is a very hard-headed businessman who doesn't mince his words. His son is a weak sort, and I can well imagine him crawling. His mother, Annabel, has always spoilt him rotten, but his father is a very different kettle of fish. I firmly believe both his parents would have forbidden the marriage if I hadn't reminded George that the child would be our grandchild, and I wouldn't want it to be born a bastard. So Victoria is very lucky she hasn't been left to bring up an illegitimate child.'

'Oh, you poor love.' Maureen stroked his cheek. 'Will you ever have peace of mind?'

'Oh yes, my dear. I have vowed many things in the past few months and made many promises. They were all to do with righting the wrongs I allowed to happen to those I love. But this business with Victoria has really hardened my heart against her and her mother. That a daughter of mine would stoop so low to trap a man into marriage, and be aided and abetted by her mother has cleared me of any responsibility I felt I owed them. And in the last few days I have made a resolution concerning myself. I'm not selfish, but I honestly believe I am entitled to some happiness in my life from now on. And you are the one person who can bring me that happiness, along with love, warmth and honesty. That it will happen so quickly is more than I dared hope.'

Robert stared down into the face he had come to love so dearly. It was an open face, one you knew at once was incapable of deceit or dishonesty. He bent to kiss her forehead before carrying on. 'Tomorrow I am going to view two properties which George Chisholm believes would be suitable for the newlyweds. You don't know Liverpool, so you won't know that both houses are in good areas and fine buildings. One in Percy Street, the other in Rodney Street. I'm keeping my fingers crossed that George and I can agree on a property tomorrow, and if it is in good decorative order, I can get cleaners in right away to clean and polish the place from top to bottom. Then I can start to deliver furniture and other essentials so my daughter and her new husband can move in immediately.'

'You are very efficient, Robert. I couldn't have coped with half the things you have. Just knowing my unmarried daughter was expecting a baby would have been enough to shatter me and render me helpless. I'm not as strong a character as you, love, so don't expect too much of me. Not at first, anyhow.'

'All I want is your love and support when we start our life together. And one day I will find enough words to say how much you have come to mean to me, and how you've helped me over the past three years to keep my sanity.'

'Good morning!' Robert entered the kitchen the next morning to find his son and daughter had already started their breakfast. 'I'm sorry if I'm late, Agnes.'

'Ye're not late, Mr Robert, it's these two who are a few minutes early. Anyway, what does it matter if yer are late? Ye're yer own boss, yer can please yerself. And I'm not ruddy well timing yer.'

'Did you sleep well, Dad?' Abbie asked, worried that her father was keeping a stiff upper lip for their benefit. 'You must have been late coming in, I didn't hear you.'

'I slept like a top, my dear, I'm glad to say. And yes, I was late getting home – it was well after midnight.'

'In a card-game at the club, were you, Dad?' Nigel was hoping there would be an opening in the conversation where he could bring up a topic without it seeming out of place.

'Something like that,' Robert said airily. 'Did you both enjoy the dance?'

'Yes, it was enjoyable, as usual,' Nigel answered, spreading golden marmalade on to a slice of toast. 'But me and Bobby were saying we might try somewhere else one night, just for a change.' He bit into the toast and licked the marmalade which had stuck to his lips. 'By the way, Dad, I mentioned to Bobby about you getting a new van, and that you'd be taking on a driver and second man. You didn't mind, did you?'

'Why should I mind? It's hardly a secret of national importance, son.' Neither man had failed to notice Abbie's quick turn of head when she heard Bobby's name mentioned. 'Why are you telling me this?'

'Well, I know how much he wants to be a heavy goods driver, so I suggested he apply for the job of second man. He pooh-poohed the idea at first, saying he would be putting you in an embarrassing position because you wouldn't want to turn him down, with him being my friend. He can be very stubborn at times, and insisted if he went after a job he wanted to get it on his own merits, not on the strength of being pally with me.'

Abbie nodded her head. 'That's Bobby Neary all over. Stubborn as a flipping mule. But you've got to admire him for it.'

'Oh, I couldn't agree more.' Robert's face was deadpan as he tapped a finger on his chin. 'I wonder how we can get around this dilemma? I certainly think he has as much right to apply for a job as any other man, but I see his point in this case. And as you rightly say, Abbie, I admire him for it. The only suggestion I can make is that he goes through the proper channels to apply. And with regards to the interview, the usual procedure is for Mr Seddon to interview the applicants. And as he doesn't know Bobby from Adam, there can be no suggestion of any favouritism.'

'I'll tell him tonight when we go for a run. He can drive as well as I can, but I told him he needs to keep his hand in if he wants a driving job.' Nigel placed his knife and fork neatly down the centre of his empty plate and pushed it aside. 'I hope he sees sense. I'd like him to get on, he deserves to.'

'I like the sound of this Bobby,' Agnes said. 'D'yer think I'll ever get to meet him?'

'Without doubt, Agnes, without doubt.' Robert didn't glance his daughter's way in case his eyes gave the game away. 'And in the near future, too.'

Robert came out of the house in Rodney Street and nodded his approval to George Chisholm. 'This would definitely be my choice. It has a warm, friendly feeling to it. It's about the right size and is near the city centre. What more could you ask for?'

'I agree, Robert, it's ideal. I'll go straight down to my

solicitor's now and have all the papers signed today and the money passed over. That is my part done, the rest is up to you.'

'The first thing I must do is engage a couple of cleaners to polish from top to bottom. The house appears clean already, but I will make doubly sure. So if I can have the keys as soon as possible I would be grateful. Once the cleaners are out, I can begin to move furniture in.'

'If you call at my office in the morning the keys will be ready for you to pick up.' George stretched out his hand. 'You and I work well together, Robert, we make a good team. Pity it had to be in these circumstances.'

Robert's handshake was firm. 'I have made up my mind that the circumstances you refer to will not spoil my life. I will do what I can to supply my daughter with the material requirements she will have need of, then I believe I will have done my duty. At twenty-three she must now take care of her own life. I will keep up her allowance for six months, as promised, and I will always be there for my grandchild. But with regards to Victoria herself . . . well, I wash my hands of her.'

'I wish Annabel was as level-headed as you. I don't think she's stopped weeping and wailing for days now. Her poor son, she cries, will have no one who understands him as she does. Who is going to make sure he has his favourite food, or his clothes are pressed to his liking? My wife really is beside herself, and I'm beginning to lose patience with her.'

'Would you pass a message on to her for me? Ask her if she'd do me the honour of inspecting the house when I have it fully furnished. Anything she doesn't like, I will remove and replace. That might give her an interest and bring a halt to the weeping and wailing.'

'I shall certainly tell her, Robert, and when you give me a sign I will bring her myself to see what wonders you have been able to perform.'

Robert chuckled. 'It's a while since I performed any

wonders, but I'll see what I can pull out of the hat. And now, before we go our separate ways, can I ask why I've always been Bob in the club, but have now been promoted to Robert?'

'You can thank your wife for that. At the dinner party the other week, she said she can't stand "Bob" – it sounds so working-class. I think she was telling me off in a nice way.'

'From now on, George, I'm back to being working-class because they have a lot more fun. The name is Bob, and I'll call into your office in the morning for the keys. Until then, take care.'

'Hang on a minute, Bob. Do the working-class *really* have more fun?'

'Come and sit in my kitchen for a few hours one day, and you'll find out. They've got more humour and a zest for life the toffs will never have. Believe me, George, they live much fuller lives. And I should know, I've had a taste of both.'

Four pairs of eyes opened wide when the back door opened and Robert walked in. 'In the name of God, Mr Robert, yer gave me the fright of me life,' Agnes said, her hand to her bosom for effect. 'I nearly jumped out of me skin!'

'I'm not staying, Agnes, I just have a few little chores to do, then I'll be off again. I came to have a brief word with my wife, and to tell you that several tea chests are being delivered in the morning. Will you see that three are taken to Victoria's room, and three to my wife's?'

The housekeeper would have liked to say it would give her the greatest of pleasure, but instead she said, 'Of course I will, Mr Robert. Now, surely yer could manage a cup of tea, if nothing else?'

He grinned. 'Go on, you twisted my arm.' After putting his hat and gloves on the big dresser, he laid his coat over the back of a chair and sat down. 'How are things with you, Pete? Well, I hope?'

'Yeah, fine, Mr Robert. There's not much doing in the garden with the weather getting colder, hardly any colour at all. But I'm turning the soil over and preparing the ground for the start of spring.'

'Good!' Robert turned to Kitty. 'I haven't seen Alf here since that day in the summer. Has he been unwell?'

'No, he's not been so bad.' Kitty was really pleased the boss had mentioned her husband. It just showed how thoughtful he was. 'He would like to come, but he's frightened of making a nuisance of himself.'

'Nonsense! How can he be a nuisance?'

'I've told her over and over that Alf's welcome,' Pete said. 'But I might as well talk to the ruddy trees.'

'Kitty, tell Alf I insist he comes to give Pete a hand. The garden is big, the air is free, so he must take advantage of it.'

'I'll tell him, Mr Robert, and he'll be over the bleedin' moon. He never complains, but he must get fed up being stuck in that little house all day. It's enough to send him ga-ga.'

'The last thing we want is to see Alf going ga-ga, Kitty, so you pass on my message.' Robert gazed down the table to where Jessie sat, eyes wide and ears alert. But her tongue remained silent, as it always did in the presence of any member of the family. 'Jessie, I wanted to have a word with you, too. I'm looking for a couple of cleaners to work in a house near the city centre, just for two or three days. I wondered if your mother would be interested?'

The eyes of the young girl became wider and brighter. 'Oh yes, Mr Robert, she'd be made-up. D'yer want me to ask her?'

'I'll call and see her myself. Will she be home now?'

'Not until twelve o'clock, when the children come home from school for something to eat. Well, she gets in before twelve, really, 'cos she's got to be there to let them in. If yer got there for a quarter to, she should be home.'

'I'll give her a knock then.' Robert drained his cup and nodded to the housekeeper. 'The best cup of tea in Liverpool, Agnes, bar none. And now I'll go and have a word with my wife.'

The four pairs of eyes followed him until he was out of

438

sight and the door closed behind him. The housekeeper could see Kitty was bursting to say something, and as soon as she opened her mouth, Agnes stretched across and covered it with her hand. 'Not one word until he's out of the bleedin' house, Kitty Higgins, or I'll clock yer one. And anyway, it's time we were all doing what we get paid to do. And don't be pulling faces behind me back 'cos I'll see yer.'

Kitty didn't reply until she was near the door, and safety. 'I always said yer had eyes in yer backside, Agnes Weatherby. Miserable sod, yer are.'

'Miserable sod or not, sunshine, don't you two be laughing and talking out there, 'cos Mr Robert will be in the drawing room having a serious talk with Miss Edwina.'

'How d'yer know it'll be serious, queen?'

'What else will it be, soft girl, with a woman who wouldn't know a joke if yer drew her a picture of it. If yer think I'm a miserable sod, what would yer call her?'

Kitty folded her thin arms across her flat chest, and cupped her chin in one hand. 'I can't think of a word that fits. I mean, what's worse than miserable? But I'll tell yer what, queen, when I'm out there not laughing or talking, I'll put me thinking cap on and come up with something, you see if I don't.'

After the little woman had left the room, Agnes moved with speed to cross the floor and stand with her ear to the door. She had to put her hand over her mouth to quieten her laughter when she heard Kitty ask, 'Ay, queen, if yer saw a woman who looked a real miserable cow, but yer couldn't call her that, what would yer call her?'

'I don't know, Kitty,' Jessie said. 'How about miserable bugger?'

'Nah, that's no good! The cow and the bugger are all right, it's the miserable we want another word for.' The voice became more distant as the two cleaners moved away, but Agnes could just make out Kitty saying, 'There's a dog in our street what looks as miserable as sin, and Alf calls him something but I can't remember what it is now. I'll ask him when I get home, save me wearing me brain out.'

Agnes opened the door and hurried after them so she wouldn't have to raise her voice. 'How can yer wear out what yer haven't got, sunshine?'

Her face a picture of innocence, Kitty asked, 'How did yer know I didn't have no vest on?'

The housekeeper looked at her as though she'd gone mad. 'What are yer on about yer ruddy vest for?'

''Cos I wore it out, that's why. So I know bleedin' well I can't wear it out when I haven't got one.'

Agnes looked at Jessie, shrugged her shoulders and held out her hands. 'I give up, I can't win.' With that she made her way back to the kitchen to double up with laughter. What a case that Kitty was. She might act daft, but by God she was far from it. She had an answer for everything.

Robert sat in a chair facing his wife. Telling himself to be calm and not let her rile him, he said: 'I'm having six tea chests delivered tomorrow, and I've asked Agnes to see that three are taken to your bedroom and the rest to Victoria's. It would help if you would start packing yours with everything you wish to take with you. I would prefer everything to be taken in the one pick-up, so there is no need for you to return to this house for anything. And when you have packed away your belongings, perhaps you can start on Victoria's. If you need help, young Jessie will oblige.'

'Am I not to be told where we are going to live?' Edwina's eyes were cold and hard. 'Or do you intend to leave it until the last minute?'

'I only found out myself an hour ago, so I could hardly have told you sooner. It is a fine house in Rodney Street, which George Chisholm is buying as a wedding present. I am to furnish it throughout. With luck everything will be in order for Victoria and Charles to move into the day they arrive back in Liverpool. If you wish to move in before, to make sure all is to your liking, I will try and make that possible.'

'And what if the house isn't to our liking?'

'Then that is tough luck, Edwina. You see, Victoria will no longer be my responsibility; she will have a husband to care for her needs. Her allowance will continue for six months, then all ties between us will be severed – except, of course, for when the child is born. I will naturally wish to see my grandchild and will make sure he, or she, wants for nothing. As for you, I will place a one-off sum of money in your name in the bank. It will be a substantial sum, and as you will be living with your daughter, and have no expenses to pay out, you should be comfortable.'

'What about my allowance? That will continue, surely?'

Robert shook his head. 'No, that will discontinue as from the end of this month. When you move out of this house we will be a separated couple, and when the divorce comes through we will cease to be man and wife. Only you and I know we ceased to be that a long time ago.' He rose from the chair and looked down at her. 'At the end of the month I will pay a large sum of money into the bank in your name. If you choose to squander it, that is your affair. But don't come to me for more, because the answer will be a definite refusal. And now I must get back to the office. Goodbye, Edwina.'

Chapter Twenty-Five

For six days Robert was rushed off his feet. He managed to get the house furnished as he'd hoped, but admitted he would never have made it without Jessie's mother, Edna. She was a brilliant worker, quick and very efficient. She moved through the house like a whirlwind, with her twelve-year-old daughter and a neighbour in her wake. Robert had been doubtful about a twelve-year-old being of any help, but Edna explained that Laura had taken over looking after the younger children when Jessie started work, and also helping in the house. 'She can clean as good as me, Mr Robert,' Edna had said. 'She's a real good kid.' And she was right. The furniture, ornaments and mirrors that Robert had delivered were gleaming before they'd been in the house half an hour. And now, apart from a few pieces that still had to be picked up and delivered today, the house was shining from top to bottom.

'Edna, I don't know what I would have done without you. You've worked very hard, and so have your neighbour and daughter. I am so grateful.' Robert grinned at her, and tired as he was, there was a twinkle in his eye. 'I'll tell you what, you can't half move. There were times when I didn't know if you'd passed me, or whether I was imagining things.'

'Can't afford to stand still when I'm getting paid for doing a job,' Edna said. 'I've got two little cleaning jobs, and if I wasn't quick I'd be out on me ear. There's a lot of people out of work so yer have to look after yer job if ye're lucky enough to have one. Besides, I'd rather be using a bit of elbow grease than standing round gossiping.'

'My sentiments, exactly.' Robert hadn't mentioned wages, so he was at a loss. 'Edna, help me out, please. I know the wages should have been discussed before you started the job, but I didn't expect you to have to stay on so long. So taking into account how hard you've worked, what would you say a fair wage would be for the three of you?'

'Give us a couple of pound, Mr Robert, and we'll share it.'

'Nonsense, you all deserve more than that.' Robert had folded ten brand new one-pound notes, knowing five-pound notes would be more trouble to change. 'There's ten pounds there, Edna, share it out as you think best.'

Her mouth gaped. 'We can't take that much off yer! I only get a shilling for a morning's work at me other jobs. This is far too much.'

'Take it, Edna, you've certainly earned it. And I'm more than satisfied I got my money's worth.'

She took the folded wad of notes and slipped it into her overall pocket. 'It's no wonder our Jessie thinks the world of yer, Mr Robert, 'cos ye're a real gent. There's not many like you around, I can tell yer.'

'Oh, I think most men behave like gentlemen when they're in the presence of a lady.'

'Thank you for that, but I have to admit there are times I behave in a very unladylike manner. It would take someone with the patience of a saint not to get bad-tempered when they're doing two jobs to help out with their husband's lousy wages, plus look after the kids and do all the washing, ironing and cooking.'

'Whenever you're feeling that way inclined, just remember this. You're a very loving mother who has taught her children the value of good manners, hard work and respect for other people. I would say that you have been very successful in your role as mother. Not everyone can say that, Edna. And I'm speaking from experience.'

Before she could answer, there came a knocking on the door. 'I'll see to it, Mr Robert.' Edna stepped back in surprise when she saw the huge van with *Dennison & Son* written in large letters at the side. 'Is this the delivery yer were expecting, Mr Robert?'

He nodded. 'Two double beds, which finally completes the furnishing of the house. Would you show the driver where the two bedrooms are, please? The bed with the pink mattress is to go in the front room with the tea chest of matching bedclothes. The blue bed goes in the back bedroom with the other tea chest.'

The driver gave a nod of respect before following Edna up the stairs. Then Robert made for the drawing room to sit and contemplate. The beds being delivered were from his own home. Never again did he want to set eyes on the big double bed which had graced his bedroom for many years but held no happy memories for him. So Edwina would be sleeping in her own bed tonight, while he slept, for the last time, on that small, cramped bed in his dressing-room. And he never wanted to be reminded of Victoria, so she and her new husband would be sleeping in her bed when they returned from Scotland the next day. Victoria, who had phoned her mother twice in the last few days, had been brought up to date with the arrangements, but Edwina had not said what her reaction had been. And Robert, physically and mentally exhausted wasn't really interested in what her feelings were. She had left Liverpool an unmarried pregnant woman, but she wouldn't waste time feeling ashamed. She had wanted Charles and she got him by means which left Robert sickened by the whole affair and wishing the next two days would fly over. He knew his daughter would be dissatisfied with everything that had been done for her. Not for a second would she think of the hard work that had gone into this house, nor the money spent by George and himself. It was a lovely house, one to be proud of. Every room was beautiful, with furniture the best that money could buy. But instead of counting her blessings, Victoria would find fault with everything. He just thanked God he wouldn't have to listen to it because he was quite sure that would be the breaking-point for him.

The door opened and Edna popped her head in. 'The van's gone, Mr Robert, so d'yer want us to make the beds up for yer before we go?'

'If you would, Edna, I'd be very grateful. I've got someone coming in an hour, and the beds looking nice would be the icing on the cake. You are an angel, my dear, and your helpers.'

'We'll have them done and be out in an hour, not to worry.' Her head disappeared for a few seconds, then came back into view. 'I'm not a bad person, Mr Robert, I always try to help someone if I can.' When she smiled he could see where Jessie got her looks from. 'But if yer heard me language sometimes, yer'd know I'm a fallen angel whose halo has slipped.'

George and Annabel Chisholm stood in the hall of the house in Rodney Street and it was plain to see they were surprised and pleased. 'If I hadn't seen the number on the door I would have thought I was in the wrong house, Bob,' George said. 'You've done an excellent job, and in such a short time. You must have worked like a beaver to have achieved what I can only describe as a miracle.'

'My husband is right, Robert.' Annabel's spirits were uplifted after being taken on a tour of the house. There wasn't a thing she could see that looked out of place. 'You have very good taste in furniture, carpets, drapes and everything. In fact, there are a few pieces of furniture I would love to have in my own home. I'm sure the children will be delighted and very grateful.'

George turned away so his wife wouldn't see the face he pulled, or his eyes being cast towards the ceiling. He loved her dearly, but she'd been so petted and pampered all her life she was ignorant of what went on in the real world. Charles wouldn't come home with his tail between his legs, because he knew his darling mother would welcome him with open arms.

However, Robert felt free to say what he thought. 'I don't expect any expression of gratitude, Annabel, because I know the reality would not live up to my expectations. My daughter is a very selfish person who thinks only of herself. And I have to say your son is very much the same. If they weren't so selfish, they would have thought of their families before engaging in an act which has brought shame on us. And they wouldn't have had to scurry off to Scotland to be married, hoping their friends, in eight months' time, will not have the brains to work out that it was a marriage of necessity.'

He saw the sadness in her face and put a hand on her arm. 'Annabel, you are a lovely, gentle, kind person who wouldn't see bad in anyone. I may be hurting you now, but if you believe what I have to say, you will be spared a lot more hurt in the future. Love your son by all means, because he will probably have need of it. But tread carefully around my daughter, who is incapable of loving anyone but herself, and can be really devious. So I warn you, as a friend, to be wary of her. Do not take anything she says as the gospel truth. You may think me a cold, cruel father to say such things about his own child, but I want to spare you the pain she has caused me over the years, and my two youngest children.'

'Bob is right, darling,' George said, taking his wife's arm. 'We have never really liked Victoria, and we would be lying if we said otherwise. So as he said, tread carefully and do not be taken in by her. And now we must be on our way because Mrs Dennison is due here at any minute. She is coming a day early to make sure the house is warm and welcoming for her daughter and our son.'

'Is it true that your wife is coming to live here?' Annabel asked. 'Doesn't that seem very unusual?'

'It is what Victoria and Edwina wished. They get along very well and I have to say Edwina will make sure the house is well run. For myself, I am glad that is the case. I am in the process of divorcing my wife, so this separation suits me perfectly.'

447

Annabel searched his face. His daughter might be devious, but Robert Dennison certainly wasn't; he was a very honest man. It must have hurt him dreadfully to say what he had, and she admired him no end for it. 'Robert, you must come to dinner one night, just so we can show our appreciation for the enormous help you've given in this most difficult and distressing time.'

'Thank you, I would like that very much. But give me a few weeks to get my life back into some sort of order. And when I come, I would like to bring a friend, providing you have no objection?'

'Not at all, old boy! We'd be delighted.' George slapped him on the back before opening the front door. 'We'll be on our way so you can finish off what you have to do. No doubt you will be glad to see the back of the place after spending the last six days in and out.'

'I won't be sorry, that's for sure. As soon as Edwina comes and has a general look around to see where everything is, I'll make myself scarce.' There was no front garden to the house, and Robert stood on the step to wave them off. They were just driving away when a taxi pulled up and his wife stepped out.

'Pay the man.' Edwina swept past him and entered the house. 'Don't give him a tip, he was most disagreeable.'

Robert paid the taxi driver and gave him a sixpence tip. There was no doubt in his mind who the most disagreeable person in that taxi had been. With a sigh, he returned to the house to find his wife standing as straight as a ramrod in the hall. Her face was contorted, as though she had a bitter taste in her mouth. Being tired and hungry, Robert felt he couldn't stand much of her company. 'I'll give you a quick tour so you can familiarise yourself with where things are. Then I'm going home – I haven't eaten all day.'

Edwina didn't even bother to take her coat off before following him up the stairs. Every room was beautifully furnished and gleaming. In the bathroom there were fresh towels on the rails, toilet rolls on the stand, and soaps in the dishes. He felt proud of what had been achieved in such a short time, but there was no praise from his wife. She huffed and grunted until he could feel his temper rising. If he didn't get away soon, he'd strangle her. When they reached the kitchen, he opened the door to the larder, then opened the cupboard doors in the big dresser to show her there was everything they would need in the food line. He even lit the gas rings so she could see how they worked. All this was done without his wife uttering one syllable. But he was determined there would be no harsh words spoken before he left. After all, how long would it be before he saw her again? Hopefully not before they were no longer man and wife. 'There is a telephone in the hall in case of emergency.'

Donning his hat, and pulling on his gloves, he turned and walked away from her towards the front door. 'Goodbye, Edwina.' He wasn't surprised when she didn't answer, he hadn't really expected her to.

Outside, he stood on the pavement and breathed in the cold, fresh winter air. Thank God that chapter in his life was over. Tomorrow was the start of a new chapter.

Agnes watched the taxi drive away before turning to walk back up the path. She was brushing her palms together as though ridding them of something unpleasant. When she saw Kitty and Jessie standing in the hall with grins on their faces, she herself had to smile. 'I don't want to speak too soon, but I hope that's the last we see of Miss Edwina.'

Kitty was almost dancing for joy, thinking of the many times she'd been treated like a slave by that woman and her daughter. 'Good riddance to bad rubbish, that's what I say. I'll not be shedding any tears for her. All that extra work we had to do, packing that stuff away while she looked on to make sure we didn't break any of her precious ornaments. And the look on her miserable gob was enough to turn the milk sour. We stayed behind every night, but did we get a smile or a thank you? Did we buggery! She thinks it's beneath her to talk to the likes of us common folk. Stuck-up bitch.'

'Well, she's gone now, sunshine, so we'll have a break to make up for the extra work we've had to do. All that bedding to be washed, dried, ironed and aired, it nearly broke me bleedin' back. I'll put the kettle on while you collect yer cleaning things, and you, Jessie, give Pete a shout, please. I made a batch of scones, so tell him there's a treat in store for him.'

Agnes and the cleaners were sitting around the table when Pete came in in his stockinged feet. 'Me feet don't smell, so don't be making any cracks,' he warned them. 'The soil's wet and me shoes were caked, so I left them outside. No point in cleaning them when I'll be going out again in fifteen minutes.'

The housekeeper sat back in her chair and folded her arms under her generous bosom. 'Me and the rest of the staff have decided we deserve a reward for the way we've worked all week, so sit back and don't bother keeping yer eyes on the clock.' The scones had been warmed and the butter was melting on top. 'There's three each, so get stuck in while they're still warm.'

Pete's mouth was watering as he reached towards the plate. 'Two treats in one day, it can't be bad. Getting rid of the Missus and a plate of Aggie's scones.' He took a bite and a look of bliss came over his face. 'If this is heaven, I'll book me seat now.'

'Go 'way, yer silly sod,' Kitty said. 'Won't do yer no good going to heaven if Aggie isn't allowed in. And to be frank, I can't see her making it.'

Pete ran the back of his hand across his chin. 'No, with my luck, I'd get a seat next to Miss Edwina, or Victoria.'

'Yer've no fear on that score, Pete, 'cos neither of them stand a snowball's chance in hell of making it up that stairway to heaven.' The housekeeper nodded her head, not only to stress what she thought, but what she hoped. 'No, they're destined for down below. And for the first time in their lives they'll have to work. The devil won't let them sit manicuring their nails all day, he'll have them throwing coal on the fire.'

'Well, I hope he doesn't give them a ruddy shovel!' The little cleaner had only bad wishes for the two departed members of the family, and who could blame her after the way she was treated. 'Let them use their fingers to throw the coal on, that'll teach them.'

'We're a bloodthirsty lot,' Agnes chuckled. 'Anyone listening would think we didn't like our dear departed friends.'

'I won't miss them.' Jessie's pretty face was serious. 'I didn't like them one little bit, and I don't like that man Miss Victoria's married.'

'What I can't understand is, why they're so bleedin' high and mighty.' This came from Kitty, who had just finished her third scone and was swinging her legs under the chair. 'They think they're better than any of us, but they're not. In fact, they're not as good as us, 'cos no matter what anyone says, I'll bet a pound to a pinch of snuff that Miss Victoria didn't elope because she thought it was romantic. Nah, she was the type to want a posh society wedding with all the big nobs there. I'll have a bet with anyone that she's definitely up the spout.'

Agnes dropped her head for a second to compose her face. When she looked at Kitty, she put on an air of being disgusted. 'What a terrible thing to say! Honestly Kitty Higgins, ye're as common as muck. Just for once, couldn't yer have been a little more genteel and say she had a bun in the oven?'

The gardener, the cleaner and the housekeeper doubled over with laughter. But Jessie sat straight-faced for a while. Then in a quiet voice, she said, 'When anyone in our street is having a baby, my mam says she's joined the club.'

The laughter increased in volume and young Jessie couldn't understand why. I mean, she was only telling the truth. That was what her mam said.

It was laughter that greeted Robert when he came through the back door half an hour later, and it rang in his ears like sweet music. After the week he'd had, it was a welcome sound.

And it was a sound he hoped would be heard often in his house.

Agnes was wiping the tears from her eyes when she saw him. 'Home at last, eh, Mr Robert? We haven't seen much of yer this week. I've got the dinner on the go, but would yer like a sandwich to tide yer over?'

'A cup of tea would be fine, Agnes, and perhaps a slice of cake if that's possible? I'll wait for my dinner until the children come home. We will be eating in the dining room tonight, and every night in future.'

The housekeeper put her palms on the table and pushed herself up. Her hips waddling, she bustled to the stove. 'Shall I bring a tray through to the drawing room for yer?'

'No, I'll have it here, if I'm not interrupting.'

'Of course ye're not interrupting. It's your kitchen, isn't it? We're having a longer break than usual because we've had a lot of extra work to do getting everything packed and the bedding all laundered. And Pete had to help the blokes dismantle those beds – two men couldn't manage it on their own they were that heavy. Still, it's over now and we can get back to normal.'

'I've forgotten what normal is, Agnes. My head's been spinning for days and my brain isn't capable of thinking clearly.'

Kitty wouldn't have dared be so forward if she didn't think her boss looked really worn out. 'Mr Robert, the children won't be home for about two hours. Why don't yer finish yer tea and put yer feet up for a nap on that couch thing in the drawing room.'

Robert closed his eyes; surely he wasn't going to smile, was he? But he couldn't help himself. That 'couch thing' the cleaner mentioned was an antique chaise longue for which he had paid a fortune. But what did that matter? Kitty, with her thin pixie-like face, had her priorities right. 'That's a very good idea, and it's precisely what I will do. An hour's rest will do me the world of good.' He pushed his chair back and got to his feet. 'I'll take the tea through with me, Agnes, and I'd be grateful if you'd give me a knock about half an hour before Nigel and Abbie are due in.'

The housekeeper waited until he was out of earshot before shaking her head and saying, 'If ever anyone deserves a better life, it's that man. Ever since I've worked here, he's put up with more than any man should have to. Let's hope that Lady Luck is going to come knocking on his door soon with an armful of happiness. I'm going to do my bit to make sure he knows how much I respect, admire and appreciate him. And I know the children will.'

'I'll do more than a bit,' Kitty said. 'Me and Alf would have been on Queer Street many a time but for him.' And her words brought nods from Pete and Jessie.

Agnes had set three places at one end of the long dining table, and Robert, after an hour's sleep, was more relaxed and tucking into his dinner. 'This is nice and cosy, isn't it?'

'You've been working too hard, Dad,' Nigel said. 'You should have let me take a few days off to help you.'

'It has been pretty grim,' his father admitted, 'but it's over now. I could have spread it out over a few more days, but I didn't want to do that. It would have meant journeys back and forth from here to Rodney Street, with your mother and Victoria coming and going as they pleased. I wanted a break, and although it has tired me out, it's over and I can start to get my life together again.'

Abbie was quiet as she pushed a potato around her plate. Then she asked, 'Will we be visiting Mother and Victoria?'

'That is entirely up to you, my dear. I shan't be visiting, unless there is an absolute need. But they are your mother and sister, so only you can decide what to do.'

Abbie turned to her brother. 'Will you be going, Nigel?'

'I'll give it some thought.' Nigel didn't think he'd ever forgive them for the way they'd treated his father. But if a child was on the way, that would make a difference because he would be the child's uncle. 'Perhaps in a few weeks.'

Robert decided a change of subject was in order. 'I'm behind with all your news, so fill me in. Where are you off to tonight?'

'I'm staying in to do some homework, Dad,' Abbie told him. 'I'm doing quite well, or so the teacher tells me.'

'I'm going down to Bobby's,' Nigel said. 'He sent in a written application for the job of second man, Dad. I haven't mentioned it to you because you had enough on your plate, but he's had a reply to go for an interview next Tuesday.'

'Oh, I didn't know,' Robert lied. He'd told Jeff to watch out for the application and had been kept informed. 'Is he nervous or excited about the prospect?'

'Both. I've told him not to worry, because what will be, will be. He's got nothing to lose as he'll still have his job at Owen Peck's to fall back on.'

'Well, I hope he gets the job,' Abbie told them. She felt she had a bigger stake in this than either of them. Bobby still treated her as he always had, but when he thought she wasn't looking she'd glimpsed a certain look in his eyes and she'd swear he felt the same about her as she did about him. Why he was holding back, she just didn't know. 'He'll be as good as any of the others applying.'

'He knows I won't be interviewing him, doesn't he?'

Nigel nodded. 'Yes, I told him.'

'I could help by telling him the questions he'll be asked,' Robert said. 'That might stand him in good stead. And as Mr Seddon will be the one interviewing him, it won't really sound like favouritism if I just put him wise on what he'll be asked.' Robert folded his napkin and pushed his plate away. 'Would you mind very much if I lit a cigar?'

'Dad, you can do as you like now, there's no one to wrinkle their nose or ask you to leave the room. Besides, I love the smell of cigars.'

'Me too.' Abbie ran to the table in the bay window, picked up the heavy ashtray and placed it in front of her father. 'If

Nigel is taking Bobby for a run tonight, why can't he bring him here? Unless you're going out, Dad?'

'No, I'm not going out, my dear, I haven't got the energy. Bring Bobby by all means, Nigel, but this house is going to come as a shock to him. And if the situation is not handled with care, you could lose him as a friend. So when you get here, come in through the kitchen and I'll make sure Agnes is put in the picture. We've got a gem in Agnes, she'll make anyone feel at home. And if Abbie just happens to be sitting in the kitchen too, it will look nice and homely. It's just a pity Kitty won't be here, she's very funny and would get on well with Bobby.'

'Kitty was still here when I came in to dinner,' Nigel said. 'I was talking to her.'

Robert's exit was hasty. He'd disappeared before Nigel or Abbie realised what he was going to do. In the kitchen he found Kitty sitting opposite Agnes and they were chatting away happily. 'Kitty, I thought you would be gone by now.'

'I should be, by rights. But me and me mate decided, as we've worked like ruddy dockers this week, that we'd sit and wind down for an hour.'

Robert pulled out a chair. 'I want to ask a favour of both of you, if you don't mind.'

'Are you sure this is all right?' Bobby asked, gazing at the big house he'd been told to stop the car outside. 'I don't think we should be doing this, it's not fair on yer dad.'

Nigel had talked all the way through the journey, telling Bobby about his mother and sister. 'My dad's worked his socks off this week, but when I told him I was bringing you here, he was pleased. But he'll want an early night, so we won't stay long.' He waved a hand at the house. 'I told you we lived in a big house, and there it is. Now come on, before it gets too late.'

It was a warm, comfortable scene that met young Bobby's eyes when they entered the kitchen. Mind you, his mam's whole house would fit in this one room, but he liked it, it was friendly. And so were the faces that greeted him.

'So at last I get to meet Bobby,' Agnes said, her homely face one big smile. 'The young man what is supposed to be funnier than me.'

'Well, your face is funnier than his, Aggie,' Kitty grinned. 'So that should even the score.'

Bobby was chuckling, and his handsome face beaming. 'Don't tell me, it's Agnes and Kitty. I've heard all about you from me mate, Nige.'

'And what about me, Bobby Neary?' Abbie tried to look put out, but she was thrilled to see him in her home. 'Have you heard all about me?'

'Oh, ye're there, are yer? I might have known it wouldn't be a show without Punch.'

'Sit yerself down, lad, and I'll put the kettle on.' Agnes pointed to the chair next to Abbie. 'And don't let Kitty lead yer astray.'

'I bet yer haven't heard that about me, Bobby?' Kitty eyed him with a twinkle in her eyes. 'I'm a real man-eater. That's why I'm so bleedin' thin, chasing after the fellers.'

'Have yer caught many?' Bobby asked, his nose twitching as he sniffed up the smell of freshly baked scones. He wasn't to know it, but tired as she was, Agnes had baked another batch specially in his honour.

'Ah, well, yer see, lad, that's the story of me life. I only ever caught one, and that's 'cos he wanted to be caught. There's times I think he regrets running so slow, that's why I tie him to a chair with ropes before I come out. I can't have him escaping on me, now can I? He says I've seen too many cowboy pictures, the ungrateful sod.'

'Watch yer language, sunshine,' Agnes said. 'Yer don't want him to know ye're as common as muck.'

'I'm sorry, queen, but I didn't know no swear words until I came to work here. It's you what taught me.' She turned to Bobby. 'Yer'll have to excuse me, lad, but I pick things up very quick and Aggie does swear a lot. Sometimes she has me blushing right down to me toe-nails.'

'May God forgive you, Kitty Higgins, yer haven't got a blush in yer.' The housekeeper set a plate of scones on the table and a dish of butter. 'Help yerself, lad. Miss Abbie, will yer give me a hand with the cups and saucers, please?'

Bobby's eyebrows nearly touched his hairline. Miss Abbie? Just in time he stopped himself from cracking a joke about it. And when Mr Nigel was asked to pour the tea out, he realised they weren't joking and was glad he hadn't made a fool of himself. But when Agnes said, 'Have another scone, Mr Bobby,' a crumb went down the wrong way and he took a fit of coughing.

Half an hour of enjoyable fun later, Bobby felt he'd known these women all his life. He didn't feel out of place with them, they were just like his mam. He kept stealing glances at Abbie, and this didn't go unnoticed by Agnes. He's sweet on her, she thought, and doesn't know what to do about it. Well, she'd try and give him a little push. 'I believe ye're a good dancer, Mr Bobby? So Miss Abbie says, anyhow.'

'Have yer ever seen Fred Astaire, Agnes?'

'Yeah, I saw him on the pictures a couple of weeks ago. Ay, he certainly knows what to do with his feet, doesn't he? Talk about fast, he was like greased lightning.'

'I'm better than him.'

Nigel chuckled. 'A slight exaggeration, I think, Bobby.'

Abbie wasn't so kind. 'You're not half big-headed, you are. And a big liar into the bargain.'

'Why not let me and Kitty be the judge of that?' the housekeeper said. 'Go on, Mr Bobby, ask Miss Abbie to dance and put yer feet where yer mouth is.'

He grinned. 'I can't dance without music.'

'We can supply the music.' Agnes didn't seem to feel as tired as she had an hour ago. It must be the young company that livened her up. 'Kitty's got the voice of an angel. What will yer sing for them, sunshine?'

'I don't know none of the latest songs, but how about "When You and I Were Young, Maggie"? That's a nice one.'

Bobby was looking bewildered. How did he get himself into this? He'd feel daft asking Abbie to dance with no proper music. But Nigel gave him no chance of refusing. 'I believe you can dance, Kitty, so why don't we take to the floor with Bobby and Abbie? You can sing and dance at the same time, I hope?'

The cleaner's face was that of a young girl looking at the sweets in a shop window and having a penny in her hand to buy what she wanted. She stood in front of Nigel, lifted her skirt slightly, and curtsied. Then she opened her mouth and out came the sweetest sound of a very popular song. And to the surprise of the youngsters, her dancing was as good as her singing. Nigel was delighted as he spun her around in a foxtrot. And Bobby just couldn't resist. 'It doesn't matter if yer don't want to, Abbie.'

'Of course I want to, soft lad.'

This was the scene that met Robert's eyes when he came to the kitchen to see what was keeping Nigel and his friend. And the sheer happiness he felt brought a lump to his throat. This was how it should always be. How it should always have been. And the song that Kitty was singing so beautifully was Maureen's favourite. He approached the housekeeper from behind. 'Would you care to dance with me, Miss Weatherby?'

'I'd be delighted, kind sir.'

Bobby couldn't believe what was happening. It wasn't a bit like he'd expected. He thought everyone would be stuffy and speak far back. But they were all smashing. Even Mr Dennison had joined in. Oh, he had a lot to tell his mam when he got home.

The song came to an end, and Abbie followed Kitty's example and did a little curtsy in front of the boy of her dreams. And she was thrilled when he held her hand to lead her back to her chair. He soon let it drop, though, so it wasn't much of a sign. But it was better than nothing.

'Kitty, you never cease to amaze me,' Robert said. 'You are a very talented lady.'

'Thank you, Mr Robert, I will oblige if I'm able.' She glanced at Agnes. 'Won't I, queen?'

'Sunshine, you'll oblige whether ye're able or not.'

'We must have a proper party next week, as I promised. Kitty, you must bring Alf, and Bobby can bring his mother. And of course, other friends will be invited. But right now I want to have a word with Mr Neary. You stay here, Nigel, it won't take long. And I want you to run Kitty home on your way back to Seaforth.' He opened the kitchen door. 'Come along, young man.'

The size of the hall, with its rich wall decorations, pictures and mirrors, stopped Bobby in his tracks. He had never seen anything like it in his life. But he didn't feel intimidated by it. Those people in the kitchen were just like him, and they weren't intimidated by it, or by the man who was watching him now. So why should he be? 'This is some place yer've got here, Mr Dennison. It's beautiful.'

'I worked hard for it, son, it didn't just happen. I was only your age when I first started and it's taken me until now to get where I am. But I have a saying, which goes,"Man maketh the money, but money doesn't maketh the man". It's nice to be able to live in a house like this and have my own business, but I only need the same as everyone else, rich or poor, and that's good friends and family, love and happiness. Now come along, let's you and me have a little chat.'

'I don't want yer to think I expect favours off yer 'cos of Nigel, Mr Dennison, because I don't. And it won't make no difference to him and me, no matter what happens. He's me mate, and always will be.'

'Bobby, a Mr Seddon will be interviewing you, and it's up to him. But I thought if you knew the questions you'll be asked, it might help. First he'll ask how many driving hours you've put in. I'm sure you'll have no trouble answering that. What gear you'd get into going up a hill with a van loaded with expensive furniture. If you know all the right hand signals, and the distance you would leave between you and the vehicle in front. If you saw a person standing at the kerb higher up the road, would you carry on hoping they'd wait until you passed, or would you change gear to slow down as soon as you saw them. That's all I can remember for now, but if you answered them correctly it would certainly help your chances.'

'I'd be all right with most of those, Mr Dennison, 'cos Nige lent me books and I know them off by heart.' His cheeky grin appeared. 'I don't think there's anything in the books about someone standing by the kerb half a mile away, but I'd definitely change gear and slow down. I mean, yer never know, do yer? It might be my mam standing at the kerb, she has a habit of doing that. I'm fed up telling her off about it.'

Robert chuckled. 'You'll do all right in the interview, son, if you remember that a driver should always err on the side of caution. I really do hope you get the job, and I mean that. Now, I'll take you back to the kitchen so Kitty can be taken home to her husband.'

'Yeah, he must get uncomfortable being tied to a chair all day. I mean, the ropes are bound to dig into him.'

Robert was opening the kitchen door when he asked, 'What ropes are they?'

'I think I'd better leave Kitty to tell yer.'

'Not tonight, lad, I'm too tired,' the cleaner said. 'I'm not at me best when I'm tired, but I'll be as bright as a button in the morning and telling anyone who wants to listen, about the feathers and tomahawk. Oh, and me Indian war dance.'

Robert followed them out to where his son's car was parked. 'Nigel, will you come straight back from Seaforth, don't stop for a cup of tea. I want a word with you and Abbie, and I don't want to be too late getting to bed.'

'All right, Dad, I'll be as quick as I can.'

'Goodnight, Kitty, and thank you for everything,' Robert said, before touching Bobby's arm. 'Goodnight and good luck to you, young man. If I don't see you before, I'll see you next week when we have a little get-together of old friends. Tell your mother I'll look forward to seeing her.'

'I came as fast as I could, Dad,' Nigel said, as he entered the study, followed closely by his sister, 'but it's a good run from here to Seaforth and back, and having to make a slight detour to drop Kitty off.'

'That's all right, son, it's my fault for leaving it late to tell you I wished to speak to you and Abbie. I could have waited until tomorrow, but as today has been a day for breaking away from the past, I wanted you to know I have plans for the future. And the sooner I get it off my chest, the sooner I'll be a happy man.' Robert opened the cigar box at the side of the desk and selected one of his favourite cigars. Then he reached into his waistcoat pocket for the clipper given to him by Maureen. He held it in his hand for a few seconds before clipping the end of his cigar and lighting it. 'What I am going to say may surprise and shock, but I hope it doesn't turn you against me.' He held up his hand when both children were about to reject such a suggestion. 'No, don't say a word until I've finished. I'll be as brief as I can, but I want you to know everything there is to know and start with a clean slate. You may recall that within the last few weeks I have been out on several occasions to meet a friend. You probably assumed it was a male friend from the club. It was, however, a lady friend. And I stress the word *friend*. There has never been any impropriety in our relationship. Her name is Maureen Schofield, she is a year or two younger than myself and has never been married. I doubt there was any lack of suitors when she was younger, but she elected to care for her elderly parents. She lives in Chester and I met her when she was helping a neighbour sell the contents of her home. I was offered a cup of tea and we chatted. She is easy to talk to, a very good listener, and I got into the habit of calling in for a cup of tea and a chat once a month when the auction in Chester takes place. That was three years ago and she has

461

been my shoulder to cry on ever since. And believe me, I have had need of that shoulder many times.' Robert kept his eyes lowered, not wanting to see the reaction of his children until he had told the whole story. 'As the time went on, I began to grow fond of Maureen, who is kind and caring. If I had to liken her to anyone we know, it would have to be Beryl Jamieson and Agnes. She has the same nature as they have, warm and sympathetic.' He looked up briefly and smiled. 'Except she doesn't swear like Agnes. In Maureen I have found someone I love deeply, and who loves me in return. We never expected anything to come of our relationship because I was a married man, and to her that meant I was out of bounds, except as a friend. Then things came to a head with your mother, who for seventeen years has not been a proper wife to me. I found I could no longer stand her attitude towards me, no longer live in a loveless marriage, and I applied for a divorce. I need a good woman to share my life with, and Maureen is that woman. I will be asking her to marry me as soon as the divorce is through. All I need to make my happiness complete is your understanding, approval and love.'

'Oh, Dad!' Abbie flung herself at him, tears running down her cheeks. 'I love you so much and nothing in this world would ever change that. I want you to be happy, you deserve that more than anyone.'

Robert looked over her shoulder to where Nigel sat. 'And what are your feelings on the matter, son?'

'Like Abbie, I want your happiness more than anything. I'm delighted, Dad, and can't wait to meet the woman who's stolen your heart. I've got a feeling she'll steal all our hearts.'

Abbie sniffed up and ran a hand under her nose. 'Are you going to bring her to meet us soon, Dad? Don't make us wait too long, please!'

'Within the next few days, I promise. She doesn't have a telephone so I'll have to go over to make arrangements. I'm having two new beds delivered tomorrow, to replace the ones I sent to Rodney Street, and I want to be here to make sure

462

they're the ones I ordered. Once that is over, I'll drive across to Chester. If Maureen is agreeable, I will arrange to bring her the following night. I want to get it over quickly because she is rather nervous and shy about meeting you. The less time she has to fret, the better.'

'I just know I'm going to like her, Dad,' Abbie said. 'I hope she likes me and Nigel.'

'She'll love both of you, how could she not?'

'I've just thought on, Dad, that's the day Bobby goes for the interview,' Nigel said. 'I know it's not nearly as important as Abbie and I meeting the woman who will one day be your wife and our new mother, but if he got the job it would be like getting two presents in one day.'

Robert closed his eyes and sighed softly. Why had he worried so much about telling his two children? Why had he ever doubted their support when he had never doubted their love? 'I think the day after tomorrow will be a day we'll remember all our lives as being one of the happiest. And now, I really must go to bed, I am so tired.'

Nigel spoke without thinking. 'Dad, why don't you sleep in my bed and I'll sleep on that small one? You need a good night's rest.'

Their eyes met and in that instant the bond between father and son grew stronger. 'No, I'll manage for one more night, Nigel, but your understanding, and offer, is much appreciated.'

Chapter Twenty-Six

'I'm so nervous, Robert, I feel quite faint.' Maureen's hands were tightly laced to stop them from shaking. 'I keep asking myself over and over what will happen if the children don't take to me?'

Robert looked in his rearview mirror before indicating he was pulling into the left. Then he switched off the engine and turned in his seat. 'Maureen, my dear, my head is at sixes and sevens also, but it is with happiness. Never once, when dreaming those dreams, did I believe this day would ever come. My heart is bursting with joy, and I want you to feel the same. You need have no fears, because you will be welcomed with open arms, and loved from the minute the children set eyes on you. Before meeting them though, you will be meeting Agnes, Kitty and Jessie. Oh, and Pete, the gardener. All of them will be on pins right this minute, dying to meet you. And I have another little surprise for you, too, which I hope you will take as a sign of my commitment to making you part of my life. Nigel is leaving work early to pick up Ada and Joe, my mother and father-in-law. I want them to meet you.'

Maureen's eyes were like saucers. 'You've told them about me?'

He nodded. 'Apart from Nigel and Abbie, they are the two people I love and care for most. I have always tried to make up to them for the disgraceful way their daughter has treated them. I have always been honest, never kept anything back, and I want them to meet the woman who will soon become my wife. I called to see them on the way home from Chester yesterday, and they were very happy for me. They treat me like a son, and to me they are my Mam and Dad.'

'There's so much happening my mind is in a whirl.' Maureen hadn't slept well last night due to an attack of nerves brought on by excitement. 'I got a shock yesterday when you walked into the shop because I wasn't expecting you, and an even bigger shock when you asked Mr Geddes if I could have this afternoon off. He must wonder what's going on with a strange man suddenly appearing in my life.'

'I'm hardly a stranger, my dear, I've known you over three years.'

'He's not to know that, is he?'

'Maureen, I really don't care what he thinks. I've made up my mind that nothing is going to stand in the way of our happiness, and that means seeing each other every day. And as the distance is too great for me to make the journey daily, I would like you to move nearer to me and my family. So Mr Geddes will have to get used to being without you. In fact, I really think you should tell him to look for another assistant.'

There was a gasp before she answered. 'You're being very masterful, aren't you, Robert? And while I find that a good quality, you seem to forget my home is in Chester. I have a fully furnished house, which I own, and I can't just walk away and leave it. Besides, I don't know what you have in mind, but I will not live with you until the day we marry. I will not change my stand on that.'

'I didn't think you would, my dear, and I wouldn't dream of asking you. But I do want to see you every day, and I want my family and friends to get to know you. I know there is a great deal of sentimental value attached to your home, and I appreciate that, but you would be leaving it when we marry, anyway. So, apart from special items you treasure, why not sell the house lock, stock and barrel? I know how fiercely independent you are, so think how much better you would feel with money of your own in the bank to fall back on. You will never have need of the money, but you'll have the satisfaction of knowing it's there and gathering interest.'

'And where would I live if I did sell my home and move to Liverpool? Have you already decided that, as well?'

'No, my dearest, I haven't. All I know is I don't want to be separated from you for even a day. I want to know you are near enough for me to reach whenever I need to see your dear face and hear your voice. I know I sound like a young man smitten by his first love, and I feel like a young man again, thanks to you. I love you with all my heart, and that is the reason I may seem to be rushing you. Too many years of my life have been wasted. Forgive me for not wanting to waste any more.'

Maureen squeezed his hand and smiled. 'That little talk has done me the world of good. I don't feel so nervous now, so take me to meet your family. Other matters can be sorted out another time.' When the car was once again on the move, she said, 'I do love you, Robert, and if your children approve of me, I will do everything in my power to fit in with your plans. My aim in life will be to make up for those wasted years.'

'My children will love you, my dear, of that I am sure.'

'Then I will be truly blessed. I've had no one to call my own since my parents died, and at my age one wouldn't expect a knight in shining armour to come along. And with him, a readymade family.' She sat back in the seat, and instead of clasping her hands, she crossed her fingers for luck.

Agnes heard the car drive down the path at the side of the house and came over all of a flutter. 'They're here, Kitty. Oh, please God, let her be nice and easy to get along with.'

'One thing's for certain, queen, she's got to be better than Miss Edwina.' Kitty looked down to make sure there were no marks on her overall, then looked at Jessie who was sitting with her hands folded in her lap. 'I think we should get up and be doing something. We're sitting like bleedin' stuffed dummies, and she'll wonder what she's come to.'

'Ye're right, sunshine.' The housekeeper pushed herself up from the chair. 'I'll be putting the kettle on, you get the cups

467

for us, Jessie, and Kitty can pretend to be wiping the cooker down.'

'You can sod off, Aggie Weatherby! How soft you are, making me do the dirty work when I've got me best overall on! No, you wipe down and I'll put the kettle on.'

'Which cups d'yer want, Aggie?' Jessie asked. 'The best china, or the ones we use for our breaks?'

Kitty was putting a light to the gas ring and Agnes was trying to make herself look busy when the question was asked. They caught each other's eye and roared with laughter. 'Ye're a belter, Jessie, that's what yer are. We've spent all day preparing for this, and now yer ask if yer should give Mr Robert's friend a drink out of a chipped enamel mug!'

'I never said no such thing, Aggie,' Jessie said. 'I never—'. The young girl stopped in mid-sentence when the door opened and a strange woman came through followed by Mr Robert.

'Maureen, this is Agnes, our housekeeper, Kitty our cleaner and young Jessie our junior maid. Ladies, this is my friend, Miss Maureen Schofield.'

The three members of staff gave a little bob while scrutinising the woman from top to bottom. It was left to Agnes, who still had traces of a smile on her face, to say, 'We're very glad to meet you, Miss Maureen. In fact, we've been looking forward to it all day.'

'And I've been looking forward to meeting you, because Robert has told me so much about you, I feel I know you already.' Maureen's lips moved, but she didn't have any feeling in them. 'I'm a bit nervous so you'll have to make excuses for me.'

She looks terrified, never mind nervous, Agnes told herself. But if I'm any judge of character, that bonny face is more at ease with a smile on it. Pulling out a chair from the table, she said, 'Mr Robert said perhaps you would like a cup of tea out here, just so yer can get to know us a bit, and wouldn't be so shy.' She watched Robert take Maureen's coat from her, and glimpsed the look exchanged between the two. They're in love

468

all right, Agnes thought, and what a handsome couple they make. I've got a feeling in me bones that me and this lady are going to get along like a house on fire.

Kitty and Jessie were looking on with more than a little interest. After all, before very long this woman would be their boss. But even without exchanging a word with her, both knew she was a world apart from Miss Edwina 'cos she wasn't stuck up, or looking down her nose at them.

The housekeeper waited until Maureen was seated, then asked, with a straight face, 'Now Miss Maureen, would you like yer tea in a china cup, a thick muggen one, or an enamel mug with a ruddy big chip in?'

It was Kitty's laugh that rang out and filled the air. 'Oh, ye're a bleedin' hero, yer are, Aggie Weatherby, stealing someone else's joke.'

Robert touched Maureen's shoulder. 'I did tell you, didn't I?'

The ice was broken and Maureen's chuckle was rich and deep. 'I'll tell you what, Agnes, I'll have what you're having.'

Again Kitty's fancy was tickled. 'That's got yer, hasn't it, queen, eh? Yer can't let Mr Robert know we use the best china cups when he's not looking, and yer hate those thick muggen ones. So it's the chipped enamel mug for you.'

Agnes turned on her. 'Do you like my scones, sunshine?'

'Yer know I do, queen, I could eat them all day and never get sick of them.'

'Well, yer won't be eating any today, yer silly sod, 'cos yer just talked yerself out of them. That'll teach yer to interrupt when I'm talking.'

'Blimey, you must have got out of bed on the wrong side this morning, queen. Ye're very touchy, so yer are. If I were you, Miss Maureen, I'd keep me gob shut or yer'll talk yerself out of some of the most delicious scones ye're ever likely to taste.' The little woman gave a broad wink. 'Mind you, it would be the price of her if she was left to eat the lot herself.'

'I don't want to miss a treat, so my lips are sealed,' Maureen said. 'I've heard all about the scones Agnes makes, and I can't wait to taste them.'

The housekeeper preened. 'That's one in the eye for you, Kitty Higgins. You can't make scones to save yer life.'

'No, but I can sing and dance, so there!' A pink tongue showed itself for a second. 'So I'll do a deal with yer, queen, shall I? One scone for one song?'

There was fondness in the housekeeper's smile. 'One of your songs is worth three scones any day, sunshine, so don't sell yerself short.'

Jessie thought it was time she said something, otherwise Miss Maureen would think she had no tongue. 'I can't make scones, or sing, Aggie, but I can do a tap dance. Would that count?'

Robert guffawed, Maureen's shoulders shook, and the housekeeper and cleaner doubled up. When Agnes came up for air, she said, 'Jessie, sunshine, for yer innocence yer can have two scones.'

'Oh dear,' Robert said. 'I can't sing or tap dance, so the likelihood of me ever getting a scone is very remote. Mind you, when I was younger, I used to be able to get quite a nifty tune playing a comb.'

'I could recite a poem,' Maureen offered.

Agnes shook her head. 'Mr Robert, you don't need to do nothing, you'll get as many scones as yer want because we love yer. And you, Miss Maureen, well, you're a visitor and we should be entertaining you, not the other way around.' Her face was smiling, but her eyes were serious when she added, 'And a very welcome visitor, if I may say so.'

'I'll second that,' Kitty said. 'Ye're as welcome as the flowers in May, Miss Maureen.' She felt a tug on her skirt and turned to find Jessie pleading with her eyes. 'And this young lady, who isn't always so shy, wants me to tell yer she feels the same.'

'That's very kind of you. I was very nervous about coming, and when Robert said there was no need to be, I thought he was only saying it to make me feel better. I know now I had no reason to be nervous, you have made me feel very much at home.'

'I'm sure you'll feel more at home when we get the cup of tea Agnes mentioned, and the much talked-of scones. They will fortify you for when you meet my two children and their grandparents.' Robert took his fobwatch out and looked at the time. 'Would you excuse me for a few minutes, I need to make a phone call.'

When he came back, he seemed pleased with himself. 'There'll be an extra one for dinner, Agnes, I hope you don't mind? Nigel took it upon himself to invite Bobby.'

'Oh, how did the lad get on at the interview, Mr Robert?'

'I'm afraid we'll have to wait until Bobby tells us, I have no idea.' But his eyes told her different and she felt cheered inside. 'Nigel is bringing him with Ada and Joe, and he's stopping at the college to pick up Abbie.' He turned to Maureen. 'So, my dear, you are to meet the whole gang in one go. Will you survive?'

'Had you asked me that this morning, I would have shuddered at the thought. Meeting the children will be the biggest strain, but I do feel a lot more relaxed now, so I'm sure I'll survive the day.'

'There's no need for you to worry yer head about the children, Miss Maureen,' Agnes told her. 'I know Mr Nigel and Miss Abbie inside out, and I can tell yer now they're going to love yer. But yer going to have to share them with me, 'cos they've been like my own children since the day I started here ten years ago.'

'I'll be quite happy to share everything with you, Agnes, except Robert. He's the only one I've got to call my own and I'm keeping tight hold.'

Bobby couldn't stop talking on the way to pick up Ada and Joe. He was so high with excitement Nigel wouldn't let him drive. 'I got it, Nige, and I feel like shouting it from the rooftops. I've got to give me notice in, though, so I won't be starting until two weeks on Monday.'

'I'm very pleased for you, Bobby, and I know my dad will be delighted.'

'Abbie will get a surprise, won't she?'

'I don't think so, because my sister believes you have it in you to achieve anything you set out to do.'

'Did she say that?'

'I'm not saying any more, Bobby, because you'll only repeat it. Anyway, what did your mother have to say?'

'Over the moon, Nige, over the flippin' moon. Mind you, I didn't have much time with her 'cos you were waiting outside, but she was delighted for me. Just think, an extra five bob a week, and that's as second man. When I get to drive, the money's better still.'

Nigel pulled up outside his grandparents' house and grinned when the door was opened immediately and they stepped out on to the pavement. 'You both look very prosperous, Gramps. You haven't had a win on the gee-gees, have you?'

'That'll be the day,' Ada said, waving to Bobby. 'I'm the only nag in Joe's life.'

As soon as they were settled in the back seat of the car, Bobby twisted round and started telling them about his new job. And he carried on until they pulled up outside the college, where Abbie was waiting for them. He couldn't wait for the car to come to a complete stop before opening the door and shouting, 'I got it, Abbie!'

'Oh, I'm so glad for you, you clever thing! Congratulations!' She bent down and kissed him on the cheek before sliding into the back seat with her grandparents, who were both highly amused but tried not to show it.

Abbie's kiss didn't only surprise Bobby, it rendered him speechless and he didn't say a word until they reached their destination. Then he pulled himself together and followed Nigel in doing the gentlemanly thing and helping the old folk out of the back of the car and up the path. They walked slowly so the couple could take in their fill of the fine house that had been their daughter's home for ten years. Never once had they been invited here, but although each of them felt a twinge of sadness, there was no deep hurt. Their daughter may have taken a lot from them, but she had given them Bob, and that more than compensated. If he'd been their own son, they couldn't have loved him more.

'We're going in the back way,' Abbie said, hurrying on ahead. 'Dad and his friend will probably be in the kitchen.' But when she opened the door there was no sign of either. Her heart dropped thinking something must have turned up to alter the arrangements.

Agnes saw the disappointment on the girl's face and hastened to reassure her. 'Yer Dad and Miss Maureen are in the drawing room, sunshine, they thought it would be better to have a bit of privacy.'

Abbie's face broke into a grin. 'I thought it had fallen through and was about to cry my eyes out. Gran and Granda are here, shall I take them through to the drawing room with me?'

'No, Miss Abbie, I'm to give them a cup of tea out here first, to give yer a bit of time on yer own instead of throwing everything at Miss Maureen in one go. But I think yer've forgotten yer manners, sunshine, 'cos none of us have ever met yer Grandma and Granda, so it would be nice to be introduced.'

While Abbie's hand went to cover her mouth in embarrassment, Bobby led Ada forward. 'Agnes, Kitty and Jessie. This lovely lady is Mrs Brady, and the handsome man with Nige is Mr Brady.' While hands were being shaken, he turned to Abbie. 'Fancy you forgetting yer manners. Honest, yer'd forget yer flipping head if it was loose.'

'Gran, will you be all right with Agnes if we leave you for ten minutes or so?' Nigel was eager to get to the drawing room, but he didn't want to plonk his grandparents down with strangers and run. 'They'll look after you, and of course you know Bobby, he'll keep you amused. But if he starts bragging about his job again, tell him to put a sock in it.'

'Oh, yer got the job, did yer, lad?' Agnes laced her fingers and put them under her chin. She was so pleased for the young man she'd taken a real liking to. 'I'm highly delighted for yer, I really am.'

'Yer not thinking of kissing me, are yer, Agnes?'

'Well, I hadn't really thought of doing so, but I will if yer want me to.'

'No, it's all right. It's just that the young lady who forgot her manners a few minutes ago, she gave me a kiss when I wasn't looking.'

Abbie blushed to the roots of her hair. 'You cheeky beggar! I was congratulating you, that's all. But I'll never congratulate you again, even if you were made Prime Minister.'

Nigel took her arm and propelled her towards the door. 'Come on, Dad will be waiting for us. We won't be long.'

Robert stood up when his children came into the room, and when they stayed motionless just inside the door, he became nervous for the first time that day. Maureen rose from her chair, and for what was only a matter of seconds, but seemed like an eternity to their father, the children stared at her. Then he broke the silence. 'Maureen, my dear, these are my two children who you have heard so much about. Nigel, Abbie, this is my friend, Maureen Schofield.'

The children saw a woman who was bonny in figure and face, and fairly well dressed. Not in the height of fashion, but her clothes were of good quality and she wore them well. They also saw how nervous she was, as she bit on her bottom lip to stop it from quivering. Then a smile broke through on the pretty face and brought the two children to life. They moved forward as one, but Abbie beat Nigel to it. Ignoring the outstretched hand, she flung her arms around the woman who she just knew would be good for her father. 'Oh, it's good to meet you after Dad's told us so much about you.'

With tears threatening, Maureen returned the embrace and

kissed the youthful face that reminded her so much of Robert. 'This is a very happy occasion for me.'

Abbie felt so comfortable she didn't want to move. This was how it must feel when you had a mother who loved you. It was a strange but wonderful feeling. But her brother thought it was time for her to make room for him, so he gently disentangled her arms. 'My turn now, Abbie, if you don't mind.'

The girl flew from one pair of arms to another. 'Oh, Dad, she's lovely. I'm so happy that you found her.'

Robert held her tight, and looking over her shoulder, he saw Nigel giving Maureen a hug and kiss. The sight moved him so much he felt a hard lump form in his throat. This scene would stay in his memory for ever. Then he heard Nigel ask, 'What do we call you? We can't call you Maureen, that wouldn't be right, and Miss Schofield sounds so stiff.'

'I really don't know, I think you should ask your father.'

'I know,' Abbie said. 'Auntie Maureen! That sounds nice and friendly. But when you and Dad are married, I'm going to call you Mum. That's if you don't mind, of course?'

'That would make me very happy.' And indeed Maureen was very happy. To be part of a family would be wonderful, and she had Robert to thank for it.

'I think we should bring your grandparents in now, Nigel. Would you bring them through, please? I very much want them to meet Maureen.'

'Can I bring Bobby, as well, Dad? He's so excited about the job, if he doesn't get to tell you about it soon, I think he'll burst a blood vessel.'

So while Ada and Joe were making friends with Maureen, Robert was showing great surprise at Bobby's news. 'I'm delighted for you, Bobby. Now you must work very hard so you can apply for a driver's job.'

Nigel and Abbie were listening at a discreet distance. And they heard Bobby answer, 'Oh, I intend to work hard, Mr Dennison. In fact I'll work that hard, I might even take your job off yer one day.'

A little later, Robert suggested the children take their grandparents and Bobby on a tour of the house. This gave him some time alone with Maureen. 'Well, my love? Did I not tell you your worries were groundless?'

'Robert, I have never known such happiness. Everyone is so friendly, and your children and mother- and father-in-law are an absolute dream. I am a very lucky woman.'

'You have met those closest to me, and you will get to know them well over the next few months. My friends you will meet next week, when I have what I call a housewarming. No society people who are only here because of their status, but ordinary people who have been my good friends for many years. It will be an enjoyable night, I promise.'

Bobby was the first one back, and he couldn't suppress his enthusiasm. 'Mr Dennison, it's some place yer've got here, all right. When me mam comes next week, can I take her around and show her all the rooms?'

'Of course you can, son, it'll be open house to everyone next Wednesday night.'

Ada and Joe came in shaking their heads. 'By heaven, lad, yer've got a grand house. We've never seen the likes of it,' Joe said. 'It's like a palace.'

'It's only what yer deserve, Bob,' Ada said. 'Yer've worked hard enough for it. Me and Joe are so happy for yer.'

'You are welcome here any time. Particularly next Wednesday when it's open house to all my family and friends. And Christmas is not far off, Ada, so you and Joe can come and spend the whole of the Christmas period with us.'

Ada sniffed up before looking at Maureen. 'Yer've got a good man here, sweetheart, so you take good care of him.'

Looking across the room to meet the pair of brown eyes that had seldom left her face, she said, 'I intend to take very good care of him, Ada.'

Robert wasn't going into work the next day, he had too much organising to do. But he still rose early to have breakfast with his two children. He was facing the housekeeper across the table. 'I thought perhaps a buffet, next Wednesday, Agnes. What do you think?'

'How many for, Mr Robert?'

'Every time I reckon up, I get a different figure. There's four from Jeff's family, six altogether from Balfour Road, Ada and Joe, mine will be four with Maureen, and then there's Kitty and Alf, yourself and Jessie. Oh, and Tilly from next door. That comes to twenty-one. But I believe Nigel may want to bring a young lady called Doreen. Am I right, son?'

Nigel flushed. 'I don't know yet, Dad. Could I let you know later?'

His sister gave him a dig. 'Why don't you tell the truth? He likes Doreen, Dad, and she is very nice. But the one he's really crazy about, but hasn't got the guts to do anything about, is Milly. Go on, admit it!'

'Is it true, Nigel?' Robert asked. 'If it is, then you shouldn't lead Doreen on.'

'Dad, Milly doesn't think of me in that way. I'm just her friend's brother, that's the way she sees me.'

'And isn't that the way Bobby sees me?' Abbie had such a determined look on her face, Agnes winked across the table at Robert. 'He's always treated me like his friend's sister. But I'm not going to let it put me off. I think Bobby is the one for me, and I'm going all out to get him. You should do the same.'

To save his son further embarrassment, Robert said, 'I'll tell you what, you can let me know in the next day or two, Nigel.'

'Yes, I'll do that, Dad.' Nigel returned the dig his sister had given him. 'I'm ready to go, are you coming?'

Abbie grinned. 'He'll hit me when we get outside, Dad. But isn't it better to go for the one you want, rather than spend the rest of your life regretting it?'

'I think so, my dear, but it really is up to Nigel. Now hurry along or you'll be late.'

The housekeeper waited until the door closed before

chuckling. 'She's got a head on her shoulders, has Miss Abbie. She knows what she wants and she'll go all out to get it.'

'I hope she's successful.'

'Oh, she will be, Mr Robert, mark my words. As sure as eggs is eggs, she'll end up with Bobby and have a wonderful life.' The housekeeper met his eyes. 'And you will have a wonderful life, too. Miss Maureen is a lovely lady, one after me own heart.'

'Thank you, Agnes. Now can I discuss a few things I have in mind? First the party next Wednesday. I don't have to ask if you can make a nice buffet for about twenty people, because I know you could do it standing on your head. If you need extra help, all you have to do is sing out. Order whatever you require from Coopers, as usual.'

'I won't need no extra help, not when I've got Kitty and Jessie. So you can forget about the party, I'll make sure everything is just right.'

'Thank you, I knew I could rely on you. Now the next thing I have in mind is the attic room opposite yours. I haven't been up there since we moved in, so can you tell me what sort of state it's in?'

'Bloody awful! Paper's hanging off the walls and it's thick with cobwebs and dust. Why?'

'I want it cleaned, decorated and furnished for Christmas. Before if possible, because Maureen has agreed to pack in her job and move to Liverpool. She's putting her house on the market today. Now I haven't mentioned anything about the attic or the spare room; she thinks I'm going to look out for a little house for her to rent until we can marry. But I'm sure I can talk her round eventually.' He grinned. 'With your help, of course, Agnes. Anyway, I want her to stay here over Christmas, and I also want Ada and Joe to spend the whole of Christmas week with us. They've spent all their Christmases on their own for nigh on seventeen years. Never see a soul, only myself – and that's only for a visit. I want this year to be special for them.'

'That's thoughtful of yer, Mr Robert, they'll enjoy being in company. I was only with them for an hour yesterday, but I fell in love with them. So yer want the attic room made ready for them?'

'Cards on the table, eh, Agnes? Just between you and me. Well, I have two spare rooms and two lots of visitors. I would offer Maureen Victoria's old room but I know she'd refuse because it is next to my bedroom and she is very careful of her reputation and afraid of what people might say. So I think it will be Ada and Joe in the bedroom next to mine, and I can't think of any reason Maureen can give for refusing to sleep at the top of the house, with you to act as her guardian in case I took it upon myself to pay her a visit.'

'We all know yer wouldn't do that. Ye gods and little fishes, Mr Robert, no one would even think such a thing.'

'Maureen wouldn't take any chances. So, although I'll offer her a choice between Victoria's old room and the attic, I know she'll choose the attic. I want to give her the best, Agnes, because she's been my friend and my anchor for three years. But I have to take her feelings into consideration. I'll just be happy she's in the same house.'

'You want me to get someone in to clean and decorate the attic room, then?'

'Please. And soon. It needs to be furnished once it's been decorated.'

They heard the ring of the telephone and Agnes jumped to her feet. 'I'll answer it.' She was soon back to say, 'It's Miss Edwina for you.'

There was no greeting from the other end of the telephone, just a curt, cold voice saying, 'You neglected to stock the cellar with wines and spirits. Will you attend to the omission immediately?'

Robert closed his eyes, his blood starting to boil. What cheek she had, this woman who had made his life hell for years. 'When will you get it into your head I am no longer responsible to, or for you? And never dare address me in that

479

manner again.' With that he slammed the receiver back into its cradle and went in search of the housekeeper to tell her if Miss Edwina rang again, she was to be told the staff weren't allowed to take messages from her. They must not let her engage them in conversation and must not answer any questions she might ask. She was no longer in a position to tell them what to do.

Chapter Twenty-Seven

The dining-room table had been extended to its full length, and the fine polished wood protected by a thick felt cloth under a beautiful white linen tablecloth which had lace insets in each corner. But the cloth was almost hidden from view by the array of trays, stands and plates, all laden with the most delicious sandwiches, pies, sausages, and slices of cooked meats. And with the housekeeper's eye for colour and detail, she had garnished each tray and stand with lettuce, onions, cucumber and tomatoes. And on the long dresser, also protected by two cloths, there were plates and stands bearing a large variety of trifles, jellies, sandwich sponges and cakes covered in different coloured icing, or chocolate.

Agnes really had surpassed herself. She and Kitty had worked hard, but both were amply rewarded by the many compliments coming their way as the visitors viewed and tasted. And they had been told by Mr Robert that they too were to partake of the goodies, and mingle with his friends. After all, he'd said, this was a gathering of all his oldest and closest friends, and they were certainly included in that category.

Robert was standing by the door with Jeff, Bill Jamieson, and Kitty's husband, Alf. And to say he was happy would be a great understatement. He couldn't stop a thought flashing through his head that this wouldn't be happening if Edwina was still here. These people definitely wouldn't be on her list of socially acceptable guests. For the first time he'd been free to invite those he liked, and the difference between this and one of his wife's social gatherings, was easy to see and hear. No stiffness, no insincere remarks, no feather boas, no one weighed down with jewellery, no ebony cigarette-holders being held by hands with long, painted nails. No one trying to outdo the other. All around him he could hear genuine laughter and easygoing conversation. Maureen was with Ada and Joe, and they were chatting to Beryl and Rose Neary. And he could see her face was lit up with pleasure. Jeff's wife, Annie was deep in conversation with Agnes and Kitty, and as she pointed to the table several times, it appeared she was asking for hints on baking.

'It looks as though our Kenny's taken a shine to that young girl,' Bill Jamieson said, nodding to where his sixteen-year-old son was talking to Jessie. 'He's starting young, but I can't blame him, she's a right bonny lass.'

'She comes from a decent family,' Robert said, 'Very well-mannered, pleasant and a good little worker. She's only fourteen, though, so Kenny would have a few years to wait.'

'How is Abbie getting on with young Bobby?' Jeff asked. 'Mr Seddon gave a glowing report on him, said he was the brightest of all the applicants.'

Robert chuckled. 'Young Bobby doesn't know it yet, but our Abbie has her marker on him and she's determined he won't get away.'

Jeff glanced over to where the four youngsters were chatting away happily. 'And are Milly and Nigel just friends, or is there something between them?'

'Oh, I'm keeping out of that,' Robert said. 'Nigel isn't as forward as his sister.'

'I think our Milly's got a soft spot for Nigel,' Bill Jamieson said, 'but I don't think he's ever asked her out.'

The men would have been surprised if they heard the conversation between the youngsters. 'Are you going to take me to the pictures one night, Bobby Neary?' Abbie asked. 'Or are you too mean?'

'Ooh, I don't know about that, Abbie.' His cheeky grin

caused her heart to turn over. 'I'll have to ask me mam.'

'We'll see about that.' Several heads turned when Abbie walked with determination down the room, to stop in front of Bobby's mother. And in a voice that was heard by everyone present, she asked, 'Mrs Neary, would you mind if I take Bobby to the pictures with me one night?'

'Of course yer can, queen.' Rose kept her face straight. 'As long as yer have him home by eleven o'clock.'

By this time, amazement had turned to laughter. Except for Bobby, whose face was the colour of beetroot. 'Fancy your Abbie having the nerve to do that!'

Nigel sighed. If only he had his sister's nerve. Then, as though she could read his mind, Milly said softly, 'We can make a foursome up if yer want, Nigel. I'd like that.'

'You would?' Nigel looked flabbergasted. 'D'you mean that?'

The girl nodded. 'I've waited long enough for yer to ask me. If leave it to you I'll be waiting for ever. But yer'll have to ask me mam.'

Once again all heads turned as Nigel practically ran down the room to stand next to his sister. 'Auntie Beryl, will it be all right if I take Milly to the pictures one night?'

'Of course it will, soft lad. I thought yer were never going to get around to it.'

Abbie dropped her head to hide a smile. She was glad she'd had that little talk with Milly. It seemed to have cleared the air.

Maureen excused herself and walked across to join Robert. 'It's been a lovely evening, dear, and quite an eventful one.'

It was Jeff who answered. He'd known of this woman's existence for three years, but hadn't expected her to be so friendly and gentle. Motherly, even. 'It's been a good evening for the Dennisons. Father and two children finding their soulmates.' He turned his head slightly and lowered his voice. 'No one is happier than I am, Maureen, that Bob has finally got the woman he deserves. I know you'll be good for him.'

She smiled her thanks before putting her hand on Robert's arm. 'I think perhaps you should spend some time with Ada and Joe. They've never stopped singing your praises, they simply adore you.'

'I have a nice surprise for them, my dear. I've been waiting for people to finish eating.' Robert lifted his brows at Alf. 'Do you think I could persuade your wife to sing for them, Alf? Ada and Joe have a special song, and I know Kitty would sing it beautifully.'

'I'm sure she would, I'll go and ask her.' His wife was with him when he came back, and she was delighted to be asked to do something she loved doing but got little opportunity for. She listened intently as Robert whispered in her ear, then nodded and made her way to stand in the middle of the room.

'I've been requested to sing a special song for Mr and Mrs Brady. So if they'll join me here, they can help me out.'

The song was 'Just a Song at Twilight', and as Kitty's clear sweet voice rang out, you could have heard a pin drop. Ada and Joe held hands as they remembered years gone by, and there wasn't a dry eye in the house. But after receiving tumultuous applause, and kisses from Ada and Joe, the cleaner went straight into a faster tempo, with 'Wait Till the Sun Shines, Nellie', and other voices joined in.

Bobby scratched his head then looked at Abbie. 'Does that mean yer want to be my girl?'

'What do you think, soft lad?'

'I think we should dance, so when I'm holding yer close, I can see whether yer've got any pimples or spots. I don't want no girlfriend what's got pimples.'

'If you want to dance, then dance.' Abbie wagged a finger in his face. 'But first I want a kiss to say you're sorry for saying I've got pimples.'

'I'm not kissing yer in front of all these people!'

'You said I had pimples in front of all these people! So you can kiss me better in front of all these people.'

Bobby looked to his friend. 'Ay, Nige, I'm going to have me hands full with this one.'

'No, you're not.' Nigel was feeling very brave. 'Just give her a peck, like this.' He bent and kissed Milly on the cheek. 'See, it didn't hurt.'

'I'll sneak it while we're dancing. Come on, wench.' As he pulled her into his arms, Bobby gave her a quick kiss after making sure the other people dancing didn't see him. 'I'm glad yer want to be my girl, Abbie, 'cos I don't half like yer.'

Abbie saw Nigel dancing with Milly and holding her very close. Things were definitely looking up in that quarter. 'Ay, Bobby, you can't *half* like me. You either like all of me or none at all.'

'I like all of yer, even that big pimple on the end of yer nose.'

It was half-past eleven when the party broke up. And then it was only because men had to go to work the next day. Nigel took Ada and Joe home in his car, with Bobby and his mother. Jeff offered to drop Jessie, Kitty and Alf off, and Robert ordered a taxi for the Jamiesons. And when all the guests had left, Maureen and Abbie gave Agnes a hand to clear away and wash the mound of dishes. When that was finished, Abbie crawled up to bed, leaving Agnes with just the kitchen table to set for breakfast.

Alone in the drawing room at last, Robert held Maureen in his arms. 'I wish you were staying here, instead of going back to Chester.'

She drew back to face him. 'Robert, today has given me much to think about. Being made so welcome by all your family and friends has given me the courage to say I want to be near enough to see you every day. As Mr Geddes has already found a replacement for me, I will finish work on Saturday. Then I'll move over here as soon as you find me a place to live. It needn't be a house, I'll be happy to rent rooms in respectable accommodation.'

'Then why not ask Agnes if you can live with her?'

She looked puzzled. 'I don't understand, I thought Agnes lived in?'

'Yes, she's a live-in housekeeper. But she has the whole top of the house to herself. It is her domain, nobody is allowed up those stairs, not even Kitty. She does her own cleaning, has her privacy, and is apparently as happy as a sand boy. There are only two rooms up there, but as you can imagine from the size of the house, they are very big rooms. Agnes only uses one of them. I'm sure she'd have no objection to you having the other room until such time as we can marry. As long as there wasn't a procession of visitors traipsing up and down the stairs every day.'

'Oh, Robert, that would be ideal! I'll run and see if Agnes is still in the kitchen.' She'd gone before he had time to take in the implication of what she'd said. Then he hastened after her.

'I was hoping you'd still be here, Agnes,' Maureen said. 'I have a very big favour to ask of you.'

'As long as it doesn't entail me being on me feet much longer, Miss Maureen, they're killing me.'

'I'm not surprised, you've worked really hard today, for which Robert and myself are very grateful. What I have to ask has nothing to do with work, it's personal. I was wondering if you would have any objection to my using the other attic room, as a bedroom-cum-sitting room? I promise I wouldn't intrude on your privacy and I wouldn't be doing any entertaining up there. It would only be until Robert is free to marry me.'

'Miss Maureen, you're welcome to the room, and to the house. Me and Kitty were only saying tonight how much we were looking forward to working with yer.'

Maureen clapped her hands together. 'Robert, did you hear that?'

'I did, my love, and I am delighted. Now go and put your coat on while I have a quick word with Agnes. I'll be through in a few seconds.' He looked at the housekeeper and they grinned at each other. 'I'm beginning to think I'm having too much good luck all in one go, Agnes, and the bubble will suddenly burst.'

'Nonsense, it's about time something good happened for yer.'

'Now can I ask you another favour? Will you ring your decorator friend tomorrow and offer him double time if he can start right away? I'll call and see Jessie's mother tomorrow and ask her to come and give it a thorough cleaning.'

'You'll do no such thing. There's three of us here, and we've got no one to look after these days, not until the evening meal. We can do the cleaning between us, never you mind paying more money out.'

Robert put an arm across her shoulders and kissed her cheek. 'Agnes, I don't know what I would have done without you for the last ten years. I think I'd be in a lunatic asylum by now. But I'm keeping you from your bed, and you must be weary in mind and body. So we'll talk in the morning when we are both refreshed.'

'You've got a long drive ahead of yer, to Chester and back. Try not to fall asleep at the bleedin' wheel.'

'I won't have to make many more journeys, thank goodness. Except once a month for the auction. And now, I'd better not keep Maureen waiting because she has to work tomorrow. Goodnight and God bless, Agnes.'

It was Christmas week and Robert was as happy as a child in a fairy grotto. Maureen was settled into the attic room now and the only time they weren't together was through the sleeping hours, and when he went into the office. They'd sat together in the drawing room in the evenings and made a list of people whom he would be buying presents for, and Maureen couldn't believe how long the list was. He didn't leave anyone out, even Jessie's younger brother and sisters whom he didn't even know. And what fun he'd had, with his arm through hers, pushing his way to the shop counters to buy a gents shirt or cardigan, or a woman's dressing-gown, slippers, scarves and lingerie. He had never known such a feeling of well-being and contentment. And looking years younger, he walked with the air of a man who had been successful in life. As indeed, he was. He had everything he'd ever dreamed of. A woman he loved, two children he adored, and friends that were dear to him.

All this was running through Robert's mind as he watched Maureen wrapping a teddy bear in bright red Christmas paper. She was kneeling on the floor and when the parcel was wrapped to her satisfaction, she would place it with great care among the other gifts under the massive Christmas tree. Then she would reach for the last gift, which was a dressing-gown they'd chosen for Abbie.

'You really are enjoying this, aren't you, my love?'

She turned to smile at him. 'I have enjoyed every moment since I came to live here. I was expecting to spend my Christmas alone, as I have done since my parents died. Instead I have been made to feel part of your family.' She looked up at the tree which had tinsel and baubles dangling from its branches, and a huge fairy with a wand in her hand perched on top, looking down on them. Then her eyes swept around the room which had been decorated with coloured lanterns, balloons, mistletoe and holly wreaths. 'Everywhere looks so festive, you can't help but feel happy.'

'The whole house looks festive,' Robert said. 'You and Agnes have worked very hard, but the result must give you a lot of satisfaction.'

She chuckled. 'The most satisfying thing has been seeing Jessie's face every morning. She said she went to a grotto once, but it didn't have three big Christmas trees like we have. It's like a wonderland to her.'

'I hope she likes the dress we've bought for her. And Agnes and Kitty, of course. You were very clever finding out their sizes without them twigging.'

'Devious, you mean, my love. I told Agnes I thought she and I were the same size. Of course she told me what size she

488

was, and then Kitty said we'd make two of her as she could get into a fourteen-year-old's dress. Jessie was easy. She told us she was only fourteen but had to get a size bigger because she was filling out.'

'She's going to be one happy girl on Christmas Eve when we give her all the presents to take home to her family. I'm glad you were with me to help choose them because I wouldn't have known where to start.'

'I would like a day in town on my own, Robert, so I can buy little gifts for you and the children, and the staff. I don't want you with me or your present won't come as a surprise.'

'You don't need to, darling, they'll all have enough without you spending your money buying them more.'

'It's what I want to do, Robert, so please indulge me. I have the money you gave me from the sale of my furniture, and although I know it's not a lot, I would like to give small gifts as a token of my appreciation. And I won't be talked out of it, dear, so will you tell me who'll be here on Christmas morning when the presents are given out?'

'The two children, Ada and Joe, ourselves and Agnes. Then at twelve o'clock I'm going to pick up Kitty and Alf who I invited to dinner because I don't like to think of anyone being on their own on Christmas Day. I invited Bobby and his mother for the same reason. Nigel will pick them up when he goes for Milly.'

'Agnes will be having dinner with us, won't she?'

'Of course! And everyone will get stuck in and help with the serving and the washing up. That is one day of the year Agnes will be a guest, not a servant.'

'You are a very caring man, Robert Dennison, and it's very easy to see why so many people, myself included, love you.' Maureen planted a kiss on his forehead. 'I'm going shopping on my own tomorrow morning, dear, and I'd like you to remember two things. That it's not the gift, but the thought that counts, and also, it is more gracious to receive than it is to give.'

489

Maureen heard a movement on the landing outside and knew Agnes was making her way downstairs to start lighting fires in the dining room and drawing room. She said last night it wouldn't be like Christmas Day without fires roaring up the chimney. It was dark in the room and Maureen had no idea of the time, but if Agnes was up and about, she should be too. So she slid her legs over the side of the bed, shivered when her feet came into contact with the cold lino, and felt her way over to the light switch by the door. It was a novelty to her to have electric, she'd only ever been used to gas. But the dim light did little to warm her up and she slipped a cardi over her shoulders before making her way to the wash-stand. She'd filled the jug with water the night before, and as she poured the cold water into the bowl she could feel her teeth chattering at the thought of having to wash in it. Agnes must be made of sterner stuff than me, she told herself, picking the soap from the dish and bravely plunging her hands into ice-cold water and swilling it over her face. A quick rub with the towel helped, but she wasted no time in dressing herself and combing her hair. Then she tip-toed down the stairs, cheering herself up with the thought of a hot cup of tea.

'What on earth are you doing up, Miss Maureen?' Agnes looked up with surprise. 'Yer should have waited until I had the fires going. The one in the drawing room seems to have caught, but the dining room always takes a bit longer. You go and sit in the drawing room and I'll fetch yer a cup of tea, the kettle's just on the boil.'

'No, I'll get the cups ready, then we'll both go in the drawing room to drink our tea.' Maureen walked towards the housekeeper and put her arms around her. 'Merry Christmas, Agnes.'

'And to you, too, Miss Maureen.' The housekeeper hugged her back. 'Ye're the best thing to come into this house since I've been here. I almost called yer sunshine then, 'cos that's what I call people who bring sunshine into my life. And you've brought sunshine into a great many lives.'

'Come on, let's take our tea through to the drawing room and get a warm before I go back to my room to get changed. I want to look my best with it being Christmas Day.'

'Ah, well, I've beat yer to it, 'cos I've got me best dress on under me overall. There's not much to do, I prepared the potatoes and veg yesterday, and made the apple sauce. So it's just a case of stuffing the turkey and putting it in the oven.' The housekeeper chortled. 'That's if it'll go in the oven, like, 'cos it's the size of a ruddy house! I can see me having to use me foot to push it in.'

'It needs to be big, there's twelve of us for dinner.' Maureen had squatted on the floor in front of the fire, which was now burning merrily, and she had her hands around the cup. 'I wonder how Mr and Mrs Brady slept? It was a treat to see their faces yesterday when they saw the trees and all the decorations. I think they're a lovely couple, the way they still hold hands and the love they have for each other in their eyes.'

'Little darlings, the pair of them,' Agnes agreed. 'Every time I look at them I want to hug them to pieces. They think the world of Mr Robert, and he has been very good to them.' She ran a finger round the rim of her cup and sighed. 'He's always talked about them, calls them his Mam and Dad, but they've never been invited here before.' There came another deep sigh. 'The least said about that the better. At least they've never gone hungry, and never will while Mr Robert's here to look after them.'

Maureen drained her cup before scrambling to her feet. 'I feel warm enough to brave the cold upstairs now, so I'll go and pretty myself up.'

The housekeeper held out her hand for the empty cup. 'And I'd better get that ruddy turkey in the oven 'cos it'll take at least five to six hours.' Her face split into a grin. 'If yer hear any shouting and swearing, yer'll know it's me having a fight with the ruddy thing.'

They parted in the hall, Maureen to climb the two flights of stairs, and Agnes to clash swords with the turkey. Two women who were destined to be friends for life.

'You look very lovely, my dear,' Robert said, his eyes admiring the dress Maureen had bought when she went on her own into the city to do her shopping. It was a deep cherry colour, in soft wool. With a round neck and long sleeves, it fitted her to perfection. She had never paid so much for a dress in her life, but she wanted to look nice on this special day.

'Yes, it really suits yer, sweetheart,' Ada said. 'The colour's put a nice rosy glow on yer cheeks.'

Joe nodded. 'The wife's right, yer look a treat, lass.'

'You both look very smart, too,' Maureen told them. 'Real toffs.'

'What about me?' Abbie did a little twirl to show off the fullness of the skirt on her sage-green dress. 'And Nigel, in his nice grey suit? I think we all look a treat, especially my Dad, who looks very handsome and debonair.'

'I've brought my camera down to take some photographs,' Nigel said. 'So will you and Auntie Maureen stand by the tree, Dad, and I'll take one of you first.'

There was much laughter as Nigel took a photograph of each of them, then in pairs, then asked his father to take one of him with Abbie. 'It would be nice to have one of all of us in a group, Dad, so we could have it enlarged and framed. Shall I ask Agnes to oblige?'

When the housekeeper came in she was rubbing her hands down the front of her pinny.

'That ruddy turkey's got a mind of its own, Mr Robert. It just plain refuses to be turned over. But it's not going to get the better of me, I'll beat the bleedin' thing if it kills me.'

'If you take a photograph, Agnes, I'll give you a hand turning the turkey.' Nigel handed her the camera. 'And I won't stand any messing from it, either!'

The housekeeper eyed his suit. 'Then yer'll have to take that jacket off and put one of me pinnies on. It's a bad bugger,

492

is that bird. He'll take one look at you and spit fat at yer.'

Robert guffawed. 'I've never known anything or anyone get the better of you before, Agnes. But before you go back to take issue with it, please remove your pinny and Nigel will take a photograph of you with the family.'

The matter of the turkey had tickled Nigel's fancy. 'I'll take one of the bird, too, so you can put it in your room, Agnes, and pull tongues every time you pass it.'

The room was full of laughter and screams of delight as the presents were opened. The only quiet ones were Ada and Joe. They were stunned as they opened their presents. Joe received a thick warm cardigan, a shirt and a pair of slippers. And Ada, she too had a warm cardigan, slippers and a flannelette nightdress. They looked at each other and there were tears in their eyes. She reached for his hand. 'Joe, we are so lucky. Our love is as strong today as it was fifty years ago, and it's helped us through a lot of heartache. Now we have the love of this family, and I thank God for what He's given us.'

Robert, wearing the rich velvet maroon smoking jacket Maureen had bought him, was fastening the clasp on the string of pearls which had been his present to her, but his eyes strayed to the old couple. There were times over the years when he'd asked himself why he had worked so hard to make money, when it had been the cause of making his life so unhappy. But without the money, he couldn't have helped Ada and Joe so much, or his mam's old neighbours. And now his life was so full, he was glad he had made enough to help a lot of the people he cared about.

'Turn around, and let me see.' He never looked into her face without his heartbeat quickening. 'They look lovely with that dress, my dear. But even they pale in comparison to your beauty.'

'Go along with you, Robert, I'm middle-aged and plump.'

Abbie heard what was said and rushed over, nearly tripping on the new dressing-gown she was trying on. 'You are not plump, Auntie Maureen, you are just right. Nigel and I wouldn't want you any different – we think you and Dad make a fine-looking couple.'

'Hear, hear,' Joe said. 'They say handsome is as handsome does, and you've got it both ways, Bob.'

'You'll have Maureen and myself blushing if you're not careful. Now, as it's turned half past eleven, I suggest we clear all this paper, strings and bows away, so Nigel and I can go and pick up our friends.'

'Good idea,' Abbie said. 'And Nigel, don't you dare come back and say you've forgotten Bobby, because if you do I'll clock you one.'

Joe sat back in the dining chair and rubbed his tummy. 'By, I've never had a meal as good as that in me life, it was delicious.'

Ada nodded in agreement. 'Yer did us proud, Agnes, even though you and the bird didn't see eye to eye.'

Rose Neary gave a big sigh. 'I am absolutely stored. I knew I was eating too much, being greedy, like, but it tasted so good I couldn't bring meself to stop. And I'll tell yer what, Agnes, I wouldn't have argued with that turkey, either. The flaming size of it, it was as big as a heavyweight boxer.'

'That's a slight exaggeration, Mam,' Bobby said. 'A featherweight, perhaps, but not a heavyweight.'

'I don't know so much.' Kitty nodded knowingly. 'Aggie asked me to pass it over to her when it was delivered, and I couldn't lift the bleedin' thing.'

Agnes began to laugh, and as the memory became clearer, the laughter became louder. 'Funniest thing I've seen in a long time, that was. The bird came in a box, and when I asked Kitty to pass it over, she slid it off the table with her two arms around it. She buckled under the sheer weight of it, and went tottering backwards. And if yer'd seen the look on her face yer'd have done no more good. She looked as though she was watching a horror film.'

'And yer really thought that was funny, didn't yer, queen?' Kitty asked, in a deceptively calm voice. 'Laughed yer little socks off, didn't yer?'

'I did that, sunshine, I thought it was hilarious. What I couldn't understand, yer daft nit, was why yer didn't just drop the bleedin' thing? Yer couldn't have done it no harm, seeing as it was as dead as a ruddy door-nail, anyway!'

Robert was sitting at the head of the table in the smoking jacket he refused to take off because he said he was going to be smoking most of the day, and if he had to keep taking it off and then putting it on again, he'd wear it out. He happened to glance at Kitty at that moment, and he caught a gleam in her eyes that told him her mind was working overtime trying to think of a way of getting her own back on the housekeeper. Agnes might be her best mate, but she wasn't going to let her get away with that! So telling himself they were in for a bit of fun, Robert sat back in his chair and waited for it.

'What!' The cleaner put on a look of shocked surprise. 'I could no more have dropped that box than fly. Yer see, queen, as soon as I set eyes on that bird me heart went out to it. Legs sticking up in the air with a ruddy big hole between them, I didn't half feel sorry for it. I felt cut to the quick, I really did. Because, queen, it had a look of you about it. Around the chin mostly, and the beady eyes. For all I knew, it could have been a relative of yours, and I wasn't going to drop one of yer family on the kitchen floor, was I?'

The loudest laugh came from Agnes. She put her head down and banged a clenched fist on the table. 'Oh dear, oh dear, oh dear. That was quick thinking, sunshine, I'll give yer that. And yer've got me wondering now whether the bleedin' turkey thought I was its mother! That would account for it having tantrums on me.'

'Well, I looked at that turkey before Mr Robert starting carving it,' Alf said, 'and I didn't see no resemblance at all. I keep telling yer to wear yer glasses, Kitty!'

'I haven't got no glasses. Same as I haven't got no false

teeth. And if yer keep saying I have, Alf Higgins, you'll be needing both.'

Maureen gazed down the table at Robert, and she tilted her head and smiled. She had never thought it was possible to be as happy as she was at this moment. It was heaven.

'Right,' Agnes said, giving one last thump on the table. 'It's all hands on deck now to clear up and get all the dishes washed and put away. They say many hands make light work, so come on and get stuck in. I want to go next door for half an hour to see me mate, Tilly. I can't let Christmas Day pass without wishing her all the best.'

When there was a mad scramble, she lifted a hand. 'No men allowed in the kitchen, they only get under yer feet. We women will have the job done in no time.'

The men retired to the drawing room, where Robert lit a cigar, Nigel and Bobby a cigarette and Joe puffed on the briar pipe which had been hanging on the tree as a special present from Father Christmas. Alf was happy to sip on the glass of whisky which Nigel had added water to because Kitty's husband wasn't a drinker and they didn't want him to get an upset tummy.

They could hear shrieks of laughter coming from the kitchen, and Bobby jerked his head at Nigel. 'Let's go and see what they're up to.'

The boys were back minutes later, with grins on their faces. 'Yer should see them out there,' Bobby said. 'They've formed a line, and as Agnes washes a plate she hands it to Kitty to dry, then it's passed to Abbie, then Milly, me mam, and finally Auntie Maureen. And they're singing and dancing while they're doing it! And sat on the table, supervising, is your wife, Mr Brady, and she's loving every minute of it.'

'It's really funny, Dad,' Nigel said. 'Plates are being waved about, Kitty's got a pan on her head which keeps falling down to cover her eyes, Mrs Neary's wearing a pudding basin, Abbie and Milly have got empty biscuit tins swinging on their heads, and Auntie Maureen has got a tea-towel tied under her chin.

They're enjoying themselves so much they didn't even see us peeping round the door.'

'I don't think we should intrude on them, do you?' Robert smiled. 'Let them enjoy themselves. It's a long time since this house has heard laughter like that, and it does my heart good.'

The women had no intention of keeping the fun to themselves, though. When the kitchen was cleared of all dishes and pots and pans, they went into a huddle to decide how to catch the men by surprise. And catch them they did. They crept through the hall to the drawing room, then, on a sign from Ada, who was waving a rolling pin as though it was a baton, they burst the door open making the most unearthly racket possible. Banging spoons on the bottom of pans, and singing 'Down By the Old Bull and Bush' with gusto. After Ada came Kitty, who looked really comical with the large pan on her head swivelling around as she bobbed up and down to the music. She had two large spoons between her fingers and she was playing them in time with the tempo. And when Rose appeared wearing the pudding basin, her son went into fits of laughter and told her she should make a habit of it 'cos it really suited her. But he and Nigel agreed Abbie and Milly were better-looking without the biscuit tins. They thought Agnes was good, though, with a large teapot standing on her head and tied down with tinsel, and banging away on an enamel tray and singing at the top of her voice. The only one not making any noise was Maureen, who was bringing up the rear. She was obviously enjoying herself, but years of shyness held her back from singing. She still had the tea-towel tied under her chin, tinsel wrapped around her shouders, and two baubles off the Christmas tree in the hall were hanging from her ears. She looked like a gypsy, but a very shy one.

When they were worn out, and their voices hoarse, Agnes called a halt. 'That's yer lot, folks, 'cos I'm off next door while I've still got a bit of breath in me.'

'Oh, don't go yet, Agnes, please,' Robert said. 'There are still presents to give out. The family have had theirs, but it was too late to give the guests theirs because it was near to dinner-time. So please stay for a few more minutes.'

'Here, I'll take some of the pans out,' Alf offered, 'if someone will give me a hand.'

There were many willing hands, and soon family and guests were seated. Nigel was sitting on the floor with Milly, his arm across her shoulders, and next to them were Bobby and Abbie. 'Will you do the honours, my dear?' Robert asked. 'You'll do it much more graciously than I ever could.'

Four of the parcels under the tree were exactly the same size, and after reading the labels Maureen gave them out. Then the two smaller parcels were given, one each, to Alf and Bobby.

Bobby's grin stretched from ear to ear. 'Is it all right if we open them, instead of sitting gawping, and wondering what they are?'

Abbie produced a sprig of mistletoe from behind her back and held it over his head. 'You have to pay for it with a kiss.'

The lad blushed. 'Ay, Mr Robert, your daughter's not half forward. She's practically throwing herself at me!'

'She takes after her brother.' Nigel took the mistletoe Milly had handed to him, held it over her head and gave her a kiss which lasted several seconds. 'You'll enjoy it, believe me.'

Bobby looked to where Rose was enjoying her son's embarrassment. 'Mam, is it all right if I give her a kiss?'

'Of course it is, lad!'

'But what if she wants another one? She's never satisfied with one kiss, yer know.'

'Go on,' Abbie said, 'tell the whole world our secrets. But not until I've had my kiss because once you start talking, you make a meal of it.'

'Excuse me,' Agnes said, 'but this parcel's burning a blinking hole in me lap, so will yer hurry up and get yer kissing done, so I can open it?'

Five minutes later, while Alf and Bobby were admiring their pale blue shirts, three middle-aged women and one young one were running upstairs, laughing with excitement, to try on the new dresses they'd been given. And when they came back to the drawing room, they paraded like mannequins. Their dresses had been chosen with great care to detail, and the fit, style and colour were perfect. They were profuse in their thanks, and Robert was showered with kisses. 'Wait until Tilly gets a load of this,' Agnes said, 'she'll be green with envy.'

Alf gazed at his wife in the dress of violet crêpe, and thought she looked lovely. 'Come here, sweetheart, and give us a kiss.'

'Blimey! This kissing lark's catching.' Bobby pursed his lips and nodded knowingly. 'All women must be the same. D'yer know, Abbie had six kisses last night and still wasn't satisfied.'

'Only six?' Milly said. 'She's easy pleased.'

Maureen whispered in Robert's ear before reaching behind the Christmas tree for a large bag with string handles. Then she began to pass small wrapped parcels around. 'These are from me, as a token of my gratitude to everyone for making me so welcome. They aren't much, but they come with my love.'

As the paper was being ripped to reveal ties for the men, and pretty headscarves for the ladies, Robert sat back and thought he must be the most contented man in the world. All around him there were people with smiling faces. He did think of his wife and eldest daughter, but it was with sadness, not a sense of loss. Nigel and Abbie had called to see their mother and sister yesterday, taking greetings cards, and presents. He had given them a cut-glass decanter to take as a present for the house, but although the children had said the presents were gratefully received, there was no enthusiasm in their voices. So he didn't have to be told the atmosphere in Rodney Street was in stark contrast to the warmth and happiness you could almost touch here. But he was glad the children went, he wouldn't like them to lose touch with their mother and sister. And, soon, of course, a new baby.

Robert was so lost in thought his mind was not on what was happening around him, and he was a little startled when Abbie touched his arm. She and Bobby were standing before him with their arms around each other, and Nigel was with Milly. The happiness on their faces was a joy to behold. His daughter held out her arm and shook it near his face. 'See what Bobby bought me, Dad? Isn't it pretty?' There was an attractive bracelet on her wrist, made up of coloured stones, and Robert reached out to examine it closer. 'It is very pretty, love, and a good choice on Bobby's part.'

'I got one too, Mr Dennison, off Nigel.' Milly held it for closer inspection. 'I'm made up with it.'

'They didn't cost the earth, Mr Dennison, but they didn't come from Woolies, either.' Bobby's face was serious, but only for a second. Then he grinned. 'When I've taken your job off yer, I'll be able to buy her diamonds, 'cos that's what Abbie deserves.'

'You'll have to go through me to get Dad's job,' Nigel laughed. 'You can have Jeff's job, and you and me will always be friends, like Jeff and my dad are.'

As the youngsters walked away, stealing a kiss as they went, Robert couldn't prevent his mind going back. He was called Bobby on that day long ago, when he'd asked Jeff if he wanted a day's work for a sixpence. Neither of them thought it was the start of a friendship that would last a lifetime. It was Jeff who shortened his name to Bob, but that wasn't good enough for Edwina, and she insisted on him being called Robert in her presence.

'Robert, you're very quiet, love,' Maureen said, bending down to look into his face. 'Is there a reason for it?'

'I've been reminiscing, my dear, and laying old ghosts to rest. But it's time for seasonal toasts now before Agnes leaves.' He gestured to his son. 'Nigel, do you think you and Bobby could bear to leave your girlfriends just long enough to see to the drinks?'

500

He raised his glass for the first toast. 'This is to wish Ada and Joe many more years of happiness and love. And to tell them I am honoured they are part of my family.'

The old couple were holding hands and smiling into each other's faces, proud as could be. They would tell Bob later that it was they who were honoured to be part of his family.

Then glasses were raised to Agnes, Kitty, Alf and Rose, who looked as proud as peacocks. 'First time in me bleedin' life, this,' Kitty's whisper was loud. 'I feel like a real toff.'

'You are a toff, Kitty,' Robert said. 'In my eyes, all of you are toffs.' Then he raised his glass, saying, 'To my two children who I love dearly. I couldn't wish for better children than Nigel and Abbie.' He chuckled. 'I better hadn't leave Bobby and Milly out, seeing as they could, one day, be part of my family.'

Bobby waited until the toast had been made, then he said, 'I think ye're right there, Mr Dennison. Because if Abbie keeps running after me, she's bound to catch me sooner or later.'

Milly had been more quiet than usual, overawed by the richness of everything around her. But she had been slowly unwinding in the warmth and friendliness, and now felt able to say, without blushing, 'I could never run fast if yer paid me, so Nigel caught me on the first corner. Mind you, it had come to the stage where I thought I was going to have to chase him.'

Robert chuckled, thinking his life would never again be dull. 'Now a toast to absent friends.' There were shouts of, 'Hear, hear,' and he waited until they'd died down before putting his arm around Maureen's waist. 'And now to the woman who has been my dear friend for three years, and who will soon be my wife. I know you will all love her as I love her.' He kissed her cheek. 'I used to dream a little dream that one day I would find happiness. Then I met Maureen, and knew my dream had come true.'

'Dad,' Nigel called. 'Your dream has brought us all happiness.'

Try a Little Tenderness

Joan Jonker

Jenny and Laura Nightingale are as different as chalk and cheese. Jenny's pretty face and lively sense of humour make her everyone's favourite girl, whereas Laura is spoilt and moody and never out of trouble. Their mother, Mary, loves them both but she's more worried about her father's new wife, Celia, who is about to bring shame on the family . . .

Then Jenny attracts the attention of two young lads in the street who both want to court her. Mick and John have been mates since they were kids but now war is declared and it's every man for himself! Meanwhile, Laura's resentment begins to build and it's only a matter of time before things come to a head. Who will learn that a little tenderness goes a long way?

'A hilarious but touching story of life in Liverpool' *Woman's Realm*

'You can rely on Joan to give her readers hilarity and pathos in equal measure and she's achieved it again in this tale' *Liverpool Echo*

'Packed with lively, sympathetic characters and a wealth of emotions' *Bolton Evening News*

0 7472 6110 5

HEADLINE

Stay as Sweet as You Are

Joan Jonker

With the face of an angel and a sunny nature, Lucy Mellor is a daughter who'd make any parents proud. But her ever ready smile masks a dark secret. For while her friends are kissed and hugged by their mothers, Lucy only knows cruelty from the woman who brought her into the world. Her father, Bob, tries to protect her, but he is no match for a wife who has no love for him or his beloved daughter.

The Walls of their two-up two-down house are thin and Ruby Mellor's angry outbursts can be heard by their neighbours. One day, Irene Pollard, from next door, decides she can no longer stand back, so she and her friends take Lucy under their wing. But sadness remains in Lucy's heart because, despite everything, she still craves a mother's love . . .

'Hilarious but touching' *Woman's Realm*

'You can rely on Joan to give her readers hilarity and pathos in equal measure and she's achieved it again in this tale' *Liverpool Echo*

'Packed with lively, sympathetic characters and a wealth of emotions' *Bolton Evening News*

0 7472 6111 3

HEADLINE

If you enjoyed this book here is a selection of other bestselling titles from Headline